Other books by Mary Duncan

Eyes of Garnet

Sightless

DOUBLE VISION

Double Vision

An Eyes of Garnet Novel

Mary Duncan

Sense of Wonder Press
JAMES A. ROCK & COMPANY, PUBLISHERS
FLORENCE • SOUTH CAROLINA

An Eyes of Garnet Novel: Double Vision by Mary Duncan

SENSE OF WONDER PRESS
is an imprint of JAMES A. ROCK & CO., PUBLISHERS

Address comments and inquiries to:

SENSE OF WONDER PRESS
James A. Rock & Company, Publishers
900 South Irby, #508
Florence, SC 29501

E-mail:
jrock@rockpublishing.com lrock@rockpublishing.com
Internet URL: www.rockpublishing.com

Trade Paperback ISBN-13/EAN: 978-1-59663-742-9

Library of Congress Control Number: 2006926207

Printed in the United States of America

First Edition: 2009

Cover Design and Interior Graphics
by Mary Duncan

For my parents

One who's still here

and one

who watches

from

another place

They always believed

in chasing dreams

Acknowledgments

I wish to thank, once again, the amazing people who keep my writing on track: Cathy Emmons, Casey Devine, Barbara Martin, Sharon Biggie, Caroline Spear, Christine Horsley, and especially my husband, Dan.

For my sister, Cathy Emmons, whose help on "birthin' babies" and medical terminology allowed me to write about the experience of childbirth.

The Boston Public Library for their help on buggery (cough) in 18th century Boston, as well as the Cape May quake.

And for all those who've stood behind the story of Catrìona Robertson and her rather insightful life, from the people who hug me at book signings, to the bookstore owners who prominently display my books and are quick to direct a customer to Cat's story, to the people who stop me on the street and tell me how much they are enjoying my books. Thank you all, and I hope the next series on Gregor Macgregor will entertain you as much as I think he will.

Part One

1

Denied Revenge

Cape Rozier, Province of Maine, September 1752

THERE WAS NO REASON why it had to go this far, but Catrìona Robertson knew deep down that this was the only way it could end. A man like Commander George Wilson could never forget a wrong against his fragile ego, especially one perpetrated by a woman; an Indian-loving Scotswoman, was how he'd described her. But at her feet lay the man. Dead. A hole perfectly placed between his unseeing blue eyes, the whip still in his lifeless hand. His powder-singed face, scarred from a close-range blast from her pistol nearly a year ago, still bore a murderous look, though impotent now.

Cat was still breathing heavily from the fray. Her deep-auburn hair stuck to her face and sweat dripped down her back, despite the coolness of the morning. It would have soaked the sark she had on, but the commander's whip had shredded it. She involuntarily shrugged as the salt stung her bloody wounds. It didn't help the pain. In the distance she heard hoofbeats. Greame and Gregor probably, panicky to locate her after hearing the shot.

How would Greame react? she wondered. Captain Greame Hay still didn't quite understand that she could take care of herself, even if it meant killing. Cat knew with all her heart he loved her, and also knew he wished she'd let *him* take care of her. He would never voice his concern, but with her power of Second Sight, it meant nothing was a secret between them. She cringed at the thought of what she would see in his eyes when he arrived.

Gregor Macgregor, on the other hand, would wear a smile from ear to ear and want to pick her up and squeeze her with a triumphant *whoop!* Being a Macgregor, despite them, seemed to make him relish the idea of killing for justice. A Highlander to the end, that one.

Crashing through the trees, Greame and Gregor reined in their horses and leapt from their saddles. Cat was sitting on a fallen log with her head in her hands and didn't look up. The adrenaline was wearing off rapidly, and she was shaking like a leaf, barely able to remain seated. All she wanted to do was sleep.

"Christ! Look at her back, Greame." Gregor peeled back the remains of the fabric of her cloak and sark to reveal four raw gashes crisscrossing the once perfect cream skin.

Greame was more interested in looking into her violet-gray eyes. Wounds would heal. Her mind was much more fragile than her body.

"*A' ghaoil,* talk to me," he whispered, as though speaking to a frightened beast. "Are ye all right?"

Cat lifted her head and looked into Greame's forest-green eyes. "I'll be fine. I'd just like to sleep for a bit," she said very matter-of-factly. "Did ye hear the shot? Is that how ye found me?"

Greame brushed the auburn locks from her face, noticing her black eye and swollen lip, and pressed a kiss on her forehead. "Aye. When Gent returned wi'out ye and Bogle, we began searchin' the entire area. Ye can sleep for as long as ye've a mind to, lass. We'll make camp ..." Looking at the body of George Wilson, he thought better of saying, *here*. "We'll make camp and ye can rest to yer heart's content, aye? But first, let's take a look at yer back."

He spoke to her like a child, calmly and softly. He knew she was in a kind of shock and he didn't want the reality of her ordeal to reach the surface just yet. This was her healing time.

Greame walked behind her and nearly gasped at the sight. Anger boiled in him, threatening to release. Without a word, he walked over to the body of George Wilson, roughly hoisted it over his shoulder, and walked into the woods. He caught Gregor's silent look and nodded. Greame would dispose of the body; Gregor was given the task of caring for Cat. For now.

A little later, Greame emerged from the woods, bloodstained and dirty. Gregor, in his usual fashion, smiled, but never asked just *how* Greame disposed of the bastard. Maybe someday he'd ask, but for now, he knew Greame had his revenge.

❧

The next morning, Cat awoke to hushed voices. She opened her eyes and looked around the clearing to get her bearings. Where was she? How did she get here? she wondered. As she attempted to sit up, the wounds on her back screamed in painful remembrance and she let out a whimper.

Greame was at her side in an instant. "Dinna move, Garnet! Ye'll open up the cuts."

"How many?" She asked quietly.

"Four. And it looks as though he was just gettin' started. Ye want to tell us how ye managed to get away?"

Gregor moved closer to hear her story, taking a seat on a nearby log. Cat stared at the two of them trying to recall the last few days. Had it really been that long since she'd run from that man? It seemed like they had just returned home from New York, back from Mohawk territory, even though it was a year past. All seemed so peaceful in their small settlement on Cape Rozier. Life blossomed all around them. Her garden flourished this past summer from the hard work of amending the bony soil of coastal Maine last autumn with seaweed and lobster shells and leaves.

The English stayed preoccupied with burning forts as fast as the French could build them in New France and New York, therefore leaving Maine and its few inhabitants alone. The Penobscot Indians came and went with the seasons, following their food sources along the river.

Cat lay on her stomach and rested her chin on her arms. Greame waited for her to get comfortable. There was no rush, none of them were going anywhere for a while. He smiled when she grabbed a lock of her hair and started twirling it, like she always did when concentrating deeply.

"When did ye realize I was gone?" Cat asked.

"When we returned from the hunt and ye werna home." He thought back for a moment, then said, "It seemed … well, as though more than just yer *self* was gone. It was more like the feelin' that yer soul was gone. Does that make sense to ye?"

Gregor was frowning at Greame, wondering how the man could feel something like he just described. He just didn't understand the powers Greame and Cat shared. Apparently he never would. Second Sight was beyond his capability of reason.

Cat smiled a little, her dimples deepening. She turned her head to face the two dearest men in her life, and said, "Oh aye, it makes sense to me. It took all o' my wits to stay a step ahead o' that madman, so I guess I took my soul along for safe keepin.'"

The smile faded from her face at the memory of the chase. A chill crawled up her spine, making the back of her neck tingle.

"It wasna long after the six o' ye had left for the hunt. Gent and Bogle must hae followed ye. Fine watchdogs they make, aye?" She snorted, but wasn't blaming her Irish Wolfhound and his wolf mate.

"I could *feel* him. Wilson." Her eyes went someplace far away. "Waitin' in the woods. I kent he wouldna wait for long. He must hae been watchin' the lot o' ye leave, and nearly an hour later, he made his move. What he didna ken was that I had slipped out our bedroom window and had crawled down to the shore. I was watchin' *him* now from the rocks on the beach.

"He wasna alone. He had three of his men wi' him, but only *he* walked in the front door. I could hear him growlin' when he couldna find me. I hope he didna break too much. I heard the crashin' o' furniture bein' tossed about." She didn't wait for an answer.

"Anyway, he bolted from the cabin and started barkin' orders to his men to search everywhere. I kent I was in trouble then. There's really nowhere to hide on the shore. Well, that's what I thought at first, until I saw the tree that had drifted onto the beach from some storm. I buried myself under it. The soldiers ne'er even came out o' the treeline. They must hae figured they could see everythin' from the embankment. I stayed buried for what seemed like hours. What persuaded me to leave was the incomin' tide." She shivered involuntarily at the memory.

"Do ye need a blanket, lass?" Gregor asked, ready at her beck and call.

Cat shook her head and continued. "I crept up the embankment and scanned the area. The woods were quiet. I couldna feel him anymore. I was about to run back in the house when I heard shouts on the beach around the point. I had to reach the pistol under the bed. All I had was my dirk strapped to my leg. I needed more. I climbed back through the bedroom window, grabbed the pistol and ammunition, and my cloak. I had a feelin' it was goin' to be a long, cold night."

"Why didna ye go into the hidey-hole? They'd hae ne'er found ye there," Gregor said, plaiting his long black hair that had starting to show streaks of silver.

"Couldna. I could hear them gettin' closer. It was my only chance to make it to the woods before they got back to the cabins. I just ran."

"Too bad Smiles at Everythin' had just left for Pasadunkec. Him and his braves would hae made it right difficult for auld George," Gregor said with a chuckle, elbowing a quiet Greame in the ribs.

Greame ignored him. He was too busy visualizing what Cat was telling them.

"I made it to the top o' the hill where we hid wi' the Penobscot when the Mohawk attacked us when we first arrived. Remember?" she asked, looking at Greame.

"Aye, I remember," he answered.

"My plan was to wait until I kent ye were back from the hunt. I kent the trail ye used, but when it got dark and I didna see or hear ye come back, I kent I was spendin' the night under the stars."

"We shot three deer," Greame explained, his voice tortured from guilt. "It took longer to get them all back. When I didna see any lanterns lit in the windows, I kent somethin' was verra wrong. It was well after ten when we got home. It was so … lonely in the cabin. I noticed yer cloak was gone, and it wasna 'til the next day that I noticed the pistol was missin.' I was near out o' my head wi' worry."

Greame ran his hands through his long, chocolate-brown hair. The frustration of the unknown freshened. "I couldna find ye."

She knew exactly what he meant. Greame was still new to the Sight. Under such duress, he couldn't get her location—couldn't *see* her. Cat's heart went out to him at the anguish in his voice, and she reached her hand over to his knee. He placed his big hand on top of it and gave it a squeeze, then looked away, unwilling to let her see his eyes.

Gregor, oblivious to the charged atmosphere, asked, "So what happened durin' the time ye were gone then?"

Cat's eyebrow lifted. "My, but ye are a pushy one."

"Ye're just takin' too long to tell the story, woman."

Despite herself, she smiled and continued. "The next mornin' I figured I could go home. That somehow I'd missed seein' yer wee band o' brothers come back. It was a quiet night. But as I started down the hill, I had the feelin' I wasna alone. I kept hearin' somethin' in the woods. Not like men, more like beasts. I thought perhaps I'd spooked some deer, but they were headed towards me, no' away. Suddenly, out o' the woods comes Gent and Bogle, all tongues and tails. I wasna sure where they came from, but at least I had some protection and could return home safely. Bogle, by herself, would be enough to frighten most men. No one really kens how to react to a wild wolf."

Gregor's brows went up, remembering his first encounter with Bogle in Cat's cabin. He, a braw man well over six feet tall, had run for his life when he had walked into their cabin unannounced one early morning to find a wolf baring its teeth at him.

"We were nearly down the hill when I heard the shot. Bogle let out a yelp and she fell to the ground. Then, two more shots were fired, tearing leaves from the branches above me. I wanted to see if Bogle was hurt badly, but every time I tried to get close to her, another shot was fired. I saw in my mind the commander wi' his evil grin on that ugly face. He had no interest in shootin' me, he kent he could hurt me more by killin' those I loved. Bastard! Gent wouldna come wi' me to the woods, he kept goin' to her side. I had to leave him."

She was quiet for a few moments, her hair being twirled at an alarming rate. Greame could see she had gone somewhere else, somewhere safe in the recesses of her mind. He motioned to Gregor to keep quiet until she was ready to speak again on her own. Apparently, it wouldn't be for a while, for she rolled onto her side and closed her eyes. Gregor got up to check on the horses. Greame watched her sleep, taking in every detail of her, committing her to memory in case this ever happened again. She always managed to find trouble wherever she went.

❧

As the golden sun fell behind the trees, Cat finally awoke. Again, she made the mistake of attempting to sit up, remembering too late the raw wounds on her back. At her sharp intake of breath, Greame was at her side.

"I need to pee."

"It certainly would hae been easier if ye'd had yer dress on. These breeks are a bugger to get down," Greame said, helping her to her feet.

"Just get me to a log so I can sit, I'll do the rest."

Greame set her down and turned his back, giving her a little privacy. After a moment of struggle, Cat felt relieved of the pressure in her bladder. As she sat, she felt her wounds tingle. It was time for an herbal poultice to make sure infection didn't set in. If they left now, they'd be home in about an hour.

"I need to get a remedy on my wounds," she said to his back. "I'd like to go home."

Greame turned to face her. His harsh features softened in the fading light. "Aye, I was just thinkin' the verra thing. Are ye able to ride?"

"I'll hae to. I canna walk that far," she said, standing to tie the flies of her breeks.

"Let's give it a try then."

Gregor was just about to stoke the fire when Greame announced their decision to leave. After a few grumbles, Gregor kicked out the flames and retrieved the horses. It took a bit of finagling to get Cat into her saddle without opening the cuts, but they managed. It was a slow ride back to the cabins, but once home, it was like a burden released.

❧

When he heard horses, Kelvin Hay looked out his cabin door and made out three riders. He rang the alarm bell he had fashioned, and within a minute, Geoffrey, Robbie and Kenny Hay burst from their cabins, lanterns and pistols in hand, and assembled on Kelvin's porch wondering what the alarm was. Kelvin sent out a thick finger into the dark and the riders appeared, as though conjured by the man. Recognizing the trio, they all ran to greet their captain, friend, and the woman they had come to love as their own kin.

In the light of the lantern, Kelvin smiled. He was not a demonstrative man. A smile on his face was an enormous show of emotion. Cat caught his greeting and gingerly lifted her hand.

"Her back's wounded, lads. Be verra careful wi' her," Greame told his cousins, reining Cat's horse as close to the porch as he could in order to let her step off.

The blanket Cat had over her shoulders fell when she dismounted, and the light from Kelvin's lantern shone on the angry gashes on Cat's back. Instantly, the mood of the men changed. Silent questions ran over their faces. Kelvin quickly retrieved the blanket, and as gently as he could, wrapped it over her shoulders. It wasn't so much for the chill in the air as it was to protect Cat's privacy. Greame put a hand on his uncle's shoulder and nodded in appreciation. The rest of the men said their goodnights and returned to their cabins. There would be plenty of time for answers in the morning.

❧

Under Cat's guidance, Greame gathered the herbs for the healing poultice. They included St. John's wort, calendula, comfrey and bayberry. Greame poured the boiling water over them and made a thick paste, then placed the brown mash in a large muslin pouch. Cat went into their bedroom to get ready.

When Greame brought the poultice in, Cat was lying naked on her stomach on the bed, the blanket just covering her legs and buttocks. The lantern light was soft, but the gashes on her back stood out in bold relief. Greame wished for a moment that George Wilson were still alive so revenge would be sweeter than what was exacted on his dead body.

"Ye canna change what happened, Greame." Reading his mind. "The wounds will heal."

He knew she'd heard his thoughts. He walked to the bed and sat beside her, unfolded the muslin pouch, gently placing it on her back. "I ken that, Garnet."

"Ye wish ye had been the one to kill him."

"Aye," he growled. "He deserved more than what I did to his body in death. A shot between his eyes was too quick for that Tom O'Bedlam!"

She chuckled. "I've no' heard someone called that since I was a wee lass. I dinna recall who it was said about—surely no' one o' my relatives—but some madman just the same."

"Dinna try to lighten my mood, Garnet. The enormity of the situation is still too fresh."

She patted his leg, "I do apologize, but it is over. Let's move forward wi' our lives, aye?"

"Perhaps in the mornin.' Get some sleep now." He stood and grabbed the lantern to leave the room.

"Greame?"

He stopped, but didn't face her.

"Thank ye."

A bitter laugh escaped from him. "For what? Once again, I'm unable to keep ye from harm." He walked out, closing the door behind him.

❧

"Well, in all fairness to the man, Ca—Garnet, he ne'er did say *which* mornin,' now did he?" Gregor jested. "I still hae a hard time callin' ye Garnet, Cat. I've called ye Cat since ye were but a wean. Do ye mind if I still call ye Cat?"

Cat was in no mood for levity. "Call me whate'er ye like, Gregor, just send Greame in here this instant."

It had been *three* mornings since Greame last said much of anything to her. Except for changing the poultices on her back, it was the only time he'd enter their bedroom.

"It's moods like this I could be callin' ye somethin' else," he grumbled as he left the kitchen.

Cat was able to walk around a little now. The poultices had done their work and the gashes were healing nicely, without becoming septic. Under her loose-fitting sark, bandages now covered the calendula-salved wounds.

Kenny, who used to be the *Revenge's* cook before settling with his captain in the wilds of Maine, was in charge of making bread for the seven souls who called this jog of land home. Cat still wasn't able to do much just yet, which she found very frustrating. Greame's self-pity was adding to her fuming mood. She knew he'd take it this way, but it made it no easier to wait out until he'd sorted it out in his mind.

She was pouring a cup of tea for herself when Greame walked in. He wasn't aware she was able to get out of bed yet, so when he saw her standing near the kitchen table he actually smiled. Cat's heart gave a little leap, despite her sour attitude, and she offered him a cup of tea, which he accepted.

"So, ye're feelin' a bit better then?" He took a seat beside her at the table.

Cat nodded, holding the warm cup in her hands. Her eyes met his, still amazed at the beauty in their green depths. "Are *ye* feelin' better?"

A sheepish grin appeared to tug at his lips. "Aye, and I thank ye for yer patience while I get o'er myself."

Cat shook her head and said, "Our timin' is a rare fine thing."

He cocked his head to the side. "What do ye mean?"

"It seems that by the time I get around to gettin' cross wi' ye for yer grumpy attitude, ye're just comin' out of it."

"Probably a good thing. Even *I* dinna want to be anywhere near the two of us if we're e'er angry at the same time. Lives could be in peril," he said dryly, taking a gulp of his tea.

Cat giggled at the scene in her mind.

"Now that's a sound for sore ears," Gregor said as he walked into the kitchen, taking a heavy seat across from Greame. "I gave Greame a couple o' minutes lead time to be sure just such a thing wasna goin' to happen when he walked in."

"Why? What did I miss?" Greame asked, looking back and forth at the two of them.

"Gregor, here, was near ready to call me a bitch when I sent him out to fetch ye."

Kenny chuckled in the background as he kneaded the bread.

"Ye ken I'd ne'er call ye that, Cat." He looked fairly scandalized at her utterance of the word.

"Oh aye, no' to my face, anyway."

"Christ, no! I'm frightened of ye! Ye might well cast some spell on me. Remember when Anna did that to me?" Gregor rocked on the two back legs of the chair, grinning madly.

"What's this about?" Greame asked, smiling at the thought.

Cat laughed. "I do remember that. It's when I was just learnin' about my powers o' the Sight wi' Anna Macpherson. Gregor had been reduced from Alexander's guard to stable hand because the rents were stolen from right under his nose," she explained to Greame. "No one kent who took them until Anna and I went into the past to see for ourselves. Gregor had fallen asleep, but we found out later that it was because his ale had been drugged at the Games."

"Aye, and a rare foul mood I was in after that," Gregor snorted. "I blamed Anna for my demotion, and ye saw it. Tried to tell me when ye were in the coach, if memory serves. Anna went back into her cott to fetch her staff, and when she came out, the storm she whipped up sent her cloak out around her like a demon's wings. She was speakin' in some queer language and all of a sudden, I felt all calm and peaceful."

"Were the rents ever found, or the culprit who stole them?" Greame asked, enthralled by the story.

The atmosphere in the room became charged at the question. Gregor and Cat looked at each other like only people who had been through traumatic events looked. They were quiet for a moment, then Cat spoke, as though it were too painful for Gregor.

"Aye. Willie Campbell stole them, then killed my Mam."

A silence washed over the world at the statement. Greame opened his mouth to say something, but closed it without uttering a word.

Thankfully, Geoffrey walked in and the world resumed its whispering sounds. The rest of the story would remain in the past. Where it belonged.

❧

It would be a day for stories. The crispness of the early autumn air was a harbinger of the long, cold winter ahead. Not long after Geoffrey came to visit, Kelvin and Robbie entered Cat's kitchen. Kelvin brought his *pìob mhor,* so they all figured this to be a long evening of tales and the pipes. Kenny went out to the root cellar and fetched a venison roast and some vegetables. They may as well eat well while listening to each other's wild yarns.

There was an easy camaraderie amongst the group. They had all shared in settling this place, which took as much to get here as it did to remain. The sea was a fierce woman, yet if it weren't for the sea, none of them would be here today. Greame, captaining his ship the *Revenge* in the waters off Baltimore, had gone after the booty of the *Marianne.* When pirating, you take what's aboard. To Greame's surprise, he'd found Cat aboard, kidnapped from Boston by the vengeful husband of the woman who took Cat in after her tragic search for her father ended.

Now, Cat was preparing to tell the group of her escape from the Redcoat Commander, George Wilson. But one more soul wanted to hear the tale. Gent was scratching on the door. Geoffrey let him in and looked around for Bogle, who was never far from him. She was nowhere to be seen. He closed the door and took his seat, rubbing Gent's ear when he sat on Geoffrey's foot.

"I couldna find Bogle," Geoffrey said absently to Cat.

"She was shot by Wilson," Gregor stated to a shocked group.

Grumbles went around the room at the tragedy. They had all grown fond of the wolf.

"I had to leave her. I ran back up the hill where we hid from the Mohawk," Cat said for the benefit of those who weren't there when she began her story a few days ago. "I heard the commander shoutin' orders to the three men he had wi' him. They were goin' to surround me."

2

Painful Memories

DAWN ARRIVED IN A FOG, casting a hazy gray over the landscape. The woods were thick, making quick movement through it almost impossible, but hiding easy. Cat had to double back without being seen or heard. She knew the area better than her assailants and worked it to her advantage. In a thicket so dense a rabbit couldn't have squeezed in beside her, she hid, waiting for a chance to escape. George Wilson and his men weren't quiet about their search. She heard them a long way off going to the top of the hill.

After a while, when the woods went still, Cat thought it was safe to start back for home. She knew the quickest way was to remain on the trail, free of branches and shrubbery that could tear clothes and flesh alike when running. Halfway home, near the fork where the big pine tree stood, the tingling along the back of her neck began.

She looked behind to see if she was being followed. The eerie fog allowed sight for only a short distance, but she saw no one. Still the tingling increased. Where was he? She knew the commander was nearby, but she didn't know how since he had led his men up the hill. Cat didn't give the man that much credit to actually plot out a strategy.

She began to run again, and at the big pine tree, George Wilson stepped out from behind it catching her in the stomach with his fist. All her breath was expelled in a gasp and she fell to the ground trying desperately to breathe. George Wilson wasn't going to wait for that to happen. He grabbed her hair and dragged her, coughing and sputtering, to a tree, then tied her to it.

George Wilson patiently waited for his men to meet him and make camp. In the meantime, the commander talked incessantly about all the ways he would make her pay for what she had done to his life.

"You ruined me," he hissed in her ear. His breath was hot and moist and sickly, making her cringe.

"My cabin is just a short way down the trail. Ye could be found at any time," Cat said in an even tone, not to incite anger, just to state the obvious.

"Do you take me for an idiot?" He slapped her hard across the face, then smiled as he saw a bloody split form on her lip.

Cat shook her head to let the lights recede, and looked around camp at the three subordinates. None was looking at her. She took that as a good sign. It meant she might have allies in camp.

The day wore on. Cat tried to reach Greame through her mind, but felt only his turmoil. With such distraction, she knew he wouldn't be able to locate her. What she did wonder was why he wasn't out searching for her by now.

By mid-afternoon, George Wilson was getting angrier by the minute. He walked over to Cat and began his sick, detailed list of tortures he had planned for her.

"You're just like those filthy savages. You deserve to be used as such, which I shall take pleasure in greatly, my dear. However, I would like very much to wait until your man gets here to witness the event. He shall be powerless to help you. He shall have to watch as I take you again and again right in front of his eyes. What do you think he'll do? Do you think it will arouse him? Do you think he'll want anything to do with you after I've finished with you?"

Cat ignored him. At this point, she knew not to speak, but wasn't afraid of the commander either. She was almost free of her ropes, then she would flee.

Suddenly, he ripped open the top of her cloak and jammed his hand onto her breast. Her eyes blazed at him with intense hatred, and he raised an eyebrow.

"So what do you think you can do with a mere look? Do you think I've not been looked at in such a way before? Don't fear, bitch, you'll like it more when you are under me," he laughed and pinched her nipple hard enough to bring tears to her eyes. This seemed to satisfy him until one of his men, the same man who took charge after Wilson was shot last year, stood and angrily rushed to stand in front of George Wilson.

Breathing heavily, Corporal Thaddeus Bakeman growled out, "With all due respect, sir, this is an illegal act against a civilian!"

The commander, with great speed, grabbed his pistol and smashed Bakeman across the face. He went down and stayed down. The other two men, clearly afraid of Wilson, ignored the situation and made busy work with tending the fire and making food preparations.

Around dusk, the corporal started coming around. Earlier, George Wilson ordered Bakeman to be tied to the same tree as Cat. He had a nasty cut over his eye, and seemed to go in and out of consciousness.

The aroma of food was making her stomach rumble. She hadn't eaten since yesterday morning. One of the soldiers stood with a plate in his hand and asked the commander if he should feed the prisoners.

"Let the two of them think about what they've done. No. They'll get no food this night."

The fog, which had remained for most of the day, finally lifted, but left everything damp. The temperature was cooling and Cat was beginning to shiver. She had to free herself of the ropes.

A groan from Corporal Bakeman signaled he was waking up. After a couple of minutes, she heard him whisper, "Don't fret, miss, I'll get us free."

Cat had to suppress a laugh. Here this man was, barely conscious, tied to a tree, and not one of George Wilson's favorite people at the moment, yet he was going to free her. Well, best of luck, she thought.

George Wilson was pacing around the fire. His hands were behind him and he was muttering to himself. Once in a while he'd stop and train his ear towards the settlement, as if hearing the sound of a rescue, but no one came. Finally, after festering for quite a long time, he needed to vent his frustration out on something … or someone.

"Why haven't your men come for you?" Wilson growled in her face.

Cat shrugged.

Once again, he slapped her across the face, making those lights explode in her head again.

Her famous temper flared at the assault. "How in Christ's name should I ken! Do ye think I can somehow conjure them up for ye!"

The commander was poised to strike her again, but Corporal Bakeman unwisely intervened. Thankfully, it only took one strike to put the corporal out again. Wilson returned to the fire and sat on a log tossing pinecones into the flames, sending sparks into the air like a thousand fireflies.

When the commander finally fell asleep near the fire, Cat continued in earnest to free herself from her bonds. She closed her eyes, and like she had done on several previous occasions, pictured the ropes. With intense concentration, she felt them loosen from her wrists, as she manipulated the rough hemp with her mind.

The two soldiers weren't paying any attention to Cat or Corporal Bakeman. When Cat began untying the corporal's wrists, she heard a small gasp of surprise from him.

"We'll wait for a while before we leave. Perhaps yer two friends will be asleep by then," Cat whispered to Bakeman. She saw him nod, the firelight making him look very young.

One by one, the two soldiers nodded off. One of them snored so loudly, it was a wonder how George Wilson slept through it all. One thing about it, Cat thought, they won't hear us leave.

The moon, nearly full, rose through the trees, casting strange shadows around the camp. After an indeterminable amount of time had elapsed, Cat looked over at the corporal and noticed he was sleeping. She nudged him, but when she did, his head bobbed onto his chest. He was out again. Cat couldn't wait any longer. She couldn't take the time to think of what the commander would do to Bakeman as punishment for insubordination, she had to think of herself.

Cat quietly stood and walked away from the tree, disappearing into the night. The two soldiers—one awake now—never tried to stop her. He just nodded and looked away, as though preparing his alibi. Cat guessed they didn't really want any part of the deed to begin with, but were too scared to do anything about it.

Just because she stayed on the trail, didn't mean it was without peril. Roots and stumps, clearly visible during the day, tripped, snagged clothes and made for a treacherous escape in the dimly lit night. At least with the fog, the twigs and leaves were damp enough to not snap when stepped on. It made for a fairly quiet getaway.

It also made it quiet enough for a stealthy pursuit.

Though Cat's wits were with her, she had been too close to George Wilson all day to not have the feeling he was still near her. She could feel him now, even though she left him sleeping a few minutes ago. She turned around at a sound behind her and saw a man coming down the trail. She quickly ducked behind a tree. As the man got closer, she heard him calling her name very softly. It was Bakeman. Cat stepped out from behind the tree.

"Were ye followed?"

"No. I left the three of them in camp. Peters was still snoring, so I'm certain they didn't hear me leave."

"What about the one who wasna sleepin'?"

"Dawson won't say anything," Bakeman assured her.

"How can ye be so sure? If the commander wakes to find us gone, dinna ye think he'll question Dawson to the point o' breakin'?"

"Let's just get you to safety. How far is it?" Bakeman said, avoiding her question.

"About an hour durin' the daylight. It'll be a bit longer in the dark."

They started down the trail once again, but Cat still couldn't shake the feeling Wilson was near. They hadn't gone more than fifty feet when Cat heard a rustle off to her right. She strained to hear it again, but there was only silence.

They continued forward, but all the hairs on her arms were now bristling to attention, sending her skin into goose flesh. He had to be near. All the warning signs were screaming at her, but she couldn't get his bearing. She quickened her pace, and Bakeman followed suit.

It was though the man could see in the dark. From behind a tree, a whip snaked out and wrapped itself around the corporal's throat. Wilson yanked on the lash with such force that Bakemen flew towards him and was beaten severely with the stout end of it. Cat threw herself on Wilson and tried to stop him, but the commander smashed his fist into her eye and she blacked out.

❧

It was morning when Cat awoke. She was tied to another tree, hugging it this time. Alone, and in a very vulnerable position, she searched to the left and right as best as she could with her body squashed against the tree. Assuming Bakeman had somehow overpowered Wilson and they were both dead now, she once again began the process of releasing her ropes.

A red squirrel scolded her from a branch above, as if she could do anything about her trespass on its territory. She was nearly free when that telltale tingle renewed itself.

"So glad you've come to, my dear," Wilson greeted her with too much niceness in his voice.

He was directly behind her so no matter how much she strained her neck Cat couldn't see him. There was something very sinister about him standing back there. Then she felt the first strike hit her back, ripping through her woolen cloak and sark. Stunned, she inhaled sharply through her teeth. At first she didn't know what had hit her. It took a moment for it to sink in that Wilson was whipping her!

Enraged, and desperately wanting to kill him, she struggled harder with her bonds. If only she could free herself. Another lash struck. This time it felt like it went to the bone. Suddenly, she heard his twisted thoughts. He wanted her to scream; that he'd get great pleasure from it.

She was almost free of the ropes when another lash, this one with the intensity for real damage, ripped into her back. She did scream. She couldn't help herself. Feeling like she would black out again, she fought it and threw up. That seemed to make the bastard very happy because he laughed, evil and malicious. While he was a bit distracted, she managed to free herself, but before she could turn around, the whip hit again with such force it knocked her back into the tree.

That's when she felt it. The one thing Wilson never did was remove her pistol. Had he continued groping her, he would no doubt have found the weapon, but now she had an advantage. Slowly, she pushed herself away from the tree.

He was still laughing like a madman as she heard him gather in the whip for another flogging. George Wilson apparently hadn't noticed that her hands were free. In an act of supernatural desperation, Cat reached inside her cloak, grabbed her pistol, cocked it, turned and pulled the trigger. There was no time to aim.

The whip was poised mid-air for another strike. In that brief instant, George Wilson saw the ball leave the barrel in a cloud of smoke aiming straight for his head. With the evil smile frozen on his face, he was mesmerized, unable to retreat from the inevitable. The lead ball struck him between the eyes, sending him backwards with such force he slammed to the ground several feet away.

❧

"That's what Greame and I heard then," said Gregor.

Cat nodded. "Aye. Ye must hae been verra close, 'cause I heard yer horses within a minute.

"Not close enough to do the killin' ourselves," growled Greame.

The room erupted with what each of the men would have done to Wilson given the chance. It took a few minutes for them to quiet down.

Cat excused herself, feeling too much of the ordeal again. She caught Greame's eye and he left the cabin with her. They walked down to the shore to let the negative emotions evaporate from them. The soothing sound of the waves began doing their magic to the harmony of their minds.

"I'm sorry, Greame."

Greame stopped short, forcing Cat to stop with him. "What on earth might ye be sorry for, Garnet?"

"I seem to invite trouble wherever I go. I canna seem to help it."

"Well, I ken from now on, ye'll no' be left alone. Someone will always be around." He noticed she was about to protest. "I dinna mean someone will be by yer side every wakin' moment, but if somethin' does arise, one of us will be here."

Cat smiled and nodded. It was a prudent gesture.

"May I be able to choose who gets the honors?"

Greame chuckled deeply. "Ye can just tell me ye want me to be the one."

Cat raised her eyebrow, and in all seriousness said, "I'd prefer Gregor."

His look of mortification made her laugh. "I'm just teasin'! O' course I want it to be ye."

He nodded and they began walking on. After a few minutes, he said, "Really? Gregor? Why him?"

Cat giggled. "One look at that Angry Giant, and no one would dare to rouse him."

"Ye dinna think I look mean enough?"

"Oh, ye're right fierce enough, but ye've got too much kindness in yer eyes."

He pressed a kiss on her cheek and held her hand for a while longer staring out at the moonlit sea.

3

Reunions

CAT'S WOUNDS WERE NEARLY healed by the end of October. On her birthday, the thirty-first—Samhain, the night when the veil between the living and dead is the thinnest—Cat wanted to do a remembrance meditation. She wanted her family around her. It was strange how sometimes she felt so alone, even with Greame's family surrounding her. She missed her mother, Anna and Lachlan the most, but would be pleased if any of her family showed up. The dead didn't remember dates.

Well after supper, after the *ceilidh* that Greame had surprised her with—including an apple pie Kenny insisted on making for her, and Highland music played on Kelvin's pipes—she set out her meditation items on the kitchen table. They consisted of a silk square of emerald, indigo and raspberry swirls, candles, fragrant herbs and the enormous amethyst crystal Greame had given to her for just such occasions.

"Would ye like me to be wi' ye, or are ye wantin' to be alone?" Greame asked.

She looked up at his rugged face, usually hard and uncompromising, now softened in the dim light of the candles, and smiled. "Why dinna ye stay, if ye dinna mind. Ye've already met them all, and perhaps they'll hae somethin' to say to ye."

He coughed out a laugh. "Garnet, ye hae a strange way o' thinkin' I've *met* them all. The only ones I e'er met while they were livin' were yer Da and Anna Macpherson. Meetin' the dead is a wee bit different, wouldna ye say?"

Cat had to giggle, too. "Aye, well, there's no' many a man who would dare go where ye hae gone wi' me, *a' ghaoil.* So, what'll it be?"

Greame took a seat next to her and laid his hand over hers. "I'll stay."

"Great! Let's begin," she glanced at the clock in the corner. "It's nearin' midnight."

She poured the boiling water over the herbs, releasing their fragrance into the air. Balsam needles, tansy and bayberry leaves gave off an earthy, woodsy smell. For times like this, she wished she had asked Far Eyes, the Penobscot shaman, for the herbal concoction he had used once that emitted an aroma that reminded her of Scotland. But the fragrance of Maine would do for tonight.

Cat and Greame held each other's hands and closed their eyes, silently saying their prayers of protection. Within minutes, Anna's cackle was heard from a far away place, making both of them smile. Cat could still see her ancient mentor, her long, steel-gray plait, those ebony eyes that held the secrets of the universe in their black depths, and the toothless smile that was ever present.

Anna seemed to appear at the kitchen table, taking a seat next to Greame. She still held her oak staff with the Celtic interlace design carved around it and the amethyst orb it held in its root ball.

"Hallò, a Chatrìona. Ciamar a tha thu?" She asked in the *Gàidhlig.*

"I am well, Mistress. And what of yerself?"

"Bored."

At that statement, Cat and Greame laughed. "Well, I hope ye're no' lookin' for us to keep ye entertained, Mistress. It's too dangerous," Cat told her.

"Och, aye, I ken all about it. And ye've kept this old woman happy, but I feel it may be time to return."

"What? Ye mean leave the other world and be reborn?" Cat asked, dismayed.

"Aye."

"But how will I get along wi'out ye, Mistress? What if I need help from the other side? Whom shall I call upon?"

"Stop, Garnet! Do ye forget why I gave ye yer name? What it means?"

Greame was always amazed that this could actually happen and that he could be privy to it. But even he was a bit dismayed at the thought of not having Anna as an ally on the other side.

"Aye, ye gave it to me because ye thought I had the qualities of a garnet: courageous, determined, fiery and independent."

"Remain steadfast on independent, Garnet. Ye dinna need me anymore. Ye are verra capable of managin' anythin' that comes yer way. Ye've proven it again and again. Stand strong, lass, and dinna use me as a crutch."

She was gone. No goodbye, no good luck, just gone. Back into the ether from whence she came. Cat was too distracted to hear from anyone else, and blew out the candles.

Greame watched her, wondering what she was thinking, but knew better than to ask when she wore that expression. She got up and paced around the kitchen, absently picking up and putting items down.

"I'm goin' to bed. Are ye comin'?" She announced.

"I'll be along shortly," he said, not moving from his chair at the table.

Cat disappeared into their bedroom and closed the door.

Greame relit the candles. He wanted to try something for himself. He heard Cat get into bed, and then he began his protection prayers.

"Da? Are ye there?" Greame whispered.

He waited a few minutes, figuring it would take longer since his father had been dead for nearly twenty years.

"Mam?"

There was no reply from either of his parents. Maybe they had been reborn already. He pondered that for a few more minutes. Who would they be now? Would he recognize them if he saw them again? He had never really considered the thought until Cat asked him if he believed in reincarnation. He told her he could consider the possibility, and after what he'd experienced with her and Far Eyes, he knew now that anything was possible. He blew out the candles and headed for bed.

"Did ye get yer answers?" Cat asked groggily, nearly asleep.

"No."

"Ye'll get them in yer dreams tonight," she said, then rolled over.

Greame closed his eyes and called up his parents' faces. In his mind, he asked if they were well, then let the question drift into the ether. Wherever they were, perhaps they heard him.

❧

The sweet, musty aroma of fallen leaves assailed Cat's nose when she walked out of her cabin heading for the privy. She breathed in deeply, filling her lungs with the fragrance. The morning was bright with no wind, a rarity along the coast. Gent had finally started acting like himself again. She knew losing Bogle was hard on him. He ran up ahead as Cat walked down to the privy. There was a strangeness in the air, as though it was waiting for something. She looked up into the sky. It was a cloud-free blue. It didn't look or feel like snow, but she could tell something was brewing.

For a moment, she wished she had gone to the Penobscots' winter camp to see Jim and Jumping Turtle and their one-year-old baby boy, who had yet to be named. The lad was good-natured and had a perpetual smile on his face. His outstanding feature was brilliant blue eyes he'd obviously inherited from Jim. Cat shuddered at the memory of Black Devil's attempt to possess that baby boy and destroy the Penobscot tribe from within. The Mohawk shaman's seed of evil perpetrated out of hate for Cat. That was over now, and she wondered if what she was feeling was the anniversary of that event, or something new. She left the privy and returned to the cabin to start breakfast. Greame was still sleeping when she'd left, and she wondered if he'd had any dreams last night.

"Good mornin,' Garnet," Greame said in a rather cheerful voice.

Cat smiled at his tone. "Ye're chipper this mornin.' Did ye sleep well?"

He was still clad just in his nightshirt. His rich brown hair, mussed from sleep, cascaded over his thick shoulders. Barefoot, he walked over to Cat and pressed a kiss on her cheek. "Indeed I did."

"Any dreams ye remember?"

He smiled widely, transforming his face into true pleasure. "Aye. My Da visited wi' me." Greame sat at the kitchen table; Cat took a seat next to him. He grabbed her hands and said, "He told me he was proud o' me, Garnet." He shook his head as though the compliment had never been told to him before. "My Da … proud o' me. Huh."

"Greame, ye act surprised to hear such a thing."

He looked at her, his eyes turning a brighter green, and nodded. His voice was choked when he spoke. "I am."

Cat hugged him, her throat catching to hold back her own tears.

He released her and said, "I was too young when he passed. There was nothin' for him to be proud of."

"From what I hear, that's no' true." Cat's amethyst eyes had a faraway look to them. "He made the special visit last night to tell ye what he couldna in life. He's always been proud o' ye, Greame. He just didna ken how to say it."

Without a word, he got up and went into the bedroom. Cat knew it wasn't just to get dressed.

❧

As the afternoon faded into evening, a wall of angry gray clouds hid the sun on the horizon. The wind picked up in earnest, whipping leaves against the windows from seemingly all directions.

By dark, small branches started crashing into the cabin. No small feat since the nearest trees were over a hundred feet away, cleared for just such occasions. The winter storms could be disastrous on the spruce and pines, uprooting them from their shallow, rocky bases. Sometimes, a pine nearly four feet in diameter, somehow managing to live its entire life straddling a boulder, would be toppled by such winds. The soil was so sparse, the bedrock so close to the surface, there was no way for its roots to go deep enough.

In the small settlement made up mostly of Greame's family, it was taken for granted that when a storm of this magnitude hit, everyone gathered in Cat's and Greame's cabin. They all went there for meals anyway, but tonight, the men brought their blankets with the intention of spending the night under one roof. Gent particularly seemed to enjoy these times. Geoffrey usually slept with him nearest the fire.

They would all tell stories of when they were lads, or older tales of when their grandsires were lads, and since they were cousins, they each knew the tales by heart. Cat and Gregor would always be asked to participate just so they could hear something they had never heard before.

Gregor had terrific stories of Alexander Robertson, the thirteenth chief of Clan Donnachaidh, also called the Poet Chief for the verse he was famous for writing. Much of it was political, much of it bawdy, and some, even though Alexander was said to despise women, was of a certain lass known only as Phoebe. No one knew anything about her, and it was speculated that perhaps she broke his heart.

As the first sounds of rain splattered against the windows, Gregor said, "I'd like to be tellin' a ghost story befittin' the ragin' storm and the significant date of the evenin.'"

Cat scanned the room full of grown men, all eager now to return to their childhood and be frightened by things they didn't understand. She smiled, wondering what any of them would think of her *real-life* experiences with the unknown. Greame caught her eye and raised an eyebrow. He must have been thinking the very same thing, and she smiled at him.

The candles flickered in the dimly lit room, as though preparing for their part in the story. The cabin creaked and groaned in the fierce wind, adding to the eeriness of the night.

"In the time of Brus, there lived a lad who was said to be descended from the King himself. The bastard child, named Simon Buchan, was no' raised wi' the finery duly belongin' to him, but he grew up strong and verra clever, despite his circumstances. He worked in his uncle's forge, learnin' the craft of iron. It was said that by the age o' ten, young Simon produced the best claymores in the glen.

"Word o' this fantastic tale reached the King himself and he wanted to see it wi' his own eyes. A royal messenger was sent to the forge wi' instructions to hae a claymore crafted by the lad fit for the King. The messenger was also instructed to watch the lad create it, just to be sure 'twas true.

"Simon Buchan was honored to hae his craft be so highly thought of, but his Uncle Henry was a jealous man, and decided to teach his young nephew that life wasna that easy. Henry would thwart Simon's efforts, but first he would take one of Simon's masterpieces that was awaitin' to be tempered and hide it for use later. Henry obtained a less than pure form of iron his nephew had ne'er used before. It was much harder and no' easy to shape.

"The Royal Messenger watched as young Simon hammered and hammered on the iron, makin' nothin' like what he was supposedly famous for. Simon's young arms werna strong enough yet to hammer such a rigid metal. After many hours, the sun went down, and the lad's arm gave out. Now was Henry's chance to usurp the lad. Deceptively, Henry helped Simon into bed, and while the Royal Messenger was gettin' a bite to eat from Simon's dear Mam, Henry retrieved the claymore creation he had hidden, and began to heat it.

"When the Royal Messenger heard the hammerin,' he went to see if the lad had regained his strength and was goin' to complete the King's sword after all. Henry pretended to be startled that the messenger was still about and that he'd been caught creatin' the famous claymore. The messenger, seein' this rare fine piece o' craftsmanship bein' created by Henry, asked if he had forged all the other claymores presumably created by the ten-year-old lad. Henry feigned embarrassment and begged forgiveness from the King. He handed the messenger the already completed sword and took all the credit for its perfection."

"Bastard," Geoffrey grumbled.

"What happened to Simon?" Kenny asked.

Cat and Greame looked at each other and hid smiles that the story was having Gregor's desired effect. The men were well into the yarn. Cat looked at Gregor, knowing him best of all, and could read his thoughts. He was ready to deliver the blow.

"Well, it took several years for young Simon to hear of his uncle's treachery. By then, he was near a man, a verra strong man. For after that day of embarrassment, he vowed he'd no' be weak again. He hammered with the largest, heaviest hammers, and his arms grew thick and strong. He was able to shape even the toughest o' metals wi'out so much as a breakin' o' sweat, which infuriated Henry.

"One day, the King's Royal Messenger returned. He looked down his nose at Simon, and searched the forge for Henry, who was tryin' his best to blend into the shadows, for he kent he was about to be found out.

"Simon bowed to the messenger and begged him to give him another chance. The messenger pondered, then nodded in agreement. This time, there was no chance for Henry to make a switch. Simon, now a braw man and skilled far beyond his uncle, chose his own iron to work wi.'"

"Did he ken o' his uncle's devious deed?" Robbie asked.

"Och, no. But once the messenger saw the craftsmanship bein' wielded by Simon, he kent he'd been deceived. This also meant the King had been deceived. Henry was taken to the Tower o' London to spend the rest o' his days in irons of a different kind."

"That wasna a ghost story," Kenny said, looking very disappointed.

"That's because I'm no' finished," Gregor said, reaching over to give Kenny a smack to the back of his head.

"Anyway … many years later, a new king released old Henry from the Tower. Whilst he was rottin' away, he cursed his nephew many times, and in his hatred, set forth that a sword created by Simon would cause Simon's death.

"Simon heard o' the curse put upon his heid by his vengeful uncle, and by this time had marrit a young maiden named Evelyn from the next village. They said she was a witch, but no one e'er found her to be anythin' but a sweet lass.

"One night when Simon wasna home, Henry paid this lass a visit. He bound her and promised to do unspeakable things to her. As he was preparin' himself, Evelyn started whisperin' words Henry had ne'er heard before. He yelled at her to be quiet and was just about to beat her, when suddenly, right in front o' his eyes, she began turnin' aulder and aulder.

"Henry couldna believe what he was witnessin.' He watched in horror as the ropes he bound a pretty young lass wi' fell away from an auld hag. She rose like a specter in front o' him, all the while chantin' the same strange words o'er and o'er.

"Suddenly, there was a poundin' on the door. Henry ran to open it, but all that stood in front of him was a claymore. He kent who had forged it, for it was perfect in every way. Then, before he could slam the door on the iron, the mighty sword lifted itself and ran old Henry through. He fell just outside the doorway, where he remained until Simon found him the next mornin.'

"'Woman,' he said to his young wife. 'How has my uncle come to be on our doorstep, dead by my claymore?' Evelyn innocently came to the door and screamed in horror at the sight. Simon wrapped his arms around his tiny, beautiful wife. He kent she couldna hae done it, for the sword was taller than she was."

Just then, a terrible gust of wind hit the cabin and made the timbers creak and pop, sounding very much like the specter claymore wanting to claim its next victim. All eyes were on the front door.

Greame couldn't help himself. He let out a high-pitched scream that made everyone in the room, including Gregor, jump out of their seats uttering profanities or prayers or nonsensical mumbles of terror.

Cat turned and slapped his arm, but Greame felt nothing because he was laughing too hard.

"Verra amusin,' Greame," Gregor grumbled. He walked over to the front door and opened it, then stepped out into the storm.

"Where's he goin'?" Robbie asked.

"Prob'ly the same place I'm goin,'" Kelvin said, tossing a scowl over Greame's way. "To relieve himself."

"No one cares to hear the rest o' the story?" Greame asked, watching his cousins get ready for bed.

"Ye always did find frightenin' the life out o' a man fairly entertainin,' Greame. Even when we were but lads, ye'd do that to us," Geoffrey said, rolled up on the floor with Gent.

"I canna help it. Ye should hae seen yer faces." Greame began chuckling anew at the memory.

"And ye wonder why we ne'er cared to tell them when ye were around," Kenny stated.

"I apologize then. I dinna ken ye'd all take it so hard."

Cat walked into her bedroom and shut the door. She'd let them work it out, but she was smiling as she got ready for bed.

❧

Sometime in the wee hours of the morning, the storm played itself out. When dawn broke, the sky was a vivid canvas splashed in colors no mortal could have painted. Cat walked down to the privy and breathed in the cleansed air, crisp and chilly. A pair of deer, clad in their grayish-brown winter coats, stood watching her at the edge of the woods. A couple of spruce trees were toppled, snapped by the relentless wind. She noticed something else, too. A pillar of smoke drifting on the water. She ran back to the cabin and alerted Greame.

Greame and Gregor went to see where the smoke was coming from. At this time of year, the only people who inhabited the Cape were in their settlement. Far Eyes and the rest of the Penobscot were in their winter camp many miles up river.

"Cat's no' joinin' us?" Gregor inquired.

"She'll watch us from the cabin." Meaning she'll *see* with her Second Sight if there is danger or just Mother Nature playing with fire.

Cat sat on her bed and began twirling her hair. She saw Greame and Gregor walking through the woods, then ventured further to locate the nature of the flames. It was more of a feeling than actually seeing the man, but there sat Corporal Thaddeus Bakeman, looking haggard and beaten, warming himself beside a fire. She had assumed he was dead when he never showed up after Wilson was killed.

What had he been doing alone out there all this time? she wondered. Were the other two soldiers still out there as well?

She grabbed her cloak and ran out the door with Gent. Kelvin was nearly bowled over as she ran around the cabin.

"Whoa, lass, where are ye goin' in such a rush?" he asked, grabbing her shoulders. "Do ye need our help?"

"No … well … perhaps it'd be prudent to fetch the men," she stammered, looking in the older man's blue eyes.

They caught up to Greame and Gregor quickly, and Cat explained what she saw. The group walked to the crude camp where they startled the corporal at the fire.

"You!" Was all he managed to say when Cat appeared from the woods.

"I thought ye were dead, corporal," she said with a smile.

"I should have been," he said, rubbing his head with a crooked arm.

"What of the other two soldiers?" Greame asked, scanning the area with a keen eye.

"I really don't think they stayed here. Wilson left me for dead. They're all long away by now."

"Let me look at yer arm." Cat squatted down beside Bakeman.

The corporal's left arm had been broken and not set back into its correct position, healing slightly crooked.

"Ye're a verra lucky man, corporal," Cat said, turning his forearm to test its range of motion.

"Please. Do not call me corporal. I no longer consider myself in the army. Not after what I witnessed." He looked at Cat with a pained stare. "Are you all right? I take it you were saved by these brave men of yours, since I was clearly of no use to you."

Before she could stop him, Gregor said, "This rare brave lass saved herself. Shot Wilson between the eyes before his whip could do its worst."

Bakeman looked sharply at her, "He whipped you?"

Cat nodded.

Bakeman shook his head slowly. "I apologize from the depths of my heart, Miss."

"It wasna for yer lack o' tryin,' corp … Mr. Bakeman."

"Thaddeus, ma'am, please call me Thaddeus."

"It's been over a month since the incident, Bakemen. Where hae ye been all this time?" Greame asked, still a bit wary of the man.

"Pretty much where I had fallen. I don't know how many days I was out, but when I came to, I tried to locate the camp. I couldn't go far. Kept passing out. When I did find camp, it was deserted. Good thing for berries or I'd have starved. I couldn't do much with this arm until recently. I've been attempting to make my way off this peninsula for the past two days. The storm last night made me long for a roof over my head."

"So what are yer plans?" Cat asked.

"Head back to Boston. From there, I'll wait for spring, then go back to Kent."

"No desire to stay in America then?"

"My family's in England. That's where I belong."

Cat glanced at Greame with questioning eyes. He just nodded.

"'Tis a long walk to Boston, Thaddeus. If ye've a mind to, why dinna ye stay the winter here wi' us?" Cat said. "After all, what would Scottish hospitality be if we didna offer?"

A confused look flitted over Bakeman's face. "But, I'm a Redcoat."

"Well, if ye dinna mind, we dinna. Besides, dinna ye just say ye werna in the army anymore?"

Gregor put a big hand on the young man's shoulder. "Ye can bunk wi' me."

"We're tryin' to make him feel welcome, no' scare him to death," Kenny said, and they all laughed.

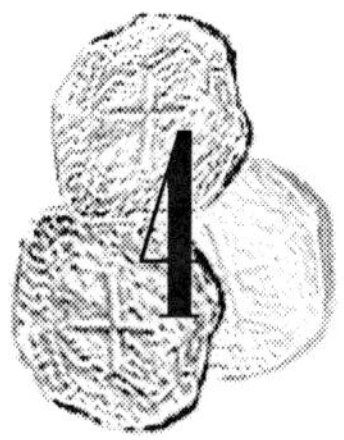

4

Nowhere to Run

WINTER WORE ON LIKE A boring conversation. Never-ending bitter winds and fierce snowstorms ravaged the small settlement from November through March.

"I really dinna ken why I had to choose to live in Maine," Cat said, staring out at the bleak, white landscape.

"Where else would ye be?" Greame asked, looking up from the letter he was trying to compose.

"That's just it, I dinna ken where else to go. Certainly no' Boston, and as much as I would cherish seein' Scotland again, I ken that shall ne'er be."

"Ne'er is a long time, Garnet." He stabbed the gull feather he used for a quill into the bottle of ink. Greame knew she was going somewhere with this conversation, and he wanted to catch all the subtleties of her thought process.

Cat turned from the wavy glass to look at Greame. "Would you consider goin' back?"

Without hesitation, he said, "Aye. So would the rest o' my family."

She didn't say anything for a minute. When she did finally speak it was nearly a whisper. "Am I holdin' ye here?"

Greame took a seat next to her on the settee. "What's this really all about?"

Cat looked at the smooth stone in her hand, a treasure she'd found on the beach last summer. It was a perfectly white oval. A jewel. She rubbed it to a soft shine. Without looking at Greame, she said, "I had a vision last night."

Silently, he waited for her to continue.

When she looked up, her expression was pained. "Death. I always see Death. I keep thinkin' there has to be a place where it wilna find me. Someplace where I can escape its grasp. I dinna want to live through another war, Greame."

"And that's what ye saw? War?"

She nodded.

"Could ye see who was involved?"

"The whole world."

His eyebrow quirked. "How could the entire world be at war with each other?"

"We already ken England, Spain and France are no' friendly at the moment. At least accordin' to Gregor. How he kens, I canna be sure, but much o' Europe will become involved soon after England and France start up again."

He was scratching his chin, pondering the ramifications of something of that magnitude. "If this comes to pass, Garnet, there'd *be* no safe place."

"I'd like to think that stayin' right here and out of sight is the best course of action, but I see the Indians involved, as well."

"The Penobscot? Who will they be fightin'?"

"The English. The whole world is fightin' the damned English!"

She got off the settee and agitatedly paced back and forth. "And to make matters worse, Greame," she stopped and glared at him. "Highlanders are sidin' *wi'* the English!"

"What!?" He shouted. "Ye canna be right about that. After all the English've done to us, and ye say we're goin' to fight *alongside* our enemies?"

Cat shrugged, started twirling her hair, and walked into the kitchen to begin supper. Greame heard pots and pans being abused and decided to remain where he was until she calmed down.

Gregor walked in just then, pounding snow off his boots in the open doorway for a minute.

"Do ye live in a barn?" Cat hollered from the kitchen.

Gregor looked at Greame with a *she's in a mood* observation. Greame nodded. Gregor closed the offending door and walked into the keeping room with Greame.

In a quiet voice he asked, "Is there somethin' I should ken?"

Matching his tone, Greame said, "She had a vision last night."

"Now what?"

"When she calms down a bit, we'll talk about it."

Kenny, Robbie and Thaddeus walked in next, and before there were any more reprimands from the kitchen, Greame and Gregor met them at the door and they all walked out to the barn. Kelvin and Geoffrey were tending to the horses and wondered who'd called the meeting.

Greame relayed the information from Cat's vision to the men. They were quiet, each turning the news over in their heads. Gregor broke the silence.

"She's right about England, Spain and France … and the Indians. Massachusetts is gatherin' militiamen, as is New York, Virginia and Pennsylvania. The French attacked an Indian tribe in Ohio this past June killin' a number of braves, includin' their chief. I'm certain that as soon as the weather breaks enough for men to march again, there's goin' to be retaliation by the Indians and English. This wilna go away wi'out a war. There's too much at stake. An entire country is waitin' to be claimed, and too many powers want it."

Gregor's words hung in the air like the snowflakes that began falling once again.

"Garnet's quandary is what to do? Do we remain here in Maine, return to Scotland, or somethin' else?" Greame let the question settle to see if there was a consensus amongst his family, then added, "Or do we fight for this country?"

"Fight who? is the question," Kenny said, rubbing a horse's neck.

The barn erupted in a debate that continued through supper. Cat listened intently while opinions were shared and fears were laid out on the table for all to pick at. By the end of the evening, they had accomplished nothing, but at least everyone knew where each other stood. It seemed time would dictate their paths.

❧

In her dream, the man was tall and young, emitting an air of command. He was an explorer of sorts, seemingly fearless. He was on a mission to speak with the French, to convince them to surrender their forts in Ohio. He wore a uniform, so she concluded that he was an English soldier.

The events that followed him would start this new war. He would fire the first shot that set the world to war.

Cat woke with a start to a dark room. Greame was sleeping soundly beside her, uninterrupted by her fitful dream. She slid out from under the bedclothes and quietly left the room. In the keeping room, she stoked the fire and sat on the settee staring at the flames as they began to envelop the logs. Gent watched her with his shaggy eyes, but never rose to greet her.

The clock in the corner struck three. The moon was making its descent through the star-studded sky, casting cool white streaks across the floor. Cat shivered, thinking of the man she had dreamed of. What would happen if he weren't there to fire that shot? Would someone else just do it instead?

"It all comes down to fate again," she said to herself, remembering her other visions that played themselves out to the end, no matter how hard she tried to alter them.

She separated a lock of hair and began to wrap it around her fingers. The softness of it always soothed her. The fire cast its light onto the moving auburn lock, making it sparkle. Maybe she was going about this all wrong. Perhaps what she should be doing was concentrating on how to remain out of the war and safe, not change the outcome of it. If her visions could tell her of the safest place for her and her family to be, wouldn't that be better than knowing who fired the first shot?

Her feet were freezing from resting on the cold wood floor. She curled her legs under her and began a meditation.

For a long while, all she did was watch the moon shadows trace their way across the room. The previous vision was still too fresh in her mind to concentrate. Her head bobbed and woke her. She would get no answers this way, and returned to bed. Greame murmured if she was all right. Cat patted his shoulder and rolled over.

❧

The waves crashed onto the ship's bow, sending water high over the deck. The winds whipped at the sails, straining the taut white canvas to its limit. Cat looked around to see that the ship was deserted. Where was everyone? She made her way below decks in search of the captain of this ill-fated vessel. Still, she found no one aboard. She searched all the cabins to no avail. It was a ghost ship.

She wondered what relevance the vision had to her. Who was this ship supposed to be for? It wasn't the *Revenge* so she didn't think it was meant for her or Greame. Who else would take a voyage in such a storm?

Cat woke when Greame touched her shoulder.

"Are you all right, Garnet?" His voice was sleep-raspy.

"Sorry to hae woken ye. I was dreamin.'"

She sat up and noticed it was getting light.

"Did ye want to talk about it?"

She turned to face him. He was up on his elbow now, watching her.

"It was a ship wi' no one aboard in a fierce storm."

He brushed a stray strand of hair from her eyes.

"Was it the *Revenge*?"

Cat shook her head. "I dinna understand it. I was trying to hae a vision as to how to stay safe from this war, and this is what I was shown. Verra helpful," she said sarcastically.

"Maybe it was at that."

Cat looked at him with a frown, waiting for an explanation.

"Think about it, Garnet. Ye were thinkin' o' leavin' Maine, perhaps even returnin' to Scotland. Either way, it would hae involved a ship, right? Dinna ye think this could be tellin' ye to stay put?"

A grin emerged on her face, and she stretched herself across the bed to plant a kiss on his forehead. He grabbed her and pulled her onto his chest. Further examination of the subject would have to wait.

There was still some snow on the ground, but the warmth of the April day made everyone in the settlement long for spring. Cat opened all the cabin windows and doors to freshen the stale, closed-up air of the interior. She had Kenny rig up a couple of lines to hang her rugs on so she could beat out the winter's dirt. He helped her drag the larger ones out and lift them over the sturdy ropes.

"Why dinna I beat these while ye do whate'er else ye need to do inside," Kenny suggested.

Cat looked at him with her head cocked. "Really? Ye dinna hae ye own chores to do?"

"No, I dinna mind helpin' ye. There's always more to do in yer cabin anyway. It's so much roomier than mine."

"Well, I was plannin' on scrubbin' the floors. If ye really dinna mind, it would save me quite a bit o' time. Thank ye, Kenny! I'll fix ye a special treat for supper tonight," she said over her shoulder as she headed for her cabin.

After a few hours of being on her knees, Cat brought out the last bucket of dirty water and dumped it. As she turned back to survey the gleaming cherry floors, a movement in the clearing caught her eyes. She squealed, startling Kenny, threw down the bucket and ran to meet Jim, Jumping Turtle and their wee son.

Kenny trotted to the barn to fetch the rest of the men and joined Cat in greeting Jim and his family.

"He's gettin' so big!" Cat said, hoisting the smiling youngster onto her hip. "Please tell me ye've given him a name finally."

Jim smiled, his blue eyes twinkling as he proudly watched his son in Cat's arms. "We have. His name is Harry Welapewet. That means handsome man, of which we have no doubt he will grow ta be."

Tears sprang to Cat's eyes remembering Jim's best friend who was killed in Boston by the English when they tried to "press" him onto the *HMS Lark* a couple years ago.

"Harry ... Oh, Jim, Harry would hae been so proud." Cat turned her amethyst gaze to Jim's Penobscot wife, and said, "Welapewet is a fine name, Jumpin' Turtle. He looks a lot like ye, except for his blue eyes. Is he still a good lad?"

Jumping Turtle smiled and nodded. Still very shy, she did manage to say, "He is very good boy."

Jim whispered something to her, and she said, "He is *a* very good boy."

"Well, will ye be stayin' wi' us for awhile?" Cat asked the two of them, as she passed Harry to Greame who'd just reached the gathering.

"Don't put yourself out, Garnet. We'll set up our wigwam in the clearing. Far Eyes won't be here for a few days yet. We wanted ta spend some time with ya before settling in at the falls."

The rest of the men were all gathered and Cat said, "Oh, Jim, I'd like to introduce ye to Thaddeus Bakeman."

Thaddeus shook Jim's hand and when he spoke with an English accent instead of Scots, Jim shot a curious glance at Cat.

"It's a rather long story. Will ye join us for supper tonight?"

Jim appealed to his wife and when she nodded, he said they'd be pleased to.

The gathering broke up and Cat enlisted Kenny and Greame's aid to put the cabin back in order while she began supper.

Geoffrey and Kelvin had been hunting yesterday and each had brought home a turkey. They had already been cleaned so Cat thought they would be perfect for the main course. Last year's trip to Boston for supplies had allowed her to buy a few more much-needed items for the kitchen. Greame's teashop in Boston was still making nice profits, allowing for all the niceties they were surrounded with. Tonight she would use the new platters, and even serve claret in the new crystal goblets to toast to the new year ahead.

As the sun disappeared, the aroma of roasting turkey wafted through the entire settlement, beckoning the men into Cat's cabin. They arrived mostly at the same time and some took their seats at the table, while others waited for Cat's instructions for dishing up the food. It was a disciplined routine.

When everyone was seated, Greame stood, crystal goblet of claret in hand raised for a toast, and looked around at the growing table of friends and family. All glasses were raised as they waited for Greame's words.

"Once again, we have our loved ones wi' us seated at this bountiful table. Our dear friends Jim and Jumpin' Turtle have returned with a name for their son. Harry Welapewet, Harry Handsome Man.

A fittin' name to be sure. And we hae a new friend, unlikely as he may be," grinning widely at the teasing gesture. "Thaddeus Bakeman, who nearly laid down his life for our dear Garnet, has made a decision to remain here in our fair settlement."

This was news to everyone at the table and handshakes and slaps on Thaddeus' back erupted the table into a festive mood.

Greame clinked his glass with a fork to settle everyone down so he could finish his toast.

"Now, all we need to do is get the rest o' ye men wives so we can really put this settlement on the maps! To a prosperous and happy rest o' the year. *Slàinte mhath!*"

The group drank their claret and ate until they could eat no more. Cat surprised Kenny with his favorite desert, a bread pudding with a sweet whisky sauce. The way it disappeared, it may well have become everyone's new favorite dessert.

Jumping Turtle helped with the dishes and the men settled in the keeping room to talk. When Kelvin brought out the pipes, Jumping Turtle's eyes lit up. Ever since the first time she heard them, Jumping Turtle has loved to listen to Kelvin play. Cat laughed and said she'd finish the dishes in the morning so they could join the festivities.

Gent and Harry were the only two in the room who seemed oblivious to the music. In fact, Harry slept through most of it. When it ended though, he awoke in a rather testy mood. Apparently, he was not used to abrupt quiet.

"This is his usual attitude," Jim said, picking up the wailing Harry. "In the village when the drumming ends, and he's been sleeping, he'll do the same thing. It's time ta sleep, little one."

When they all left, the quiet was deafening. Cat wore a smile to bed, feeling, for the first time in a while, like she was where she was supposed to be, doing what she was supposed to be doing. As if tonight, the stars were aligned in her favor. It felt good.

She slept straight through the night in a dreamless rest. When she awoke, Greame was dressed and watching her from the doorway. It was light out, sunny, in fact.

"What time is it?" she asked, stretching her arms and back.

"Half eight, sleepy head."

She sat up straight. "I've got to get breakfast started!"

"Already done," he said. "Kenny did it."

She was angry now, scampering out from under the covers and slipping into her breeks. "Why did ye no' wake me?"

"Because ye've no' slept well for days and ye needed the rest."

"Damn it, Greame, I'm young. I'm certain a few days' lack o' sleep wilna harm me."

"Perhaps no,' but ye sure look good," he said before leaving the bedroom.

Her eyebrows rose. How could she argue with that?

❧

The dishes were just where she left them last night. She wasn't sure if she was glad for that or not. It would have been nice not to be faced with the stacks of them, but she knew she would have been upset if Kenny had done her job. Even more than he already had.

By the time the last of the dishes were dried and placed in the cupboards, she wanted nothing more than to go out and enjoy another warm early-spring day. It must have remained warm through the night, because there were only traces of snow left in the deeply shadowed areas. The smell of the air was so fresh she wanted only to breath it in and never exhale.

Gent was barking at something near Jim's wigwam. When Cat walked over to see what it was, she stopped and smiled at the sight. Harry was holding himself up by grasping a sapling, and Gent, who towered over the lad, had his rump in the air with his tail wagging furiously, hoping he had someone to play with.

Cat walked over to find no one else around. She looked in the wigwam and it was empty. She called out several times, but no one came, except Thaddeus.

"Is there something wrong, Catrìona?"

"Hae ye seen Jim or Jumpin' Turtle?"

"Jim's in the barn with the rest of the men. I haven't seen Jumping Turtle." He looked at young Harry and realized why Cat was so distressed. "She just left him here by himself?"

"I dinna care for this, Thaddeus. Would ye look around for her? I'm goin' to the barn."

Cat picked up Harry—much to Gent's dismay—and carried him into the barn. One look at Cat's face and everyone was on alert.

"Where's Jumping Turtle?" Jim asked, already racing out the door.

"I was hopin' someone could tell me."

The men poured out of the barn and began to search the woods for any sign of the lass. They called out in all directions, going deeper and deeper into the woods. Cat waited with Harry beside the wigwam, hoping Jumping Turtle would return on her own, but she already had a very bad feeling that something was terribly wrong.

5

Misguided

SHE CAME TO IN AN UNFAMILIAR place. Her head hurt, and when she tried to get up, she realized her hands and feet were tied. The gag was tight enough that screams were useless. As she searched the wooded area with wild eyes, it didn't look like anyone was around to hear her anyway.

Jumping Turtle tried to remember what had happened. Her last recollection was when she was in her wigwam with Harry. She went outside to begin her stew, and since Jim was with his friends, she would have a chance to do some more beadwork on the buckskin jacket she was going to surprise him with for their second wedding year. Jim called it an anniversary. He seemed to hold some dates very sacred, and this was one of them.

She had just finished cutting the meat into chunks and sliding them into the pot, when she heard a twig break behind her. Thinking it was Jim, she smiled, pleased that he couldn't remain far from her for long. Before she could turn into his arms, everything went black.

Who would do such a thing? she wondered.

As Jumping Turtle struggled with the rawhide bonds, she heard voices and footfalls getting closer. From out of the woods came three men, two whites and one Indian. The Indian looked Huron. What would he be doing this far east? And what did she have to do with it?

The two white men pulled her to her feet, eyeing her up and down. She looked at the Huron, who seemed unconcerned with her plight, and sent him hateful daggers with her eyes. He smiled maliciously and held up a small bag. It jingled when he shook it. Now it became horribly clear what it had to do with her.

She was to be sold as a slave.

❧

Like a dog, Jumping Turtle was kicked and shoved for miles through the woods to a clearing where five other women were being held. Only one was white, the rest were from different tribes. She was shoved to the ground at the women's feet. Her hands were still bound in back when the Huron viciously grabbed the rawhide, wrenching back her arms, then further intimidating her as he let the knife graze her throat before he sliced the leather and pushed her to the ground once again.

She untied her gag, licking her lips in an effort to remoisten them, then rubbed her swollen wrists to bring some feeling back to her fingers. As she looked around at her frightened companions, she noticed one thing. Each of their eyes held the same conviction: *we will not go willingly.* Jumping Turtle might not be a brave woman on her own, but with a group facing the same ominous fate, she knew she would do what was necessary to escape.

The small group remained quiet until dark. The Huron threw some wood at them, indicating it was their job to keep themselves warm. A little while later, he tossed in a leather pouch of water. It was barely enough for all of them, since they had not drunk anything since their capture.

Jumping Turtle told the women her name, and for the benefit of the white woman, she said it in English, much to the woman's surprise. The rest of the captives followed suit. The white woman said her name was Susan Bradford; the others were named Corn Woman, Yellow Leaf, Weeps for Child, and Mali.

Susan was a tiny woman of about twenty years old. Her hair was the color of an autumn field, all golden and light. She scooted closer to Jumping Turtle so she could speak to her in English, since the other women spoke only French or their native tongues.

"Where were you taken from?" Susan asked, chewing her fingernails to the quick.

"The place called Cape Rozier. What about you?"

"Pentagöet. My husband and I had just moved there from York." She gave a disgusted snort before continuing. "Reginald said he wanted to settle a wild and untamed town. As though York was a bustling community!"

Jumping Turtle frowned. "How long ago were you taken?"

"Five days, now." She looked at the other women around her, then pointed to Yellow Leaf, and said, "Apparently, she was the first one to be taken."

The fire cracked loudly as the spruce sap exploded in one of the logs, startling Susan. After a moment, she said, "We must find a way to escape."

"Not worry," patting Susan's hand. "My husband has many friends. They will find us."

"We can't wait that long, Jumping Turtle!" she hissed. "Don't you understand? They mean to sell us, since they haven't," she paled in the firelight at the thought. "Scalped us yet."

Jumping Turtle held Susan's hand tightly and smiled weakly. "Not worry."

❧

They had scoured the area for hours and came up empty. Jim said the few hoof prints they had found behind his wigwam were impossible to track. The horse's hooves had been covered with animal skins, leaving virtually no trail to follow beyond where the scuffle took place to capture Jumping Turtle. The men were all gathered in the keeping room now, waiting to see if Cat could get an indication of where she'd been taken.

Cat had put young Harry down for a nap in her bed. She was

sitting in her rocking chair; amethyst crystal in one hand, hair twirling in the other, trying to see where Jumping Turtle was. Her head hurt, so she knew her friend did not go willingly.

The vision placed her at a campfire. As Cat looked around, she saw Jumping Turtle and five other women. For the moment, they all looked unharmed. Cat took a seat on the log beside one of the native women. The one they called Yellow Leaf seemed to acknowledge her presence. The Indian woman wasn't afraid, but she kept looking at Cat as if she were really there. Cat smiled at her and was amazed to see Yellow Leaf return the gesture. Yellow Leaf must be a medicine woman. Far Eyes had told her of women with powers such as hers. Cat had never met one, until now. It was the only explanation for the woman's ability to recognize Cat through the ether.

Cat turned her attention to Jumping Turtle and a white woman named Susan, who were discussing where they thought they might be.

"I heard one of the men say that we were going to be transported south, which means that somewhere there are ships awaiting us," Susan whispered.

Cat looked at Yellow Leaf and asked, "Can ye tell me where ye are right now?"

Yellow Leaf nodded and closed her eyes. She had obviously done this sort of thing before and knew that sending images through the ether is the quickest way of communicating.

It took a few minutes for Cat to take in all the landmarks, and when she saw the hills on the western shore of the bay where the Panawanskek River emptied in the sea, she had a better notion of where they were. It was further south than she recalled ever being, though. In Cat's travels, the only time she remembered the vantage point she was shown was when they first sailed to the Cape. She could see the island archipelagoes to the west, that meant the ships would be waiting further south on this peninsula, a place she had not explored yet. So, unless Gregor had been down there on one of his many secret excursions, it was uncharted territory.

Cat patted Yellow Leaf on the shoulder and told her help was on the way. "Oh, and what tribe are ye from?"

Yellow Leaf said, "Huron."

Greame was standing in the doorway patiently waiting to see what information Cat had garnered in her meditation.

Cat looked up and said, "We'll be sailing at first light."

"Far Eyes or Smiles at Everything would ken the area best," Gregor said. "I tend to go north and east in my 'excursions,' as you describe them, Cat," his eyes twinkling mischievously.

"But they're no' expected for another couple o' days, and I dinna think we can wait that long," Cat argued.

"We canna wait," Greame said, spreading out his charts on the kitchen table, moving the lanterns closer to chart the best route. "We'll be ready at first light. It shouldna take more than a couple hours to reach the southern tip," he traced his thick finger down the map Hector had made when they sailed up from Boston a few years ago. "I only hope this map is accurate. We dinna ken how far this Eggemoggin Reach goes. We've ne'er been that far down. For all we ken, this southern end may be an island."

"Well, if that's true, that it's an island, I mean," Cat began, scanning the chart. "They would've already had to hae sailed. Right?"

Greame nodded, then looked at Cat. "Can ye see if they're bein' held near the shore?"

Cat closed her eyes for a minute, revisiting her vision with Yellow Leaf. It was too dark to see far, so she trained her ears on the sounds she heard when she was there. The fire, the distant peepers, but she couldn't hear waves near the shore. Of course, if the wind was right and they were any distance at all from the water, she wouldn't have heard them anyway.

"Damn it!" she hissed, scowling at her inability to get an answer. "I canna tell."

Gregor put a big hand on her shoulder. "We'll find her, Cat."

Jim walked over with Harry in his arms, and said to the group, "Jumping Turtle may seem shy ta ya, but she doesn't scare easy. If I know her, she'll already be planning her escape."

Cat didn't want to say it aloud, but that's what she feared the most. Her captors weren't the type to let an escape happen, or go easy on her if the attempt failed. It would be just as easy to put a bullet in her to set an example to the rest not to attempt such foolishness.

Kenny and Jim volunteered to remain in the settlement with Harry, just in case Jumping Turtle did manage to escape and find her way back. By dawn, Greame and Cat, along with the rest of the men, were aboard the *Revenge* and underway. The sky looked threatening, but for the moment, it remained dry. Within an hour, Geoffrey was making amendments to Hector's charts. The southern part of the peninsula was indeed an island.

"We could be trailin' ghosts," Greame said.

"Not sure what ye mean," Cat said into the wind.

"The Reach is a long stretch of land. They could be anywhere along it."

Cat and Gregor looked down the length of the rocky, tree-lined shore. The wind was cold and the sky was lowering. If it started raining or the fog settled in, it would make spotting anything nearly impossible.

"If ye think like them," Cat asked, shivering. "Where would be the best place for a ship to pick up the women?" Pulling her cloak tighter around herself.

Greame thought for a moment, the wind whipping loose strands of hair from his queue. He closed his eyes, recalling Hector's map. "If they are indeed goin' to take the lasses south, and *if* they aren't meanin' to capture any more along the way, then 'twould be daft to sail them to the island just to pick them up on the southern end of it."

"Aye," Gregor agreed. "If there were other settlements on that island, I'm sure we'd hae heard about 'em by now."

Cat nodded in agreement, then frowned. "How does that explain what I saw in my vision?"

"Could it be ye were mistaken, lass?" Gregor asked, stepping away from her in case her temper lashed its talons at him.

Cat looked at Gregor, but didn't hit him. "I'll be back in a few minutes."

She sat in Greame's quarters, glad to be out of the wind. From her pocket, she pulled out the amethyst crystal and placed it against her forehead, clearing out any distracting images and thoughts.

She concentrated on the best way to locate the women without actually sitting with them again. Perhaps Yellow Leaf gave her the wrong information. The most logical idea would be a bird; unobtrusive and therefore undetected. So Cat selected a lock of hair and began the metamorphosis of becoming the eagle.

In her mind, she called up the eagle's image, with its pure white head and tail like bookends on a dark brown body. Within a moment she was soaring on the wind with barely a beat of her six-foot wings. Her yellow eyes peered down through the trees, seeing details with amazing clarity. The breeze took her down the length of the Reach in just a few minutes, making short order of the search.

Cat saw no sign of the women or their captors. Could they have ventured onto the island? she wondered. It would only take a few minutes to find out.

The experience was exhilarating. She could actually feel her body rise off the seat, as though airborne herself. Banking her wings, she followed the coastline, with all its coves and points, until she reached the southern end of the island. There was no sign of any human activity. She flew back up a little further inland to no avail. They were nowhere. Could she have been totally misled and they were still being held on the Cape? But why would Yellow Leaf do that? Was she in on the kidnappings? she pondered. If so, why?

Cat had assumed the Indian girl was a shaman: it never occurred to Cat she'd be deceived. Yellow Leaf's life force is what she needed to focus her sight on now. If Cat could locate her, she would find the rest of the women.

Cat flew back up to the Cape, again hugging the shoreline. She soared into all the coves until, suddenly, not more than a few miles from the settlement, smoke from a campfire was spotted. It was coming from deep inside one of the larger coves located at the northeastern side of the Cape.

❧

Jumping Turtle didn't get much sleep. Her captors kept a tight watch on the women, so there was no possible way to escape under those circumstances. She put another log on the fire to ward off the damp air. At dawn the Huron threw some dried venison at them. His malicious black gaze lingered at little too long on Yellow Leaf, prompting Jumping Turtle to move closer in a protective gesture.

But, suddenly, she had an odd feeling that he and the Huron woman were already acquainted. There was no fear in Yellow Leaf's eyes. Maybe seducing her captor was Yellow Leaf's plan for escape.

Jumping Turtle shook her head. If that were true, it was a very risky plan, one that was selfish and could get the rest of the captives killed. But apparently, Yellow Leaf wasn't thinking of the rest of her fellow prisoners. Jumping Turtle looked skyward to watch an eagle soaring along the shore. She wished *she* could sprout wings and fly away.

❧

This made no sense to her. Cat returned to her own body with more questions than answers. Yellow Leaf had led her on a wild goose chase. Why?

She went up on deck and gathered the men.

"What?" Greame shouted. He didn't need to order the ship to turn around; Kelvin was already making adjustments to the steering.

Gregor was silent. Not good.

Cat watched him for a minute, then asked, "What are ye thinkin,' man?"

Gregor stared at Cat for a moment before answering, "I'm tryin' to figure why she would lead us away from the settlement on a fool's errand. What's the real reason for misguidin' us? They would hae to ken we would see their ships comin' for them, *if* they really intended on transportin' them somewhere else." He scratched his bearded chin.

Greame was now the silent one. He had his hands folded together in back of him and was pacing the deck. Periodically, he'd open his mouth, as if to say something, but would close it again without uttering a word.

"What's in our wee settlement they would want?" asked Kelvin from the helm.

Cat, Greame and Gregor all stared at each other open-mouthed.

"We've been there for three years," Greame said, tucking a windswept lock of hair behind his ear. "There's been no findin' o' treasure, so it's doubtful they want somethin' from the land."

He didn't sound convinced it couldn't be a possibility, though.

"What if we're too close to it for them to retrieve wi'out us interferrin'?" Cat asked.

The only sounds were from the howling gale and the sails being snapped taut in the wind, but if one listened hard enough, the wheels of thought could also be heard whirling out scenarios.

"To the settlement, Kelvin!" Greame ordered.

6

A Not-So-Jolly Roger

JIM EMERGED FROM THE privy and headed back into the main house with Gent happily in tow. When they entered the cabin, Kenny was on the floor with Harry rolling a ball. In a flurry of fur, Gent snatched the ball up before Harry could grab it and trotted into the spare bedroom, sending the lad into squeals of laughter.

"He's a fine lad, Jimmy," Kenny said, grinning.

Jim nodded, but even his son's laughter couldn't shake his feeling that something was terribly wrong. Kenny caught the silence and stood to pour them each a cup of chicory.

"Hae yerself a seat, man."

Jim sat and warmed his hands on the stoneware cup. "There's something amiss," he said, not looking at Kenny.

"I dinna understand it either, but they'll find her, man," mistaking Jim's statement.

"No, it's not that. Something doesn't *feel* right. I've been thinking on it all night. Her captors must've been watching this place." He looked up at Kenny. "I don't think it was a random act."

"What would they want wi' Jumpin' Turtle?" Kenny rubbed the back of his neck, then a thought came to mind. "Or do ye think they were after Garnet, and Jumpin' Turtle just got in their way?"

Jim shook his head. "No, if they were after Garnet, she'd have known about it. No, that's what has me in such a quandary. I don't for one minute believe they were even after Jumping Turtle."

"Ye mean," Kenny looked around. "The settlement?"

Jim nodded.

"But we've been here for three years. What could possibly be here that they want that we haven't found already?"

"That seems to be the question, now doesn't it, boys?"

Kenny and Jim whipped around to see two men in the doorway. Before Kenny could grab his dirk, a knife hurled through the air and into his upper arm.

Jim stood and put his hands out to indicate he was unarmed. "Please, may I get my son?"

A fair-haired man with piercing gray eyes nodded, but trained his pistol on him to make sure there'd be no trickery.

Harry and Gent were playing with the ball in Jim's old room, oblivious to the danger lurking about. Jim bent to lift Harry and scanned the room for any kind of weapon. He found none. "Fine watch dog ya are, Gent," he muttered under his breath.

Gent wagged his tail, his tongue lolling to the floor.

He closed the door to keep him inside. Cat would have his head if something happened to the beast. He walked back into the kitchen and waited for commands. He would do nothing to aggravate these men, for Harry's sake.

"So, judging from the conversation you two boys were having when we walked in, you haven't found it," the tall, dark-haired man said.

Through gritted teeth, Kenny asked, "What is it we didna find? Just so's we're o' like minds, aye?"

"It hardly matters now, since you'd've known if you'd seen it," the dark one said. "Now we can do this the easy way, where the three of you live … or …"

"That would be preferable, sir," Jim said, not needing to hear what the *or* was. "Just take what ya came for and leave us, if ya please."

The dark one smiled and nodded. "A wise boy, to be sure." Without so much as a glance at the fair-haired man, he said, "Tie them securely."

A length of rope was produced. Blondie brought around one of the chairs and placed it up against the back of the chair Kenny was sitting in, then indicated to Jim to take a seat. He never spoke, but Jim knew not to antagonize him, and did as he was instructed. Harry sat on Jim's lap and Blondie proceeded to tie them all together. Gent finally started barking, startling Blondie enough to grab the pistol from his waistband. He released it, realizing now why Jim closed the door. He turned and audaciously winked at Jim.

When his task was complete, he grabbed the hilt of the knife still protruding from Kenny's arm and pulled it out, ignoring Kenny's hiss of pain, then wiped the blood on Kenny's sark before returning to stand in the doorway.

"Now that the rest of your friends are out of the way, sailing for God knows where," the dark one said, chuckling that his plan worked so well. "We'll be doing just that. Ta, boys!"

And they were gone.

"Are ya all right, Kenny?" Jim's voice was ragged.

"Oh, I'll live."

"I'll try ta loosen the ropes. Harry may be our saving grace. He's a wiggler. If I give 'im enough time, he can get out of anything."

❧

"There's something wrong wi' Jim," Cat said, her eyes seeing something no one else could.

"They're at the settlement already?" Greame asked. "They hae to be watchin' our every move."

The wind picked up in intensity, sending whitecaps crashing into the hull.

"How are we goin' to get back wi'out them seein' us then? We're goin' to hae to get ashore before the point and walk in," Gregor continued, answering his own question.

"No," Cat said. "Go further up, then we'll walk from there. They'll see us no matter what, but may think we're doin' somethin' else if we sail past."

"Kelvin, go up to the deep cove around the point," Greame shouted.

The rain started just as they dropped anchor. Gregor, Greame, Cat and Robbie rowed to shore in a long boat, while Kelvin, Thad and Geoffrey continued further around the Cape to get the *Revenge* out of the weather.

"We hae to stay to the woods. I feel two men in the settlement who shouldna be there," Cat told them when they pulled the long boat up onto the beach.

The four of them ran through the woods following the trail system they had created over the years. As they closed in, Gregor and Robbie shifted off to the left. They were all within sight of the cabins now, stopping to see if they could spot the culprits. All seemed quiet enough.

Cat heard Gent barking from what sounded like inside a cabin.

They all inched their way silently through the open land surrounding the settlement. Once to the cabin, Gent was heard clearly now. Gregor chanced a quick peek in the window of Jim's room. He saw Gent inside with the door closed. Robbie hugged the log walls and reached the kitchen window. He quickly popped his head up to see if anyone else was in the house. Cat and Greame were just stepping up onto the porch, staying tight against the logs as well. Robbie mouthed Jim and Kenny's names and pointed to the kitchen. Greame nodded and everyone had pistols at the ready.

Greame opened the door and slipped in, much to the surprised wide-eyed looks of Jim and Kenny.

"'Bout time ye got here, Greame," Kenny growled.

"There's no one else inside?" Greame whispered.

"No. They tied us here about half an hour ago," Jim said.

Cat grabbed her dirk and cut the ropes that held the trio in the chairs. She looked at the wound on Kenny's arm and went to her herb cupboard, grabbed some linens and a bottle of whisky, placing everything on the table.

"There were two of 'em," Jim continued, setting Harry on the floor. "They said there was something here in the settlement that belonged to 'em. I don't know where they went, but I think it may be along the shore."

Greame, Gregor and Robbie were out the door.

"All right, Kenny," Cat said in a soothing voice. "Let's hae a look at yer wound." She cut off his sleeve to get better access to the injury. The blade had sunk deep into the bicep muscle, but it looked like a clean cut with no damage to the arteries. "Jim, would ye fetch me a glass, and pour some boilin' water o'er these herbs?" She handed him the mortar with the herbs she had prepared. "Just enough to make a paste, aye?"

Cat poured a healthy dram of whisky into the glass and handed it to Kenny. He shot it down in one gulp.

"I'm going to hae to clean this wound, and it'll pain ye some, mind. Are ye ready?" Before Kenny could answer, Cat poured some whisky directly onto the slice.

Kenny hissed through gritted teeth, following it by a string of muttered *Gàidhlig* curses.

Jim picked up Harry from the floor, walked into the bedroom where Gent was being held prisoner, and sat Harry down on the floor to keep him company. He walked back into the kitchen and took a seat to watch Cat finish ministering first aid to Kenny.

All three of them jumped when shots were fired.

Jim spared no one a glance, just bolted from the cabin. Cat and Kenny weren't far behind.

❧

The Huron and his captives were huddled around the fire trying to stay warm in the cold rain. They all looked at each other when they heard the shots. The Huron glared at Yellow Leaf. Jumping Turtle now was positive the two were in this together. He shot to his feet and viciously grabbed Yellow Leaf's arm, hoisting her to her feet. With the back of his hand he smashed her face. He threw her to the ground and ran off in the direction of the shots.

"You help these men?" Jumping Turtle spat, standing over Yellow Leaf.

Yellow Leaf nodded and smiled through a bloody lip that was already swelling. Jumping Turtle had no remorse when she kicked the traitor hard in the stomach, knocking the wind out of her.

Jumping Turtle turned to the other women, and said, "I am going home. Susan, you come with me. Pentagöet not far from where my friends are." Without waiting, she fled toward the shots she knew came from the settlement. Susan was right behind her.

❧

The dark-haired man lay on the beach with two holes in his chest. Greame and Gregor had each found their mark. The fair-haired man was nowhere to be seen. Robbie was trailing him, but returned a while later with no results.

"And neither one ever said who they were?" Gregor growled.

Jim shook his head. "This one," gesturing his head towards the dead man. "Was the only one who spoke. Blondie never said a word, but seemed mighty handy with a knife. I was much more worried about him than the dead one."

"Great. And somehow I dinna think we've seen the last of him," Greame said, rubbing the back of his neck.

Cat was sitting on a large rock on the shore. "Ye're right, Greame, they'll no' give up that easy. I feel Jumpin' Turtle has been freed, but we're no' safe from them yet." She walked over to the dead man and looked around. "Did ye find what they were lookin' for?"

"They'd started several holes, but unless the other one has whatever it was they were willin' to go to these lengths to get, no one's found naught," Greame stated.

"C'mon, Kenny, let's finish patchin' ye up, aye?" Cat said, guiding Kenny back to the cabin. "Besides, wee Harry's been left wi' Gent. No' that he's a bad guardian o' weans, but probably no' wise for long."

❧

Jim stood on the porch watching dusk settle in as he waited for Jumping Turtle to return. He poked his head in the door and asked Cat once again if she was certain that his wife had been released.

"Let me see if I can get her whereabouts. It does seem like she should hae been back by now," Cat said, finishing the last of the dishes.

She wiped her hands on a linen, grabbed a lantern and went into her bedroom. Before she was even seated in the rocking chair by the window, Jumping Turtle was in her mind. The white woman was with her and was very scared. Someone was chasing them through the woods. Cat waited to see if she could identify the pursuer.

She frowned when she saw another woman running after them. An Indian woman. Surely this had to be yet another one of the captives running from the unseen assailant. When the Indian woman ran passed Cat, she recognized her as Yellow Leaf. It was beginning to make some sense now. Yellow Leaf was in on the kidnappings to throw everyone off the trail of the men who wanted what was hidden on the settlement. That's why she was shown the wrong location. Yellow Leaf must have had great powers to be able to see her so clearly, then send the image of a place Cat had obviously seen, but had to travel a distance to get to. But what about the other women? Why were they taken if not for the purpose of slavery? They had nothing to do with the settlement. Again, there were too many questions unanswered.

Jumping Turtle knew the Cape very well and that to make it back to the settlement without crossing freezing bogs and rivers, she'd have to take a longer route to safety. But that didn't allow for the extended time. There must be something else wrong.

Cat thought about the fair-haired man Jim described and wondered if he was giving up this deed, or if he would try to reconnect with the others. She could not get his whereabouts, but knew Jumping Turtle needed help. It was turning cold, and she must be soaked from the heavy rain. Cat tried to get a bearing on where Jumping Turtle was and which trail she would likely take to get back.

Before she could find out, Cat heard talking outside. She opened her window to find Far Eyes and Smiles at Everything on her front porch talking to Jim. She bolted from her chair and ran passed a startled Greame, who was talking with Gregor and Kelvin at the kitchen table.

"What's wrong?" he asked, jumping up out of his seat.

"Far Eyes is here!" she shouted over her shoulder as she ran out the door.

"Far Eyes was just telling me that he saw Jumping Turtle in danger and came earlier to help," Jim said, relieved that more people were involved.

Cat gave her Shaman friend a big hug, and over his shoulder, said, "Hallò, Smiles at Everything."

"What wrong? Have dream. Not good." Far Eyes said, holding Cat's shoulders.

The rest of the men began congregating on the porch. They all knew plans were about to be made and they would all be involved.

After everyone relayed Jumping Turtle's plight and the mysterious men looking for who-knew-what, Far Eyes told them what he saw.

"I see Jumping Turtle with bad men. Then more bad men come here," indicating the settlement. "Many summers ago, when my father was a boy, a ship came here. Men in strange clothes not speaking French or English dug many holes in ground by shore. My father watched from distance. Wooden boxes, very heavy, put into holes and covered. Some of my people dig up boxes when ship leaves."

Cat, Greame and Gregor all looked at each other with wide eyes.

"So what was in these heavy boxes, Far Eyes?" Gregor asked, trying not to get too excited.

"Gold."

The porch erupted in a frenzy of speculation.

Greame held up his hand to quiet the men so Far Eyes could finish his story.

"Is the gold still here?" he asked.

"Some."

"What happened to the rest of it?" Cat asked.

"My father said my people not have much use for yellow metal. But not all thought that way. Some come back to take some. Before long, one box empty. Next summer, when strange talking men return, they see much gold gone. They search area for many weeks, killing all they find. Not matter if have gold or not. They kill."

"Did these men get all their gold back?" Greame asked.

Far Eyes shook his head. He lifted the amulet he wore around his neck and opened the leather pouch. From inside, he pulled out a gold coin and held it in the palm of his hand.

"May I?" Greame asked, plucking the coin from Far Eyes' hand.

It was a flat, odd-shaped piece of gold stamped with a cross. What looked like royal lions were inside the upper right and lower left quadrant of the cross, and crowns were in the upper left and lower right. Small dots encircled the coin. It was about the size of the first knuckle on Greame's thumb.

Greame passed it around so everyone could get a closer look at it.

"So, this is what a doubloon looks like," Gregor said.

"What did ye call it?" Cat asked, feeling its weight in her hand.

"A doubloon. It's Spanish gold," Gregor explained. "The men who brought this here were pirates. Perhaps Spanish themselves."

"Oh, aye, then Cap'n," Kelvin said looking at Greame, "why is it we've ne'er found any of these?"

The men laughed.

"Aye, well, it certainly would hae made things easier if we had."

"Would it, now?" Cat contested. "It didna make anythin' easier for Far Eyes' people when they had any of it."

"She has a point," Gregor said laughing, handing the coin back to Far Eyes.

"And to prove that point," Cat stated. "Look what it's already doin' to the settlement. Kidnappin,' knife-play and dead men on the beach. I say let them hae it. If it will keep them from e'er returnin' here, let them hae it."

And with that she walked back into the house. The men were all quiet knowing Cat was absolutely right. There would be no peace here with the lure of treasure in their midst.

"So how do we find this gold, what do we do with it, if and when we do find it, and who do we return it to?" Thaddeus asked.

"I know where to look," Far Eyes said. "But not know about rest."

Jim was the only other person to be thinking straight when he said, "I think the first order of business should be finding my wife."

7

Turning the Tables

JUMPING TURTLE AND SUSAN were huddled together, shivering under a rock escarpment in a thicket of dense cedar. They could hear the Huron and Yellow Leaf talking nearby. Jumping Turtle thought for sure she would be in the safety of Jim and his friends by now, but her pursuers had gotten too close. She'd found this hiding place and here they would remain until help came or they could escape once again.

"I cannot believe you have let them escape, Yellow Leaf," the Huron said in his native tongue. "Yellow Hair wants all women back. Says ship comes tomorrow to sail south with women. Brown Hair dead so more gold for us, but only if we find the other two."

"The Penobscot has a powerful friend watching out for her. I tell you this woman crosses worlds and can see what we are doing."

"What white woman can do this?" he scoffed. "She has no power over you!"

A loud slap was heard, then a thud. Yellow Leaf must have received another beating.

"Hit me once more, Matchitehew, and you will find out just how powerful I am," Yellow Leaf growled.

"What will you do, Yellow Leaf? You told me where the gold was, and that was for both of us. And just because you are happy to open your legs for me does not mean there are any feelings further than that one thing you do for me."

Jumping Turtle heard Yellow Leaf spit. It must not have been on the ground for more sounds of punching and slapping were heard before the Huron ran off, leaving Yellow Leaf on her own, crying softly.

Susan was sobbing silently against Jumping Turtle's shoulder. They both heard Yellow Leaf pull herself together and run off after the man who beat her.

"We are alone again, Susan. We wait to be sure, then go for settlement. It will be dark soon."

"I am so glad for your guidance, Jumping Turtle. I honestly do not know what I would have done without you," Susan whispered between sniffles. "How far to the settlement?"

"Not far."

Suddenly, screams were heard in the distance and the skirl of the Highland pipes.

Jumping Turtle laughed. She knew that sound. It was the sound of freedom!

"Dear God! What is that noise?" Susan asked, clearly frightened again.

"We are safe now. That is my friend, Kelvin!"

Just as they emerged from their hiding spot, a shot was fired, stopping them in their tracks. It was too late to dive for cover; Yellow Leaf burst from the trees almost running into Susan. In a quick action, Yellow Leaf grabbed her and pressed a knife to Susan's throat, effectively putting an end to Jumping Turtle's rescue effort.

Matchitehew was next to explode from the trees, but he was bleeding and limping badly, apparently from a bullet in his leg. He wasted no time on Yellow Leaf's attempt to save herself. She was on her own. When Jumping Turtle saw the reaction to his coldness on Yellow Leaf's face, she knew it was the time to react.

She grabbed Yellow Leaf's arm that held the knife on Susan.

With all her strength, Jumping Turtle tried to wrench Yellow Leaf's fingers off the hilt, but in the tussle, Yellow Leaf managed to take a swipe at her, slicing across her shoulder through the deerskin dress. Jumping Turtle let out a hiss, then dove onto her assailant. Susan was thrown free and scrambled for cover.

Jumping Turtle was sitting on top of Yellow Leaf with both hands around the hilt of the blade. Yellow Leaf bucked trying to dislodge her, then kneed Jumping Turtle in the back, causing her to fall forward. Still holding the knife, Yellow Leaf rolled on top of Jumping Turtle and in a desperate attempt to gain control of the weapon, bit Jumping Turtle's arm hard enough to make her scream out in pain.

Jumping Turtle had no option but to give Yellow Leaf a headbutt. While it made her see white spots in front of her eyes, it also made Yellow Leaf release her teeth from Jumping Turtle's arm. Jumping Turtle managed to get back up on her knees and started beating Yellow Leaf's hands against the rocks and tree stumps, anything to get her to release the blade. Yellow Leaf growled in aggravation then spit in Jumping Turtle's face.

Just in time, Susan reacted by grabbing an oak branch the size of a rolling pin and slammed the heavy stick down on Yellow Leaf's forehead. The knife was released. Jumping Turtle grabbed it, and in one fluid motion, slit Yellow Leaf's throat.

From behind her, bursting from the trees like madmen, came Jim and Smiles at Everything, followed by the rest of the settlement. Jumping Turtle lay on the ground panting from the exertion. Jim knelt and lifted her into his arms.

"Are ya all right, bug?" he asked, using his favorite endearment.

Between breaths, she said, "I hear Kelvin's pipes and I know I am safe."

Cat ran to Jumping Turtle to see if she was wounded. The cut on her shoulder wasn't too deep, but would need a couple of stitches. "Are ye hurt anywhere else, Jumpin' Turtle?"

"She bite me," she said, rubbing her upper arm.

"We'll check it out when we get ye back to the settlement, aye?" Cat said.

Jumping Turtle nodded, then turned to Susan, who was cowering in the cover of the cedar. "This is my friend, Susan Bradford. She is from Pentagöet. We will bring her home, yes?"

Suddenly, all eyes were on Susan, just realizing she was there. Geoffrey was beside her in a second, holding out his hand to help her up. "Are ye all right, lass?"

Susan's light green eyes released the torrent they'd been holding back, and she threw herself into Geoffrey's arms with deep, wracking sobs into his shoulder.

Geoffrey crooned to her, stroking her hair and rocking her like a babe. Robbie patted him on the back as he turned with the others to return to the settlement.

❧

The inhabitants of the settlement remained in Cat's cabin for the night. Three men were posted on guard in shifts, just to be sure the slavers stayed clear.

By morning, it was as though nothing dire had happened the day before.

Geoffrey never left Susan's side, eliciting smirks from several of the men. It was Gregor who finally emphasized the point that she was already spoken for.

"Susan, lass, when would ye like us to take ye back to yer *husband?*"

She looked up at him, her green eyes wide, and said, "My husband?"

Gregor's eyebrows shot up with curiosity. "Aye, ye did tell Jumpin' Turtle ye were marrit, did ye no'?"

Susan shook her head as if to jog her memory. She glanced at Geoffrey, then bowed her head. "Ah, yes … Reginald." She said his name like she only just remembered him, and wasn't all that pleased to have done so.

Geoffrey caught the tone, then asked quietly, "Perhaps ye'd like to remain here while we fetch him for ye, Susan?" He looked up at Gregor with a pleading look in his eyes.

Gregor scratched his head and nodded. "Well, it may be wise, just to be sure Himself is unharmed."

Cat and Greame looked at each other and smiled. Neither one would have taken Gregor for a romantic, but it goes to show how some things are taken for granted.

"I'll take Smiles at Everything with me and fetch him for ye, lass."

"Thank you, sir," she said timidly. "That's very kind of you."

Gregor put his hand on Smiles at Everything's shoulder and they turned to go.

"Might I join you?" Thaddeus asked, watching the two leave. "I'd like the chance to know the area better."

"More the merrier," Gregor replied, and the three of them headed for the barn.

For the rest of the day, small pockets of quiet conversations spread throughout the cabin. Jim and Jumping Turtle spent the entire day behind closed doors in Jim's old room. Harry and Gent were content to spend time with each other on the floor. When luncheon was cleared away, Cat told Greame she was going in for a nap.

"Go. Ye look done in, *a' ghaoil,*" pressing a kiss on her forehead.

Cat closed the door to her bedroom and stepped out of her breeks. She crawled under the bedclothes and was asleep within minutes. It was a lazy, dreamy sleep of soft colors and shapes. No horror, no death, no messages, only rest. When she woke, it was dark outside. She sat up in bed and listened to the sounds of the cabin. Hushed voices and periodic chuckles made her smile. She reached down to retrieve her breeks and heard hoofbeats outside. Slipping into the heavy canvas britches quickly, she went to see if Gregor had found Mr. Bradford.

When Cat and the rest of the household poured out onto the porch, they saw just three men. No one spoke. Gregor dismounted, and with a serious expression on his face, walked up to Susan. Geoffrey had his arm around her waist, as if holding her up.

Gregor took her by the shoulders and said, "We found yer husband, lass, and we buried him."

Susan seemed to melt into Geoffrey's arms. Geoffrey lifted her and carried her into the cabin. The rest remained on the porch to hear Gregor's explanation.

"He was on the ground when we got there. He'd been scalped."

"A gruesome sight," Thaddeus said, shaking his head.

"The cabin was burned. The lass has naught to return to." It was Gregor's turn to shake his head.

"She'll be welcome here," Cat said softly, looking into the house at Geoffrey comforting Susan. "It looks like Geoffrey is taken wi' her."

"Aye, from the moment he laid eyes on her," Gregor chuckled softly.

❧

Supper was a quiet affair in deference to Susan's loss. Jumping Turtle looked rested after her long nap and was helping Cat with the dishes. The men began leaving for their cabins, but were asked to stay in pairs all night. There were still two men out there with gold fever who would apparently stop at nothing to retrieve it.

Far Eyes had shown Greame and Robbie where to dig earlier in the afternoon. Sure enough, the wooden box, now severely rotted, was found and the gold removed. There still remained a vast quantity of the precious metal, and it was very heavy. It took eight satchels to remove it all. It was now stored in the hidey-hole in the root cellar. They covered the wooden box back up and covered the freshly dug area with grasses and branches. It was quite a ways from where the slavers had dug, so if they did return, it may take them a while to discover their loot was missing. That was the hope, anyway.

8

A Fragile Peace

IT HAD BEEN NEARLY TWO months since the dastardly kidnapping and the discovery of gold on Cape Rozier. The weather was perfect: warm, sunny and breezy. It was midsummer's day and Cat could tell Greame was aching to be on the water. There were days when he was so distracted he was useless for anything else.

"Why dinna we take a sail today," she suggested.

Greame had been trying to hammer a bit of iron to rig up a better latch for the barn doors, but his mind was out to sea more than it was on his work.

He tore his gaze from the shimmering blue water to look at her and smiled sheepishly. "Are ye readin' my thoughts, lass, or did ye really want to take a sail?"

Cat walked behind him and wrapped her arms around his waist, hugging his back. "It's a perfect day. All this can wait, can it no'?"

He chuckled deeply, "I dinna imagine that it's life or death to complete it today." Dropping his hammer, he patted her arm. "Why dinna ye go gather anyone else who'd like to join us and I'll clean up here, aye?"

Cat pressed a kiss on his cheek and ran out of the barn in search of a crew.

She returned with the entire settlement in tow just as Greame was exiting the barn.

Geoffrey and Susan were inseparable now, and seemed very happy about it. Kenny had actually moved in with Kelvin and Robbie to give them the privacy young lovers deserved. If this kept up, they'd have to build more cabins.

As the crew boarded, Greame asked Cat where she'd like to go. He was at the helm and Cat stood beside him with her arm around his waist.

"How about 'round the island we didn't make it to a couple months ago."

"Fine idea, Garnet. Maybe do a bit of explorin'?" He glanced to see her face light up. She always loved to explore.

"Oh, aye!"

"I ne'er did ask Far Eyes if he kent of any settlements down there," he said. "Did ye?"

Cat shook her head, putting her hair up in the Chinese sticks with the miniature dragons on them to keep the blazing locks from flying in her eyes.

"Ye should wear yer hair up more often, Garnet," Greame said in her ear. "It suits ye." He nibbled her earlobe, making her squeak.

"I thought ye wanted to sail?" she said coyly, knowing full well what he really wanted.

"We've ne'er made love on my ship, ye ken."

Cat looked into spruce-colored eyes that crinkled at the corners when he smiled. "Ye're a bad influence on me, *a ghràidh*. I may hae to take ye up on that offer."

"Kel—" he started to shout, but Cat quickly covered his mouth with her hand.

"Not *now*!" she giggled. "Christ, Greame, what will they all think?"

He would not be deterred by her hand, and began pressing kisses to her palm and doing interesting things with his tongue between her fingers.

"Kelvin!" she shouted, a bit breathlessly.

❧

The knock on the captain's door froze Cat and Greame at a most inopportune moment.

"This had better be verra important," Greame growled at the less-than-timely intruder.

They heard Gregor's chuckle on the other side of the door before he said, "Pardon, love birds, but ye may want to see this."

Cat slid her sark over her head and slipped into her breeks, trying to hide her smile at the look on Greame's face. He was grumbling curses in *Gàidhlig* as he got dressed. He looked forlornly at his wife, shaking his head.

"C'mon." He blew out a frustrated breath. "Let's go up and see what's so goddamned important we couldna be left alone."

Greame couldn't decide if the billowing white sails heading out to sea was important enough to warrant the rude interruption. He put the telescope to his eye and it brought the ship to a more reasonable distance. It flew no colors, so it more than likely wasn't a naval ship on anyone's side.

"The slavers?" Kelvin asked from the helm.

"Hard to be certain, but I would entertain the thought pretty highly," Greame said to his uncle. "We're too far away to do anythin' about it in any case."

"With any luck, they'll no' return," Gregor said. "I just hope they didna take anyone wi' them."

Cat stared after the ship. She didn't care who was on it, as long as it was sailing away from here. She glanced over at Susan and noticed she was crying. Geoffrey was rubbing her back trying to console her. Cat could tell she was thinking that it could have been her on that ship bound for who-knew-where.

A little while later, they were at the southern end of the island. They drifted into a sheltered, mottled-gray granite cove surrounded by a myriad of small islands and shoals. Robbie took over the mapmaking duty and was busy making sketches of the rock formations and islands before the rising tide covered them. Thaddeus was on the bow watching for underwater shoals that could rip out their hull.

"Ye can drop anchor anywhere ye'd like, Kelvin," Greame suggested. "We'll go ashore and see what we can find."

The long boats were lowered and the nine of them disembarked in the natural harbor. The entire area was solid rock, worn smooth by time and the elements, with very little ground covering any of it. They had to climb from the shore, as the land rose steeply overlooking the sea.

"Smiles at Everythin' told me that his people have fished from this island forever," Gregor said to Cat, while taking a seat on a flat rock in the shade.

Cat looked down on him and asked, "But there aren't any whites down here, are there?"

Gregor shook his head. "No. The sheltered coves make it easy to fish from their canoes wi'out waves capsizin' them."

Greame had gone a little ways into the woods. "Here's where they camped."

Cat and Gregor walked over to see who "they" were. A new fire ring was at the edge of the woods and the coals smoked when prodded. Several rabbit carcasses were strewn around.

"Looks like there were just two people here," Greame stated. "Probably means there werena any women wi' them."

"That's a relief to hear," Cat said. "I'm certain that word will get around to the villages to be watchful o' slavers from now on."

From the other side of the cove, Robbie shouted, "Come look at this."

The group gathered around an enormous shell pile that was nearly ten feet across and four feet high.

"Well, Smiles at Everything did say his people hae been here forever," Cat said, walking around the mound of mussels, winkles, scallops and clamshells. The pastel colors made it look like a work of art. "It must hae taken many years to make such a pile."

"Look at the pink scallop shells, Garnet," Susan said. "Some of them have rays on them." She picked a couple of beauties out of the pile.

"This one has an enormous barnacle on it," Cat said excitedly, reaching to pluck it from the mound.

By the time she and Susan stopped grabbing souvenirs, they each had about twenty of the six and seven-inch shells in various shades of pink and ivory. The men had disappeared into the woods or around the cove, each enjoying the warmth of the afternoon and the freedom to just walk the beach. Several hours later, by some internal clock, or the fact that it was nearing suppertime, everyone began returning to the longboats. The group rowed back to the *Revenge* and set sail for home. It had been a perfect day. Several harbor porpoises tagged along, skipping through the water like shiny stones. When the *Revenge* dropped anchor in the cove on the Cape, the dark gray mammals continued on their way, seemingly satisfied that they had the privilege to escort the fellow seafarers home safely.

Greame's face had turned a reddish-brown from the afternoon of sun. Cat's was a screaming red and stinging. She made a tea of chamomile and let it cool, then soaked a linen to apply it to the sunburn. Then she applied some calendula salve to relieve the tightness.

"Ye look a bit like a lobster, Garnet," Greame said as he pulled his sark over his head and untied his queue.

"Pretty much exactly how I feel," she said, pulling the Chinese sticks from her hair and letting the long auburn locks tumble to her waist. "A cool bath is what I'd like."

"Well, unless ye plan on swimmin' somewhere, a bath I canna grant ye."

"Perhaps on our next trip to Boston we can bring a copper tub home wi' us, aye?" She poured some water from the ewer into the basin for Greame.

"'Tis a fine idea," he said, looking around the room to see what size would fit, as he rubbed the washcloth over his chest. "We could put it here in the corner, if I move the chest o' drawers a little," making mental measurements.

Cat sat on the edge of the bed and pulled off her breeks. Her long legs caught Greame's attention and suddenly the tub was forgotten. He walked over and stood in front of her, then loosened the laces of her sark. He reached down and grabbed the hem and lifted it over her head. Cat leaned back on her elbows, naked, and smiled.

At dawn the next morning, Smiles at Everything was on the porch when Cat opened the door.

"Well, good mornin,' Smiles at Everythin.' What brings ye here so early?" she said smiling.

"Wait for Gregor."

"It somethin' wrong?" The smile faded from Cat's face.

His grin was wide, but somehow didn't reach his eyes. "No."

Before she could question him further, Gregor strode onto the porch from around the side of the cabin. He had his horse saddled and packed.

"Oh, good. I was just comin' to tell ye I'm leavin' for New France. Be back in a couple o' weeks."

Smiles at Everything disappeared behind the cabin, reappearing astride his horse. Gregor mounted his own saddle, smiled, waved and was gone.

Greame stepped out onto the porch fully dressed and looked around. "Who was just here?"

"Mystery man and his best friend."

Greame laughed at her analogy, but knew exactly who she referring to. "Where's he headed this time?"

"New France. Said he'd be back in a couple o' weeks, then was off." She shook her head. "I probably dinna even want to ken what he's up to, do I?"

"Doubtful," he replied over his shoulder, heading for the privy.

Cat started the fire under the wash cauldron outside, then returned to the kitchen to begin breakfast. The morning air was still cool, but the breeze smelled warm so she left the door open. She planned to wash the sheets today, and it would be a perfect drying day. As she placed the water on the stove to boil for porridge, she saw in her mind's eye the tall young man she had dreamt of a few months ago. The one who would fire the first shot of the war that was imminent.

Cat sat at the kitchen table and began twirling a lock of her hair and watched the vision play out in front of her. She heard Greame walk in, but he must have seen that she was having a vision and remained quiet.

The young Englishman was speaking with an old Indian chief. The chief wasn't dressed like any Indian she had ever seen, though.

He wore a blue coat, resplendent with gold lace, and a blue tricorn hat. His face was badly scarred. He was very angry with the French and wanted them out of his territory. Cat didn't know where his territory was, but assumed it was west of here, in Ohio, perhaps. The chief told the young man that he would remain loyal to the English. She wondered how many more Indian nations would turn against the French.

Then the vision was gone. Her eyes refocused and Greame's face was all she saw across from her.

"Gregor?" he queried.

Cat shook her head. "No. That same Englishman I saw who would fire the shot that started the war."

Greame waited to hear the rest of the story.

"He's meeting with an old Indian chief who wears white man's clothes. His face is scarred. They seem to be combinin' forces against the French."

"Ye ne'er cease to amaze me, Garnet," he said in awe, running his hand through his hair. "Should Gregor ken about this information?"

"He's no' headin' west, is he?"

"I dinna ken, ye're the one he talked to. New France is rather large, but to only be gone for two weeks, he couldna make it too far west, aye?"

"Right," she said, though not convinced for some reason. "I'm no' goin' to worry o'er him. He's old enough, big enough and, hopefully, smart enough to stay out o' trouble."

Greame snorted and got up to pour himself and Cat a cup of chicory. Cat added the oatmeal to the boiling water and stirred it in. Greame put his arms around her waist and kissed the back of her neck.

"What else are ye thinkin'?"

"That obvious, eh?"

"Aye. I can feel yer mind workin,'" he said softly.

"Do ye really think we can remain out of this war if we stay right here?" The spoon stopped stirring for a moment.

Greame blew out a breath and let her go. "I wish I could say aye with all confidence, but truthfully, I dinna ken."

Cat just nodded and resumed stirring.

❧

Greame watched her at the stove. Since she was distracted at the moment, he could think freely without her reading his thoughts. His gaze started at her face and continued down the length of her trousered legs. She had no idea what she did to him. His heart was filled to the brink of bursting with adoration for her. That didn't mean she'd stopped scaring the hell out of him; no, hardly a chance of that after this morning's news, but there seemed to be less of that of late. At the moment, life was secure, and he felt blessed to share the relative peace with her. Sure, the odd kidnapping here, a spy network within walking distance there, but all in all, a very good life. They would be safe here; he felt it. He wished he could have told her that with the certainty he believed, but she was too good at reading his mind. She would have seen that it would be his *will* that would keep her safe, and he couldn't bear having her take that away from him. He would protect her this time. Or die trying.

9

Mr. Macgregor Goes to Washington

GREGOR COULDN'T TELL CAT the real reason he called upon Smiles at Everything to ride with him. Word had reached the Penobscot, that in April, the French had marched an army of over two thousand men to Ohio to rid the English from what they deemed to be their territory. At this point, even the Mohawk were alarmed.

He'd instructed Smiles at Everything to keep him informed of any and all western unrest. Gregor figured the more he knew, the more he could keep the settlement safe. He also didn't want Cat to know where he was going; that's why he gave her the two-week time limit. She would assume he was heading north, not west. He didn't want to alarm her any more than she could alarm herself with information she received in her visions. Greame updated him regularly about what she saw in case it pertained to them directly.

They were going to meet the Iroquois chief, Theyanoguin, an older man of over seventy years. Gregor absently wondered if Cat had seen him in a vision yet. Apparently not, because Greame would have told him. If only he had a little more information on the man.

Far Eyes had told Smiles at Everything that if the Iroquois wanted to align with the Wabinaki against these foreign invaders, he wanted to hear what they had to say. Gregor and Smiles at Everything were meeting Far Eyes on the other side of the Cape. Eight of the Lobster Clan of the Penobscot were going to Ohio.

❧

Cat had spent the past two weeks in a state of absolute happiness. Susan and Geoffrey had officially announced their wedding plans just after Gregor left, effectively eliminating any thoughts for what he was doing or why he wasn't back yet.

The date was set for the first of September.

"D'ye regret not gettin' marrit, Garnet?" Greame asked as she lay in his arms that night.

"I'd say we are marrit as we need to be, unless ye feel havin' a ceremony would make it official."

He kissed her forehead. "Official to whom?"

"Precisely."

Greame chuckled. "Will ye be helpin' Susan wi' the plannin' then?"

"Aye. I've offered to help her wi' her dress. I'm givin' her whate'er fabric she wants from what Rose left me." Referring to Rose Carlyle, her friend from Boston who had left Cat all her bolts of fabrics from around the world when she died a few years ago.

"Does she hae any family she'll want to invite?" he asked, sleepiness making his voice gravelly.

Cat was quiet for a moment. "I dinna ken. I've ne'er asked her. She's from Charles Town … I think. I'll hae to find out tomorrow." She rolled out of his arms and onto her side. "Good night, *a' ghaoil,*" she whispered.

Greame was already breathing deeply.

As tired as she was, there was something nagging at her. She couldn't put a finger on it, but something wasn't quite right. After a few minutes of pondering, she gave into the sleep her body insisted upon.

He sat tall on his horse, this Englishman. He wore a scarlet coat with white lace and had on shiny black boots over his white breeks. The men he led were shabby and ill fit for combat, many not even wearing shoes. Yet they marched ever closer to the French, who outnumbered them by far. They met with an Indian chief different than Cat had seen before. They joined forces and snuck up on a sleeping French camp and began firing and scalping, killing most of the troops.

Cat woke flailing her arms, waking Greame in the process.

"What is it?" Greame asked, placing his hand on her shoulder.

She explained the dream and sat up on the edge of the bed, rubbing her forehead as if trying to erase the memory. "I need some air."

"D'ye want some comp'ny?"

"No … no."

Cat left the room and walked out onto the porch. The night was warm and filled with sounds. Crickets chirped, and a pair of nearby owls called back and forth to one another in a treetop gossip session. There was little in the way of a breeze to stir the air, but its scent was cleansing. Cat breathed it in. The moon was bright and she could see the shadowed forms of small creatures scurrying around the cabins.

It was getting closer, this war. She thought of Gregor, who should have returned by now, and wondered where he was. She didn't feel that he was in any danger, but would have preferred him to be home. She knew he kept Greame apprised of the state of affairs going on in the west. She was pleased about that, even though neither of them included her in the update meetings. They were staying informed for the safety of the settlement, and she knew they would tell her if danger was imminent.

But why the Englishman? What did he have to do with her? Then it dawned on her. Gregor. He would be involved with this Englishman somehow, she felt certain of it. The Indian chiefs she had seen; that's how he would be involved.

She blew out a deep breath. "Damn it, Gregor," she muttered, then returned to bed.

It was the end of August and the summer had been very dry so far. Cat resorted to hauling buckets of water from the stream to water her garden. Gent was making loud lapping sounds as he stood beside her in the cool trickle of water when he abruptly looked up at something only he could hear. Cat followed the direction of his attention and waited. When his tail started wagging, she knew it was friendly company.

She trudged back to the garden with the last bucket, and into the clearing came Gregor. Two weeks had turned into ten. He hadn't noticed her yet, enabling her to watch his progress undetected, noting his weariness.

When he got a little closer he caught her observing him. Sitting up straighter in his saddle, he smiled and waved, looking more like the Gregor who was inexhaustible. He couldn't fool her, though. She had seen his fatigue.

He reined his horse in close and smiled down at her.

Cat looked up and said, "What news hae ye then, *duine mor?*"

Gregor chuckled at the endearment. "Can I no' dismount, get somethin' to eat and hae a couple days' rest first, lass?"

"That's all I need to hear," patting his leg, still in the stirrup.

"Really?" He gave her a quizzical look.

"Oh, aye. If there was any dire news, ye'd hae been ridin' in as if the demons o' hell were after ye."

Gregor dismounted and pressed a kiss on her forehead. "I love a woman that can keep her wits about her."

Cat giggled. "Susan's made stew for luncheon when ye're ready. Biscuits are almost done."

Gregor nodded and headed for the barn.

Less than an hour later, everyone was sitting in the dining room listening to Gregor share his news.

"His name is Theyanoguin. The English call him Chief Hendrick; not sure why." He pondered for a moment. "Anyway, he's an old man who's fought many battles, and has the scars to prove it."

"Was his face badly scarred?" Cat asked.

Gregor nodded, biting into a biscuit. "Aye. Crisscrossing his cheek," he indicated with the flaky roll. "And around his eye on the left side of his face. He's been to England twice! King George gave him a blue—"

"Coat wi' gold lace and a tricorn hat to match," Cat finished, looking at Greame, verifying her vision of the man.

Gregor's mouth opened, a curious look on his face.

"Garnet saw him in a vision after ye left," Greame said to clarify.

Susan crossed herself. She was afraid of Cat's powers of Sight. No one begrudged her her beliefs.

"Aye, that's him," Gregor nodded, swallowing his food. "A Christian convert. Hates the French, but isna very happy wi' the English right now, either."

"So is he takin' a side, or waitin' to see what'll happen?" Greame asked.

Gregor wiped his mouth and stifled a belch. "Good stew, lass," he said to Susan, who smiled and bowed her head. "Seems the Indians dinna jump into anythin' wi'out lots o' talk first. There has to be a consensus before the Nations can act. Though there are displaced Indians who've been known to take opposite sides or remain neutral. A chief named Tanaghrisson leads one of these smaller tribes called the Mingo. He also hates the French, said they boiled and ate his father."

Shocked and mortified mutters went around the table and Susan ran out with her hand to her mouth.

"Christ, Gregor!" Cat said angrily. "No' verra nice dinner talk!"

Geoffrey, tossing a scowl at Gregor, ran after Susan to be sure she was all right.

"Pardon. Wasna thinkin.'" He shrugged, but wasn't terribly distressed that he'd caused such a ruckus at the table.

"Oh," he continued. "But let me tell ye of an English Major name George Washington. He delivered a letter from the English to the French Commandant, a Paul Marin de La Malgue, telling him to vacate Virginia's lands."

Cat shook her head, as if she didn't hear him correctly, and frowned. "Wait, Virginia's land? Where is Virginia?" She turned to look at Greame. "That's where Charles Carlyle was havin' me transported to when ye found me. I'm confused as to who owns—or think they own—what."

"Aye, well, lass, ye're no' alone in yer quandary," Gregor told her, leaning back on his chair. "If ye ask a Pennsylvanian, they think they own Ohio. And ne'er mind about the Indians. It's been their territory for longer than they can remember, but that doesna stop the whites from clearin' their huntin' grounds o' trees, planting crops, and buildin' homes and forts where'er they please. Those whites dinna want to live in peace wi' the natives, they want to hae it all for themselves. The Indians believe ye canna own the earth."

"I quite agree wi' them," Cat said, getting agreements from around the table. "We may live here, but we dinna displace the Penobscot, we asked to live *with* them."

"Invadin' countries dinna see it the way we do. Ownin' the land's all that matters."

They sat in silence to finish their meal, each man thinking his own thoughts. One-by-one, they left the table to resume their chores outside. Gregor was just about to leave when Cat stopped him.

"By the way, Gregor, Susan and Geoffrey are to be marrit on the first o' September, and ye're invited." She looked for Susan outside. Geoffrey was holding her. "At least I think ye are."

"I'll go apologize … again," he said sourly and left.

Cat smiled and watched as he walked towards the pair. Whatever he said, it made her smile, and Geoffrey shook Gregor's hand. Peace reined in the settlement once again.

Greame came up behind Cat and wrapped his arms around her waist. "No one else could hae made him do that, ye ken."

"Fear is a wonderful thing to hold o'er a man," she joked.

Greame snorted. "Do ye think he's afraid o' ye?"

Cat nodded, "Aye. He still remembers what Anna could do." She paused for a moment and smiled wickedly. "And I've ne'er enlightened him to the fact that I dinna possess those powers."

Greame laughed and said, "Ahh, well, yer secret's safe wi' me."

He kissed the back of her neck and released her. "I've sent Robbie to invite the Penobscot to the weddin.' Is everythin' ready then?"

"Aye. We finished Susan's dress a couple o' days ago. Kelvin said he was goin' turkey huntin,' so that will be dinner. The apples may be a bit early, but I'd like to go to Pentagöet tomorrow and pick some for pies. I'll just use a little more maple sugar if they're too tart."

Greame helped her with clearing the table. From the dining room he said, "Kenny told me he'd help ye in any way he can, so be sure to put him to work."

"Susan wants to hae the ceremony by the water, and ye ken ye're marryin' them, right?" Cat asked, hands in the basin washing the dishes.

"Aye, Geoffrey asked me already," handing her the last of the plates. "Oh, I nearly forgot to tell ye, but he wants to go to Boston and buy some things for his cabin. I told him we'd go next week, after the weddin.' Ye didna hae any plans, did ye?"

Cat smiled and shook her head. "No, and it'll be nice to see Claire and Emily again. I wonder how they're gettin' on in that big house."

"Probably taken in a few folks by now, dinna ye think?" Greame asked, picking up a linen to dry the plates.

"I've no doubt. Makin' a boardin' house was a perfect idea to keep them busy. Wi' Boston growin' so quickly, there must be plenty o' folk who need a place to room while they settle in."

The rest of the warm afternoon was spent in small chatter. Susan came in later, and she and Cat detailed what was needed for her cabin when they went to Boston. Cat enjoyed having a woman's company. Today also seemed like a good day to learn a little more about Susan Bradford.

"All of my family have been in Charles Town for over seventy-five years now," Susan stated. "My father was the captain of a merchant ship that sailed to the Carolinas with supplies. He was lost at sea six years ago."

Cat poured a cup of tea for the both of them and sat at the kitchen table. "Sorry to hear. What was yer maiden name?"

"Witherspoon. My mum was a Henry. She also passed away two years ago, just after I got married to Reggie."

"Sorry to hear that, too. Hae ye any brothers or sisters then?"

"I have an older brother. He's also a merchant sailor, and I don't see him for years at a time." Susan looked at Cat and asked her the same question.

A hint of pain clouded Cat's eyes for a moment, but she blocked it. "I had three fine brothers, but they were all killed in the Risin.' My Mam and Da are also gone."

Susan nodded sympathetically, "We have a bit in common then, don't we?"

They sat in silence for a moment.

Cat sipped her tea, then said, "Isna there somethin' else ye want to be askin' me?"

Susan flushed a pretty pink. Her light green eyes looked deep into Cat's amethyst ones, then looked down again. "How … when … oh, dear. I'm making a complete fool of myself."

"I had my first vision when I was eleven," Cat said, saving the poor woman from herself. "I had no idea what was happenin' to me, but my Mam did. Her Mam was a great Seer for our clan." Cat didn't want to tell her too much to frighten her, so only disclosed the barest of details.

"So that's how you knew where to find me and Jumping Turtle? You *saw* us?"

"Aye." Cat watched the emotions play across Susan's face. She also noticed Susan had her fingers crossed under the table, as if to ward off any demons Cat might be possessed by. Christians were a superstitious lot.

"The evil Indian woman, Yellow Leaf, said that Jumping Turtle had a very powerful friend who crossed worlds watching out for her. She meant you, didn't she?"

Cat nodded. "Jumping Turtle and I hae become verra close since she marrit my dear friend Jim. That's what happens when I get close to people. I become connected to them and can see when somethin' is wrong."

Susan gazed out the window for a moment, composing her next question. Cat could hear it already, but waited for her to ask.

Susan's gaze held Cat's eyes this time. "Do you see me and Geoffrey safe?"

Cat smiled and patted her hand. "For the foreseeable future, aye."

Susan let out a relieved breath.

"I've got to take in the wash," Cat stated, rising from her chair. "Then I was goin' to see if I can catch some lobsters and dig some clams for supper tonight. Care to join me?"

10

Tying the Knot

AS THE SUN ROSE IN A peach-colored sky, Cat opened her eyes and smiled. Greame was watching her from the pillow next to hers.

"What's got ye smilin' so early?"

"I'm lookin' forward to the weddin' this afternoon." She threw off the bedclothes and sat on the edge of the bed looking out the window at the deep blue of the sea. No breeze stirred the water in the cove yet. It was mirror-like before a loon's wake carved a v-shaped ripple.

When Cat turned around, Greame was already into his breeks. "Which dress are ye wearin' for the event?"

"I was thinkin' about the deep red paisley silk."

Greame nodded, "A fine choice." Then he squinted a little.

"What?"

"Well, I'm just hopin' ye'll no' look so lovely as to take away from the bride."

Cat giggled. "And what is it ye need me to do for ye to warrant such a fine compliment?"

Greame clucked his tongue and scowled. "A fine thing to be sayin.'" Then pulled his sark over his head and walked out of the bedroom.

A moment later, as Cat was making the bed, his head appeared in the doorway wearing a sheepish grin. "Would ye locate my dark green waistcoat and tan coat when ye get a chance?"

Cat threw a pillow at him.

Footfalls were heard on the porch and Cat hurriedly got dressed. When she emerged from her room, Gregor was in the kitchen pouring a cup of chicory for himself and Greame. Kenny was putting wood in the stove, and Kelvin and Robbie were in the doorway.

Cat put her hands on her hips and smiled at the houseful of men. "Bring me what ye want brushed, mended or otherwise need for the ceremony," she said to the innocent looking faces, "and I'll hae them ready for ye."

Appreciative words were spoken all around as breakfast was cooked and eaten. The men left in a mob and returned with their finery. Robbie was the only one who seemed a bit reserved. He was the last one to drop off his clothes. Cat picked through the pile he laid on the table and opened his coat, noticing the stained, moth-eaten fabric. His waistcoat and breeks were in the same condition.

Without a word, Cat went into the spare bedroom and opened Greame's trunk where he kept a little of everything. First, she pulled out the clothes he wanted to wear and placed them on the bed. She rifled through what appeared to be an entire wardrobe of apparel and pulled out a dark brown coat and pair of ivory breeks. She went in again searching for a bit of softer cloth. When she felt the fine fabric, she brought it out to see what she had. It was an ivory silk shirt with a beautiful jabot of lace in the front. She was holding it up to the coat when she heard Robbie at the bedroom doorway.

"But those are Greame's," he said, looking thoroughly embarrassed.

"I dinna think he'll mind, Robbie. We canna let ye wear what ye brought," she said in as kind a voice as she could muster. "I'll make ye a new suit of clothes sometime, but I certainly dinna hae the time to do it today, aye?"

He nodded.

"Come here then. Let's see if these will fit ye," holding up the coat to his shoulders. He was a couple of inches taller than Greame, but not as wide. "I'll let ye try these on. Oh, wait, ye'll need a waistcoat." She went back to the trunk and held up embroidered gold brocade that would look very nice with the brown coat. "This, too," handing the vest to him before exiting the room.

Several minutes later, while she was brushing out Greame's coat, Robbie walked into the keeping room that was mounded with clothes to be tended to for the Hay clan.

Cat looked up and smiled warmly. Robbie's face was tinged with scarlet.

"Och, Robbie, ye look rare fine," she said, getting up to check the fit of the coat.

"Dinna fret, Garnet," he said, looking mighty uncomfortable.

"There's naught to fret o'er. It fits ye right well." She walked around him looking him up and down, nodding her approval.

Greame walked in then and looked at his cousin with a frown. He shook his head and walked back out again.

"I'd best go change now and get back to my chores," Robbie said, clearly unaccustomed to such close scrutiny.

Cat suppressed a giggle and went about brushing Greame's coat. When Robbie returned with his regular work clothes on, she noticed he held his new suit away from himself so as not to get it dusty.

"Thank ye," he said softly, and quickly walked out the door.

Greame must have been watching and waiting for his cousin to leave because he walked in not a minute later.

"Was that my suit Robbie was wearin'?"

Cat walked over to where Robbie left his "best" suit and held it up to Greame.

Greame's eyebrows went up and he shook his head. "Looks like Robbie needs a new set o' clothes."

"I dinna think ye'd mind if he borrowed some o' yers, considerin' the circumstances."

Greame chuckled. "Did ye see how red his face was? I do believe it may hae been the first time a woman e'er looked that closely at the man."

"Dinna poke fun at him. What would he need such a fine set o' clothes for anyway? He's no' one to be out socializin' with royalty, aye?"

"No, ye're quite right," said Greame, his fingers stroking his gold embroidered waistcoat admiringly. "But e'ery man should hae a good suit."

"Well, I'll see what I can do to rectify that situation, just no' today."

Cat finished checking all the men's clothes, making repairs and airing them out. When the clock struck eleven, the men started filtering in to fetch their finery and head back to their cabins to get ready. Susan came in at half eleven, and disappeared into the spare bedroom to get dressed.

Cat glanced outside to see Kenny tending the turkeys on the spits, and Far Eyes going over to talk to him. Most of the Lobster Clan was amassing in the yard now. Sings Like Bird, Far Eyes' sister, brought in some bread, and Jumping Turtle pulled out a platter from the cupboard and laid an expertly cooked venison roast on it. They asked Cat if they could do anything to help. Cat thanked them, but declined the offer.

She was just putting the apples into the two piecrusts and rolling out the tops when Susan emerged from the bedroom in a white cloud of brocade and lace. Sings Like Bird and Jumping Turtle gasped.

"Susan, ye look lovely," Cat said.

"Beautiful," was all Sings Like Bird could say.

Jumping Turtle smiled and hugged Susan.

The crusts were pinched and Cat slid the pies into the oven. "I've got to get dressed now or I'll be late for the celebration."

About twenty minutes later, Cat came out of her room in the form-fitting deep red paisley silk dress, which enhanced her tiny waist. She had her hair up in the Chinese sticks with long fiery tendrils left curling down her back. The women all gasped once again. None of them had ever seen this side of Cat before. She usually wore breeks and a loose-fitting sark.

"Dear God, Catrìona, you look stunning," Susan said.

A flush brightened Cat's face, and she smiled then curtsied. "Thank ye."

Greame was the last to find his way in to get dressed. He saw Susan and smiled, lifted her hand to his lips and pressed a soft kiss on it. "Ye look lovely."

Susan blushed at the show of affection and smiled. When he turned to go into his bedroom where Cat was still standing, he was stopped short.

Only Cat saw his face and the blazing look he gave her. Once again, her face turned pink as she backed into the bedroom, stopping only when the back of her legs hit the bed. Greame closed the door, not giving the ladies in the kitchen another thought.

He reached her in two steps and wrapped an arm around her waist, while his other hand held the back of her head. He kissed her thoroughly and both of them were breathless after his lips left hers.

"I ken it would happen like this. It wouldna matter if ye stayed in yer breeks, ye'd still outshine the bride," he said huskily, holding her away to look her over. "I'm verra much lookin' forward to gettin' ye out o' this dress later tonight," nuzzling her neck and brushing the tops of her breasts with his lips before she pushed him away.

"I'm goin' to go make sure Susan is ready to walk down the path," she said reaching for the doorknob. "Now hurry up and get dressed or ye'll be late."

Cat took a couple of deep breaths and tried to act normal when she reentered the kitchen. She was quite certain her cheeks were more flushed than they should be.

Thankfully the only person left in the kitchen was Susan, who smiled a knowing smile, but never said a word. A moment later, Greame opened the bedroom door and stepped out into the kitchen, presented a formal bow to the two of them, then left the house for the flat stone at the end of the path to preside over the ceremony.

Cat made sure he was in place, then handed Susan her bouquet of wildflowers. She grabbed her own bouquet and stepped onto the porch ahead of Susan.

Kelvin, who was waiting on the porch, took his cue and began playing the pipes as he led the procession.

Greame stood at the end of the path with Geoffrey. As Cat walked down the grass track, she kept her eyes straight ahead, looking only at Greame. She reached his side, then turned to watch Susan walk the short path.

Susan gazed radiantly at Geoffrey, allowing a soft smile to play over her lips. Cat glanced at Geoffrey to see that he indeed only had eyes for his bride. He held out his hand for Susan and she placed her hand on top of his. There was no need to bind the hands with the traditional tartan, as they were doing more than hand fasting. Greame was as close to clergy as their little settlement would ever see, but they would be legally married.

The pipes went silent and Kelvin took his place beside Geoffrey.

Susan and Geoffrey looked intently at Greame, who still resembled a sea captain, even in his finest clothes.

Greame cleared his throat and began in the *Gàidhlig*.

"*Mìle fàilte dhuit le d'bhrèid, fad do rè gun robh thu slàn. Mòran làithean dhuit is sìth, le d'mhaitheas is le d'nì bhi fàs.*

"For Susan and our Penobscot friends: A thousand welcomes to ye wi' yer marriage kerchief, may ye be healthy all yer days. May ye be blessed wi' long life and peace, may ye grow old wi' goodness, and wi' riches."

Greame looked at Geoffrey now and asked, "Would ye like to say yer vows, Geoff?"

"Aye."

He turned to face Susan and held out his tartan with the Hay clan brooch to her. She looked at it and nodded, then Geoffrey placed the tartan over her shoulder, signifying her acceptance into the clan.

In a clear, proud voice he began in his native tongue.

"*Tha mise,* Geoffrey Alexander Robert Hay, *a-nis 'gad ghabhail-sa* Susan Marie Witherspoon *gu bhith 'nam chéile phòsda. Ann am fianais Dhé 's na tha seo de fhianaisean tha mise a' gealltainn a bhith 'nam fhear pòsda dìleas gràdhach agus tairis dhuitsa, gus an dèan Dia leis a' bhàs ar dealachadh.*"

He turned, faced their guests and repeated in English.

"I, Geoffrey Alexander Robert Hay, now take ye Susan Marie Witherspoon to be my wife. In the presence of God and before these witnesses I promise to be a lovin,' faithful and loyal husband to ye, until God shall separate us by death."

Greame nodded then directed his attention to Susan now. "Would ye care to say yer vows now, Susan?"

She nodded and looked longingly into Geoffrey's storm gray eyes.

"I, Susan Marie Witherspoon, do take you Geoffrey Alexander Robert Hay to be my husband. In the eyes of God and before these witnesses I do promise with all my heart to love, honor and be faithful to you, until death shall separate us."

She had nothing to give him except the love in her eyes. She grabbed his coat, stood on tiptoes and kissed his lips.

Through a grin, Greame said, "Ye're now husband and wife. Be good to each other."

Kelvin began playing the pipes, leading the newlyweds back down the path and into the house. The crowd of well-wishers clapped and shouted. The Penobscot set up their drums in a circle and started hammering out a beat and singing. Many of the younger girls began dancing. They all wore their finest embroidered clothes and moccasins. Beads were strung in their hair, making them look like small, colorful birds.

Cat and Kenny began dishing up the food and setting it out on the tables for all those who wanted to eat. One of the barrels of whisky Greame had been saving was opened, and for the rest of the day and well into the night, the festivities continued.

It was nearly dawn when most of the men found their way to their cabins. The Penobscot slept wherever they found a good spot, sharing cabins or simply under the stars.

Cat and Greame had retired long before many, taking great pleasure in removing the deep red paisley dress.

11

The Past Catches Up

JEREMIAH BRADFORD WAS understandably upset over the death of his brother, Reginald. That the letter arrived nearly six months after the fact is what so enraged him. Susan wrote that there had been no way to get the news to him any sooner. She had apparently just arrived in Boston after having been in the wilds of Maine for nearly two years: his brother's ridiculous idea, and look where that got him. He had no idea how she managed to return, but he had to find her. It was most likely she would be in Charles Town, at her family home.

He reread the letter as he was boarding the ferry. It didn't tell him how Reginald had died, only that their house in Pentagöet had been burned and all of their possessions lost to the flames.

Then there were the last two sentences. *Don't try to find me. I have moved on with my life.*

What did that mean? Susan knew how he felt about her. Why she chose Reginald over him he would never know, but now that she was a free woman, and a widow at that, she would be in even greater need of him.

When he disembarked from the ferry, he strode up to the Witherspoon estate on the hill, which had a commanding view of the bay. He knocked on the door and waited a moment before one of the servants answered.

"I'm here to see Susan," he said to the older woman brusquely, twisting his thick moustache.

She gave him an odd look, and told him that she was in Maine.

Jeremiah thrust the letter in her face and told her that he'd just received it and that she had to be here.

"No sir, she hasn't been here," she said. "Master Thomas has returned, though," pointing to the study. "If you'd like to speak with him."

He grunted and rudely pushed by her to the study. When he opened the door, Thomas was sitting at the large desk writing in a ledger. He looked up at the intrusion, then lay his quill down.

"What do you want, Jeremy?"

"Where's Susan? I just received a letter from her saying she is in Boston, now that my brother is dead six months gone."

Thomas' eyes widened. He hadn't heard his sister's husband had died, nor that she had returned to Boston.

Jeremiah stood rooted to the floor, but could tell from the look on Thomas' face that he didn't know what was going on either.

"So it looks as though we are both in the dark over this situation," Jeremiah stated while taking a seat across from Tom.

"What happened? May I read the letter?"

Jeremiah handed it over and waited for him to finish. Jeremiah could tell when he read the last of it because Tom eyes, so much like Susan's, held many questions.

"She's moved on? What does that mean?"

Jeremiah gave a disgusted snort. "I should truly like to have that answer."

Tom sat back in his chair and pondered for a moment before asking, "Where else would she go? Does she have any close friends in Boston?"

Jeremiah stood abruptly and started pacing the oak floor. He just kept shaking his head, apparently eliminating all possibilities.

His gray eyes blazed at Tom. "I can't think of anyone she knew there. We must find her!"

Tom smiled condescendingly. "Why, Jeremy? If she doesn't want anything to do with you, any more than she did when you tried to make her choose you over Reggie, why would she have a change of heart now? Let her be." Tom picked up the quill and continued writing.

It was a dismissal, but Jeremy wasn't ready to be dismissed yet. He strode purposefully over to the big desk and pounded both fists onto its dark wooden surface, startling Tom, and angering him as well.

"I shall ask you to leave now," Tom said in a quiet voice that barely held his temper in check. "Or I shall be forced to remove you myself."

Jeremy wasn't a big man, but he was burly enough. Tom, however, stood nearly six feet and was a fighter. One had to be to captain ships and men.

The little man scoffed and swiped a few papers from the desk before taking his leave. Before he reached the door, though, he turned back to Tom and said threateningly, "You'd best let me know if you see her."

Tom ignored him.

❧

Emily and Claire were thrilled to have Catrìona's extended family stay with them for a few days while they gathered supplies for the winter. The house on 35 Newberry Street was much the same as Cat had left it a few years ago. In a stroke of luck, there were no guests staying at the Rose Guest House, as it had come to be known.

Greame and the rest of the men went down to the Worldwide Tea Emporium, his teashop, to see how the rest of his family was faring and how the business was going. That left the women to have tea in the best room.

"Soo, hoow's our Jimmy-boy?" Emily asked Cat in her thick Glaswegian accent.

"Oh, fine, Emily. Ye should see his wee son; they named him Harry. His eyes are just as blue as Jim's. His wife, Jumpin' Turtle, is doin' verra well, also."

"Our Harry would hae been right proud." Her hand went to her enormous bosom. "And, Susan, ye say yer a Witherspoon, aye? D'ye ken a Henrietta Morrisey then? She lives in Charles Town, too?"

Susan's eyes flew open in surprise. "Yes, she lives just two houses down from my family's estate! Heavens, if you know Henrietta, then you must have known my parents, James and Elizabeth Witherspoon?"

"I remember 'earin' Miss Rose talk of 'em," Claire chirped. "They're both gone, now, aren't they?"

Susan nodded, "Yes, but my brother Thomas owns the estate now and stays there when he's home. Merchant seamen are away quite often."

"Ye were marrit before, if memory serves, werna ye, Susan?" Emily ventured.

Susan paled a bit at the question, but nodded. "Yes, to Reginald Bradford."

"Bradford? From right here in Boston?" Emily asked.

"Yes, did you know him, too?"

Before she answered, she asked, "Does he hae a brother named Jeremiah?"

Susan's light green eyes darkened for a moment. "Yes. A rotten man," she nearly spat.

Cat looked deep into Susan for a moment to get a clearer picture of the man while she spoke.

"Jeremy wanted to marry me. He even tried to have Reggie … well, let's just say he tried to place him in a very compromising position, and have me find out about it. He figured I would call off the wedding and marry him instead."

"Why doo men think that women need their protection?" Emily asked, making Cat and Claire laugh.

"Em, no' all women are as brave as we are, eh?" Claire giggled, remembering fighting off Charles Carlyle's men with frying pans and rolling pins.

"Did I miss something?" Susan asked the room of madly laughing women.

"It's a terribly long story, but the short of it was that these two fine women," Cat said, wiping tears from her eyes. "And I saved Rose, the woman who owned this rare fine house, from a husband who enjoyed his rum and usin' his fists on her whene'er he came home from sea."

"Ooh, it was a right freein' experience too sit doown on a man's chest an' point oot all his shortcoomin's too his face!" Emily said, intensifying the giggling.

"Perhaps that's what Jeremy needs to have done to him. I felt compelled to write him a letter telling him his brother was dead, but I do not plan to ever see the man again."

❧

John, Thomas, Edward and George Hay, Greame's cousins, had remained in Boston to run the Worldwide Tea Emporium when Greame and the others left for Maine. Greame was in the shop with the rest of his cousins, and there was a great deal of friendly boasting and serious information being talked about. Gregor told the Hay clan what he knew of what was happening in the west, while the four Bostonians told of the local events.

"There have been a great many people in the area comin' down with small pox," George told them. "Many are dyin,' and I fear it isna finished yet."

"That's a verra large concern o' our Indian friends. Many o' the tribes hae been nearly wiped out because o' that plague," Greame said somberly. "I dinna ken why some whites can survive it, but no' them."

"We'd best be verra careful no' to bring it along wi' us. I couldna bear seein' the Lobster clan killed from that terrible plague," Robbie said.

"Aye," Greame stated. "Let's all be sure to hae our clothes washed proper before headin' home."

"Do ye still like it up there, Cap'n?" John wanted to know.

Greame glanced at Gregor, then smiled and nodded. "Aye. There's such a freedom up there. No one bothers us," he raised an eyebrow and grinned. "Usually … and wi' wee Geoffrey now takin' a wife, our settlement has just grown by one."

The roomful of men congratulated Geoffrey, and George brought out several bottles of whisky to celebrate. By the time the men had returned to Newberry Street, it was suppertime. The women had cooked a feast. Several smaller tables were brought into the dining room to accommodate all the men, and the celebration lasted well into the night. It was like having a more formal wedding reception.

Cat and Greame were the last to retire. They would sleep in Cat's old room, the green room, as Rose used to call it. The featherbed was covered in a sage green quilt, and rosy-pink pillows rested against a rich, tiger maple headboard that arched high against the wall. At the top was a carved scallop shell gilded in gold. There were two chairs near the window, upholstered in silk in the same shade of green as the quilt, with thin pink stripes. A wool rug in a darker shade of green with burgundy flecks rested beside the bed on the wood floor. An enormous armoire and a chest of drawers matching the wood of the headboard finished the room. In the looking glass that topped the drawers, Cat noticed her reflection. She looked happy.

Greame began undressing, and in the candlelight, his features softened. She walked over to him and touched the scar he'd received from an English soldier at Falkirk in the '45 that traveled from the back of his right ear all the way down across his right pectoral muscle.

"In the presence o' so many English, does this tingle?" She asked softly.

He grabbed her wrist and stopped her. "The only reason it's tinglin' now is because o' yer touch. It's burnin.'"

When Cat looked into his deep green eyes, it wasn't the only thing burning. His lips searing hers did nothing to extinguish the flame.

❧

The next morning dawned brightly. The green room faced the harbour and Cat awoke to see Greame standing by the window looking out to sea. He was naked. She secretly scanned his body, once again marveling at the wide breadth of shoulders tapering down to a small waist. His square buttocks flared out again at his thick, muscular legs.

He turned with a grin on his face, knowing she was looking at him. "Are ye enjoyin' the view?"

Cat laughed and pushed herself up onto her elbow. "Oh, aye, ye ken I am."

Just then, someone knocked on the door. Greame shook his head and shot a remorseful look at Cat. "What is it?" he asked none too kindly, making no move to get dressed until he heard if it was something dire or could wait.

"It's me, Robbie. George just came up from the shop wi' news ye may want to hear."

Greame blew out a breath and raked his hand through his deep brown hair. "I'll be down in a minute."

Cat was already out of bed. They both dressed and went downstairs to find Susan sitting on the settee a little paler than she should be.

Cat went and sat beside her. "What's wrong?"

Susan's light green eyes were threatening to overflow. "George just told me that there was a man searching for me. I can only guess that it's Jeremy."

Geoffrey was standing beside her with his hand on her shoulder. "I told ye, lass, that he'll no' harm ye, nor will he find ye. Ye're safe here."

Susan looked up at him and said, "But you don't know what he's capable of, Geoff."

This was news to Greame. "If someone would kindly fill me in as to who this Jeremy is, and why he's lookin' for Susan, I'd be obliged."

For the next thirty minutes, Susan explained to the roomful of Scots a great deal of her background, that up until now only Geoffrey knew anything about.

"He was always jealous of Reggie," she began. "Jeremy even tried to poison him when he was a child! Reggie was three years younger than Jeremy, and so different. Where he was kind, giving and adventurous, Jeremy took everything the wrong way, tried to bend people to his will, and is just … just so arrogantly hateful.

"Two weeks before we were married, he drugged Reggie and brought him to a friend's house on the other side of town. He then arranged for some … women … to … to take advantage of him, and I was brought there to *find* him in that compromising position."

The air in the room seemed to be charged with emotion, but no one spoke.

Susan raised her head a notch and thrust out her chin. "But I knew it was all a lie. Reggie wasn't like that. Then I found out from the gentleman who owned the house that it was all just supposed to be a prank, but I knew that it was more than that to Jeremy. When he saw me rushing out of that room, he tried to console me by saying that I should leave Reggie and marry him instead. He said that he would never treat a woman like that." She stood abruptly, suddenly looking like if he were standing in front of her right now he'd be in for a bit of abuse.

"What did ye tell the scoundrel?" Emily asked with a scowl on her face. She would take care of this little problem with no remorse in maiming the man.

"I told him that if he were the last man in the colonies, he'd not have me for a wife."

"What did he do after that?" Gregor asked, grinning like a dog eating bumblebees.

A flush reddened Susan's cheeks, but she continued the story. "He tried to force the issue by telling me that just one kiss and he'd be the only one I would ever think of again."

"Sounds like someone else we knew, doesn't it, Greame," Geoffrey stated, meaning their cousin Hector who'd said nearly those same words to Cat a few years ago, with dire consequences.

Susan stared at Geoffrey and asked, "What happened?"

Cat fielded the question before the answer frightened Susan more than she already was. "No' anythin' anyone would care to repeat."

"So what shall I do about this? I had no idea he would still be feeling this way after this long," she said, sitting back down as if the weight of it was too much to bear. "I don't want this mess to go any further than here. I just want to buy some necessities for our home and get back to Maine as soon as possible."

Gregor spoke up. "Dinna fret, lass, he'll no' even remember yer name after we *speak* to him."

Everyone knew there'd be no speaking involved.

12

Foreseeing the Future

SUSAN WASN'T ALLOWED TO go anywhere by herself. She, Cat and Geoffrey had bought quite a few of the essentials needed for their cabin at Walker's Mercantile. The pots, dishware, cutlery, linens, fabrics, bedding and other items were to be delivered right onto the *Revenge*. Robbie and Kelvin waited on Long Wharfe for the afternoon to be sure they were indeed delivered. That left Greame, John, Kenny, Thaddeus and Gregor to patrol the streets for one Jeremiah Bradford.

It didn't take too long to locate the man, as he was causing a ruckus wherever he went, insisting to the shopkeepers that Susan had to have been there. Jeremy was found in a public house having a bit of luncheon and a pint. Gregor was given the honors, as he so enjoyed the sport of frightening the life out of mortal men. Greame and the rest of the men took tables with the best views on either end of the room to watch the outcome.

Gregor took a seat directly across from Jeremy, startling him and nearly making him lose his grip on the ale he had just taken a swig from.

"Here, now! What do you want? Do I know you?" Jeremy bellowed, clearly unaccustomed to company.

"Ye are Jeremiah Bradford, are ye no'?" Gregor asked in a belyingly soft tone.

Jeremy regained a little composure and sat up straighter in his chair. "Yes, I am he. What may I help you with, sir?"

Gregor reached into his coat pocket, pulled out an envelope, and laid it on the table. Jeremy's gray eyes narrowed, looking from Gregor to the envelope as if something would spring from either one of them. Gregor slid it across the table towards Jeremy and waited.

"Who are you? What is this?" he demanded in a booming voice, as though wishing someone would come to his rescue.

"Must ye be so loud, Jeremy?" Mockingly putting his hands over his ears. "Canna ye just read the letter so I can hae meself a pint in peace?"

Jeremy wiped his thick moustache of foam from his ale, snatched the letter off the crumb-laden table and opened it. As he read it, his face turned a vivid scarlet, and a deep, raging scowl contorted his face as he turned the page. All the while Gregor watched him with a straight face that seemed to be hard to maintain, for his mouth twitched every so often.

When Jeremy finished the letter, Gregor could have sworn he could hear the man growling. Before Gregor knew what hit him, Jeremy was on his feet and actually grabbing Gregor by the throat. He obviously had no idea how big Gregor was, but found out quickly he had done the wrong thing to the wrong man.

Gregor stood, taking the little man with him, who was now not just trying to strangle Gregor, but trying to hold on for dear life as his feet where well over a foot off the ground. He was a bit like a rabid dog that once his teeth were sunk in, his eyes rolled up into his head and pure hostility took over.

Gregor had the audacity to look over at Greame and wink just before he pried the little man's fingers from his throat and tossed him to the ground. Jeremy wasn't to be discouraged so easily though, and jumped back to his feet for another attack.

Jeremy raged toward Gregor headfirst, but Gregor neatly sidestepped the man, grabbing a fistful of collar on his way by. It nearly took Jeremy off his feet. Gregor hoisted him up by the front of his coat and said, "Wee man, I dinna come here to harm ye. My task was just to deliver the letter, but if ye insist on this behavior, ye'll be gettin' just what ye ask for."

Jeremy took a few swipes at Gregor, finding his mark, but not making a dent in Gregor's fortitude. Gregor threw him across the room. The wall stopped him, and Jeremy bounced right back into the fray without missing a beat.

Men made room for the cocky little bantam rooster and the smiling giant. Whoops were shouted and bets were taken around the pub. Jeremy managed to fling a chair at Gregor who once again sidestepped it easily, causing it to crash at Greame's feet. Greame casually bent over and righted it.

Jeremy threw himself once more at Gregor's midsection and, once more missing his mark, landed hard on the sticky plank floor.

Before there was any other damage done, or someone retrieved the militia, Greame shouted to Gregor, "End it!"

Gregor moved quickly and caught Jeremy by the scruff of his coat, then grabbed the waist of his breeches and lifted him off the ground, carrying him kicking and flailing over to the front door—which someone had thoughtfully opened—and tossed him into the street.

The militia apparently had been summoned because as the men poured out of the tavern, three armed guards were racing up the street, surrounding the group with bayonets as Jeremy lay panting on the ground.

Gregor had a favourable compliment to pay the man, and bent to his ear. "Mr. Bradford, ye're a right durable man."

Gregor was detained for questioning, but with everyone corroborating his story of how the man went mad after reading a letter, Gregor was sent home.

"Ye dinna really believe that will be the end of it, do ye?" Kenny asked, watching as the militiamen hauled Jeremy down the street to the gaol.

"Nope. But anything he does now will only make him look guilty," Greame stated. "We'll wait. He wilna be in gaol for too long. I want this ended here, no' brought to the settlement."

When the men all returned to Newberry Street, and were seated around the dinner table, Gregor boldly asked Susan what the letter had said to provoke such a rage in the man.

Susan blushed fiercely.

"Gregor!" Cat squeaked. "Ye dinna ask a woman for that kind of information!"

Geoffrey couldn't help it and burst out laughing.

Gregor looked at him and said, "Ye ken, dinna ye?"

Geoffrey's eyes widened at the sharp kick he received under the table and the glare of a scowling wife with murder in her eyes.

Emily and Claire seemed to have reverted to their servant days and hastily began asking if anyone wanted more fish, or potatoes, or bread, or …

Not another word was spoken of the incident as they ate supper. In fact, most of the men made hasty excuses and left directly after they finished their meal, either to escape the thick air of the room, or to release their laugher in the privacy of their own company.

Cat, Emily and Claire began clearing the table. Susan began washing the dishes, but it seemed as though even she wanted nothing more than to be in her own room without all eyes upon her.

Soon, it was just Cat and Greame who remained downstairs. All the others retired to their rooms for the evening.

"I fear Geoffrey may be in for a bit of a tongue lashin' tonight," Greame said quietly, stoking the fire.

Cat giggled as she wiped the table of crumbs. "Oh, ye think so?"

"Ye should hae seen the man," Greame said, smiling and shaking his head with the memory. "He was bloody fearless. Even though Gregor was more than twice his size, he attacked like a mad man." He stood beside the hearth in silence for a moment, then turned to Cat.

She was watching him with her hands on her hips and a mock scowl on her face. "Dinna even think of askin' me what was in that letter," she admonished. "I dinna ken, and I dinna wanna ken."

Greame held up his hands with an expression of total innocence.

They both laughed.

"I think our wee Susan will do right fine in the wilds o' Maine," Cat stated.

"Oh aye, she may be small, but her pen carries a fair amount o' weight, judgin' from the look on wee Jeremy's face when he read that letter."

Cat walked over to Greame and hooked her arm through his. "Let's go to bed, I canna wait to get out of this dress. I dearly wish I could wear my breeks around town," she elaborated. "This corset may well be the death o' me."

❧

For the next two days, there was no word from Jeremy Bradford. The late September sun was still warm, and the days were filled with browsing through shops and quickening life's pace in the bustle of town. Cat couldn't wait to get back to Maine.

"So, we'll leave tomorrow then?" Cat asked as she stared out at the harbour from her bedroom window.

"Aye, if Susan's finished with her task," Greame replied, shaking out his waistcoat.

"She told me she has but a few more items to purchase." She spoke to the window. "I'm hopin' we'll get that done today. We fair ladies are plannin' a day speakin' wi' a furniture maker Susan's family kens."

Greame glanced at Cat's less-than-enthusiastic expression and grinned. "What would *ye* care to be doin' instead?"

Cat turned from the window and smiled, "Anythin' but that. Shoppin's ne'er been a favorite task for me."

"I think ye may be the only woman in Boston to say such a thing," Greame said, walking over to wrap his arms around her. "Is there naught ye would like to hae for yerself? A wee bit o' jewellery, or a new pair o' shoes, perhaps? A copper tub canna be the only item ye purchase on a shoppin' spree."

Cat thought for a moment. "D'ye think there might be an apothecary shop in town?"

"Isna there one on Summer Street, right beside the bookshop?"

She nodded and smiled. "I think ye may be right. Would ye care to join me for a wee bit o' shoppin' then?"

"Just tell me when," he said, kissing her cheek. "I've got to go over some things wi' my cousins right now, but afterwards ..."

"I'll be here waitin' for ye then."

❧

Wilmont's Apothecary might have been the most interesting store Cat had ever been in. Rows upon rows of wooden shelves were loaded with jars of the most amazing array of herbs she'd ever seen. Many were imported from around the world, much like Greame's teashop. Blaisdell Wilmont was behind the counter helping an elderly man with his gnarled hands. Cat and Greame walked around the store reading the labels of everything from ordinary goldenrod to the extraordinary manroot.

Cat was sniffing a beautiful dusty green, round-leafed stem that smelled curiously fresh yet musty at the same time, when Mr. Wilmont came around the counter to speak with her.

"I see you have found my eucalyptus," he said in a high, feminine voice. He had no wig on his head, but his thick silver hair fell in deep waves over his shoulders.

Cat turned to him and noticed his clear, light blue eyes that seemed to tell the story of his entire life in a quick flash. He seemed to note a similar quality in Cat's dusty violet eyes.

"Say it again?" she asked. "U-ka … what?"

"Eucalyptus, my dear. It grows in Australia."

"What's it used for then?"

"Mostly to keep rather large spiders and scorpions from entering one's home," he said with a pleasant smile.

Cat held up her hand, "I dinna think I even want to ken what a scorpion is."

Mr. Wilmont chuckled. "I am Blaisdell Wilmont. What is it I may help you with?"

"I'm Catrìona Robertson, from Loch Rannoch, Scotland, sir. This is my husband, Greame Hay," she said, laying her hand on Greame's arm. "There are many fine plants there for healin.' Unfortunately, Maine doesna seem to hae those same plants. Since ye seem to hae a verra fine selection, I was wonderin' what ye might recommend for substitutes."

For the next two hours, Blaisdell Wilmont, Cat and Greame talked about everything each other knew about botany, herbals and healing. Greame, who hadn't nearly the education Cat had in what herb was used for what ailment, got quite a lesson.

Cat purchased armfuls to replenish her waning supply with everything from astragulus to wood betony.

When she was nearly out the door, she turned back to Blaisdell and risked a question.

"Oh, Mr. Wilmont? Would ye by any chance carry crystals?"

His bushy silver brows lifted, and again, Cat was getting the impression that he was much more than he seemed.

"I, uh …" He walked over to the front door, locked it and put the "closed" sign out.

Cat and Greame looked at each other with raised eyebrows of their own.

"One cannot be too careful when it comes to what you are asking for, my dear."

"What do ye mean?" Cat asked, putting her packages on the counter.

In a very quiet voice, as if someone were listening who shouldn't be, he said, "In many circles in this town, that question would be construed as witchcraft, my dear. One shouldn't ask those sorts of questions without proper knowledge of whom you are asking."

"Here, too?" Cat retorted angrily. "Is it still happenin'?"

Blaisdell started at her vehemence and shook his head. "You've not heard of the nineteen who were falsely condemned of witchcraft just over sixty years ago?"

Cat and Greame once again looked at each other, and they both shook their heads.

"It happened in Salem, just north of town, when a group of young girls who mysteriously became entranced decided to spread a rumor that a few people were witches. It escalated into a statewide frenzy culminating in the hanging deaths of many a good folk whose only crime was that they went to the wrong church or sided with the wrong beliefs."

"Christ," Cat whispered. "So it's no' happened since then?"

Mr. Wilmont shook his head, "No, but I shall not try to spark the issue, if you understand my meaning."

"We understand just fine, sir." Greame was rubbing the back of his neck.

"But!" Mr. Wilmont said a little too loudly, making Cat and Greame jump. "I do have what you're asking for. Come with me."

For the third time, Cat and Greame looked at each other with eyebrows raised, and followed the man. He took them into a small back room and closed the door. Inside was a small, simple wooden desk and chair, surrounded by wooden crates. Each crate had a number and a tiny symbol on it. Blaisdell sat in the chair, folded his hands on the desk, and asked Cat what type of crystals she was looking for.

"What d'ye mean, what type?" Cat asked.

"For what purpose will you be using them, my dear? Healing, balancing, seeing?"

Cat opened her mouth, but no words were uttered. She was fairly stupefied. "I had no idea, sir, that the wee stones could do so many things." She paused for a moment, tapping her cheek, then said, "Hae ye something for protection then?"

Blaisdell's eyebrows raised high. "Protection?" He rubbed his chin, then asked, "Protection from what?"

Greame snorted and folded his arms over his chest. "From everything, sir. Seen and unseen."

"Seen and *un*seen?"

A keen light shone in Blaisdell's eyes then, Cat noticed. Before she said anything else, she looked inside him to be sure he was truly what he claimed to be. What she saw was rather startling. Blaisdell Wilmont was a very old soul. There was a mystical quality to his heart and mind, and he was sincerely interested in what she was doing with such powerful talismans. He had more abilities than he knew.

"I am a Seer in my country, Mr. Wilmont. I am also a healer." She waited for that to sink in. Seeing that he was unfazed by the revelation, she continued. "I've had experiences wi' the other side, good and bad."

"It's a gift," Greame stated.

"Not such a gift, at times, is it, Mrs. Robertson … or is it Mrs. Hay?"

Cat smiled. "Mrs. Hay, or Catrìona, will be fine, sir. And no, more times than no,' I would call it a curse."

"Yes, well then." He turned and began looking over his crates as though the numbers or symbols told him what he was searching for. "Ah, here we are."

Blaisdell lifted one of the crates and placed it on his desk. He stood then and opened the lid, removing bits of straw. Then he reached inside and took out five small wood boxes inscribed with the names of the stones, and placed them in front of Cat.

"Open them," he instructed. "You will know if any has the power you're looking for."

Cat reached for one of the boxes and lifted the cover, reminding her, for an instant, of when her brothers gave her the garnet and silver ring she wore on her finger. She carefully plucked out the stone and set it into the palm of her hand.

The blue and green clump of crystals was called Azurite-Malachite.

"It's properties are said to see through illusions, and it aids in communication," Blaisdell told her.

Cat laid the stone on the desk and opened the next box. This one was called Rhodizite. It was a cluster of yellowish-green crystals.

"That one unlocks blockages so one may see clearer."

The next one contained Tiger Eye, an iridescent multi-hued brown stone. Cat liked this one, and looked at Blaisdell for its attributes.

"I knew you'd like that one. It's a great protector of the mind and aids in clarity."

Cat set it down and picked up another box. This one had a bright red stone that seemed to be pockmarked. Coral, it read.

"You'll definitely want to take that one, Mrs. Hay, as it protects against evil."

Greame snorted again. "Oh aye, ye'd best sew that one into yer clothes. Better yet, wear it like Far Eyes does in a pouch around yer neck."

Cat glared at him then opened the final box. It was labeled Obsidian. It looked like a piece of black glass. Its edges were sharp and translucent, and the stone was smooth and shiny.

"And what is this one for?"

"Obsidian is generally a protective stone, and it may work well for what you need," Blaisdell replied, watching her curiously.

Cat looked at all the stones presented. She picked them all up and held them in the palm of her hand. She closed her eyes and felt the power they radiated. She did a little experiment by removing one stone at a time, seeing if it changed the power. It did. It was definitely more powerful with all the stones together.

"I'll take them all, Mr. Wilmont."

Blaisdell nodded, and was still watching her intently. "You could feel each stone, couldn't you? Their power, I mean."

"Aye."

"Did you see anything when your eyes were closed?"

Cat's head cocked a little, looking him in the eyes. "Colors."

Greame's head was going back and forth to Cat and Blaisdell as they spoke.

"What colors?"

"Green, yellow and blue."

"No red or orange?" he asked.

Cat shook her head.

"Interesting. The colors you see are peaceful and spiritual. It tells me the stones you have chosen will keep you harmonious."

Cat's dimples deepened. "That's all I can ask for then."

"I'll wrap them up for you." He stood and began placing the stones back in their boxes, then stopped. "One more thing, Mrs. Hay." He began scanning the crates for something, then opened one of them way in back, and rifled through its contents. When he faced Cat again, he was holding up a nearly clear, pink crystal ball. "Might you have use for this?"

Cat gasped at the six-inch sphere. She looked at Blaisdell with wonder in her eyes. "May I hold it?"

He handed the stone to her, watching her face. "I obtained that from a gypsy in Poland many years ago. Never thought I'd have any use for it."

"A gypsy?" Greame asked, rubbing a finger over the smooth surface.

"She told me the right person could see what was to come in its depths."

Cat looked up at him sharply. "Hae ye been able to see into it?"

Blaisdell shook his head and chuckled warmly. "No, my dear. I have no such powers."

She offered nothing to dispute him.

Looking at the orb, she experienced a warm vibration in her hands. She looked up at Greame, who seemed to be mesmerized by it, and said, "Hold it."

Without taking his eyes from it, Greame held out his hands and cupped the sphere. His eyes got wide and he glanced at Cat. She was smiling.

"Aye, Mr. Wilmont, we've use for it," she said, patting Greame's shoulder.

❧

Cat and Greame brought their plunder directly to the *Revenge*, as neither wanted to explain why they had just purchased stones and a gypsy's crystal ball to anyone.

Greame waited until they were aboard ship in the privacy of the captain's quarters before asking his questions.

"Did ye feel the vibration, Garnet?" He was placing the packages on his bunk. "It was as though it was alive and breathin'! And I felt verra odd, like … somethin' was tryin' to get inside o' me."

He glanced at Cat to see her reaction. She was sitting at his desk watching him, but not seeing him. He waited for her to re-enter this reality.

Cat heard him, but as he was speaking, she was getting a vision of the gypsy the crystal had belonged to. She was very old, with long white hair covered by a deep blue, heavily beaded shawl that wrapped around her neck. She was looking directly into the sphere with eyes as black as Anna Macpherson's used to be. Colors spiraled out of the crystal and undulated around her, dancing with a distinct rhythm. When Cat gazed into the ball, she actually saw Greame. The old woman did too, and smiled, covered the crystal with a red silk square, sat back in a heavily carved wooden chair, and died.

Cat shook herself out of the vision and looked over at Greame, who was watching her intently. He raised an eyebrow in question.

"The crystal was meant for *ye*."

He frowned, not quite certain she said what he thought she said. After a moment, he asked, "How? What did ye see?"

"It was as though the old woman was directin' the ball to find ye, and that's why ye had such a powerful reaction to it when ye held it."

That didn't really answer his question. "How?" he asked again.

Cat just shook her head and shrugged. "I dinna ken. This is new to me."

"So, ye're tellin' me that an old woman, what? placed a curse on the ball?"

Cat snorted, "A curse? Why would ye say that? Is that the pirate in ye talkin'?"

Greame scowled, "No, it's no' the pirate in me, but I ken what I felt."

Cat frowned, "Did ye feel evil then?"

He thought for a moment before he answered. "No, it wasna evil. It was … well, the best way I can describe it is that it felt like somethin' was pressin' on me." He rubbed the back of his neck. He looked at Cat and put his hand to his chest. "Here."

Cat stood up and walked over to him. She placed her hand on his chest and closed her eyes. After a moment she said, "I dinna see anythin.'"

"Wait, let me hold it again and see if ye see anythin' then." He opened the box and pulled out the ball, holding it in his hands. "Try it now."

Cat did as she was told and waited, but saw nothing. She looked up at Greame when a frown furrowed his brow.

"What is it?" Cat asked, removing her hand from his chest.

He was staring at the ball. "I dinna feel it anymore."

"I think it was familiarizin' itself to ye. I think that's what ye felt."

"What do ye mean?"

"The old gypsy, she kent yer … spirit somehow. When ye held the ball, it combined its powers wi' ye. A bit like findin' its destined place."

"But *how*? I've ne'er met a gypsy. How would she ken who I was to place this … this … power into this ball and assign it to me?"

Cat shrugged. "I dinna ken."

He bent to return it to its box, but stopped when Cat said, "When ye look into it, tell me what ye see."

He held it in his hands again and looked into the stone. "Cracks. Pink. A bit of milky color."

"No, dinna look *at* it, look *into* it."

Greame frowned and sat down on his bunk. This time he cleared his mind before looking into the stone. After a few moments, he began to see little sprites of color dancing around it. Inside, the sphere began to get cloudy and shapes began to appear.

Cat watched in his mind, as she could not see any changes in the sphere.

Greame kept his eyes on the stone and his ship appeared. As he watched, angry storm clouds surrounded it and enormous waves pummeled the *Revenge's* hull. The gale ripped the sails from their masts and the *Revenge* foundered into the raging depths.

Greame nearly dropped the ball into his lap. He looked up at Cat with horror on his face. Her face almost matched his.

"We're no' goin' anywhere tomorrow," he whispered.

Cat shook her head. "I wonder if I'd hae received the same information later tonight to spare ourselves that journey to hell."

Greame was visibly shaken. "So, that's what ye would see when somethin' bad's about to happen?"

Cat nodded.

Greame shook his head slowly from side to side. "I dinna think I want to be able to see into the future. Perhaps we should return the orb to Mr. Wilmont."

He placed the orb back into its box, pulled Cat to sit beside him, and held her tightly until both of them regained their composure.

13

Death and Taxes

THE NEXT MORNING, Greame awoke to a sky of crimson and scarlet and purple. They were the colors of death. He stood at the bedroom window watching the colors fade into a dark, malevolent gray. The wind was calm for the moment, as the harbour was treacherously still. If he hadn't seen with his own eyes the storm that waited for him out at sea, he'd have risked returning home today. The thought made him shiver. He turned to find Cat watching him from the edge of their bed. She wore an uncharacteristically serious expression.

"Did ye see what I saw, Garnet?"

"Aye." She stood and walked over to the window with him. "It was nearly the same vision, wi' a few details added, just to be sure the point got across."

He crossed his arms over his chest. "I dinna care to hear the details, if ye dinna mind. I saw all I needed to make us stay in port 'til this storm passes."

They stood side-by-side for a moment pondering their own thoughts.

Greame then turned to her and asked, "Will the *Revenge* be safe where she is, or will we need to be findin' a more sheltered cove?"

Cat touched his arm. "No, it'll fare well where it is."

His gaze returned to the harbour, to the ships that were leaving, braving the impending storm. "How will those poor ships fare, though?"

"Ye canna save everyone, Greame," she stated softly. "They've made their own choices. Ye can tell most will remain in port today. The smart ones ken what's out there waitin' to take them down. The others …"

"Once again, I am awed by ye, Garnet," he stated softly. "How ye've been able to live wi' this … *knowin'* all yer life." He turned to her and pulled her sleep-warm body against his chest. "And ye're still able to smile and laugh and be cheerful about life."

Cat looked up at him and smirked. "Oh aye, verra cheerful. Ye're just wonderin' why I havna put a pistol to my head."

Greame snorted humorlessly. "Well, I'm no' certain I would no' hae."

"Perhaps that's why the Sight comes to ye when ye're young. It gives a person time to adapt to it. In yer case, since ye've just acquired the skill, I can see where it would be a bit more difficult to adjust to." She stepped out of his arms and began to dress. "Give it time, *a' ghaoil*."

"Or stop lookin' into the crystal ball," her muffled voice uttered from under her shift.

❧

By mid-afternoon, the gale lashed the ships in the harbour, and a heavy rain battered the windows of the Rose Guest House. Cat sat near the window in the best room and watched the rivers of muddy water wash down the cobblestoned streets, cleansing them of all debris. Greame was at the teashop to be closer to his ship, if needed. A sharp clap of thunder made her jump, and Susan, who was on the settee doing a bit of needlework, squeaked in surprise.

"Dear Lord!" she cried, her hand delicately covering her heart. "I hate such storms. Boston is notorious for them this time of year."

"Oh, aye. In Maine, they tend to be more in October through February."

"I do wish Geoffrey would have stayed with me," she said, looking out the window. She caught Cat's glance and blushed a bit. "Selfish, I know."

Cat smiled and shook her head. "No, no' selfish. I was wishin' Greame would hae stayed, too."

Through the kitchen door, Emily emerged with a tray of tea and scones with boysenberry jam, and set it down on the table.

"Thought this might be makin' us all feel a bit less jumpy, aye?"

"An' for those of us who need a bit more ..." Claire chirped, holding up a bottle of sherry.

All of them laughed. Claire laced each cup of tea with a nip, and the rest of the storm faded from memory.

It was well after dark when the men arrived home. The storm's fury had passed, leaving the moon's glow to steal in through the windows, darkened now and again by cloudy remnants that whipped across the sky.

Nearly everyone was heading up to bed. Gregor and Kelvin were the only two to remain downstairs to talk and polish off a bottle of fine whisky Gregor brought home.

Cat slipped under the bedclothes to watch Greame undress in the moonlight. Geoffrey and Susan's room was right next to theirs, and Cat smiled when she heard their lovemaking noises.

Greame slid in beside Cat and pulled her close to him. Either he didn't hear them, or he wasn't in the mood for romance.

"Talk around town is that the Crown is imposin' an excise tax on Bostonians for the consumption of wine, rum, liquor and other such goods."

Cat got up on an elbow. "Only for Bostonians? Surely, that wilna effect yer teashop?"

"Aye, just for Bostonians. And they are requirin' householders to swear an oath—an oath!—if ye can believe it, to the exact quantity of rum drunk in their houses per year! 'Tis gettin' out o' hand, if ye ask me."

She could see him in the moonlight scrubbing his face with his big hands.

Greame was quiet for a moment, rolling it over in his head before he spoke, then propped himself up on his elbow. "Supposedly, Gov'nor Shirley's no' goin' to sign the bill, but it seems to me that the General Court's gettin' too big for its breeches and enactin' taxes for their own convenience without the people's consent. It might be time for us rebels to take a stand."

"Us *rebels*? Is that how ye see us?"

His teeth shone white in the moonlight when he smiled widely. "I despise being told what to do."

Cat laughed. "How well I ken that! But seriously, Greame, what if they start taxin' tea? Will ye sell flour instead?"

"Aye, well, it may just be easier to make sure the tax doesna go through."

"Now that's the kind o' rebel talk I prefer." She leaned across and kissed him. "The stay-out-of-it kind. I dinna need ye to land in gaol for treason while we're in Boston, aye?"

He rolled onto his back and chuckled. "No, perhaps that wouldna be the best way to handle it. But . . ." His voice took on a more severe tone. "I will be speakin' wi' the merchants to see what we *can* do about it. There's a town meetin' tomorrow evenin' that I think I'd enjoy attendin,' if ye dinna mind waitin' to return to Maine until the followin' day."

"With yer business at stake, I think it'd be a wise course of action."

❧

The town hall was crammed with people and anger hovered thickly in the stale air. From the middle of the room, Cat recognized many of the merchants. She had never taken part in any sort of election process. It was dizzying as merchants shouted at legislators, and the legislators shouted louder in return volleys. After several hostile hours, the officials of the General Court, evidently oblivious to the people's desires, passed the Excise Act in spite of what was said would happen to the townsfolk. It all came down to money, and making certain it came out of the pockets of the townspeople, not the country people. Apparently, there were even smaller factions that divided the state. Cat was awed by the corruptness of it all, and the fact that the people let it happen. Who voted the General Court in, anyway? she wondered. Weren't they elected to represent what the people wanted? This political method seemed to be quite a farce. She left on Greame's arm more confused than ever.

"At least in Scotland, when there is but one ruler, the Clan Chief, he could be murdered so another can rule fairer," she said in all seriousness when they returned to the teashop before heading home.

Greame and Gregor looked at her with unbelieving eyes, then burst out in hysterical laughter. The other men smiled, but weren't altogether certain she was bluffing.

"So, that's yer solution to the problem, lass? Murder the General Court? Lord, I ken there was a reason we got on so well!" Gregor was wiping the tears from his eyes.

"Well, it's no more unjust than what I just witnessed!" She was pacing the room like a caged beast and twirling her hair.

Apparently, taking her along wasn't as wise an idea as Greame had assumed it would be. Cat wasn't one to let the blatant disregard for justice triumph. It was a good thing they were returning to Maine in the morning. Who knows what she'd do if she remained here for too long. He smiled a bit, pondering the notion of Cat on a rampage in the General Court. They wouldn't know what hit them!

❧

The next morning was particularly cool when the *Revenge* and her crew sailed back to Maine. Cat looked a bit haggard when she said her farewells to Emily and Claire just after dawn. She hadn't slept well, reliving the anger from the town meeting and feeling a need to rectify the situation.

"It's just plain unfair," she muttered, pacing around the deck.

Greame took the helm to keep up the premise of distraction to navigate around the ships in the crowded harbour. But really it was just so he could watch her. He could hear her muttering when the wind was right, and he wondered if she'd stew all winter over this. It would be a very long winter, if so. Before they sailed, he'd asked George to get word to him somehow if things escalated further to include tea under taxation. In that case, he would have to rethink his options to remain in business.

When they were well out to sea, Kelvin ambled over to take the helm.

"Where is she?" Greame asked.

Kelvin shrugged. "Last I saw her, she was talkin' wi' Gregor."

"Great. The man kens how to site a riot well enough, but I still dinna think he kens Cat's temper first hand."

Kelvin chuckled and lit his pipe. The sweet aroma of it blew away in the wind.

Three perfect days later, they arrived at the settlement. It took nearly a full day to unload all the goods Susan had purchased in Boston.

"Where are they goin' to put all that fancy stuff?" Gregor asked, watching from Cat's porch as trunks and crates and furniture poured into Geoffrey's wee cabin.

Cat giggled. "I'd imagine we'll be buildin' a bit of an addition soon."

Gregor stole a glance at her to see if there was a hidden meaning in that information. He was certain there was. "She's with child?"

Cat glanced at him and nodded.

"Does Geoff ken about it yet? He's no' mentioned it to me?"

"NO!" she hissed. "And dinna ye say a word, mind?"

That sly grin that indicated a useful tidbit of information was just received crinkled his eyes. "My lips are sealed, lass."

"Hmm."

14

Choosing Sides

The letter arrived at the end of December 1754 in quite a dilapidated state. There was no telling how many hands it had passed through from Boston through the Maine wilderness.

In George Hay's scribbling hand, he wrote that only a couple of weeks after Greame had sailed back to Maine, a delegation had returned from the Albany Congress with The Albany Plan of Union. It was promptly circulated to towns affected by the Excise Tax to garner people's opinions and advice. What the plan included was a Crown-appointed president and legislator representing each of the colonies with the power to tax and raise troops.

Greame read a bit of the letter out loud to Cat.

> "... *Thank Bride, the consensus saw it for what it was: a way to take more from the people and give it to the Crown. As though the Crown isn't meddling in our Business enough these*

days. It would have given them the power to not only take what little money we have, but to take men for Military use for the Crown. Do they not understand why we have left England? While I am not certain what side would be taken by Bostonians, I have a suspicion it would not be with the English. Either way, Cousin, this time even the General Court rejected the plan.

Another fair note is that the Businessmen in town have formed a Merchants Club, and they are working with the Caucus to have harmony at the Town Meetings. They often get a bit violent with disagreements."

"So I take it to understand that the town meetin' we attended was a well-behaved gatherin'?" Cat asked, rolling her eyes at the lengths politicians will go through to get what they wanted imposed on the people, whether voted in or not. "That's no' what I would call a democracy."

Greame snorted. "Well, I'd hae to agree wi' ye on that, but perhaps it does best havin' a King rulin' o'er us, and we havin' no say in the matter whatever."

"One day, the people wilna take it anymore. What will happen then?"

He looked at her for a moment to judge if what she had just said was a premonition or just her opinion. Either way, his own feeling was that it would come to pass that the colonists would rebel against the Crown. And the only way to win that battle would be to fight.

Would it be worth a war to separate completely from England and become their own country?

He thought, yes. Cat would surely have something to say on the matter, but in his mind, freedom would be worth the fight.

❧

Cat was watching Greame's mind at work. She knew what she said had sparked an entire series of ideas, none of which she liked, except the final outcome. Freedom from the English. Would it be worth it to go to war to be free? She walked to the kitchen window to ponder on that for a moment. She didn't hear Greame walk up behind her. He slid his arms around her waist and rested his chin on her shoulder.

"So, would it be worth it?"

She didn't have to ask what he meant, she knew. She shook her head slightly, and patted his arm.

"Perhaps. But I think we'll need to deal wi' one war at a time."

"Ye dinna think the impendin' battle will hae anythin' to do wi' a rebellin'?" He released his hold on her to get a better look at her face.

Cat shook her head again. "No. No one's angry enough yet. Everyone's still makin' the effort to compromise and work things out." She turned to face him and searched his green eyes for a moment. "It'll only happen when both sides stop wantin' to settle."

Greame touched her cheek. "Aye. I'll hae to agree wi' ye. No one is near angry enough. In addition, there's no real leadership. Each colony is ruled by differin' opinions. No one has a consensus on anythin,' much less havin' a basis for change." He took a seat at the kitchen table.

"People are much like sheep," she said, leaning on the counter. "They're willin' to be led almost anywhere. Sheep are no' what will take this country from the English … or French, or whoever is the victor in this war; it will be the fearless, the strong, the ones willin' to make a change that even sheep will see is right and just."

"I fear it will take more than one man to do such a task," he said, running his hand through his hair.

Cat grinned. "Aye. It'll take a woman, as well."

Part Two

15

First Born

GREGOR LEFT WITH THADDEUS and Smiles at Everything at the first sign of good weather. This time he gave Cat and Greame his full itinerary, and no promise of a return date. It was 3 May 1755.

"I canna believe ye didna try to stop him," Geoffrey said to Greame at the dinner table that night. Apparently, Gregor only told Cat and Greame about his venture to New France.

Greame snorted, pouring himself a glass of claret. "Oh aye, I'd hae made him change his mind? Even Cat couldna do that this time."

"She tried then?"

Greame shook his head. "No. There was no point."

Cat brought the tureen of fish soup to the table and caught Geoffrey's eye with a scowl. Greame did his best to hide his grin, but Cat flashed a look that effectively wiped it from his face.

"There will be no more talk of Gregor, understood?" She addressed the room with hands on her hips and an expression even Gregor would have comprehended. "Now eat."

It was a quick and quiet supper.

Susan, now sporting an enormous belly, stood to help with the dishes, but Cat sent her home. "Ye're nearin' time, Susan. Get some rest, aye?"

Rubbing the small of her back, Susan's attempted smile looked more like a grimace. She patted Cat's shoulder and waddled out the door. Geoffrey followed, but Cat touched his arm with an indication to wait a moment.

"Be sure to keep the water boilin' tonight, aye?"

The blank expression on Geoff's face made Cat elaborate. "The babe's comin' and I'll be needin' clean, hot water. Get lots o' linens ready, too, and fetch me when she starts her pains."

Geoffrey's eyes got big and excitement flitted across his face. He pressed a quick peck on Cat's cheek and ran out the door to catch up with his wife.

Greame chuckled from behind Cat as he watched his cousin help Susan into their cabin.

"Are ye sure it's tonight, Garnet? She's still a month away."

Cat turned a knowing smirk on Greame. "Oh no, she's right on time."

A dawning light washed over Greame's smiling face, and he chuckled deeper. "Ye'd best get some rest then. Ye'll be needin' it." When Cat started to refuse, he added, "I'll tend the dishes." She went into her room without further hesitation.

❧

The moon rose large and full, much like Susan's uterus. Cat was awakened by a rather blood-curdling shriek. She rose without anyone having to tell her she was needed.

Greame was sitting at the kitchen table writing in his journal. He'd been concentrating so hard on his entry he didn't hear Susan's cry. He looked up when Cat walked into the kitchen and watched as she prepared a satchel with herbs, a small, sharp knife and some gut sutures. Then she did something he didn't comprehend. She poured a dram of whisky and set it on the table.

She smiled as his eyes went from the dram to her face and back. "Not for ye."

"Is it time?" He asked, confused. "Geoff isna here."

"I heard her first pain. He should be here—"

The thundering footfalls on the porch indicated Geoffrey's timely arrival. He practically flew into the house like a wild beast, frantically searching for Cat.

"I'm on my way, Geoff. Ye stay here wi' Greame, aye? Ye can see yer daughter when she gets here."

The look on his face was one of bewilderment, fear, rapture, and well … more fear.

"I want to be wi' her!" he said raggedly, wringing his hands.

"No, ye dinna. Trust me, Geoff, ye'll both be better off in separate places till the deed is done."

"C'mon, man," Greame said gently, guiding Geoff towards the table and the dram of whisky Cat so thoughtfully set out.

She grabbed her satchel and an old blanket and walked out into the night.

When Cat walked into Susan's room, three lanterns lit it brightly. Susan was pacing the floor with one hand on her lower back and one rubbing the lower part of her belly. She was naked, which made Cat smile.

"I can see ye've seen a birth before, aye?"

Susan smirked. "No sense in ruining perfectly good clothes."

"Where would ye like to have her? In bed?" Cat asked, putting down her satchel and holding out the old blanket.

An odd expression came over Susan's face, but it was due to a contraction rather than the question.

"Jumping Turtle said birthing a baby sitting up is much easier," Susan said, expelling a long breath. "Is she correct?"

"I've seen it done both ways, and I'd venture to say whate'er is more comfortable for ye is how ye should do it."

"Then I think I should like to sit up."

She looked at Cat for a moment, realizing what she had just said. "A girl?"

Cat smiled and nodded.

Susan grinned brightly, then scanned the room for something

stable to lean against, and settled for the side of the bed. "Here, I expect will do."

"Get comfortable then. I'm goin' to make a tea, make sure I have enough linens, and get a basin of cool water. I'll return in a moment."

Cat had nearly completed her tasks when she heard Susan gasp, then a splash of water hit the floor.

"Garnet? Would you hurry, please?"

"Comin'!" Cat called from the kitchen, wiping her hands.

When Cat reached Susan, she was already leaning on the side of the bed, squatting over the old blanket.

"Any pains?"

Susan nodded.

"I'll be needin' to feel how open ye are, all right?"

Susan nodded again, and Cat's expert fingers slid into Susan's vagina to feel for dilation.

Susan's face was flushed and she was breathing heavily, then her eyes got wide and she let out a long moan from deep within herself. Cat wet a linen in the cool water, wrung it out and dabbed Susan's face with it.

"Oh, that … feels … good."

"I'm afraid ye still hae a bit o' time yet, Susan. Ye've still got to drop some more. Can ye stand? Walkin' tends to settle the wean and will get her into the correct position."

She helped Susan to her feet and they paced the room for nearly half an hour, stopping when a contraction hit. Cat always found watching a baby move about inside the womb fascinating, and this wee lass looked as though she was doing a Highland fling!

"From the looks of her, she's turnin.' She's gettin' herself ready."

"I need to squat again." She settled herself against the bed and laid her head back while Cat placed the cool cloth on her forehead.

Suddenly, Susan's eyes flew open as a violent contraction racked her body and she screamed.

Cat rubbed the lower part of Susan's belly, letting the contraction ease before rechecking for dilation. She was a little more open, but still had a ways to go. Up to walk some more. The contractions were happening more regularly now at about ten minutes apart. More walking, more screaming, more checking.

As dawn crested, Susan was ready to push.

❧

"She must hae had it by now!" Geoffrey growled as he paced the floor again.

Greame was at his wits end. Every time he'd get to sleep, Geoffrey would start muttering again. "Geoff, if ye dinna sit down and shut up, I swear I'm gonna kick ye! When the wean gets here, it gets here! Not a moment before then!" He was sorry he barked when he saw the worried look on his cousin's face, and got off the settee to make some chicory. "Look, Garnet kens what she's doin.' She's birthed quite a few bairns. If there was any trouble, she'd hae come to get us. It just takes time, man."

Geoff had dark circles under his eyes and looked panicky. "Maybe I'll see if I can get some sleep then," he said, walking into the guest bedroom and practically falling into bed.

"Good thought. I'll fetch ye when it's time."

The men began trickling in shortly after. Kelvin's cabin is nearest to Geoff and Susan's and he said he could hear "quite a ruckus" coming from it throughout the night.

❧

The sweat slid down Susan's brow from the exertion of pushing. The pain nearly sent her beyond her limits. She was fully dilated, yet the child wasn't ready to leave the safety of her warm quarters. Susan leaned up against the bed, panting, and waited for another contraction to ravage her insides.

Cat mopped Susan's face with a cool cloth, and walked over to open the window all the way. The stifling aroma of a heated body was becoming overwhelming.

"Is everything all right with the babe, Garnet?"

Cat turned and faced Susan. Her face was flushed and her spring-green eyes bright. Cat looked at the swollen belly, still alive with movement, and she smiled.

"The babe is fine, lass, it's ye I've concern o'er. How are ye feelin'?"

Susan looked hard at Cat at the subtle meaning. "I'm quite tired, but I've try in me yet, so don't worry about me."

Cat nodded. "I'm glad to hear it, 'cause it may be awhile yet. Yer wean seems verra content to stay where she is for bit longer."

"But the contractions are less than five minutes apart, why is she not coming out?"

"It's just not her time yet, is all. She's in the proper position, but apparently, she's waitin' on somethin' to move her down further. Do ye feel like walkin' a bit?"

"Lord in heaven, it feels like that's all I've done!" Her tone was a bit abrupt, but she lifted her hand for Cat to help her up and together they paced the house for another hour.

By noon, Cat heard a soft knock on the front door. Susan had just resumed her squatting position by the bed, and was resting there.

"I'm goin' to let Greame ken how ye're doin.' I'm sure Geoffrey's mad wi' fear for ye."

Cat closed the door behind her and answered the front door.

"Are ye needin' some help, Garnet?" Greame's eyes were tired, and his expression was worried.

Cat shook her head and wiped her forehead with her sleeve. "No, the babe's just no' ready yet. She's fine and so is Susan, tell Geoff." She placed her hand on his cheek and smiled. "It may be awhile yet. Susan's holdin' up well. We just hae to be patient while the wean decides to make her grand entrance in her own time."

"All right then." He placed his big hand over hers and dragged it to his lips. "Ye look verra tired, Garnet. Can I bring ye some food?"

A deep, animal groan drifted out from the window and Greame's eyebrows rose.

"I'd better get back in." She turned to go inside, then turned back to face him, "Thank ye for checkin' on us."

He nodded and told her he'd let Geoff know his wife was fine.

Cat walked into the bedroom and with a fresh set of eyes, saw the beginnings of wear on Susan's face. Cat had seen births last for two full days, and half the time the mother didn't survive the ordeal. She couldn't let that happen.

"I'm going to hae ye lay on the bed so I can get a better idea of where the babe is, aye?"

Susan slowly managed to get herself up and lie on her back with her knees in the air. Cat placed a hand on Susan's lower belly and, using her practiced fingers, went inside to see if she could feel the wean's head. She had to go deep, but felt the hardness of the small skull.

Suddenly, Susan screamed. She got up on her elbows, and with a growl fit for a she-bear, pushed. Cat was still between Susan's legs and saw the head crown, stretching the labia to impossible tautness.

Cat reached into the basin of water for the small knife she'd brought, and with quick precision, cut the flesh before it tore. The baby's head nearly popped from its confines.

Cat grasped the head, turned it to the side and told Susan to push again. Susan screamed and gave another long push. The shoulders slid out and Cat guided the rest of the tiny body from Susan's womb. She cut the umbilical cord and washed the child of mucus and blood before wrapping her in a large cloth. Sarah, as she was to be named, announced her arrival to the world with loud, angry, wonderful wails. Cat set her on Susan's belly, and watched Susan's weary eyes flow with tears at the sight of her child, still a bit purple and prune-like, with miniature fists batting the air angrily for having left the comfort of home.

"Thank you, Garnet." It was just a whisper, all she could muster.

After Cat stitched Susan up, she covered her in a sheet to let her nurse. The clock struck three. A warm breeze blew in through the open window, and sounds of spring voiced its approval of the newborn.

"I'll go fetch Geoff, if ye're of a mind to see him just yet."

Sarah made greedy sucking noises at Susan's breast. Susan smiled contentedly and nodded.

When Cat walked into her kitchen, all the men were sitting around the table looking as though they were the ones who had gone through the birthing ordeal. Each of them seemed to have aged ten years, looking tired and cranky.

"Wee Sarah's arrived and both she and Susan are doin' right splendid."

Geoff looked up at Cat as though expecting to hear bad news. His eyes filled with tears, then he bolted from the house to see his family.

The rest of the men let out a collective sigh of relief and slowly began to smile and pat each other on the back like they had just single-handedly thwarted some menacing world threat and were congratulating themselves for a job well done.

Cat snorted, shook her head, poured herself a whisky and went directly to her bed.

16

Engaging the Enemy

THE HUMIDITY IN THE late June air was stifling, making it easy to smell the English camp well before they arrived. The fetid odor of unclean and dying men living too close together meant sickness was ravaging the camp. Hiding in a thicket of laurel, Gregor caught sight of Smiles at Everything's grimace and choked a laugh.

"Why Whites not know about clean village?"

"Damned English are too soft, livin' their lives in cities where it smells much like this." Gregor remembered Thaddeus then, and threw a quick, "pardon, Thad," in his direction.

Thaddeus just shrugged. "I tend to agree with you about our cities, but apparently those soldiers aren't digging proper latrines. The bloody flux must be rampant down there."

"I'd wager Duquesne's camp is clean," Gregor replied, referring to the French fort that sat on the Ohio and Monongahela Rivers in southwestern Pennsylvania.

The trio had traveled nearly seven hundred miles in almost two months, through sparsely populated English colonies in New Hampshire, New York and Pennsylvania. The countryside was remote and the terrain rugged, but now they were in French territory where the mountains were reduced to rolling hills.

Along the way, they had passed no fewer than ten burnt out homesteads. These charred remains reminded Gregor very much of the aftermath of Culloden, as he and Cat crossed the Scottish Highlands in search of her father, taken prisoner by the Hanoverians nearly ten years ago. He shuddered in his saddle, and thought for a moment about his home country, one he knew he'd never see again. What had become of Scotland now? he wondered.

The three rode past the blackened ruins in utter silence, unwilling to disturb the dead and stir up ghosts. Each man discreetly made protective gestures according to his own beliefs, and none thought it odd to see the others do so.

Gregor wondered what he would do if a foreign people tried to move in on his property. Whites were encroaching on Indian land in this part of the country at an alarming rate. They just planted their homes anywhere that looked like a good site, having no regard that it might have been prime hunting ground or farming land for the Natives. Indians didn't seem to matter, and Gregor could see their way of life being altered forever with the coming of Europeans.

On his belly in the cool moss, Gregor spied the camp through his telescope taking a head count, when none other than George Washington strode out of one of the large tents reserved for the ranking officers. He, too, looked like he wasn't well. His clothes hung loosely on his skeletal frame and he was the color of aged linen. Gregor scoffed and shook his head, then noticed something.

"Seems our friend Washington has earned the rank o' Lieutenant Colonel since we've seen him last, lads."

Before he could continue his one-way conversation, Smiles at Everything tapped Gregor's arm and pointed to three Mohawk braves arriving in camp.

Gregor fiddled with his telescope. "I'd give anythin' to hear what they hae to tell the Colonel."

For the rest of the sticky afternoon, the three men remained well hidden watching the camp's activity. By dark, they decided to move on. Just as they were about to leave their shelter, they saw the three Mohawk braves skulking out of camp with one of the Oneida scouts. The three men decided to wait a bit to see what the Natives were up to.

When it was full dark, with just a crescent of a moon to light the night, Thaddeus caught movement in camp. He tapped a napping Gregor on the shoulder, and pointed.

"Now where do ye suppose those lads are headin'?" Gregor whispered, watching the soldiers attempt to wander from camp in secrecy.

When the soldiers ventured into the trees, Smiles at Everything gave a sign to Gregor that he was going to find out, then he disappeared into the night.

Less than five minutes later, musket fire shattered the quiet. The camp swarmed like bees in a disrupted hive. Several scouting parties were dispatched to locate the missing men, and not long afterwards, shouts came from the woods. Smiles at Everything scampered into the laurel with news that the three soldiers were found scalped. The entire camp was roused. Gregor didn't want to be anywhere near this place when the troops were let loose to locate the murderers.

"Time to go, lads." Gregor was already mounting his horse.

❧

On a cloudy morning at the beginning of July, Gregor, Smiles at Everything and Thaddeus located a large Indian camp near the French Fort Duquesne. Here, a dozen nations were represented, from Delawares to Ottawas, to Hurons, Abenakis and Ojibwas. Smiles at Everything led them in, and since many spoke French, Gregor could follow along in conversation.

"There must be close to eight hundred Indians here," Thaddeus mused, looking around the encampment at the variety of dress each nation wore. Colorful headdresses, beads and feathers, to say nothing of the face paint they wore, made them stand out as brilliantly as the Redcoats, but when placed in nature's arena, they would blend in completely, as though they were part of Her.

That evening, as the group took their meal, a French Captain named Daniel Beaujeu walked into camp. He had fought alongside these Indian nations for more than twenty years, and he knew them well.

Gregor and Thaddeus tried as best they could to blend in with the natives so as not to rouse suspicion. This became easier when many of the Indians crowded around the captain to hear what he had to say.

"You all know me, for I have served with you all these years. I come now asking the chiefs of these many mighty nations to fight with me against the English!"

A murmur rippled through the camp. Gregor and Thad looked at each other with the same *perhaps we should leave now* look on their faces.

Several of the chiefs moved closer to the captain, and one of them was designated spokesman through some unspoken precept.

"The English are more than four thousand men," said the Indian whose face had seen many years. "We are but eight hundred and you wish us to attack them? You have no sense." He folded his arms across his chest, the international sign of *end of conversation.*

The murmur grew to a cacophony, and the Indian spokesman held up his hand, apparently hearing objections. "We must have until tomorrow to decide."

The chiefs all went back to their meals, and the captain returned to the fort.

"What will they decide?" Gregor asked Smiles at Everything, who was chewing the last bit of meat off a bone.

A shrug was all Gregor received in reply.

"Will ye stay and fight wi' them if they choose it?" Gregor asked again.

Smiles at Everything looked at Gregor with mischief in his dark eyes and a smirk on his face. "Why you ask me this? Why not just say you want to fight?"

Gregor tried with all his heart to look innocent, but it wasn't working on either of his mates.

"I'll have to sit this one out," Thad said. "I won't fight against my countrymen."

"After what they did to ye?" Gregor scoffed. "They left ye for dead, if ye'll permit me to remind ye."

"Whites have strange loyalties," Smiles at Everything chided, tossing the bone over his shoulder.

"Not all whites," Gregor replied testily.

Smiles at Everything just shrugged again, then rolled over to sleep.

❧

In the morning, Captain Beaujeu and his men returned to the Indian camp with every confidence of leading the Natives to battle. A crowd of Indians once again encircled the Captain and gave him their answer.

"We will not go with you," the Indian spokesman told him.

True to his rank, the Captain would not let an opportunity pass without trying to gain the Indians' alliance, this time using a bit of persuasion. He met each of the chiefs' eyes, letting them know he could see into their hearts, then shouted, "I am determined to meet my enemy." He paused for effect, then continued. "You will let me go alone?"

As last night, murmurs swept through the camp. Suddenly, a runner split the crowd and breathlessly announced that the English had crossed the Monongahela River and were marching towards the fort.

Shouting ensued, and a Delaware hollered from the crowd that they should shoot them all! War whoops sounded around the crowd, and warriors rushed to the wagons the French had brought with them, to fill their horns with powder and arm their bullet pouches with flints and shot. Within minutes, nearly all the bands had joined the Captain and were headed down the path in a French and Indian mob to fight the English.

Gregor patted Thad's shoulder and let out a war whoop of his own, then bolted out of camp with the rest. Smiles at Everything was right behind him.

"Bloody hell." Thad picked up his rifle and trotted down the path.

❧

By noon, they heard music.

"Grenadiers March?" Thad asked Gregor. They were on their bellies under a large hemlock looking down from a rock escarpment.

"Only the English would stop a fight to play a tune," Gregor snorted.

"They haven't stopped," Thad pointed to the soldiers marching four abreast, with a small detachment of horsemen in the lead.

On either side of the column were flanking parties, slashing away at the underbrush to widen the path for the main body of men and cannon to follow. Smiles at Everything whistled and shook his head.

"How Whites win any war? Too slow, too much …" he was waving his hand, but not finding the word he wanted.

"Frill."

Smiles at Everything smiled questioningly at Gregor and waited for an explanation.

"Extra, indulgence, nonessential."

Smiles at Everything nodded. "Yes, that is what I mean."

Thad chuckled. "It's the art of war, gentlemen. Something we English have excelled at for centuries."

Before anyone could comment, Captain Beaujeu gave the order to charge and, with his men, burst like demons through the brush down the hill to engage the enemy. The Indians screamed at the tops of their lungs in a frightful display that reminded Gregor so much of the Scots' method of fighting, he plunged headlong into the fray, as if with his own countrymen. With a command, the French and Indians hit, then disappeared back into the thick wood, like deadly phantoms.

With military precision instinctual with the English soldiers, they fell into a four-man front with their bayonets fixed and fired ahead. After the first volley, the front ranks stepped back and the ranks behind took aim and fired, then the third and the fourth. On the third volley, Captain Beaujeu was shot in the head and fell to the ground, dead.

Another captain took his place and sent his men to flank the English, killing them by the dozens. The English captain lost control of his men. They fired indiscriminately into the woods at the unseen assailants, cutting down their own men who were trying to get back to the road.

It was total bedlam. The Redcoats scattered like sheep being pursued by wolves. The French and Indians had a special passion for officers, and not long into the fight, nearly all of them were dead or wounded.

Gregor had just smashed through the brush up the hill to take a breather, and was about to head back down, when he noticed George Washington atop his white horse. It was as though the man were invincible. Lead was flying all around, tearing at the leaves, ripping men from their horses and ending scores of lives, but there he sat, tall in his saddle, saber held high, barking orders to the cowards fleeing the fray. For a moment, Gregor had great admiration for the man, but only for a moment.

Back the English fled, abandoning everything, including artillery and the dead and wounded. Still, the French and Indians pursued them, hacking men down all the way to the river, where it ran red with English blood.

Thad sat at the top of a knoll looking over the battle scene. Carnage was strewn the entire distance of the road the English had built. Now, the fallen soldiers were being scalped and stripped of all they wore. The prisoners would wish with their last breaths that they had died on the battlefield, rather than be put through the tortures that lay ahead in the Indian camp.

Before night fell, Smiles at Everything located Gregor, and together they met up with Thad. They made camp away from the terrifying screams of the men taken prisoner. Thankfully, the drumming drowned out most of that noise. By morning, they were on their way home.

"I think I care not join you on any more of your excursions, Gregor." Thad was riding at the rear. He'd been grazed by a lead ball on his side, and was attempting to keep it to himself. In secret, he'd managed to clean it out and apply a bit of moss to prevent infection so as not to draw the attention of Gregor or Smiles at Everything.

Gregor chuckled and turned in his saddle. "Ye canna tell me honestly that ye didna enjoy yerself, Thad."

"I can, and I will."

"He not say that if he not get shot," Smiles at Everything said over his shoulder to Gregor.

"What?" Gregor bellowed before reining his horse to see just where Thad had been hit.

"Is there no privacy around here?" Thad scolded.

Smiles at Everything just grinned and shook his head.

Gregor lifted Thad's bloodstained sark.

"Oh, for heaven's sake!" Thad said disgustedly. "It's not but a scratch!"

"Scratches fester."

"I am completely capable of tending myself, if you've noticed."

Gregor pealed off the moss to see that is was just a scratch, and placed the dressing back on. "Ye'd best tend to this every day. Cat would hae me heid if she kent ye didna care for it proper."

Thad looked into Gregor's angry blue eyes and saw a kind of fear there. He grinned, and couldn't stop himself from saying, "You're actually afraid of our dear, sweet Garnet, aren't you?"

Gregor's eyes grew darker and a wall was placed over his expression. "Careful, Bakeman. Ye've no idea what she and I hae been through. She's the strongest person I've e'er kent. Stronger than any man; braver than any man." He roughly kicked his horse to move ahead of Smiles at Everything.

Thaddeus was very curious now. He'd seen Cat's bravery first hand, but what else was there to that amazing woman to make a man like Gregor become so defensive? He pondered for a long time on that question, and the only feasible answer was that the big man loved her. Not the lusting kind of love, but the fatherly type. Thad wondered if she knew how much the men around her cared for her. He imagined she did.

17

At One with Thyself

GREAME LEANED ON THE doorjamb and watched them from the threshold. Cat was sitting with wee Sarah in the rocking chair humming a song her mother probably used to sing to her when she was a child. Cat's eyes were closed and a slight smiled played over her lips as Sarah lay in her arms.

It was a sight he'd never get to witness with his own bairn, but this would do. He took in every detail of the picture: from the fine blonde hair fluffing out around Sarah's head, to her long, fair eyelashes just sweeping the tops of her round, rosy pink cheeks in the angelic bliss of sleep. The way one of Cat's hands softly rubbed Sarah's bottom, while the other cradled the back of her head, her thumb absently playing with a strand of fine hair.

He wondered if she craved a child of her own. They'd never spoken of it; no need when it was an impossibility, with him, anyway. The childhood caber accident saw to that. But, did she have feelings of motherhood that he didn't know about? She guarded her secrets well. There were still many things he didn't know about her, things she'd refused to speak of, like her oldest brother, Seumas.

Greame knew Seumas had been married and had a bairn. What happened to his wife and child after Culloden? Cat never spoke of them. Did they die? Did they go to live with her family? Did Cat even know?

Footfalls on the porch signaled the end of his pondering, as it was time for luncheon and all the men were coming to eat.

Cat's eyes opened and she saw Greame standing in the doorway.

"How long hae ye been watchin' me?" Her voice was sleep-raspy and very seductive as she rose from the chair.

"Just long enough to see a peaceful scene and burn it to my memory," he said quietly, walking into the bedroom to kiss Sarah's fuzzy, sweet-smelling head.

Cat smiled at the questions in Greame's eyes. "We'll talk later, aye?" She lifted Sarah off her chest and placed the still sleeping child into Greame's arms. "Hold her while I tend to the men." Their eyes met and held for a moment, then she walked into the kitchen; the spell was broken.

Kelvin and Kenny walked in, and knowing Cat was watching the bairn today, remained quiet. Just as Kelvin opened the door, Greame walked out of the bedroom with Sarah sleeping in his arms.

"Ah, there's the wee lass," Kelvin whispered, running the back of his thick finger over her smooth cheek.

Cat watched silently as she dished up the fish soup and a couple loaves of bread, amused at the tenderness the men showed the new babe. Poor Sarah probably didn't even know who her Da really was the way they all must hold her every chance they got. And Kelvin was the worse. He couldn't get enough of her. Greame relinquished his time and handed her to his uncle. Kelvin expertly transferred Sarah to his thick chest without so much as a stirring from the lass.

Life was good, Cat thought, as she glanced around the table at her family, all the people she loved. The day was warm and the breeze blowing in the windows smelled of the sea. She was smiling, and about to take her seat, when her glance caught movement out the window. She stopped in mid-motion as she observed three ships far out on the horizon.

Having spent enough time together, Cat never even had to speak; Greame caught the look on her face.

"Trouble?" he asked, as he and the rest of the men walked over to the doorway to see what had captured Cat's attention.

They all stepped onto the porch to get a better look. Greame brought out his telescope and noticed the ships flew English flags. "Two more are following," he told them.

"Now, what d'ye suppose they're doin'?" Kelvin handed Sarah to Cat and taking the telescope Greame offered to him. "Another, still," he announced. "This canna be good."

Cat quietly went to her room, laid Sarah on the bed, then sat in the rocking chair and pulled a lock of hair from under her kertch. As she twisted the auburn lock around her fingers, she concentrated on the English ships and their destination.

She saw that there were many more than the five they'd seen. Thirty had set sail from Boston loaded with militiamen and supplies. They were going further north, to Nova Scotia. In her mind's eyes, Cat saw a fort. All around it was farmland and peaceful people tending to their land. Her brow furrowed in anger when the English forced these peaceful people onto the awaiting ships with the intention of sending them to some far-flung land they were unfamiliar with.

Cat slammed her fist onto the arm of the chair. "Damn it!"

Greame had been waiting in the doorway for her return. He poked his head in the bedroom when he heard her swear.

"What is it?"

She relayed her vision to him as she picked up Sarah, who'd started fussing.

"Garnet, perhaps we should be grateful the English are botherin' someone else, and no' us, eh? They could verra easily get a bee in their bonnets about Maine, then what?" He rubbed the back of his neck and watched her relax a little.

"Oh, I suppose ye're right," she said, pressing a kiss on Sarah's forehead. "But it just makes me verra angry that they can just take o'er wherever they want, wi'out consequence."

"I agree, but perhaps we can remain out o' their sights here and live happily."

Cat smirked at his romantic vision, and walked over to kiss his cheek. "Ye paint a lovely picture, Mr. Hay."

When Sarah reached for him, he took her from Cat's arms. "I do try, my love, I do try."

❧

Later that evening, when the cabin was quiet, and Cat was lying in Greame's arms, she answered the question that was on Greame's mind.

"I canna say that I wouldna mind a bairn of my own, but I dinna hae an all-consumin' urge for one."

He rubbed his hand over her arm, but remained silent.

"Tell me," she whispered, running her fingers through the hair on his chest.

He was quiet for another moment, "Ye were so peaceful this morn' wi' the babe on yer chest hummin' softly to her, it made me feel as though I'm deprivin' ye of a woman's need."

She pushed herself up onto her elbow. "Do ye think that's all I want from life?"

He snorted, "That's no' what I meant, and ye ken fine that I dinna view women as brood mares."

"Good, 'cause I feel like I'm losin' my powers as it is wi'out havin' to care for a wean o' my own."

"Losin' yer powers?" He turned his head to face her. "What got that idea into yer heid?"

"The ships. I should hae seen them comin' much sooner than when they were at our doorstep."

"They meant us no harm. Maybe that's why ye didna."

She rolled onto her back and stared out at the half moon. "Do ye sometimes feel like ye dinna hae enough space?"

"From ye?"

"Aye. From everyone."

He thought for a moment and got up onto his elbow. "I go to my ship when I feel the need to be alone."

Cat turned her head to look at him. "So ye do feel that way, too?"

"Oh, aye. To be alone is one o' the best things in life." He blew out a breath. "Then again, the better thing is when I'm wi' ye."

"Quite a quandary."

"No' really, Garnet. If ye e'er need to be away from all of us, ye just tell me. I can sail ye out to one o' those islands and leave ye there for as long as ye like."

She chuckled, then thought how wonderful it might be to spend an entire day all alone. No one to tend to, no one to speak to, only her own mind to have conversations with. Oh, how she missed that.

"I may hae to take ye up on yer offer someday soon." She stretched over and kissed him, then rolled onto her side. "Good night."

"Ye're no' goin' to speak of him, are ye? Seumas ..."

"Nope."

"Just answer me this one question, and I promise to ne'er bring the subject up again."

She rolled over to face him. "What."

"What happened to his wife and child?"

Cat was quiet for a moment. She'd hoped to never have to return to that day. That day from hell itself, when her entire life crumbled before her eyes and all she had in the world was gone.

When she had returned to *Slios Mìn* after Culloden, she went to check on Seumas' croft to see if Charlotte and wee Teàrlach were all right. They were gone. Everything was gone. Cat had no idea what had happened to them, but what little her brother and his family owned had been removed. The croft stood empty. Door open to the wind and desolate, just like her heart. To this day, Cat didn't know if they were alive or dead. It was as if they had fallen off the earth itself.

"Some things are to remain a mystery, Greame."

"Ye've ne'er tried to find them?"

"Gregor had that honor, and failed."

"Did ye look for them in yer mind?"

"Of course." She rose onto her elbow. "Seumas and I werna close after he found out I had the Sight. I ne'er really kent her well. Charlotte was her name. She was sweet and shy and quiet, and I was fond of her, but ne'er kent her family, bein' as she was from up around Gairloch. Teàrlach was just a wean, no more than two years old at the time. Each time I'd try to feel them, find them, there was no response. I figured they had to be dead, otherwise I'd've been able to *see* them."

She rolled so her back was toward him. When he began another question, she said, "Good night, Greame."

She smiled when he blew out a heavy sign, indicating he knew she wasn't going to say another word, then he, too, rolled over.

❧

Two days later, she was aboard the *Revenge* on a perfect summer day, heading for the largest of the islands just off shore. She'd packed her satchel with provisions for an overnight stay, left Kenny in charge of meals in the settlement, and bid her family *adieu*.

"Now, just light a fire when ye're ready to come home, aye?" Greame said, as he and Robbie rowed her to shore. "But if I see no fire after three days, I'm comin' to get ye."

Cat laughed. "I ne'er said I wanted to leave ye forever, Greame, just a day … or so."

He helped her out of the longboat and walked her to the trees. He placed her satchel under a low, sprawling oak and grabbed her shoulders, searching those dusty violet eyes of hers.

"Ye'll be all right?"

Cat smiled and kissed him. "I'll be fine. Talk to me tonight."

His face showed confusion for a second, then he smiled, remembering he could speak to her in his mind. His bright green eyes twinkled with mischief. "I'll make ye wish ye stayed home."

Her eyes widened and she let out a roll of laughter. "That's no' playin' fair."

"I'll no' be makin' a midnight pickup, either," he said in a voice as smooth as silk. "Ye'll just hae to make do on yer own."

"It works both ways, aye?" she said softly in his ear. "Now off wi' ye."

She patted his butt when he turned to go, making him chuckle deeply. "Ye'll pay, my love."

Cat watched from her private pebbled shore as the longboat reached the ship and was hauled up by Kelvin and Geoffrey. She waved, then returned to the trees. The sun was hot, but the breeze was much cooler out here. She laid out a blanket under the oak and lounged in the dappled light. It was perfect. Gulls floated above, eyeing her to be sure she wasn't some wonderful carrion washed up on shore to feast on. She could hear the splashing of seals, and when she gazed out at the water, a pod of porpoises arched their backs as they broke the surface to breathe. Her mind was still reeling from activity, but she knew she'd quiet it down in short order. For now, she just wanted to enjoy the peace.

She must have dozed off, because the sun had drastically changed its angle. A few puffy clouds dotted the soft blue sky, and the tide had retreated from the seaweed line by quite a few yards. Sitting up, she could see the sunlight reflecting off the windows of her cabin across the way. She absently wondered that if she could see them, who else could when sailing past.

Alone. Her mind was empty. That's what it felt like. And she didn't want to fill it up with anything for a while. It had been a very long time since she had this feeling and, she had to say, she liked it. A lot.

She sat up and stretched, arching her back until it popped. Then she stood and decided a walk would be nice. She scoured the beach for shells. Mostly, it was lined with millions of blue mussels and earth-toned winkles, with an occasional scallop or oyster, just for color.

As she walked around the west side of the island, she saw how many more small juts of land there were. Some were just rock, but others were large enough to be covered with spruce and oak.

On the south side, she saw more open water, but also larger islands further out. It was a bit warmer on this side, and she stopped to watch tiny shore birds scamper with the waves, stopping periodically to catch whatever bug caught their eyes.

She absently wondered about the treasure that was buried on the settlement. Why didn't they choose one of these islands instead? Her mind went to her brother, Lachlan, and how, as children, they loved to explore and find treasures of their own.

"I miss ye to this day, Lachlan."

She could hear him chuckle in her head, then say, *I'm wi' ye always, a' ghaoil mo chridhe.*

"Oh aye, but it's no' the same." Her eyes welled up at the loss.

She slid out of her moccasins and rolled up her pant legs. The water was frigid, but she stood there for a few minutes and let the waves lap her toes. The shock of it cleared her head of things she didn't want to think about.

Her face was beginning to burn, she could feel her skin tightening. It was time to return to her camp. When she rounded the west side of the island, she noticed a wall of clouds over the hills across the bay. She sniffed the air, but there was no fragrance of rain on it.

Not for tonight, anyway. Tomorrow might be a different story. She didn't want to have to cut her trip short due to the weather. Greame wouldn't let her stay out here without adequate shelter, anyway.

When she returned to camp, she foraged around for some wood for a fire, then searched out a spot for her lean-to, and busied herself. Once she had a cook fire going, she heated some water for tea. It would undoubtedly get cool this evening.

The sunset was spectacular, all crimson and apricot and purple. Night birds began to make their appearance, and she could hear the tiny peeping frogs begin their nighttime serenade. The breeze was just enough to keep the bugs at bay, so she peeled off her breeches and settled under her lean-to in just her sark. The moon could still be seen faintly through the light clouds, and she watched it for a while. As it grew darker, the little field was ablaze with the sparkling twinkle of fireflies. When she closed her eyes, she wore a smile of contentment on her face.

She expected Greame to begin telling her what she was missing any time now, and was a bit disappointed when all she heard him say was, *Good night, Garnet.*

Good night, Greame, she replied back in her head.

❧

She woke with the first light of day, having slept like the dead. She crawled out from under her lean-to and stretched, feeling very energetic. She dressed and foraged around for more firewood and, given the cloudy start to the morning, reheated the tea she made last night.

Once some of the hot liquid was inside her, she sat cross-legged near the fire and began a meditation, something she rarely got a chance to do anymore.

Even though she was out here to get away from the settlement, it was still the first place her mind visited. Greame was still asleep, as was nearly everyone else. Sarah was being fed, and Geoffrey, being the good husband he was, was making breakfast.

Next, she ventured over to Far Eyes' camp on the other side of the peninsula. They were at their summer village now. She smiled when Far Eyes greeted her in her mind.

I see you are well, Garnet, and taking some time for the mind.

Yes. My mind was becoming too busy. I couldn't see what I should be seeing anymore.

A difficult task with so many wanting its attention.

Perhaps I should have come to you instead, and taken a sweat.

She heard him laugh in her head, then say, *You hate taking a sweat.*

Yes, but it does clear the mind.

It does.

Then she could feel his confusion.

Where are you?

It was her turn to laugh. *On an island across from the settlement, all by myself.*

He was quiet for a moment, then said, *Which island?*

That western-most island about a mile offshore.

Again, he was quiet, and she began to wonder why. Without having to voice her feelings, he answered her.

That island is known to the Penobscot as the Place of Shadows.

Cat looked around. The only shadows she saw were under the trees.

Why?

> *In my grandfather's time, two canoes of men were fishing around that island. A storm came up on them too quickly for them to make it back to the mainland. They paddled as best they could to get to the island, but the seas were fierce. The two canoes were pounded onto the shore. The men never returned. It is said they live there now as shadows.*

Cat felt no presence. She closed her eyes to see if she could get any remaining pieces of their souls. There seemed to be nothing left of the men who perished here.

I feel naught of them, Far Eyes.

Ah. Then perhaps they have finally found the rest they needed. You have visitors.

There was a short silence, then Far Eyes returned. *So I have.*

I will let you get to them. Good to speak with you, my friend. Weliwoni.

But before she was able to close the conversation, Far Eyes had a piece of advice.

Garnet?

Aye.

You do not have to leave to get away.

Cat smiled at his wisdom. *Weliwoni, Far Eyes.*

Cat poured herself another cup of tea, then, in her mind, told Greame she was ready to come home. She wanted a long soak in her copper tub.

18

The Past Returns like a Bad Penny

THE TREES HAD STARTED TO turn a muddy olive color, signaling autumn's quiet slide-in. It was Cat's second favorite time of year, spring being her favorite. There was a certain smell to the air, a slowing down of life. It wasn't full-blown just yet, but it lurked behind the façade of perfectly blue skies, warm days and flowers still in bloom.

She absently wondered if Gregor, Thad and Smiles at Everything would be home before it got cold. She hoped so. The trio was fine, she knew, managing—despite Gregor—to remain out of harm's way. She smiled to herself at her larger-than-life friend, picturing him now, hair wild, full beard, eyes full of the devil himself. She shook off the mind-wandering to continue her chores.

The morning was fresh and promised to be warm. She was hanging sheets out on the line when she glanced over at Gent on the porch. She'd been noticing for a few months now that he'd not been himself. He barely left the house, wishing, it seemed, not to expel extra effort on anything but breathing. Even eating was only barely interesting to him now. Cat knew the day would come. He was well past the usual age when a dog his size died, but it didn't make it any easier.

It was another link to Scotland she would be losing. Alexander had given Gent to her as a pup when Anna had died and she'd moved into Anna's cott to take over as clan Seer. He was for protection, Alexander had told her. That was two years before the Rising, but war was brewing, and the Hanoverian patrols had been harrying Alexander more than normal. A young, beautiful woman a mile from anywhere and all alone wasn't a responsibility Alexander wanted on his head, especially since she was also his cousin. Not to mention what her father, Angus, would do if anything happened to her in Alexander's care.

She chuckled to herself how naVve she was to believe that a dog could protect her from a patrolling group of Dragoons. Then again, in those days she had the Sight much clearer than she had today. She saw everything coming, like it or not.

The last pin was pushed onto the sheets and she had just bent to pick up her basket when a tingle went up her spine. Instantly on the alert, she searched the area for the reason. From out of the clearing came three men on horseback. A squeal of joy escaped her throat and she tossed the basket to the ground and ran for the field.

"I oft' wondered if I could e'er sneak up to surprise ye," Gregor said, smiling to see her so happy to see him.

"No' a chance, big man! How are ye—all o' ye?" Her eyes took in Thad and Smiles at Everything.

"Faring well, Cat," Gregor said. "But I canna wait to eat something a woman cooked."

Cat giggled. "What, between the three o' ye, no' a one can cook?"

"I cook just fine," Thad spoke up. "He's just worked himself up into a frenzy over the last hundred miles, making each of our mouths water for an apple pie."

Smiles at Everything wore his usual grin, licked his lips and nodded.

"Well then, I guess that'll be for dessert. Robbie shot a few turkeys yesterday and I was planning on that for supper. I imagine I could set three more places," she said, teasing.

"God, woman, it's goin' to be a long afternoon," Gregor said, stepping down from his horse and taking her hand in his.

Cat looked up and noticed he seemed tired, but didn't mention it. She said instead, "Good to hae ye home."

Dinner with all the fixings was served to the entire settlement. Gregor sat at the head of the table holding Sarah. He was, as were all the men, entranced. His enormousness simply dwarfed her as she looked up into Gregor's hairy face, unfazed by yet another man in her life.

Cat and Susan walked into the dining room with platters of food and the sight stopped Susan in her tracks. She smiled broadly, set the platter on the table and patted Gregor's shoulder, before returning to the kitchen.

As the group ate with enjoyment, they talked of what had gone on while Gregor was away. Nothing, it seemed, as exciting as what Gregor and his entourage had been through. Thankfully.

"See, Garnet. I told ye it was best the English were botherin' someone else and leavin' us be," Greame said, waving a turkey leg at her.

"Ye did at that," she agreed, then turned to Gregor. "So, who, in your opinion, is goin' to take America as their own?"

The silence around the table was absolute. It seemed that that was the ultimate question everyone wanted answered.

Thad looked at Gregor with a certain knowledge in his eyes, as did Smiles at Everything, who was, for once, not smiling.

After a few minutes of collecting his thoughts, Gregor spoke.

"I think that the French hae much more experience wi' this country, and the natives. They seem a part of the land, as they've been dealin' with the Indians for a hundred years already." He paused when Sarah grasped his thick finger. His face lit with a kind of awe. His pleased look made everyone at the table smile.

Gregor looked up when the silenced stretched a little long, to see everyone he loved sharing the same moment.

"She's a verra special lass," he said in an uncharacteristically soft voice, speaking directly to Susan and Geoff.

They both just nodded.

"Ah, where was I?" he asked, returning to himself.

"Ye were just extollin' the fine traits o' the French," Greame said after taking a sip of his whisky.

"Aye, that I was."

"Hae ye anythin' to say of the English then?" Robbie asked.

"First, thinkin' o' poor Thad here, I apologize once again, as he's already heard all the badmouthin' I've done about the English. So, to lay it out for ye, they've no idea how to make it through the winter. The blood—" he stopped himself, refraining from using the coarser name at the dinner table for a change. "The dysentery runs through their camps wi' abandon. If left to their own devices they might all perish from it, leavin' the French and Indians to take o'er wi'out so much as a shot fired."

"That's no' really answerin' the question, is it?" Greame said, watching Cat's reaction to this line of questioning.

Gregor laughed. "I sound a bit like one o' them politicians, don't I, Thad? Sayin' lots o' words wi'out sayin' anythin' o' merit." He laughed again, making Thad and Smiles at Everything grin at some secret meaning.

"I s'pose the answer is ye can ne'er tell what the English might hae up their sleeves. I ken that most of the Indian nations are sidin' wi' the French, but I dinna ken if that will hae much bearin' on the final outcome, as the Indians fight as they wish, unwillin' to be put to command in a legitimate, disciplined manner."

"All ye had to say was that ye didna ken," Robbie said sourly, dishing up some more potatoes.

Gregor scowled and returned to his meal.

"We'll be needin' to make a trip to Boston to pick up supplies for the winter soon," Greame said, changing the subject, and trying his best to keep the smile from his voice. "I want to be sure we get back before the weather turns. Make yer lists and we'll plan to leave the middle of the month."

❧

Far Eyes had invited the settlement to a gathering before they left for their winter camp far up river and the settlement sailed to Boston.

It was dusk when Cat returned to her house with Greame. She wore a contented smile.

"I still canna believe how big Harry's gotten o'er the summer. He's grown like a weed," she said, walking around the house lighting lanterns.

Greame chuckled. "And Jim's got his hands full wi' him."

"Oh, he's a good lad. Sort of," she giggled recalling how Harry had walked around to each of the adults and sprinkled a bit of dirt on each of their plates of food when they weren't looking.

"I really thought Kenny broke a tooth when he bit into his stew." Greame shook his head as he put some wood in the fireplace. It would be chilly enough for a fire tonight.

"Then to have him be watchin' the results o' his devious actions wi' that devilish smile o' his." She shook her head knowing if the elder Harry were still here, he'd probably be proud of his namesake.

"He sure did wail when Jim found out and paddled his behind wi' a stick."

"See, aren't ye happy we dinna hae children?" Cat said. "It's just nice to be able to tend to them when ye want, then return them when ye're finished."

Greame's eyebrow lifted and he nodded. "Perhaps ye're right, under the circumstances."

The fire in the fireplace took hold, and Cat took a seat beside it to put the finishing stitches in the waistcoat for Robbie. His new suit of clothes was finally complete. It had taken nearly a year to get him to come in and have measurements taken. Kept telling her that he really didn't think he'd ever have a call to wear a good suit again. After long prodding, Cat coaxed him by saying he could be the next man in the settlement to get married.

"And who would this lass be, Garnet? There's no' a woman anywhere near here."

"I'm quite sure Geoff thought the very same. Look at him now, aye?"

Susan did just sort of fall from the sky into Geoff's arms. Apparently, Robbie thought the possibility of it happening again was good enough, and allowed Cat to take his measurements.

Greame sat at the table and wrote in his journal for a while, then heard something outside. Gent was out there and didn't bark, so it couldn't have been anything out of the ordinary.

Cat caught his curious expression and questioned him with her eyes. Greame shrugged, but walked to the door to see if he could pinpoint the noise.

Just before he reached for the latch, Cat hissed and blew out the lantern. Greame instantly knew something wasn't right and backed away from the door. He turned to Cat, who'd been standing by the fireplace, and followed her into the spare bedroom where the pistols were stored.

"What is it?" Greame whispered.

Cat shook her head, then said, "I've felt his presence before, but I canna remember from where. I do remember he wasna a person we wanted around here, though."

"Crawl out the window and fetch Gregor and the rest. I'll keep talkin' like we dinna ken anything's wrong. Go!" he whispered.

Cat did as she was told. It was full dark now with no moon, so she was able to quickly make it to the Gregor's cabin undetected. She stealthily maneuvered around to the door. When she opened it, the light pooled onto the porch, illuminating the night. Gregor and Thad were sitting at the kitchen table having a cup of chicory. Gregor looked up to see who'd walked in and a smile creased his face.

"To what—." Seeing the look on her face, he immediately knew something was wrong, and went to her.

"Someone's outside my door and I need yer help. I canna see who it is, but he's no' friendly."

Thad was already gathering weapons and passing them to Gregor, then they all snuck out into the night. Cat went to Kelvin's cabin, then Geoffrey's, leaving Gregor and Thad to handle the situation with Greame.

Before Cat and the rest of the men reached her house, shouting was heard. The Highlanders poured into the house to find Greame and Gregor wrestling the culprit to the floor. Kenny instantly recognized him.

"That's the bastard who knifed me last spring," he spat, giving him a good hard kick to the ribs.

"He's no' alone," Cat said.

All eyes simultaneously did a head count, then Geoffrey ran out the door. In unified realization, knowing someone was still lurking about and Susan and Sarah were alone, all but Cat and Greame followed him.

❧

When Cat came into their cabin looking for Geoff, Susan knew something was amiss. Sarah had just been fed and put down, and she and Geoff were enjoying some quiet time of their own.

Now, Susan was in the nursery, fearing the worst. There was danger here; she could feel it. She picked up Sarah and had a sudden urge to flee, but that was foolish. Sarah sensed her mother's frightened emotion and started to fuss. Just then, the porch step creaked. Someone was out there. Susan began to panic and Sarah began to wail.

From the nursery, she could plainly see the front door. It slowly began to open. Susan frantically searched for a hiding place, but there was none. She slipped behind the door and tried to sooth Sarah, but she wasn't having any of it and kept crying.

Through the crack in the door, Susan saw him walk into her house. When she realized who it was, at first she was stunned, then she was furious. She stepped out from behind the door with all the fury of a she-bear, and set upon him with a verbal berating fit the Queen.

"What in bloody hell are you doing in my house, Jeremy Bradford!?"

She set Sarah back into her cradle, deaf to her cries. Susan walked into the kitchen, where a very angry-looking Jeremy stood. His menacing glower had no effect on her. She had plenty of her own daggered looks that were much more effective. With her hands on her hips, she glared, waiting for an answer. "Well?"

Suddenly, Jeremy's stance relaxed and he smiled. "Nice arrangement you have here."

Susan wouldn't be fooled into letting her guard down. She knew his tactics better than he did. When he took a step towards her, she held her ground.

"Get the hell out of my house this instant, you bloody sod, or you'll be very sorry," she hissed, knowing any second the troops would be on her doorstep.

"But I've come all this way to see you, my love. Won't you at least show some common courtesy and ask me to sit down?"

She didn't have to see him to know he was there. Without giving anything away, Susan watched as the door slowly opened, and Geoffrey walked in and stood directly behind Jeremy. The rest of the men stood just outside the door.

Jeremy took another step towards Susan. "Let me take you home where you belong."

"That wilna be happenin' anytime soon," Geoffrey said in an icy voice.

Jeremy's eyes grew wide and he whipped around to see six pistols aimed at his head.

He turned to face Susan once again with fury in his eyes, made even more acute when he noted the smirk on her face.

"What did you think, that I was being held against my will up here? You just don't understand, do you, Jeremy? Why in the world would I want anything to do with you? You are a selfish, contemptuous, weasel of a man. Didn't my letter explain everything to you? But no, you have to have everything your way. Well, I'm telling you one last time, do not *ever* try to contact me again, or it'll be the last thing you do." She turned to tend to Sarah, who was still crying, but whirled back around. In a venomous voice she said, "And I'll not let my husband do the killing! Now get out and never let me see you again!"

Her tone made Geoffrey's brows rise, as he wasn't accustomed to it. He smiled that she scoffed at Jeremiah's attempts to kidnap her.

Gregor laughed, "That's a lass!" Then he walked over to the little man, put his enormous hand on Jeremy's shoulder and said, "See, we hae strong women up here, Bradford. They're no' afraid o' wee incidents, and apparently, she considers ye just a wee incident." Then Gregor's eyes hardened and he bent and whispered something in Jeremy's ear. Whatever he said made Jeremy's eyes widen in horror. When Jeremy tried to step away, he was stymied by a vice-like grip that held him in place, making him wince.

Jeremy was hauled rather forcefully out of Geoff 's cabin and brought to Cat's.

Greame was quite surprised to see Jeremy be tossed onto the floor to land beside Blondie. He looked back and forth at the unlikely pair and had to ask. "How in the world did the two o' ye meet up together?"

Neither man answered.

"Hae it yer way then." Greame looked at his men and said, "Put them in the barn and tie them up. We'll take them back to Boston with us the day after tomorrow and let the authorities tend to them."

"I'm going to see to Susan for a bit," Cat said to Greame.

"Tell her there's no need to fear. They've been apprehended."

Gregor chuckled, "Ye dinna need to tell her no' to be frightened. Our wee Susan gave Bradford the ultimatum."

Cat and Greame looked quizzically at Gregor.

"What ultimatum would that be?" Cat asked.

"She said she'd kill him if she e'er laid eyes on him again."

Greame rolled out some laughter and Cat smiled broadly.

"She'll do, aye?" Gregor said.

"She'll do," Cat and Greame said in unison.

❧

But nothing's as easy as it should be.

Gregor decided he didn't like Blondie. There was something in those cold gray eyes that told him to be extra wary. He took it upon himself to ask each man to rotate on watch every two hours. He knew the quiet man was far more dangerous than Bradford. What was his reason for associating with Bradford? It had to be much more than taking Susan away. He didn't believe for a second that it was the only motive.

He also knew Blondie's sort, and getting him to talk would probably never happen unless drastic measures were employed. Certain Cat and Greame wouldn't go for that method, he explored a different option. One much simpler.

Get Bradford to talk.

He was pretty sure he could make the wee shite squeal without too much difficulty or bodily harm. Gregor remembered that Bradford was a fearless and scrappy brawler, but put real pain in the equation and he figured he'd fold quickly.

He'd wait till morning to test his theory.

Gregor climbed into the loft for the night as backup if anything went wrong. Kenny was on first watch.

The two prisoners were tied back-to-back to a beam in the center of the barn. Kenny was entertaining himself by throwing horse dung at Blondie. Gregor listened to him chuckle for two hours before being relieved by Robbie, who was considerably quieter. Quiet enough to get a little sleep.

When Gregor woke at dawn, Greame was on watch, and the two men were still attached to the beam. Gregor climbed down from his perch and decided now was as good a time as any to get some answers out of Bradford.

"'Mornin,' Greame. Mind if I speak to these two?"

"As ye please," he told him, dropping his quill in the bottle of ink he was writing with, standing to blow out the lanterns.

A wary-eyed Jeremy said, "I'm not saying a word to you until I am allowed to relieve myself."

Gregor winked at Greame and began untying the rope that bound the wee man.

"We are civilized men around here, Bradford!" Gregor scowled when Jeremy began untying his flies. "Ye'll use the privy or hold it."

"Fine."

They walked out of the barn together.

"D'ye mind perhaps, answerin' a few questions for me, as I'm terribly curious about things?" he asked, draping his arm over Jeremy's shoulder.

Jeremy had to tilt his head pretty far back to look Gregor in the eyes. "I don't have to answer to you, or anyone."

"Awe, dinna be like that," he patted Jeremy's shoulder in camaraderie. "I just want to ken what possessed ye to think Susan would just up and leave wi' ye."

Jeremy was silent. They reached the privy and Gregor opened the door with a flourishy bow to allow Jeremy to enter. While he waited for Jeremy to do his business, he leaned up against the rough wood and tapped out a beat.

"Really, Bradford. She's marrit now," he said to the wooden structure. "Has a bairn wi' Geoffrey. And that chatty fella ye're ridin' wi. What's he got to do wi' ye? Ye ken he was wi' the slavers that came through here last year, didna ye? Took our mate, Jim's wife. Was gonna sell her somewhere, for Christ sake! What are ye doin' wi' him?" The berating lasted even after Jeremy exited the privy.

Finally, Jeremy raised his hands in a show of helplessness, and said, "Do you never shut up?"

Gregor's brows rose and he grinned like the cat that ate the bird.

"Even if I wanted to tell you anything," Jeremy continued. "Which I clearly do not, I would not be able to get a word in!"

Gregor saw the beginnings of the fury Jeremy tried to contain. It was time.

"I'll give ye a chance then to say yer piece." He paused for a moment knowing full well the little man wouldn't say a word. "Well, ye see, this is my problem wi' ye, Bradford. I give ye a chance and ye dinna take it. Now, because my captain doesna hae near the patience I do when dealin' wi' folks, I'm gonna hae to hurt ye to get the answers out o' ye."

Before he let Jeremy even think about what he'd just said, Gregor balled up a fist and sent it straight into Jeremy's stomach.

All the air in Jeremy was let out in a painful gasp and he fell in a heap to the ground. Gregor let him struggle with his breath for a minute before dragging him up by his collar to set him on a large rock.

He peered into Jeremy's face, beet red and still coughing. "Well?"

Jeremy shook his head, held up his hand and coughed some more. In a wheeze, he told Gregor, "He'll kill me if I say anything to you."

Gregor chuckled, then his face turned hard. "All right, then I'm goin' o'er to tell my captain that ye spilled yer guts to me, told me yer plans and then let ye go."

Jeremy's eyes opened to enormous proportions. "You, you can't do that!" he stammered. "Did you not hear what I said? He'll *kill* me!"

"Oh, aye, I heard ye just fine. But see, Bradford, I dinna care what happens to ye. My life—and Susan's—would be much better off if ye were dead."

"But …"

Gregor held up hand. "However. I'll protect ye if ye tell me everythin' ye ken about the man ye're ridin' wi' and what his plans are up here."

Just as Gregor suspected, Jeremy's feisty attitude and total lack of common sense prevented anything informative from coming to the surface. He folded his arms over his chest and stared boldly into Gregor's eyes.

Perhaps he thought Gregor was joking. The joke was on him when Gregor hauled him to his feet by the collar and nearly dragged him to the barn.

Greame looked up and grinned at the disheveled little man standing bravely in front of him.

"He talked then?" Greame stated.

Jeremy's eyes grew wide with fright once again.

"Told me everything. Wasn't near as difficult a task as I would hae hoped for." Gregor glanced at Blondie for a reaction. It wasn't much, but for a second, a fire burned in those light gray eyes. Jeremy had apparently seen it as well because he was swearing on everyone's heart he could think of, denying Gregor's accusation.

Just as a guess, Gregor threw out an obvious scenario just to let Blondie know Bradford really had said something. "See, Bradford had the idea that he could hae this gentleman," nodding over at Blondie. "Kidnap her. Then Jeremy would ride to her rescue, and Susan, bein' as she's just a stupid woman, would run into his arms and be his wife forever more."

Apparently, Gregor hit the nail on the head. Jeremy's jaw dropped, and Blondie tried with all his might to get loose of his bonds so he could get his big hands on the little man.

Greame stood with his fists on his hips in a stance that could not be mistaken. "We simply canna tolerate these actions, Mr. Bradford." He looked over at Gregor. "Tie him back up." He started for the door, then turned to issue one more order. "Oh, and be sure to tie him nice and close to his friend."

19

To Be or Not To Be

CAT STOOD ON A ROCK AT the edge of the shore letting the water rush over her bare feet in a frothy torrent. The coolness of it took her mind off the morning's discovery. The body of Gent was found in back of her cabin. He had apparently died of natural causes, that being the reason two men could sneak up on the settlement without being announced. It was a wonder she hadn't tripped over him when she'd escaped out the window to get help last night.

Greame and Geoffrey had just finished burying him. Geoffrey actually had tears in his eyes. She had just returned from placing some wildflowers on the fresh earth. Her tears dampened the rock she'd placed at his head.

As she scanned the horizon, her soul seemed to wander, searching for something she was unaware was missing. What had she lost? she wondered. It wasn't a tangible thing she could name, but she felt its loss as acutely as if it were her arm. There was still the nagging question of her place here in Maine. Perhaps she was homesick.

She thought about Scotland then. About Loch Rannoch and *Slios Mìn*. Some days she longed for the place so deeply that it was an all-consuming ache, but she hid it well, buried it deep. She wondered how Greame managed to free himself from his homeland. She knew he wanted to return someday, but was waiting for her to decide what she needed to accomplish here. She wondered if she would be as patient if their roles were reversed.

"No," she said softly to the sea. "And I've no right to ask him for the same."

It had been quite some time since she'd had a vision of any kind without actually making herself go inside and search one out. Look how close the settlement had come to another kidnapping, and right on her front doorstep. She had no advanced warning, not an inkling that anything was amiss. What good was the Sight when it gave no advanced warning?

When she was a child, she remembered the auld people telling of how the Sight left a person the longer they were away from Scotland. Add to that the fact that she wasn't living alone, as a Seer should to hold her powers. She had an entire family living with her. Cat was convinced that was what was happening to her, why she was losing her abilities.

All the souls who lived in the settlement were heading to Boston today on a wee ship on a very large sea. Anything could happen during the week it usually took to get there, yet she could see naught of the voyage. She felt blind, and it scared her more than she cared to admit.

Her contemplation was broken when she heard footfalls coming up behind her. She knew it was Greame before she turned around. She snorted. Well, at least she still had that skill.

"Are ye all right, Garnet? Ye seem to hae more than Gent on yer mind." He wrapped his thick arms around her waist.

"Are ye ready to leave then?" Ignoring his inquiry.

"Aye. You, me and Gregor are the last to board. Hae ye a feelin' something's to happen?" He said it quietly and nonchalantly, but Cat heard the seriousness behind the words.

She turned in his arms and stared deep into his forest green eyes.

Those eyes that captured her from the moment she first saw them. Those eyes that asked silent questions, never doubted, twinkled with mischief and held a love so deep, only death would sever it.

She shook her head. "No, and that's the problem. I see naught. We could be in terrible danger and I couldna tell ye."

He stared at her for a moment, then rested his brow against hers.

"Garnet, ye ken I love ye, dinna ye?"

She nodded.

"Do ye think the reason I love ye is because o' yer special gift?"

She blew out a breath, then shook her head slowly from side to side.

He took her by the shoulders and held her away, then looked into her smoky amethyst eyes. "Then can we get on with just livin' like two normal people? It matters naught that ye canna see into the future anymore." He tightened his hold when she was about to argue. "It matters naught. Ye've done more wi' the Sight than any one person should've had to. Ye've used it to change more lives than ye probably can recall, aye? But now it's time for ye to do as ye please wi'out givin' so much of yerself away." He kissed her forehead and whispered, "It's time for ye."

Her eyes burned holding back the tears. Why should this be so upsetting? Couldn't she now just become a regular person and do what Greame said? Live?

In typical Greame fashion, he knew her nearly as well as she knew herself, and said, "Do ye want to return to Scotland now that yer purpose for bein' here is the same as anywhere?"

Cat stared at him for a long moment, then threw her arms around his neck and hugged him tightly. "Aye, Greame. I do."

❧

There was an enormous weight lifted from her heart at the thought of returning to Scotland. A cool, late summer wind blew in her face as she stood under the billowing white sails of the *Revenge.* They hadn't discussed when they would return, but just the idea of it made her so happy she thought sure she would burst. Nearly ten years. That's how long she'd been in the colonies. Perhaps next spring they would sail home.

She hadn't felt this good in years. Finally something to look forward to. Something good; not a mystery, not a scheme, but a real, touchable event, and she felt the smile bloom on her face.

❧

Greame watched his wife come back to life right before his very eyes. He hadn't seen such pleasure on her face since … well, he really couldn't remember when. When he thought of it that way, he was a bit taken aback. Had she really been that unhappy all those years and he hadn't seen it? The thought of it made his heart ache.

It seemed her entire life was lived to guide others; family, events, wars. She had never been able just to be herself. Every vision was to keep someone else from harm. He understood now why it was so difficult a thing to lose. It was like losing *herself* because she'd never known what it was like not to have to care for anyone else. All those months she'd struggled to regain the Sight because it was the only thing she'd ever known. He hadn't realized how it drained the life out of her.

He made a vow right then and there that he would help her find herself, the part of her that he loved more than his own life. The part he was seeing emerge right now. As if sensing he was thinking of her, she turned to him and flashed a smile so brilliant, he couldn't help but return it. All he ever wanted was to make her happy. It seemed that now he would get his chance.

❧

There were no storms or mishaps during the voyage to Boston. The two prisoners were bound and confined to a small cabin under lock and key. Their horses remained at the settlement as payment for their bad behavior.

When they arrived in Boston Harbour, there were more ships than they had ever seen. Long Wharfe was littered so thickly with them, Greame instructed Kelvin to see if one of the smaller quays had space to dock. They found an opening on Charles Wharfe, northeast of the major hub.

Cat emerged from below decks with her dress on instead of her breeches. She was carrying Sarah, as Susan and Geoffrey had more than they could transport on the walk to the Rose Guest House. Cat was making Sarah giggle, which in turn made all who heard the child's laughter, smile.

The gangplank was lowered and one by one they strode onto the dock, weighed down with satchels and gifts for Claire and Emily. Kenny and Robbie stayed aboard ship to keep watch on the prisoners, while the rest of the men immediately went to the teashop. Cat and Susan walked up to the Rose Guest House on their own, admiring the brilliant fall colors of the trees and grasses and wildflowers.

Hugs and kisses were passed around when they walked into 35 Newberry Street. Claire instantly bonded to Sarah and had to be bribed to let Emily have a turn holding the happy bundle.

"'Tis soo good to see ye," Emily gushed. "Is everyone well?"

"Oh, aye," Cat told her, hanging her wrap in the hallway.

"I'm takin' it the men are at the teashop."

"Or the gaol."

Emily's eyes widened. "What?"

"I 'ope it's not our Gregor," Claire said, looking a bit distraught.

Emily scowled at her. "Now why would ye say such a thing? Foolish woman."

Claire ignored her friend and waited for Cat to explain. Susan was the one who spoke up.

"Jeremy Bradford and some scoundrel he no doubt found on the docks tried to kidnap me … again!"

Shock and indignation appeared on Emily's and Claire's faces. As was now becoming tradition, they all went into the best room and Claire broke out the spirits to hear the full story. It was near suppertime when they finished catching up on all the news.

The men appeared at dusk. The Rose Guest House was now full, noisy and very happy. Supper was served, and since the beds were like heaven itself, most retired early just so they could lie on the deep, soft mattresses for as long as they could.

When the sun rose the next morning, it brought with it the sounds and smells of the city. Ships being loaded and unloaded could be heard from Cat's window facing the harbour. When she awoke, Greame was still sleeping. His chocolate brown hair spilled over his wide shoulders in deep waves, making Cat reach over to skim her hand over it.

Without opening his eyes, he smiled. "Why is it ye need to touch me when I sleep?"

Cat scooted closer to him and pressed a kiss on his forehead. "Ye make it impossible for me no' to, lookin' all innocent like ye do."

He cracked open an eye and snorted. "Oh, aye? Innocent, ye say?"

Before Cat had a chance to react, Greame grabbed her and rolled her on top of him, holding her tightly in case she had any thoughts of leaving. Her fiery hair fell in his face and she smiled down at him with mischief in her eyes just before she lowered her lips to his.

It was quite a while later when they finally made it downstairs to breakfast. They joined Gregor and Robbie who were just finishing their eggs and sausage at the table.

"Jeremy's out," Gregor said after downing the last of his coffee.

It took a minute to process what he'd said.

Cat and Greame said in unison, "How?"

"Seems his family's got connections," he said sardonically. "He was released this mornin' and his only punishment is to apologize to Susan and her family for causing undue emotional distress."

"Oh, for Christ's sake!" Cat blurted. "Does Susan ken about this?"

Gregor shook his head.

"Where is she?"

"Still up in her room." He pointed to the ceiling with his cup. "Seems wee Sarah finds the beds here mighty comfortable as well. There's no' been a peep out o' her all night."

"She and Geoff, I'd imagine, could use a good bit o' sleep. Sarah didna take to the ship verra well," Cat said, pouring coffee for everyone at the table.

Robbie snorted. "The lass has a right powerful yell."

"Dinna blame her a bit," Cat said seriously.

"So what are ye thinkin' o' doin' about wee Jeremy, Cat?" Gregor asked, studying her face intently.

Cat caught the look. It was as if her answer was a test of some sort and she wasn't playing. "I'll do naught. Susan has a fair mind of her own and she and Geoff can handle it as best they see fit."

Gregor smiled grandly. "Glad to hear it, lass." He rose from his chair and stretched to the ceiling. "I'm off. George is takin' me huntin.'"

Cat and Greame exchanged curious glances.

"Hunting what?" Cat's eyes narrowed on the big man.

"Oh … ah, I may hae neglected to mention that Jeremy's companion was also released. They had naught to charge him wi.'"

This time it was Greame who became upset. "What!?"

Cat let her head fall to the table in silence.

"So ye and George are goin' after him? Then what?" Greame asked angrily.

Robbie looked back and forth at the two men, sensing trouble brewing.

Gregor shrugged. "We hae to find him first."

"What he means—" Robbie started.

"We ken exactly what he means, Robbie." Cat's voice sounded muffled on the table. "He'd just rather no' tell us what he's goin' to do when he finds him, this way we'll all sleep better when he just ne'er shows his face around the settlement again."

Gregor chuckled. "That's why I love ye, lass." He bent and kissed her head. "Ye ken just what I'm about and let me be meself anyway."

With that, Gregor left.

Greame almost stood up, but Cat lifted her head and put a staying hand on his arm. "Let it be, Greame."

"Aye, maybe ye're right," he said, raking his hand through his hair. "What else would he do around here anyway?"

Cat lifted a brow.

"And Robbie. What are ye doin' all dressed up in yer finery?" Greame asked, changing the subject.

Robbie smiled and said, "I'm gonna find me a woman."

Cat was so proud of Greame for not laughing, because she had a hard time squelching a giggle. He kept a serious face on and asked, "Do ye hae a plan on where to look then?"

"I was thinkin' the bookshops. Woman seem to frequent them. Then if that doesna work, I'll hae myself a cuppa at a teashop and wait for one to come in."

"So ye plan on findin' one today then?" Greame remained perfectly straight-faced.

"Shouldna be too difficult, do ye think?"

Greame shook his head from side to side and pursed his lips.

"Nope. A fine lookin' young man such as yerself shouldna hae a difficult time whatsoever."

Robbie looked pleased as he rose from his chair. He stifled a belch, patted down his hair and headed for the front door.

Cat and Greame waited to hear the latch lock, then burst out into hysterical laughter.

"Shouldna be too difficult," Greame mocked with tears running down his face.

"What are the two o' ye laughin' about?" Geoffrey asked, walking into the room bouncing Sarah on his hip.

Cat and Greame couldn't stop to tell him. In the end, Geoff went in search of some breakfast, shaking his head. "Daft is what they are, huh, Sarah."

❧

Susan was furious.

"We're going to Charles Town, Geoff, to see my brother. If Jeremy thinks for one minute an apology will make things right, he's sorely mistaken." She stormed around the house, wringing her handkerchief as if it were Jeremy's neck.

Geoffrey sat at the table feeding Sarah and watching his wife pace. He was pretty sure he even heard her growl once or twice.

"Darlin,' ye need to be calmin' yerself a bit. This will only feed his case. It'll be much easier to convince anyone listenin' that ye may hae exaggerated about Jeremy attemptin' to kidnap ye if ye go in screamin' like a *bean sìdhe*."

Susan growled for sure this time, balled up her fists and stormed upstairs. She found Cat in her room sitting in a chair in the sunlight reading a book.

Without looking up, Cat said, "He's right, ye ken."

Susan walked over to the bed and sat on the edge. "I know he's right, but I can't believe the audacity of the man—Jeremy, I mean."

Cat set the book on her lap and looked over at Susan. "Remember the first time we met?"

Susan frowned, remembering that day in the woods being found by Cat and the rest of the settlement. She nodded.

"Remember how frightened ye were? Ye were timid and quiet and afraid of everything."

A small smile played on her lips when she understood where Cat was going with this.

Cat picked up her book and resumed her reading. She heard Susan leave, then smiled to herself. This is so much easier than trying to save the world, she thought.

20

Vengeance Is Mine

THE OCTOBER AFTERNOON was bright as Susan and Geoff sat in Thomas Witherspoon's best room and watched as Susan's brother entertained Sarah.

"She's a lovely girl, Sue. Is she always this well-mannered?"

"Most of the time," Susan replied, getting up to pour herself a sherry. She lifted the bottle with raised brows to see if anyone wanted to join her. Geoff and her brother shook their heads.

"I'm so pleased you brought her by, and perfect timing, since I'm leaving in two days for the West Indies. You will stay the night, won't you, sister?"

"We'd appreciate it, Thomas, as I've a favor to ask of you."

"Oh?" he said, as he lifted Sarah into the air over his head making her giggle.

"Seems Jeremy's at it again."

He set Sarah on his lap. "At what?"

Geoffrey told him the story and what had happened at the gaol. Thomas stood and set Sarah in Susan's arms, then poured himself a now needed sherry.

"What is it with the man? Doesn't he understand the word no?" They were merely rhetorical questions. "The Bradford name is rather high in social prominence around here, but only pertaining to Jeremy's parents, not for him. He's not well liked, as though I needed to point that out to you."

"What can be done about him?" Susan asked, taking a sip of her sherry. "It's not as though his getting caught in a compromising position with a woman would do him any great harm."

Thomas sat in his leather chair and swirled the smoky burgundy liquid in his glass, lifting it to his nose to savor the aroma every once in a while. Slowly, a plan began forming in his mind and his face nearly lit up at the thought.

"I was just recalling a rather bawdy article in the *Boston Post* a couple years back. It was all about sodomites in the Masons."

"Buggery in the Freemasons?" Geoff asked, startled.

"Yes. It seems the article was meant to throw slander on the Masons to make them seem less masculine in hopes men would cease joining." He flicked his hand in annoyance. "You know how prudish people are around here, and frightened of anything they don't understand."

"What's this got to do with Jeremy? Is he a Freemason?" Susan asked, not really knowing what one was.

Thomas raised an eyebrow and tapped his chin. "Perhaps he is. But what I'm thinking is to give him a taste of his own medicine."

Geoffrey caught on quickly and smiled a bit sadistically.

"What? What?" Susan asked, bewildered, looking back and forth at the two men.

Geoffrey patiently explained and laughed at her shocked gasp.

She seemed to get over the scandalousness of the plan quick enough and replied with great delight, "Well, that would certainly tarnish his reputation, now wouldn't it?"

Geoffrey left for Boston the next morning to summon his family and friends for the task at hand. He told his wife he'd return the morning of Thomas' departure.

❧

"I'm going to be truly sorry to miss this," Thomas said. "I've so little time for fun these days." He was packing his satchel for his voyage this afternoon.

"Well, Jeremy shall have a different view on it, I'm sure." Susan stood by the window waiting for Geoff to return.

Thomas glanced at his sister and noticed dark circles under her eyes. "Are you having second thoughts?"

She turned to face him and he noticed her face harden. She had definitely grown up in the last couple of years. No longer a timid girl. She'd grown into a strong woman.

Susan shook her head and crossed her arms under her breasts. "I just want him out of my life once and for all."

"All right then, it's all planned. You're certain your friend Greame will see it through?"

Susan snorted. "Oh, to be sure. And if Gregor has returned from his hunting trip with Geoff's cousins George and Edward, it will be even better. I do so wish you could postpone your sail for a few days."

"I really mustn't. Vicious storms still torment the southern waters even this late in the season and I can't chance my cargo."

She turned again to face the window in time to see Geoff arriving with everyone she'd come to rely on. It seemed fitting that they all would once again come to her rescue.

"Oh, they're all here! Good! I wanted you to meet them all. You'll have much in common with them, since they're, ah … seafarers, too." Not wanting to divulge the fact that they were more of the pirating sort than merchant seamen.

She ran to the door and let them in. Geoff kissed her cheek and started introducing his cousins and friends to Thomas.

When Thomas came to Gregor, he still had to look up, even at his height. "Well, I certainly can see why my sister hoped you'd be back from your … hunting trip," he chuckled. "And she tells me Jeremy actually attacked you?"

A twinkle entered Gregor's eyes and he smiled at Thomas. "Oh, he's a scrappy wee fella, that Jeremy. Give him a good bit o' credit for it, but I must compliment *ye* more on yer fine imagination." He scratched at his chin. "Not sure I coulda come up wi' anythin' nearly as devious."

"Ye've a friend for life now, Thomas," Greame laughed when it was his turn to shake hands. "Gregor here has a great fondness for revengeful ideas."

Thomas laughed. "Well, I only hope it works as we've planned."

"We've a man who'll, as he told me, be honored to bugger wee Jeremy," Gregor stated in all seriousness.

"Might I ask how you found him?" Thomas asked with as straight a face as he could muster.

"Robbie," Greame began. "My youngest cousin, who a few days ago decided he was goin' to find himself a woman. He, too, had a plan, only his didn't work quite as well as he thought it should."

George, Edward and John snorted, and Geoffrey burst out laughing.

"Seems our Robbie stumbled in to what he thought was a teahouse, where there'd be women ripe for the pluckin.'"

Thomas was getting the picture quite clearly in his head now and grinned widely. "Please don't tell me he walked into the Black Angus Social Club."

"Oh aye, that'd be the place." Greame chuckled. "Sat down and ordered himself a cup o' tea. He told me it took a few minutes of serious searchin' before he realized there wasna a woman in the place."

The entire Hay clan had now joined Geoff in all out laughter.

Gregor, still somehow managing to keep a straight face said, "And there Robbie was lookin' like a dandy in his best suit and all. Must o' caused quite a stir."

Thomas burst out laughing at that, and Susan, though fairly mortified, was giggling.

"Poor dear Robbie," she said, grinning. "Geoffrey flew upstairs when I was feeding Sarah, red as a rose from holding in his laughter. Robbie had burst into the house demanding Greame do something about the atrocities that were going on at the Black Angus Social Club. I could hear Robbie shouting, 'Do ye ken what they asked me to be doin'?'" She imitated Robbie's accent to a tee, making even Gregor burst into rounds of hilarity. "'I'll no' be doin' that wi' another man's cock!'" she continued, turning a flushed pink when she realized what she'd said out loud.

"Cat had the forethought to pour him a large whisky," Greame said, trying to catch his breath. "Just to calm him down. He was near ready to burn the place, 'back to Hell where it came from,' he'd said, all fired up and scandalized."

"I have just one question," Thomas asked, attempting seriousness. "Who went in to … ah, employ our new sodomizing friend? Surely not Robbie."

The room went very quiet for a moment, then one by one, they turned to Gregor and burst out laughing all over again.

"Oh, bloody hell," Thomas said, grinning madly. "What's a couple more days. This is just too good to pass up."

"So you'll stay, Thomas?" Susan asked, hiccupping, wiping tears from her cheeks.

"It may be the most interesting thing to ever happen around here. I simply must."

❧

Cat couldn't remember laughing that hard in years. It felt so good. Greame placed her in charge of making sure the "right" people caught Jeremy in the act. She played the role of being an outraged citizen, and told a magistrate what she'd heard Jeremiah Bradford liked doing in his free time.

"That, and he's," she looked around and lowered her voice conspiratorially. "A Freemason."

The magistrate, whose powdered wig looked too small for his round head and kept slipping to the side when he made quick moves, squirmed in his seat, implicating his own involvement in the brotherhood. Cat had a hard time keeping her dimples from showing during what she tried to make a very serious conversation.

"Well, madam, if you are correct in this … this abomination, then we must stop it at once," he told her in his most outraged voice.

"I wholly agree, indeed, sir." Looking around once again, Cat slipped him a piece of parchment with the address and time of the deed.

When the magistrate read it, his eyes grew wide and a scowl crinkled his face. He looked up into Cat's eyes. "You do know that you have given me the address of a very prominent social club."

"Well, pardon my ignorance o' where these sorts o' things *should* take place sir, but this is where the illicit act will take place." When she read doubt in his eyes, she pulled out all the stops. "I have it on good authority, sir. Thomas Witherspoon has heard it himself."

At Thomas' name, the crooked-wigged magistrate cleared his throat. "Well, then, if Witherspoon has said it, I shall make certain Bradford is apprehended."

"That's all I ask of ye, sir. Thank ye. We canna tolerate this sort of indecency."

❧

The night was velvety black with a bit of a misty fog rolling in off the harbour from time to time. It was cool, but the crickets still chirped loudly in the common. The heels of one Jonathan Birmingham, aka "Janet," clicked on the cobblestones of King Street as he walked alongside Gregor. Gregor had already paid "Janet" half of the arranged amount and was making certain he would go through with thc plan.

"You know, Mr. Macgregor, there's always room for …" looking Gregor over from head to toe. "Large men, such as yourself in my line of work."

"Oh aye," Gregor replied in all seriousness. "But I dinna fancy such dallyin' around me cock, nor does the thought of buggery make me pine for the craft."

Jonathan laughed gaily, sounding very much like a woman. When he rested his hand on Gregor's arm, Gregor didn't shake it off. They arrived at the Black Angus just then and Gregor opened the door for Jonathan with a sweeping bow, again making him twitter.

"Please do reconsider, sir, for you have such a flair for this." His soft brown eyes nearly batted.

"Just do as ye were paid to, and the rest of this gold," he jingled the bag slightly in his pocket. "Will be yers, aye?"

"Oh, aye," Jonathan mocked, patting it, then headed for the stairs to ready himself for the evening's entertainment.

Gregor watched Jonathan sashay up the stairs, making him shake his head and snort. "Christ, the man walks more like a woman than Cat!"

❧

The note had arrived at Jeremy's house the day before. It was an invitation to an almost too good-to-be-true business deal with a top-shelf wine and spirits distributor he'd been trying to worm his way into for several years, run by an older gentleman who seemed bent on running it into the ground. Jeremy saw great potential there and was now being handed a deal he couldn't refuse to capitalize on. He was to meet one Jonathan Birmingham, Esquire, at the Black Angus tonight at seven o'clock "for drinks and conversation." He was only too happy to oblige.

He looked himself over in the large looking glass in his room. Tonight he was dressed to impress; his finest diamond stickpin on his dark green coat, under which he wore a gold embroidered waistcoat. His breeks were form-fitting and his boots were polished to a high sheen. He looked every bit like a wealthy businessman, thinking perhaps he could make the men who frequented the Black Angus club look at him in envy.

Jeremy glanced at his gold pocket watch and decided it was time to leave. The weather was fine, so he planned to walk the six blocks to the club instead of calling for a carriage.

When he arrived, a large man with a shock of golden hair asked for his name, which riled him. Didn't know who Jeremiah Bradford was, eh? Well, that was about to change, he thought.

"I'm to meet Jonathan Birmingham, Esquire, here, sir. Has he arrived yet?"

For a moment, Jeremy thought he saw a smirk play along the man's stern features, but he had to have been mistaken.

"Ah, yes. He's waiting for you up the stairs in the last room down the hall. Shall I take your coat, sir?"

Jeremy waved him away and headed for the stairs. He took a moment to look over his shoulder at the smoke-filled room below, with the groupings of leather chairs, tables filled with decanters of spirits that he was going to be filling from now on, and Boston's fashionable elite talking business or just relaxing after a long day's work.

Yes, he thought, this would be his place very soon and men would be looking to him for business services. He smiled and climbed the rest of the carpet-covered stairs. He strode past many rooms with closed doors. Behind them he could hear sounds of lusty lovemaking, and wondered where the women were. All taken, he sniggered, finally coming to the door at the end of the hall.

He knocked purposefully and was greeted by a man he swore he'd met before. The man remained silent and took Jeremy's coat and hat.

The room was comfortably appointed with a settee and several leather armchairs surrounding a low, ornately carved wooden table holding a silver tray with more of the fine decanters of liquor. It was actually a suite of rooms, as Jeremy found out when a door opened and a young, almost beautiful man dressed in elegant clothes stepped out.

He extended his delicate, lace-surrounded hand. "I'm Jonathan. So very pleased to meet you, Jeremiah."

Jeremy shook Jonathan's hand, trying to keep a grimace from his face. God, he hated men of this sort. "Pleased," was all he said.

"Take a seat, Jeremiah. I'm waiting for one more gentleman, then we may proceed. Would you care for a drink?"

"Love one."

The quiet man who took his coat stepped over and poured two glasses of whisky into crystal glasses. He kept his back towards Jeremy while he poured, then turned and handed Jeremy his drink.

Jeremy took a large gulp and waited for the burn of the liquid to straighten his head. Something didn't feel quite right about this meeting.

"When my uncle told me he wanted nothing more to do with this business, well, frankly, I didn't know what to do," Jonathan said, taking a seat directly across from Jeremy, then crossing his legs.

"So old man—" he stopped himself. "Mr. Nevells is your uncle?"

Jonathan twittered, "Yes. And I quite agree with your assumption of him. He is rather old."

Jeremy shifted uncomfortably in his seat and took another large swallow. The drink was finally starting to relax him.

"So tell me what his plans are, or must we wait on this other fellow before we can talk?"

"Oh, no, we can talk all you want. Uncle Walter wants to sell out. I have heard through my sources that you've been pining for a piece of this business for quite some time."

"You'd be correct," he said, slightly slurring his words. He heard it in his voice and barked out a laugh. "If this is the quality of the whisky you sell through your company, you just name your price, sir. I want in."

Jonathan's eyes twinkled and he licked his lips most seductively. "Then you are in, Jeremiah. You most definitely can get in."

With that, Jeremy's sight blurred and he laughed again. He felt himself being lifted from his seat. His eyes went in and out of focus, but when he was placed on a large four-poster bed that was a soft as a woman's breasts, he let out a little sigh. He didn't mind having his clothes removed, it was gentle and loving in the task. He didn't even mind it when he was rolled onto his stomach, and with sashes of silk, his hands were tied to the bedposts. Then he felt his legs be spread apart and his ankles bound with the same smooth silk, then anchored firmly to the posts at his feet.

He was nearly asleep when he felt soft hands on his back. It was as blurry as a dream, for he had no sense of where he was. He took a moment to scan the room and shook his head, making himself dizzy in the process. Well, wherever he was, the woman at his back was going to give him some pleasure, that's for certain. He wasn't sure how *she* would benefit with him on his belly, but he was always willing to try new things. He adjusted himself by lifting his hips off the bed to let her know he was ready for whatever she wanted to dish out.

A smile played along his mouth as she ran her tongue up his legs, all the while playing with his arse. But even in his slurred state of mind, what he wasn't ready for was when those soft hands spread him open and plunged into him with what he could only describe as a stake.

He let out a yell, and when the soft body in back of him seemed to writhe with the same motion as the stake, his outrage cleared his mind completely.

He heard the twitter of Jonathan's laughter in his ear, the man's soft breath heating his shoulder. He bucked and jerked and hollered, but this only seemed to excite the twisted man riding him. Jeremy screamed as he was abused over and over, until suddenly, the door burst open and militiamen rushed into the room. Gasps of horror and disgust filled the heated air, then all went quiet.

Jeremy surveyed the room but everyone had left. Good, he thought. The fucking sodomite was being arrested, and now if someone would just untie him, he could try to get out of this wretched place with a little dignity. It was still dark. No one had to know he'd been here. No one had to know what had happened.

A sound in the doorway made him stretch around to see who was going to set him free. What he saw made the blood drain from his face. The magistrate—bought and paid for by the Witherspoons only because his father didn't get to him quickly enough—strode into the room and cut the silk bonds at his feet, then at his wrists. Jeremy rolled onto his back and off the bed with great speed, but not quick enough for the magistrate to miss his cock at full attention.

"Enjoyed it, did you, Bradford?" The magistrate asked with a sickened look on his face.

Jeremy grabbed his breeks and pulled them on. "I dare say to you sir, that this was none of my doing. It was a trap. I was drugged and ..." flipping his hand towards the door. "Whoever that was had his filthy way with me. He told me it was a business deal. That's why I came here. I do not do this sort of thing. I'm not a bloody sodomite!"

The more he explained the more the magistrate turned a deaf ear. The militiamen entered the room once again and this time took Jeremy to the gaol.

❧

It had all been worked out. Gregor was waiting in the pub across the street. Jonathan strode in, took a seat across from Gregor and called for a pint.

"Nice ride, then?" Gregor asked casually with a devious twinkle in his eye.

"One of the finest arses I've had the pleasure of man-handling," he twittered under his breath.

Gregor slid the leather bag of gold across the table and stood to go. "'Night, Janet."

"So soon?" Jonathan pouted.

Gregor raised an eyebrow, tugged on his forelock and walked out into the night.

21

A Shot in the Dark

IT HAD BEEN TWO WEEKS since Jeremy was caught at buggery. Greame hadn't intended on staying this long in Boston, but he and the rest of the good people from the Maine settlement had to be sure Jeremiah Bradford remained behind bars.

Word of the upcoming trial was like candy to Bostonians. It fed their secret desire for scandal and the town had a festive atmosphere. Nothing like the ruin of a prominent man to bring out the socialites.

Cat wanted nothing to do with it. She told Greame she was just going to take advantage of the quiet town tomorrow when everyone else was being entertained in court. Greame didn't really want to go either, and decided he might just stay in and take advantage of Cat while the house was quiet. Yes, that's just what he'd do. A far better use of his time, he thought.

Greame walked into the best room and found Cat having what appeared to be a rather serious chat with Claire. He couldn't hear what she was saying, but they were brow to brow so something was out of sorts. He felt, rather than heard, her ask him to not interfere just yet.

He walked into the kitchen and took a seat on a stool to watch Emily knead bread dough.

"Soo, they're still at it then?" Emily said, pounding the dough into submission.

"Just what is it they're at?"

Emily looked at him through the flour-strewn sunlight. "Claire's in love."

He raised an eyebrow. "And who might the lucky gent be then?"

"Ye dinna ken?" She smiled and shook her head. "Men. Ye can be near blind when it coomes too affairs o' the heart." She continued pummeling the dough.

He watched her for a moment, waiting for an answer, then the shock dawned on him. "It's no' me, is it?"

Emily barked out a laugh. "Noo, noo laddie, though ye'd be a right fair catch, even though ye're already spoke for."

"Who then?" He shifted in his seat, relieved.

She ceased movement of her hands for a moment, then told him. "Gregor."

It was Greame's turn to bark out a laugh. He shook his head and shoved his hand through his hair. "The man leaves a trail wherever he goes."

"Are ye tellin' me he's got himself a woman up in Maine?"

"No, none serious that I ken about, but for some odd reason women find him attractive."

"Hae ye even looked at the man, Greame? He *is* attractive!"

Greame rubbed his hand under his nose to keep from smiling, then cleared his throat. "So I take it our Claire hasna told Gregor how she feels then."

Emily shook her head. "She's twelve and twenty an' ne'er had herself a man."

"What about ye, Emily. Why haven't ye e'er marrit?"

She blew out a breath and in total seriousness said, "I'm too much woman for a man."

There was no way he was going to laugh, but it took every ounce of his being to will himself to think of something else. After a moment of composing himself he said, "I can see where that would be a problem. So Claire's askin' Garnet for advice on how to go about gettin' Gregor to notice her then?"

Smoothing the bread dough into a round ball, she placed it into a bowl and covered it. "That's what she's tryin' to decide."

"What's to decide?"

Emily blew out another breath as if readying herself to patiently explain to a child. "He's a man o' the world, Greame. He takes far too many chances gooin' ooout too New France scoutin' for trouble, leaves on a whim, and canna seem too take root anywhere. Our Claire's a homebody. And I canna see her traipsin' all oo'er the countryside wi' him, nor stayin' home waitin' for his return. 'Tis noo way for a marrit couple to live."

Greame nodded, accepting her sound rationale, then looked her in the eyes. "But the heart, Emily. The heart doesna ken o' these things, the heart only kens what it wants and ne'er pays the head much mind, aye?"

Emily wiped her dough-covered hands on her apron and smiled with a twinkle in her eyes. "I ne'er kent ye were such a romantic, Greame. Noow if our Claire had a man like ye she could fall in love wi, it'd be soo much easier on her."

Greame chuckled and rose from his seat to drape his arm around her round shoulders. "There isna another man like me in all the new world, my dear lass."

Emily gave him a friendly elbow in the ribs as they strode into the best room to see how Cat was doing with Claire.

"Well then, what's the verdict?" Emily asked when she saw Claire and Cat in a more relaxed position on the settee drinking tea.

Cat looked up and smiled. "I told her all the bad things about him, all his crude ways, the way he broods around most o' the time, and the fact that he still thinks he's but sixteen, and," she turned to look at Claire. "She still wants him to ken how she feels."

Claire began wringing her hands together. "Maybe I can make him change 'is ways." She didn't really sound all that confident about it but was apparently willing to give it a go.

"If anyone can, Claire, ye can," Greame said, making Cat smile.

Later that night, Cat wanted a long, hot bath. She began the process of heating the water and hauling it up the stairs to the copper tub. She poured some lavender oil into the water and the smell of it floated on the air like music. When it was deep enough, she piled her hair on top of her head and left her clothes in a heap on the floor. Nearly everyone was tending to their own business and even Greame was at the teashop so she had time to herself. She dipped her toes into the steamy liquid to test it, then slid the rest of herself in up to her shoulders. A sigh escaped her and she closed her eyes in warm bliss.

The soothing aroma made her sleepy. There's a moment between being awake and full sleep that the mind is able to go other places yet still be conscious of it. Cat was in this state when she saw her brothers. It was when they were all much younger and happy in their ignorance of the world around them. They were in the woods near Loch Rannoch hunting for rabbit. It was early morning and the sun penetrated the thickness in soft, golden rays that illuminated the forest floor in fingers of light. Cat was sitting high on a large granite boulder watching Seumas, Iain and Lachlan skulk around the underbrush. She didn't know how many rabbits she saw dart away from the intruders, her brothers being oblivious to the fact. She was grinning widely when Lachlan happened to notice her.

"And what's got ye wi' such a brilliant smile on yer face?"

She giggled. "If only I'd had a net to scoop up the rabbits that've scampered past me, we'd already hae supper for two nights." She laughed harder at the look on his face.

"Ye could hae told us."

"Then I wouldna hae such a brilliant smile on me face, now would I."

His only response was a good-natured smirk. Iain and Seumas weren't as forgiving.

She changed the dream because she knew what was coming and she only wanted to think good thoughts.

Her next reverie was sailing on the *Revenge* on her return trip to Scotland. This time the voyage was easy. Certainly there were summer storms, but not the fury of the North Atlantic in late fall. The sailing was fair for most of the two-month trip. She was going home and took this vision to be a good omen.

There was no telling how long she was in her bath, but the water had begun getting cold. She opened her eyes to see Greame sitting on the edge of the bed staring at her with a crooked smile.

"Ye looked so peaceful, I couldna bear to wake ye."

Cat smiled and rose so she could get dried off. Greame brought a linen over and wrapped her in it. His warmth was welcome and she melted into his arms.

"I followed the scent of lavender till I found ye, *a'ghaoil*," he said in a husky whisper. "And now that I hae ye in my arms, naked as the day ye were born, I think perhaps I should lay ye down and see if I can keep that pleasured look on yer face, aye?"

Cat was still smiling as she looked into his eyes. "Do yer best, Captain."

❧

The front door slammed sometime in the middle of the night, sending nearly the entire household downstairs to see who the intruder was.

Gregor sat on the floor with his back resting against the door and a dazed look on his face. No one noticed the bloodstain on his waistcoat until Greame and Thad tried to lift him to his feet. Actually, it was his groan of pain that alerted them to the bullet wound.

Kenny opened the big man's coat. When Cat saw the blood-soaked waistcoat, she flew up the stairs to get her herbs and bandages. Claire and Emily were already heading for the kitchen to get linens and hot water started. It was a silent, well-organized dance that looked as though it had been performed a thousand times. Each knew their routines and what was expected of them without a word being uttered. A bit like battlefield medics.

Greame and Thad got Gregor to the kitchen and removed his waistcoat and blouse. He was sitting on the butcher block in just his breeks when Cat got there. She stopped for just a second to look into his dark blue eyes, passing some unspoken message to him. Then her eyes dropped to the bullet wound.

"Geoff, would ye fetch me some whisky, please?"

"There's still some laudanum left from when Miss Rose was ill," Claire stated, looking as frightened as Cat had ever seen her.

"Would ye fetch it?"

Cat looked behind Gregor and saw that the bullet had indeed

gone through his side, but what damage it wreaked to his innards was what worried her. It went through his left side just below his ribs.

"Ye ken what I hae to do, dinna ye *duine mor*?"

"Aye, but if ye dinna mind, I'll be waitin' for Claire to bring me the laudanum first."

As if on cue, she walked in with a nearly full bottle and handed it directly to Gregor.

He drank down a few long swallows leaving the bottle less than half full.

Cat swiped it out of his hands. "Ye may be big, but that'll do. Now let's get ye laid down." She looked around, doing a mental tally of all she would need.

"Susan and Emily, I'll be needin' ye to keep changin' the linens and keep the water hot. I hae to go inside the wound and see if there's anythin' that needs stitchin' up. Kenny, would ye thread some catgut on a couple o' curved needles for me?"

Gregor was lying down now and his eyes were closed. Cat lifted his hand and let it fall to the table with a thud. He appeared to be out. She'd know for certain when she poured the whisky on his wound.

Geoff arrived with the amber liquid and Cat laid a linen under Gregor's side and poured right from the bottle. He flinched, but never woke from the opium, then poured a little over her knife and hands for good measure.

Cat took a deep breath, let it out, then proceeded to open the wound. She wasn't distracted too much when she heard a thud behind her, along with shuffling feet as Claire was carried out. The bullet tore its path of destruction through mostly muscle. It looked as though it hit the last rib and bounced out, making Gregor one very lucky man. It did nick a bit of his gut though and she stitched it up while Kenny and Greame held open the incision. It was gruesome work made more so when Gregor started coming out of his drug-induced state while Cat was still stitching. All hands were removed from the wound and Emily poured more of the laudanum down Gregor's throat. After a few minutes, suturing continued and after an hour, Gregor was closed up, bandaged and resting under a blanket on the table, snoring.

"At least *he's* gettin' a good night's sleep," Geoff said, yawning.

"We'll be needin' to take shifts watchin' him," Cat told them. "I'll take the first. He should be sleepin' for at least another hour, but in case he wakes, I want to be here."

"I'll stay wi' ye," Greame told her. "The rest o' ye go to bed. I'll fetch ye when it's time."

Emily guided Claire back to her room, stopping first to check on Gregor. Claire gently laid her hand on his cheek then continued on her way.

Cat sat heavily in a chair and Greame stepped behind her to rub the tension from her shoulders.

"Who do ye think …" She waved her hand. "Oh, ne'er mind, I dinna want to ken."

"I'm sure he'll hae quite a story to tell when he wakes. Why dinna ye go and rest on the settee. I'll watch him."

Cat patted the hand that kneaded the taught muscles and nodded. "Wake me if there's any change, all right?" Then she moved in a dazed shuffle to the best room.

Greame sat on the stool and stared at the big man on the table. "So auld man, what is it ye've been up to this time that ye got yerself shot o'er, eh?"

Gregor didn't answer.

"No' a woman, I hope, 'cause Claire seems to hae fallen hard for ye, man. No' that ye'll e'er notice any more than I did, but that's the truth of it. What ye do's yer own business, but ye could do worse," he chuckled. "She, Claire, looked verra frightened for ye tonight. She couldna watch when Garnet started cuttin' ye open. She, Garnet that is, did a fine job on ye, too. Stitched yer insides up so ye'll be just as good as new. Lucky, if ye ask me. But I surely would like—"

"I surely would like it if ye'd shut up," Gregor said in a sleep-raspy voice.

Greame shot off the stool and stood beside Gregor. "Was hopin' my badgerin' would ensure the likelihood of yer wakin' up."

"Aye, it did," he said trying to get up.

Greame's hand pushed on Gregor's chest. "No' so fast, *mo charaid,* ye've had to be stitched up, and if Garnet finds her handiwork ruined, ye'll hae more than a bullet wound to contend wi,' aye? Now stay still and tell me what ye did to get yerself shot."

Gregor rolled his head to face Greame and smiled groggily. "Oh no, this is too good to tell just one man. I want the whole settlement to hear this one so ye'll just hae to wait till mornin.'"

"What'll hae to wait till mornin'?" Cat asked from the doorway, wiping the sleep from her eyes.

"Gregor was just about to tell us what happened last night."

Gregor scowled at Greame, then turned his face away from Cat's penetrating stare.

Greame chuckled. "Ye may as well start talkin,' man. It'll be the easy way out."

Cat walked over to the stool, pulled it up close to Gregor and sat down.

Gregor knew he had to talk. She would sit there until he did, and he wasn't in any shape to win this battle of wills. Hell, she was sitting so close he could feel her breath on his neck. He slowly turned his head and looked at her with daggers in his eyes.

Cat just raised an eyebrow and waited.

He clucked his tongue. "Oh, all right then!"

Greame pulled up a stool of his own and got comfortable.

Gregor cleared his throat making a ceremony out of it, till he caught the look on Cat's face.

"I was havin' me a pint down at the Green Dragon Public House down near the quay." He looked over at Greame with a devious twinkle in his eyes. "Ye ken the one wi' the barmaid wi' the big—"

Cat cleared her throat loudly.

"Pardon. Anyway, I was sittin' at the corner table mindin' me own business when a couple o' gentlemen I'd made acquaintance wi' came in and sat down wi' me to hae some supper. We were enjoyin' a fine conversation when three gents rushed in shoutin' 'bout somethin' bein' amiss down on Long Wharfe.

"My supper mates apparently thought it was worth a look 'cause they flew out o' their seats as though the hounds from hell were heavy on their heels. I downed me ale and followed." He looked sheepishly over at Cat. "At a safe distance, o' course."

Cat shook her head and smiled, despite herself. Greame snorted.

"I hid behind some crates at the end o' the dock. I could hear shoutin' and bangin' a ways down. Sounded more like just a fisticuffs so I started down the quay to get a better look. That's when the shootin' started."

Cat could swear his eyes lit up at the memory. She hid her smile. He needed no more instigating.

"I dove for cover when I heard wood splinterin' beside my heid. Then I heard lots o' runnin' feet comin' towards me. Whoever it was bein' shot at or doin' the shootin' wanted off the quay and in a hurry. Probably ten men ran past me. I waited for a minute before comin' out o' the hidey-hole, but I neglected to see the gent bringin' up the rear.

"He was near the same size as me and held a pistol on me. I raised me hands and told him I was unarmed and was only comin' to see what all the fuss was about. A right nonbeliever, he was, and cocked his pistol. I dropped my heid and ran into his gut hopin' to knock the gun from his hand. I succeeded and the pistol landed somewhere behind the crates I'd just come out o.'

"We had ourselves a fine scuffle. Tore me best shirt. Ye ken the one wi' the lace jabot—"

"Who was the man ye were fightin' wi,'" Cat asked, tryin' to keep him focused.

"Huh? Oh, we werna introduced proper. Anyway, I threw a punch and sent the man sprawlin' out on the dock, and I dove into the crates for the pistol. When I emerged, he was on top o' me again and we struggled for control of it when it went off harmlessly into the air. Useless now, I threw it into the water. That's when out o' the corner of me eyes, I saw a flash o' metal in the moonlight. Before I could react, I heard the shot and felt a burn in my gut. The fella who I was fightin' wi' took off and ne'er looked back. I fell back into the crates holdin' me side. Could feel the blood. The fella who shot me stopped, looked at me, then walked away.

"By this time, whoever was left on Long Wharfe ran past me for their lives before the militia showed up. I managed to get up and walk for a ways, but had to keep sittin' down to gain me strength."

"No one stopped to help ye?" Cat asked with anger in her eyes.

"Considerin' the circumstances, lass, I wouldna hae either."

"And ye've no idea what it was all about?"

Gregor shook his head.

"What about yer supper mates? Did ye see them again?" Cat asked, noticing he was getting pale.

"No. They might hae taken back to their ships for safety."

"Could it hae been a press gang?" Greame asked.

"Doubt it. I saw none o' the Crown's men, but sailors were involved for certain."

Greame pulled out his pocket watch and noted the time. "I'll see what I can find out in a couple hours. But for now, it looks as though ye might need some sleep, auld man."

"Aye, and another swallow of laudanum."

One step ahead, Cat passed him the bottle. "One *swallow*," she told him sternly.

Gregor did as he was told. Before long his eyes got heavy and he was snoring happily.

"Go on upstairs," Cat said to Greame. "I'll watch him till dawn, then I'm certain Claire will want to take over."

"I'll watch 'im now, if ya don't mind?" Claire whispered from the doorway. "Why don't ya both go upstairs an' get some sleep."

Cat smiled and nodded. Greame touched Claire's arm, then guided Cat out of the kitchen.

22

Conspiracy Theory

"DO YE FIND IT COINCIDENTAL that Gregor was pretty much singled out and shot on the dock?" Cat asked Greame. "I mean, it sounded like there were plenty o' men to choose from, but Gregor was the one who took a bullet."

Greame looked up from the bed at his wife standing in front of the window looking out over the harbour. He'd managed to get only an hour's worth of sleep and was in no mood for speculation. He sat up, scrubbed his hands over his face and blew out a sigh.

Cat turned to face him, noticing his frame of mind wasn't one to be trifled with at the moment. "Never ye mind."

She stepped closer to stand between his legs. Her arms wrapped around him and pulled his head to her bosom. He captured her waist as her fingers began kneading his skull. The sigh he exhaled this time was one of contentment.

"My Mam used to do this to my Da and got the same results."

He chuckled. "It's my thinkin' that a woman's touch can cure many an ailment, but seems to hae a particular knack wi' a frustrated man."

"Frustrated, are ye? Dare I ask?"

"No. No' right now, anyway. I'll need a clear heid for this kind o' thinkin,' and mine's nowhere near that." He nestled further into her body.

"Is that due to lack o' sleep, or the wantin' o' what yer heid is restin' upon?"

He chuckled again, then reached up and pulled her shift down over her shoulders to get better access to her breasts, making his answer quite obvious.

❧

A couple hours later they emerged downstairs to the usual household activities. Well, except for Gregor, who was lying on the settee being fussed over by Claire to the point that he nearly ordered her out of his sight.

"Cranky in the morn,' ain't 'e?" Claire muttered, but smiling, carrying the tray of food and tea back into the kitchen.

Cat gave Gregor a scowl.

"What? The woman's gonna drive me mad!" Gregor ranted. "Eat this, drink this, let me check yor bandages," he mocked.

"She's just scairt for ye, ye auld lout. The least ye could do is be thankful anyone wants to care for ye," Cat hissed, sitting hard on the settee right beside him, jostling him painfully. She smiled at his discomfort. "I wasna goin' to talk to ye about this until ye were feelin' a bit stronger, but if ye're sendin' those who care about ye away, I'm goin' to hae me words wi' ye right here and now."

Greame watched as Gregor sat rigidly on the settee trying to ignore her. Greame smirked at her tone—a no-nonsense chiding as if scolding a horse only capable of understanding the sing-song sternness. Apparently, Gregor had now been reduced to the level of a dumb beast.

"I've done naught that I need to explain to ye," he told her through hooded eyes.

"Why were ye the only one to be shot? What are ye no' tellin' us?"

He attempted to fold his arms over his chest, but winced at the pain in his side.

"I'm no' goin' anywhere, and I'm no' the one who's still in need o' this." She held up the bottle of laudanum.

"Bi—"

"Oh, dinna ye dare call me that." Her voice went very cold and steely.

"I dinna ken why ye're making such a fuss o'er it."

"O'er what?"

"Bein' shot. Isna that what ye want to ken?" he said facetiously.

Cat sent him a glare fit to kill, but it only made him smile, which infuriated her.

"There's more to it and ye ken o' what I'm speakin.' Just tell me why!"

"Why? Ye mean why Blondie decided to take his revenge out on me? Hmmm!" he tapped his chin. "Could be that he took a bit of offence 'cause we threw him in gaol! I dinna ken! How would ye hae reacted?"

Cat's mouth was set in a rigid line and her eyes blazed at him. "Why didna ye just tell us it was him? We could hae prepared for it—been ready for somethin' like this to happen. Yer lack o' judgment has put us all in danger."

"Ye canna be serious, Cat." His brow furrowed with anger. "I truly canna see why ye're so upset. I take—took," pointing to his side. "Responsibility for me actions. No one else was placed in danger. No' ye, no' anyone!"

"Ye kept it from me, hid it from me, as if I wouldna find out about it, then ye nearly got killed because of it," she shouted.

Gregor looked up at Greame for some kind of reason for her temper tantrum. Greame lifted a brow and shrugged.

"What's the real reason ye're so bloody angry, Cat?" he growled.

She abruptly stood and stormed from the room. A moment later, a door slammed upstairs.

Gregor's eyes remained on the spot where she'd disappeared.

"Can ye tell me what just happened, man?" Gregor appealed to Greame.

He, too, was watching the spot where she left the room. He felt heaviness in his heart. Gregor was right. There was something much deeper than just Gregor's usual irresponsibility bothering her.

"Pick yer battles, man," Greame muttered to himself. "And this isna one ye're gonna win." He left the room and headed to the waterfront to post guards on his ship for fear of what Blondie might be thinking of doing to it. Just in case. He for damn sure wasn't going upstairs.

❧

The trial was set for noon. Cat and Gregor were the only two who remained in the house. Greame didn't think Cat would be very good company after what had transpired earlier, so he too went to see what verdict would be handed to Jeremiah Bradford.

❧

Cat remained in her room, pacing mostly, sometimes throwing small items, sometimes crying. Her heart hurt. Her head hurt. Her soul ached. Only one other time had she felt betrayed like this.

Tears streamed down her face at the loss of her brothers, the waste of precious life for a cause they didn't even believe in. All for the glory of a goddamn war.

Now Gregor. It was difficult to put into words how angry she was. No, not angry. Enraged. For a second, she wished him dead, but sobered and just wished him immense pain. Pain to rival what she was feeling. She wondered if that were possible. She sat down in her chair overlooking the harbour and thought of all the pain she'd like to beset upon him. Yes, that would make her feel better. Lots and lots of pain.

❧

Gregor was confused. Of course there were things he'd done in his life he wasn't all that proud of, but he was the only one affected. He answered to no one but himself. But she knew, didn't she. She knew he was hiding something from her, that's why she questioned him so relentlessly. But he also knew her better than she thought he did. There was something else bothering her. A nerve was struck that hadn't healed from some other mishap. It was deep and painful, but he didn't think it had anything to do with him.

He began wondering who had hurt her that badly. Badly enough for the wound to be reopened by his actions. He wished he had Greame's powers to see into her heart. Perhaps then he would understand why she was so distraught.

The afternoon wore on, and the more Gregor wracked his brain, the further from the solution he got. He finally fell asleep more mystified than ever.

❧

The trial was over in just a few hours. Buggery was a hanging offense. It simply was not tolerated, especially in puritanical Boston. Strange though, how such tender sensibilities ate up each word of what went on behind the closed doors of the Black Angus Social Club. Near rapturous looks were on many a face as the men and women slowly filed out of the courthouse. If someone asked any of them what the verdict was, they probably couldn't even say. And it didn't matter. Some wished perhaps that Jeremiah Bradford be let go in order to possibly find his way back to scandalize another day. All the public wanted was a distraction, the utterance of the obscene to titillate the senses, the fantasy of the taboo.

Jeremiah Bradford's parents still had enough money in their pockets to see that their last remaining son wasn't hung. Jail time was mandatory, though, and he would be behind bars for many years. The magistrates still had to make it look like they were doing their jobs.

❧

It was two days before Cat ventured out of her room. The colors of the darkening sky looked as bruised as she felt. She wasn't usually one to wallow in self-pity, but she couldn't seem to shake herself out of it.

Her stomach growled. She couldn't remember the last time she'd eaten. Apparently, it had been a while. She opened her bedroom door and was assailed by the aroma of supper. Laughter drifted to her from the family she'd come to love. It was a good sound. When she emerged in the best room and saw everyone carrying on with life, it seemed to snap her out of her self-absorption.

Gregor noticed her first. Their eyes met and seemed to cling to each other. Cat walked over to her dearest friend and pressed a kiss on his raspy cheek.

The room went silent, as if waiting for something else to transpire, like a slap to the other cheek. Greame motioned for everyone to leave the two warriors alone. Quietly and discreetly, they filed out of the room.

Cat sat on the edge of the settee and lifted Gregor's sark to check his bandages. They apparently looked satisfactory because she put his shirt down and gently smoothed it over his side.

Gregor took her hand and brought it to his lips.

"Forgive me," she whispered in a choked voice.

"Just tell me, Cat. Why did my usual mischief upset ye so this time?"

She looked up at him for a long moment. "I … oh this is goin' to sound stupid now, but … I felt like ye betrayed me."

Hurt crossed his eyes and he shook his head. "How? Ye ken I'd ne'er do anything to hurt ye, lass." His voice was low and gravelly.

Cat bowed her head. "I ken that. It's just that it brought back the same feelin' as when Iain and Lachlan left me sleepin' at the inn to go off and fight wi' Da at Culloden."

Gregor's eyes flew open in surprise. "What?" He lifted her chin so he could see into her eyes. "I had no idea that's how it happened, Cat. Ne'er did understand how they came to be in the thick o' things. Last I kent, they'd made a promise to ye to stay out of it. Yer Da was right proud o' ye for findin' the strength to carry out yer Mam's last wish for yer brothers no' to fight. Most o' yer brothers promised, anyway."

Cat snorted humorlessly, "Aye. They did. But, apparently the lure o' war was stronger than their word."

"Christ, Cat," he said, rubbing his hand over his face.

"Ye kept it from me, Gregor. Hid it like I didna need to ken about it."

"I ne'er let ye in on anythin' I'm doin,'" he said quietly. "Why, all of a sudden did this set ye off?"

She looked into his eyes and smiled sadly, "Because this time I almost lost ye."

23

The Wrath of the Gods

NOVEMBER WAS SLIPPING AWAY. Gregor was taking longer than normal to mend, according to Cat. He kept flirting with infection and the medicines he needed to keep it at bay were much easier to obtain here. She didn't want to risk him getting a full-blown outbreak aboard ship.

Besides, the long stretch of perfect weather made for an enjoyable time in Boston.

For a month now, the word had circulated along the docks to watch for Blondie. Greame had a suspicion it wasn't the end of the man, and there was no way he was returning to Maine while that culprit was lurking out there somewhere. He wondered how long it would take to locate him. Sailing this late in the season did not thrill him in the least.

When he arrived at the teashop late that afternoon, he was surprised, and pleased, to see Cat there. She sent him a radiant smile and he went over and kissed her cheek.

"Out for some air?" he asked.

"Aye, that and gettin' some tea for the settlement. It's nice to have a variety, dinna ye think?"

Greame nodded. "Get what ye need then." He turned his attention to his crew and told them they'd have a meeting after supper to discuss a date to leave by. He waited for Cat to fill her satchel, then walked her home.

Greame noticed Cat kept looking down at her feet. The expression on her face was curious, as if trying to discern something.

"Wanna tell me what's goin' through that mind o' yers, Garnet?"

"Do ye feel it, Greame?"

He looked at her with questioning eyes as they neared Newberry Street.

"No' sure what ye mean. Feel what?"

"In yer feet." She saw his look of incomprehension and elaborated. "I feel a rumble. A sort of jump now and then. Ye dinna feel it?"

He stopped for a moment, concentrating on his feet, then shook his head.

Dogs were barking all through the neighborhood and horses were misbehaving.

"There's something amiss, something queer about this evening. I dinna care for the feelin' in the air."

Greame looked up at the clear sky turning dusky. The north star was already shining brightly through the leafless trees. He could sense nothing out of the ordinary.

"Sorry, *a ghràidh*, I dinna feel anything."

Cat shrugged it off and they walked into the house.

After supper, Greame gathered all his crew and talked about the return trip to Cape Rozier.

Gregor announced that he was fit enough to sail, no matter what Cat said.

"I've been able to walk for near a week now wi'out much pain. The last batch o' that bitter tea she made seemed to stop the puss from leachin.'" He made a grimace that made everyone laugh. "We can leave tomorrow, if ye've a mind."

"I'll no' leave wi'out Garnet's consent. She's the one that has to tend to ye," Greame stated.

"He's right," Cat said from the doorway. "That last batch o' tea did seem to clear the septic from him. I think he's ready to sail."

"Fine then. We'll sail in the mornin' if that's all right wi' the rest o' ye."

The consensus in the room was to return to the settlement immediately, to beat the winter storms.

❧

Everyone seemed pleased to be returning home. Blondie had not been located anywhere in Boston and that was a hopeful sign that he'd moved on.

In the predawn hours, Cat woke to the feeling of movement. The local dogs once again began to bark and there seemed to be a sense of agitation in the air. She looked over at Greame in the moonlit room. He was sound asleep. What was going on?

Then she heard it as well as felt it. A deep, groaning rumble emanated from the earth itself, growing louder and stronger. It seemed to be racing directly towards her! This time Greame woke up.

"What in bloody hell is goin' on?"

The entire house began to shake, making creaking noises as if it were being torn apart, and they flew out of bed. From down the hallway Cat heard Susan scream and Sarah wail. The big grandfather clock downstairs in the best room was chiming to its own time. If anyone had looked, it was half four.

Everyone stumbled out of their beds and staggered into the dimly lit hallway, clinging to the walls with looks of horror on their faces. Someone emerged with a lantern to guide the way. As they raced down the stairs, Emily and Claire—lanterns ablaze—met them in the front foyer. They piled outside in their nightclothes and met with neighbors in the same predicament.

From their high vantage point and the bright moonlit sky, they could actually see the nearby church steeples sway violently, some toppling from the pitching action. From every street, crashing of chimneys onto roofs and cobblestones was heard. China and crystal smashed from cupboards and shelves. Crying and praying and screaming added to the cacophony. And the dogs! They ran through the streets willy-nilly trying to get away from the unseen growling beast that pursued them.

Cat and Greame clung to each other, unsure what to do.

When the shaking ceased, Cat's face lit up at the thrill of the event. Greame was amazed to find no fear in her eyes as he did in everyone else's. Even when another round of shaking occurred, though not as violent as the first, the fear of God showed on the faces of the people surrounding them. Cat stood with her legs apart, braced, as if riding some underground wave. At times, there was even a smile on her face. He just shook his head, feeling that sometimes she was so in tune with nature, it was frightening.

The movement seemed to last forever, but it was really just about a minute, they would later find out. An earthquake they called it.

When the sun came up a few hours later, people were still in the streets, afraid to return to their homes. They stumbled through the town dazed and confounded. With so many chimneys destroyed or damaged, it was impossible to cook or heat their homes. Many roofs sustained damage from the falling bricks, and structures not soundly built toppled from the violent swaying action.

Greame instructed Robbie, Thad and Kenny to see if there was any damage to the Rose Guest House chimneys, of which there were four. Gregor, Geoffrey and Kelvin surveyed the house for structural damage, and the women righted the house on the inside.

All reports came back with little or no damage to the structure or chimneys. This house was built to last. Others in the neighborhood weren't so lucky. Everyone pitched in to help each other the best they could.

George, Edward, Thomas and John arrived later that morning with reports of damage done to the teashop. It was mostly shelving coming down and tea strewn all around, but the roof in the backroom sustained a hole where the neighbor's chimney came down on it.

Now Bostonians, being the puritanical lot they were, were assured that this was a sign from God for the sins they incurred. In the following days, churches were filled to the brim with repenting souls all begging God to never let this kind of catastrophe befall them ever again. They would be good from now on. They promised.

A day after the quake, a fishing boat sailed into port, its crew telling tales of a shock so strong they thought they'd run aground nearly two hundred miles out to sea. Accounts filtered in from towns further away telling of large cracks opening up in the ground and sand and water spewing forth from them. Some farmers described springs on their property drying up, while their neighbors discovered new springs on their land.

The days went by filled with busy work for those less fortunate. At breakfast, two weeks after the calamity, Greame announced they had done all they could here and were setting sail the following morning to return to Maine. Everyone breathed a sigh of relief. With any luck, they'd be home the first week of December.

❧

The morning they were to sail home, Greame was watching Cat sleep. There was a slight smile on her face and he wondered what she was dreaming.

As if sensing his gaze, she opened her eyes.

"Are ye staring at me?" she asked huskily.

"Uh huh."

"Was I droolin'?"

Greame chuckled. "No. I just wanted to ask ye somethin.'"

She rubbed the sleep from her eyes and got up on her elbow.

"How … when … werna ye scairt, even a wee bit?"

Cat grinned widely. "The earthquake, ye mean? Oh, at first I was frightened. I didna care to be in the house. But when we all got outside safely, it was the single most thrillin' thing I've e'er witnessed in my life!"

Greame was smiling at her enthusiasm.

"Did I e'er tell ye I was caught in a hail storm once?"

He shook he head.

"I may hae been fourteen. I was miles from Anna's tendin' to a septic finger. Gorse thorn. Anyway, thunder began splittin' the air and bolts o' lightnin' struck the trees right next to me, explodin' them. My horse bolted, leavin' me on the ground nearly a mile from home when the hail started comin' down." She sat up cross-legged in bed, keeping the covers over her legs.

"When I fell off the horse, the wind was knocked from me, so I was just tryin' to breathe. It felt like someone was throwin' rocks at me.

The batterin' I was takin' began hurtin' bad so I started crawlin' towards Anna's cott. When I finally got the air back in me chest, I ran.

"Anna was outside tryin' to get Clot Heid into the barn." When she noticed a question in Greame's eyes, she said, "That's what the horse was called after that day."

He laughed.

"Anna was hollerin' at me to hurry, as if I need any more incentive. I made it to the house soakin' wet and battered. Anna peeled off my dress, wrapped me a blanket and stood me by the fire. She went to put on some tea, then came back and started rubbin' me down like a horse."

"That must've hurt a bit."

"Tcha! I told her to stop and pulled away from her. When I did, my blanket remained in Anna's hands. When she saw the bruises all o'er my body, she understood why I got cross wi' her. But it was an incredible experience to see what nature can do, dinna ye think?"

Greame raised his eyebrows. "I suppose I've ne'er looked at it that way before. To me, the earthquake was a frightenin' ordeal that I'll ne'er forget, but it *was* a bit excitin,' too. And I'll only admit that to ye. To see such fear in everyone's eyes, then to look at ye wi' a smile on yer face. Well, it could be seen as a bit o' witchcraft by some."

Cat's eyes darkened and the happiness fell away from her face. She got out of bed and stood by the window. The sun wasn't quite up yet, but the colors in the sky reminded her of thistles. For a moment she remained quiet, then turned to Greame.

"I suppose I canna help what I am." She walked over and sat next to him on the bed.

"I didna mean anything by what I said, Garnet. I just want ye to be careful." He put his big hand on her leg and gave it a squeeze. "I love ye. And I'm sorry for taking away from yer happy story."

She snorted and patted his hand. "No, ye're right. And I canna wait to get back to Maine so I can be myself, so let's get movin,' aye?"

❧

It was cold, but sunny when the *Revenge* left Boston Harbour with the tide that morning. The wind was favourable and they made good time getting out to sea.

Cat was below decks in the captain's quarters reading a book when the vision hit. It was as if she were going backwards to London, remembering when she sailed from that port so long ago. This time, instead of seeing the land grow smaller, it was getting closer. She could see the buildings as they drew nearer.

Suddenly, she was sailing past the Thames and heading further up the coast. Towards Scotland. Towards home. The air was cool, and the feeling of home was so strong it made her smile. When she reached a small port on the eastern coast, the heather was blooming all along the braes, turning them a dusty rose-purple. The season must have been late summer.

She walked through the moors breathing in the scents she'd thought she'd never smell again. No other place could compare with her homeland. Her heart filled with joy.

A knock on the door brought her out of her dream.

"Come in."

Thad poked his head in and smiled. "The captain requests your company, Miss Garnet."

Cat raised an eyebrow and put her book on the desk. She wrapped her cloak over her shoulders. Thad offered her a steadying arm and she took it with appreciation. Sea legs took her a long time to settle into. Usually they were already at their destination when she finally felt comfortable enough to walk around and not bump into things.

Once up on the open deck, she released Thad's arm and made her way to Greame, who was at the helm.

"Christ O' Jesus it's cold up here," she said through chattering teeth.

Greame chuckled and folded her in his arms. "I wanted to speak wi' ye about Scotland. I think—"

"I just had a vision about our return voyage," she cut in.

"Did ye see the heather all a-bloom along the hillsides near my home?" he asked from behind her with a smile in his voice.

Cat turned her head with a smile of her own. "Aye, 'twas lovely. So, it wasn't a vision, just somethin' ye wanted me to see then?"

He nodded. "I just wanted to ask ye if ye've still a mind to go back."

"If I didn't before, I do now. As usual, ye paint a grand picture, my dear. I could even smell the place."

He hugged her closer. "We'll ride out the winter in Maine, then return in the spring. I've no idea what condition my auld croft will be in, but we'll make do."

"*Slios Mìn*, unless destroyed by the Hanoverians, should still be standin.' There's six thousand acres there." Then added, "But it's no' on the coast."

"Well, that could be a slight problem gettin' the *Revenge* in and out o' the water," he chuckled. "Six thousand acres? I dinna recall ye e'er tellin' me ye were a wealthy land owner."

"*Pffftt!* Oh aye, I'm right wealthy," she said sarcastically. "I dinna ken if it's even mine to be talkin' about anymore."

"It'll need to be looked into when we return."

"Hae ye spoken wi' the rest?" indicating their extended family. "How many do ye suppose will want to uproot again and go back wi' us?"

Greame was quiet for a moment. Cat could feel his heart beating on her back as he held her close.

"I think perhaps most will want to return. Geoff, I'm no' sure of, wi' Susan's family bein' here and all."

"Let's discuss it tonight at supper. This way everyone can be makin' their plans, aye? Now, if there's naught else ye need me for, I'll be returnin' to our cabin to get the feelin' back in me toes."

❧

Greame watched her make her way below decks. What he didn't tell her was that the gold they'd found would go a long way towards securing proper land in Scotland. It was his turn to watch over her, to make a life for her, and he'd do it whatever the cost.

Part Three

24

Quandaries

THERE WAS OVER SIX INCHES of snow covering the ground when the *Revenge* and her crew returned to the settlement. It took the better part of a day to unload the ship and fill the cabins with the bounty brought from Boston.

While there was a bit of daylight left, Cat began rearranging her bedroom for her long-awaited treasure: the copper tub. It was a little larger than she had imagined, taking up the entire corner, and it took all the men to get the enormous basin into the house.

She had Kenny and Robbie move the big chest of drawers to the far side of the room and was eyeing her new addition with a smile on her face while dreaming of long, leisurely soaks. She reckoned it was actually large enough for two. Very cozy during the long, dark months of winter, she thought.

Someone entered the house with all the stealth of an elephant. Cat went into the kitchen to see what the fuss was about.

Gregor had just set down an armload of crates on the floor when he saw her emerge from the bedroom.

"Pardon the noise. Where's Greame?"

Cat cocked her head and squinted, "Why? What's wrong?" She could see it in his face.

He wasn't going to hide anything from her on this subject. "Footprints in the snow where we havna been yet."

"Fresh?"

Gregor shrugged. "Within a day or two. It's been cold, so possibly a little longer."

"In the barn." Cat wrapped the cloak around her and went out with Gregor.

Before she reached the barn though, she veered off towards the beach.

"Where are ye goin'?" Gregor asked, stopping to see what she had in mind.

She didn't answer him, so he followed her.

When they reached the beach where long-ago pirates had buried the gold, the banking was littered with holes. Someone had been here all right and now it was clear what he wanted. Cat looked up to see Gregor's face. It was enraged.

Before she could say anything he trotted away, heading for the root cellar. He needed to see for himself that the gold was still safe in the hidey-hole he'd built.

There were no prints in the snow anywhere around the entrance. He breathed a sigh of relief. Cat caught up to him and noticed the same thing. She patted him on the back.

"It's safe, but I'd appreciate it if ye told Greame. I've things to do in the house, if ye dinna mind."

Gregor nodded. "Be sure someone's wi' ye and Susan all the time, aye? We still dinna ken if he's around or no.'"

❧

Sitting in her rocking chair in her bedroom in the waning light, Cat attempted to sense the whereabouts of the unknown man who'd trespassed on her property. Was it really Blondie? Or did someone else know about the gold? She really wished whoever was looking for it had found it. At least then the settlement could get back to its peaceful existence.

Her mind wandered restlessly, unable to even call up the man's face. What she did see was the heather-strewn landscape of Scotland. She gave into it and began exploring the vision. What she saw must have been Greame's land because she didn't recognize it. The rocky coast, the windswept barren land: harsh and unforgiving. Ruins of a once-great castle clung to the cliff as though ready to leap into the rolling sea far below. It was breathtaking. Cat inhaled the sea-scented air: cleaner than the foulness of Boston, and not as cold as Maine.

Then she was at *Slios Mìn* looking out from her childhood bedroom window at the high rolling shielings covered in gorse and broom. She walked down to Loch Rannoch remembering how the water changed each hour of the day. Usually still in the morning, with the mountains and trees reflecting in it so clearly one couldn't tell which was real and which was the mirrored image. Other times the wind whipped it into a frenzy, sending white-capped waves crashing onto the pebbled shore.

Suddenly, the vision became overlapped with her place in Maine. There was no doubt she loved it here, but what was the prophecy trying to tell her? She couldn't have it both ways, it was either Maine and staying through the war, making the best of this wilderness while staying clear of the hostile factions; or it was returning to Scotland, to the place she held so dear in her heart. But wasn't her homeland going to be just as war-torn as America when the English decided to dominate the entire world? Didn't she already see Scotsmen fighting alongside the English? Was she risking sending Greame and his family to a fight they didn't want to be in? And what if Gregor was right about having to decide where they stood here? To fight for this country against the English. It was like a double vision. Damned if she did and damned if she didn't.

Cat rose from her chair in a huff. This was going nowhere and dedicating more time to it right now was a waste. She walked into the kitchen to find Kenny sitting at the table with a cup of tea. The smell of stew and biscuits permeated the softly lit house.

"Might I join ye?" she asked.

Kenny smiled. "Ye ken ye ne'er hae to ask, Garnet." He took a sip of the steaming liquid. "Ye look a mite perplexed, though. Anything I can be helpin' ye wi'?"

"Oh, that obvious, is it?"

He shrugged.

Cat decided since her quandary affected him as well, she might as well ask what he thought.

"I've something to be askin' ye, and I want ye to be honest in yer answer." She waited for his nod. "Greame and I are thinkin' o' returnin' to Scotland." She watched his face closely. "What would ye do if we did?"

Kenny's eyebrows lifted and a smile blossomed on his face. "I'd go home in a heartbeat."

"Ye dinna care to think on it for a bit?"

He shook his head. "No."

She ventured further questioning. "What about Robbie and Kelvin and the rest?"

"Robbie and Kelvin go where their captain says. But no' just that, they'd be happy to return to Scotland, too. I canna say about Geoff, or Johnny, Tom, Edward and George in Boston."

Cat twirled a lock of hair as she sipped her tea, lost in her own little world. Kenny slipped away from the table unnoticed to tend to supper.

❧

The next morning, Greame and Gregor assembled a scouting party to locate the trespasser. Greame remained in the settlement, and Susan and Sarah moved into the spare bedroom for safety's sake.

Gregor, Robbie and Thad followed the footprints, while Kelvin, Kenny and Geoff set up watch posts around the woods and beach. If the intruder decided to return, they'd see him.

Greame was cleaning his pistols at the kitchen table. Cat was beside him filling horns with powder and putting flints and shot into pouches.

"Do ye ken how to use a pistol, lass?" he asked Susan.

Susan was holding Sarah on her shoulder. She shook her head with a look that said *and I don't want to know.*

Greame read her face and soothed her by saying, "'Tis all right. Cat and I are crack shots. Ye dinna need to worry."

Susan just nodded and observed as he slid the ramrod in and out of the barrel. She noted how Cat readied the ammunition with a practiced hand, wondering if she'd ever feel as comfortable with the wildness and dangers of this place as Cat did.

Sarah began to fuss, so she took her into the bedroom to feed her.

When the door was closed, Greame whispered to Cat, "She's frightened."

Cat nodded, looking at the closed door. "I think she's more afraid because o' Sarah. She's fiercely protective, though. She'll be fine."

❧

It looked like they were ready to start their own war. Pistols, dirks, and even a blunderbuss Gregor procured in Boston were added to the stockpile.

The sky had lowered during the morning, looking more and more like snow. The men would be freezing when they came in from their posts. Greame had instructed them to come home one at a time to get warm and get something hot in their bellies before returning to the cold.

Greame was heading out to patrol around the cabins. The snow made for easy tracking of anything that wandered into the settlement, four-legged or two. So far, there were only the four-legged types, with a rafter of turkeys added not long ago.

When he rounded Geoffrey's cabin nearest the woods, he felt rather than saw an intruder. He scanned the dense fir trying to see who or what it was. In his head, Greame discounted a bear, as they were pretty much all hunkered down for their winter's sleep. He'd seen no wolf tracks since Bogle died, and any other beast out there was pretty much harmless. But that didn't stop the hair on his neck from rising.

The wind was in his favor and he took a deep breath in an effort to smell the culprit. He walked closer to the timberline, pistol at the ready, and inhaled again. Still nothing. It was too cold and the wind was too strong to hold a scent. Closer he walked, and this time a low menacing growl emanated from within the underbrush. Perhaps all the bears weren't sleeping yet.

Slowly he backed away, not wanting to tangle with the unknown beast. He had other things to worry about. Whatever it was probably wouldn't let anyone else get near it either. Sort of like another guard, he thought to himself.

He turned and cautiously walked towards the other cabins, feeling eyes on his back. Suddenly, from behind him came the breaking of branches as the beast crashed out from its hiding place. When he looked back, a cat the size of Gent leapt from the brush, eyes trained on him. At first, Greame was struck by the beauty of the beast. Its tan-colored coat and long, graceful gait was a thing to marvel at. It was fast and covered more ground than he could in twice the time. As it got closer, Greame saw its golden eyes intent on making him the meal for the day. He didn't want to kill it, but he couldn't reach the safety of anyone's cabin before the cat was upon him. Without hesitation, he lifted his pistol and fired.

The cat's body made an unnatural shift as the bullet hit it in the throat. It stumbled to the ground and slid the rest of the way in the snow to rest at Greame's feet, blood pumping from the hole in its neck. He stepped back a few paces, just in case, but the cat wasn't moving. He inched his way closer to inspect the beast. Such a shame he had to kill it, but it gave him no choice.

Cat heard the shot nearby. She grabbed her pistol and flew out of the cabin. In the snow-silenced settlement she listened hard, trying to gauge where the discharge came from. She crept around each of the cabins, finally reaching Geoff's, when she saw Greame bent over a large … something.

Greame heard the crunch of the snow and looked up to see Cat standing there.

"I had to kill it. I think it wanted me for dinner."

Cat stepped closer and bent to touch it. "I didna think a cat could get so big. Did ye?"

Greame shook his head as he stroked its ears. "Lovely fur. I dinna want it to go to waste. I'll get a horse to drag it to the barn and we'll skin it later."

"Hae ye e'er seen tracks for this beast in the area before?"

"No, but Far Eyes has a drawin' of one in his lodge, so they must be fairly common. If memory serves, I think he called them *bitt-ohn-lo*. It means long tail."

"I canna imagine what any of us would hae done if we'd run into such a beast in the woods," she said, eyeing it for its size. "It must be near six feet long."

"Aye, no' something I care to think about."

Just then, Kenny and Geoff came bounding around the cabin, stopping short when they saw the cat.

"Good God, what is that?" Geoffrey asked, his eyes wide with a mixture of fear and curiosity.

"A big cat is all I can tell ye," Greame said. "He came after me as I was walking towards the woods. I had nowhere to go and it was too quick to outrun."

"Fine pelt," Kenny said, reaching down to stroke the tawny fur.

"Aye, let's drag it to the barn where we can tend to it later." Greame looked around. "Did Kelvin come wi' ye?"

"Havna seen him," Geoff said.

"Well, let's get this done, and since ye're both here, grab some food and warm up a bit. I'll continue my watch," Greame said.

❧

Kelvin heard the shot and saw Kenny run towards the cabins. No need for him to leave his post; besides, he wasn't feeling well. Trudging through the snow seemed to take everything out of him this morning. Perhaps he was getting too old for this kind of work. "Hardly," he mumbled to himself. In a little while he'd go back and get Garnet to make one of her herbal concoctions; then he'd be good as new.

He'd found an enormous boulder nearly hidden with fir trees. It was a perfect perch to watch the surrounding area from, sheltered from the icy breeze his cloak wasn't warm enough for.

Another scan of the area again came up empty. He wondered if Gregor and the lads had tracked down the man yet. All of this might be for naught and he would be sitting out here freezing for no reason whatsoever, he chuckled. He ached to light his pipe, but knew its fragrant smoke would give him away.

A snap of a branch from behind had him whirling around in time to see a club swinging at his head. It was the last thing he saw.

25

Security Breach

GREAME STOMPED HIS snow-covered boots on the porch before walking into the house. One look on Cat's face told him something was amiss.

"What's happened?"

"It's nearly time for luncheon and Kelvin still hasna come in from the cold."

"Has Kenny or Geoff seen him?"

She shrugged, worry written all over her face.

"Stay here wi' Susan and the bairn. Keep the pistols close. I'll go check on him."

"Greame?"

He turned to look at her. She couldn't voice her fears, but he understood the look in her eyes.

"I'll bring him home." He closed the door behind him and headed back into the woods.

Kenny had told him where Kelvin was posted, so he started out in that direction first, hoping they were sitting together and everything was all right.

When he reached Kenny's post, there was just Kenny.

"What's wrong?" he asked Greame quietly.

"Kelvin's no' come in yet. Hae ye seen him?"

Kenny shook his head. "Hae ye checked wi' Geoff?"

Greame was staring into the woods and shook his head. "Where is he?"

Kenny pointed in the direction he'd last seen Geoff, and Greame took off.

The forest was nearly silent. Snow had begun to fall and made small tapping noises when the flakes hit the brown, withered oak leaves clinging to the ancient trees. Greame scanned the woods, hoping for a sign of his kin.

He stopped for a moment, feeling, rather than seeing, a person nearby.

"Are ye lookin' for me, Greame?" Geoffrey whispered from over his head.

Greame looked up and grinned. "What are ye doin' in the tree, man?"

"Besides freezin' me ballocks off? Watchin' for strangers, I'm guessin.' What are ye doin' out here? Somethin' wrong?"

"Hae ye seen Kelvin? He hasna come in to get warm all mornin.'"

Geoffrey shimmied down the old pine in seconds. "No, I havna seen him. Best we go hae a look then, aye?"

Greame was already walking back towards Kenny.

Kenny was doing up his flies when they got there. "No sign then?"

"We'll split up and meet back at the house when we're through," Greame said, already choosing a direction. Before he got two steps, he turned and said, "Keep yer pistols ready. I dinna care for this."

He headed for the thick woods closest to the shore. He just needed to cut Kelvin's trail and follow it, then it would lead him right to his uncle. It was snowing harder now. If this kept up, tracking him would be impossible. He crossed deer track several times. They knew the storm was coming and were eating now so they could bed down and wait it out.

Greame wasn't sure how long it was before he finally saw footprints, but breathed a sigh of relief when he noticed they were heading back towards the settlement. "Tough auld man," he chuckled to himself.

He followed the tracks to within sight of the cabins, but stopped when they took a turn towards the shore. Something wasn't right. Why would Kelvin go to the beach? Scanning the snow, he noticed faint footprints that led into the woods. These must have been Kelvin's when he first went to his post. Greame turned around and followed them at a trot.

From the looks of the prints, Kelvin was trying to keep his path concealed as much as possible and walking closest to the trees. A few rabbit and squirrel tracks had crossed his uncle's impressions in the deepening snow. The woods thickened and Greame looked up to get his bearings. He noticed a boulder nearly hidden in the spruce and pine. The trail led right to it.

Greame noticed the newer prints were coming from the boulder. It had to have been Kelvin returning to the settlement, but …

Leaving nothing to chance, Greame bushwhacked his way into the thick undergrowth. As he reached the boulder, he saw them. Boots, unmoving on the other side. He ran to his uncle. The deep cut over Kelvin's eye turned the snow around his head a deep crimson. Greame let out a roar of frustration and anger, then shot a round into the air to let the others know he'd found him.

He put his hand on Kelvin's chest under his cloak to see if he was still breathing. There was a faint heartbeat. He was so cold. He felt around to see if there were any other injuries he couldn't see, but all else seemed to be in good order.

"Kelvin. Can ye hear me, man?"

Greame took off his cloak and laid it over his uncle. A little ways away, he could hear branches breaking signaling the return of Kenny and Geoff.

"O'er here!" he shouted.

Within a minute, his cousins were at his side.

"We've got to get him inside," Greame said.

"We'll hae to carry him." Geoff was already lifting a shoulder.

Greame got on the other side and Kenny grabbed his legs. It wouldn't be easy carrying him such a distance, but there was no other way.

When they had gone a few steps, Kelvin moaned. The three looked at each other and continued towards the settlement.

❧

Sarah was fussing and wasn't satisfied with anything her mother was doing to rectify the situation.

Cat came out of her room and went directly to her herb cupboard. She searched for a few minutes before pulling down a jar of licorice root. She pulled out a long root and washed it up well, then handed it to Susan.

"Hae her chew on this. It'll help wi' the pain."

Susan looked at the root with a raised eyebrow, shooting a look at Cat. "What pain?"

"She's gettin' her teeth in."

"Oh." Susan put a finger in Sarah's mouth and felt around the gums. They were indeed hard and her little round cheeks couldn't have gotten any redder. Sarah stopped crying while her gums were being massaged and was drooling amply from the stimulating action. Susan gave her the root and Sarah began gnawing on it contentedly.

"I'm sorry she disturbed you. I hadn't realized."

"It's fine, but if ye dinna mind, I'll be in my room."

"Garnet?"

Cat turned in the doorway. She didn't have the answer Susan wanted yet and didn't want to worry her. "He'll be all right." She closed the door and sat in her rocker.

"At least I hope so," she muttered to herself.

Twirling her hair and watching the snow fall with increased fear that everything *wasn't* all right, Cat tried again to get Kelvin's whereabouts and condition. She just couldn't see him.

"Fine time to lose the Sight, when everyone's countin' on ye to find him."

Out of the corner of her eye, she caught a movement near Gregor's cabin. She ducked behind the curtain and watched. All was still. Had she imagined it? No, because whoever it was had now entered the cabin. She strained to see if it was indeed Gregor, or someone who shouldn't be there.

She ran out of her room and made certain the front door was

bolted. There were four pistols on the table ready and waiting. Cat absently felt for her dirk and patted it on her leg.

Susan caught her actions and said, "It's time?"

Cat looked her square in her light green eyes and nodded. "Take Sarah into the dinin' room. Oh, wait. Here." She thrust a pistol at her.

"I don't know how to use this," shaking her head, refusing to take it.

"It's half cocked now. If ye need to fire it, pull this back once more," indicating the hammer. "Point and shoot."

The look of horror in Susan's eyes made Cat try to calm her fears. "'Tisn't likely he'll get this far, I'll make sure of it. Please. Take it."

Susan did as she was told and took Sarah into the dining room.

Cat skulked through the rooms searching out the windows for who entered Gregor's cabin. There was still no sign of him: no movement anywhere. She had just entered the spare bedroom when someone pounded on the front door, making her jump. Susan screamed from the other room and Cat bolted into the kitchen with her pistol trained on the door. She took a quick look out the window overlooking the porch.

"Damn it, Gregor!" she yelled as she ran to unbolt the door.

"What's goin' on here?" he boomed, fear in his voice.

"Were ye just in yer cabin?"

"No, we followed the tracks back to the settlement and I wanted to make sure everyone kent he's here somewhere."

"Where's Robbie and Thad?"

"In the barn. Where's Greame and the rest?"

"Searchin' for Kelvin. He hasna come in since this mornin.' And I think someone's in yer cabin."

Without a word, Gregor stole out the door. Cat watched from the doorway, the pistol still in her hand.

Not long after Gregor disappeared behind the side of the building, a shot exploded. Without thinking, she flew out into the snow and was nearly bowled over by one very angry stranger. She righted herself and took aim. She fired, and when the smoke cleared, he was gone.

She rushed into Gregor's cabin to find him sitting up against the door with a knife protruding from his stomach. He looked up with a sheepish grin and a wince.

"Good thing he was expectin' someone shorter or I'd've taken it in me chest and might no' be chattin' wi' ye right now."

"Oh, shut up! Christ, Gregor, what were ye thinkin' goin' in big as life?"

"He's got a bullet in his shoulder. Did I hear ye fire a shot at him, too?"

"Aye," she said, inspecting the damage from the blade. "But I dinna think I hit him. Ye all right for a minute? I dinna want to leave Susan alone." She turned to leave, but stopped. "And dinna pull out that blade!"

"Go," he flicked his hand. "I'll no' be leavin' anytime soon."

❧

All three of them heard the shots and looked at each other with concern in their eyes. They were nearly to the clearing before the cabins. It was a tortuous decision. Should they leave Kelvin, possibly to die, or let Cat fend for herself, possibly to die?

They picked up the pace, breathing heavily from the dead weight of Kelvin and trudging through the deepening snow trying to keep from tripping on unseen sticks and fallen logs.

When they broke into the clearing, Geoff pleaded with his eyes to Greame and Kenny.

"Go! We've got him." Stopping to maneuver Kelvin's full weight into his arms. "If everything's all right, give us a shout, aye?"

Geoff just raised his arm and raced towards the cabins.

Greame and Kenny struggled by themselves, but within a few minutes, Robbie and Thad were rushing towards them to help carry Kelvin.

"What news hae ye? Is anyone harmed?" Greame asked anxiously.

"Dinna ken," Robbie said. "Thad and me were in the barn and before we could get out to see what happened, Geoff raced by lookin' mighty frightened. We stopped him and he told us to come help ye wi' Kelvin."

"C'mon, then, let's get him into the house so Garnet can tend to him. Then we'll see what happened."

When they arrived, Geoff was holding his frightened wife and Cat was gathering bandages in the spare bedroom.

They laid Kelvin on the table and began removing his cloak.

Cat appeared in the kitchen with an armload of supplies, took one look and said, "Oh no! What happened?"

Greame filled her in with as much as he knew.

"Get him out o' his wet clothes and get him warm. Keep light pressure on his wound. And see if ye can wake him. I'll be needin' ye, Greame," she said ominously, already heading for the door.

Greame followed without question.

"What's wrong?" he asked when out of earshot of everyone.

"Gregor took a knife to his gut."

"Blondie?" he growled.

"Most likely so," she said as they walked in to find Gregor in the same sitting position Cat left him in.

"How are ye, *duine mor*?" Cat bent to check on the wound.

"Great, thank ye for askin.'" It was said with as much sarcasm as he could muster.

Ignoring his wit, Cat looked around for a place to lay him while she worked.

"Help me get him onto the table, Greame."

Even with the two of them, it was a struggle getting the big man upright. When Gregor was standing, Cat took off his cloak and sark, having to tear it a bit more to go over the knife without disturbing it.

Gregor sat on the table and Cat pulled off his boots.

"I could learn to like havin' ye undress me, lass."

If he didn't look a bit too ghostly for Cat's liking, she might have taken offense, but he was scaring her. The whole bottom half of his sark and the front of his breeks were soaked with blood.

"Lay him down. I forgot the laudanum. I'll be right back."

The cold air snapped her out of her near-panic attack. When she stepped back into the house, she fetched the laudanum, and Robbie and Kenny.

She re-entered Gregor's cabin in a *whoosh* of frigid air. "Here," handing Gregor the bottle. "Drink."

A brightening of his eyes told her he'd be fine, but this was going to be very touchy. She'd known many a man not survive from a stomach wound. An awful lot could happen in there when she pulled out that blade.

After Gregor was rendered insensible, Cat instructed Robbie to fetch some hot water that perpetually simmered over the fire; Kenny to thread the needle with the new silk thread she'd purchased during her stay in Boston; and Greame to help her with the actual wound and its repair process.

"What are his chances?" Robbie asked when he set the basin of hot water within Cat's reach.

Cat didn't look up, just said, "I canna tell ye just yet, Robbie, but I'm goin' to do everything I can."

Slowly, she began pulling out the knife. It resisted her efforts, as if caught on something. She stopped, not wanting to pull on organs and cause more internal damage. Bleeding started in earnest. Cat placed a large linen around the blade and pressed.

"Kenny, would ye gather a handful o' lamb's ear and yarrow, along wi' some o' the moss and pummel it to make a poultice?"

Without a word, he did as instructed.

Knowing Cat's routine, Greame reached for the whisky and watched while awaiting her approval to pour the blistering liquid onto the wound.

Cat gingerly lifted the blood-soaked linen and nodded to Greame. He poured the whisky onto the gash, and even though Gregor was out cold, he moaned.

She looked into Greame's worried eyes. "Would ye fetch me the new wee knife we got in Boston? I hae to open the wound further to see what the blade's caught on."

Greame handed her the small, very sharp knife, and she made an incision on either side of the entangled blade.

Robbie stepped closer as Cat gently tugged on the knife. With it came Gregor's intestine. She cut into the grayish-white gut and saw why it wouldn't free itself as it should have. Blondie's knife was broken before it went into Gregor's belly. The end was jagged and barbed. An impossible task to remove without disemboweling the patient if the healer was without surgical skills.

"Robbie, would ye hold the knife steady for me? Dinna pull on it, just put enough tension on it so I can work around it, aye?"

With Greame holding open the slice and Robbie keeping the blade steady, Cat cut a little further and suddenly the blade slipped free.

"Good. Now pour a little more whisky on it," she instructed Robbie.

As the fiery liquid washed away the blood, Cat probed deeper to see if there was any further injury. She saw none.

Kenny was standing beside her ready with the suture. He held out the needle, the silk thread so light the air in the cabin made it sway. Cat took it from him and began to stitch the slippery intestine, then closed the wound.

When she finished, she went outside into the cold. Once again, it brought her senses back. She took deep breaths, then sat on the snow-covered steps and buried her head in her hands.

Greame came out and sat beside her, rubbing her back.

"All right then?"

Cat nodded then turned to face him, exhaustion etched on her face. "I dinna ken how much more o' the man's innards I care to see."

Greame snorted. "I'm certain he feels the same."

Then a serious look came over him. "Tell me what happened."

"We'd best see to Kelvin. I'll tell ye on the way."

26

Fear Not

THE SPLIT OVER KELVIN'S EYE was deceptively mild in contrast to his comatose state. It had been three days since whatever happened to him had happened. The bruise was the color of a winter sunset, and the large swelling of his forehead indicated to Cat there was something more inside that she couldn't see or treat. All she could do was wait and hope he regained consciousness soon. The longer he remained comatose, the harder it would be for him to come out of it.

Kelvin was remanded to Cat's spare bedroom so she could keep a close eye on him day and night. Thad kept a vigil over Gregor, who was mending well. She made sure Thad kept feeding him the bitter tea remedy that worked so well on his gunshot wound so he wouldn't become septic.

Greame was concerned his wife was trying to do too much. She only slept in fits and starts wherever she could, and the darkness under her violet eyes was telling him to intervene.

"Here," he handed her a dram of whisky. "Drink this down in one gulp, then get into bed."

Standing at the sink of dirty dishes she was trying to muster the ambition to do, Cat looked from him to the golden liquid.

"Go on then, take it. I'll tend this mess. Ye need some decent sleep, Garnet."

She took the glass and did as she was told. After the burn in her throat faded, she asked, "I look that bad, eh?"

Greame smiled and nodded, then swept her off her feet and carried her to their bed. With the spoonful of laudanum he'd added to her drink, she'd be out in no time. He laid her on the bed where he'd already turned down the bedclothes, removed her boots and breeks, and kissed her goodnight. She was already sleeping when he closed the door.

He put on his cloak and walked over to check on Gregor. When he entered the cabin, Thad was dishing up a broth he'd gotten from Susan.

"Care for some supper, Greame?" Thad asked, pausing his hand over a bowl.

Greame shook his hand, "No, had mine already. Just came by to check on the auld man."

"I may be carved up a bit, but there's naught wrong wi' me hearin,'" Gregor bellowed from his bedroom.

"How is he?" Greame whispered to Thad before going over to see for himself.

"Doing quite well," Thad smiled.

Greame set the supper tray on Gregor's lap, then perched on the edge of the bed, folding his arms over his chest.

Gregor eyed the steaming soup. "Says I canna hae anythin' solid till I mend a bit more." He dipped his spoon into the clear brown liquid and dropped it there. "How's a grown man to survive on this wee amount o' food?"

Greame kept quiet. Cat knew what she was doing and he wouldn't question her, but he was glad he'd eaten his fill at home.

"Says my gut canna take it. Ballocks! I need meat! Look," he complained. "No' even any bread."

Then, Gregor sobered. "How's Kelvin?"

Greame shook his head at the abrupt turn. "Still no change. That's what I wanted to speak wi' ye about. Ye told Garnet that ye shot Blondie in the shoulder, aye?"

Gregor nodded and took a spoonful of broth.

"Where would such an injured man hole up while he's mendin'?"

Gregor swallowed and scratched his beard, pondering. It was like he was checking off likely spots in his mind because, periodically, he'd shake his head.

"Nowhere that I ken about. It's cold—too cold to survive wounded out in the open. There aren't any caves in the area, nor are there any other cabins."

"He could no' hae gotten far then." But where? he wondered.

Suddenly, Gregor looked at Greame with eyes rounded with possibility. "What about the *Revenge*?"

"Christ!"

Greame flew from the cabin and rounded up all of his cousins, arming them to the teeth. They set out for the *Revenge* as twilight deepened overhead in a brilliant display of star-filled sky. As the group gathered on the shore overlooking their ship, they waited for any sign of occupancy. Their breath came out as vaporous clouds in the moonlight.

Sound carried over the water with crystal clarity. If the man so much as yawned, they'd hear him.

It didn't take long before low moaning and steady pacing was heard on the ship's wooden floorboards.

"All right, we ken he's aboard ship and in no condition to sail her on his own," Greame whispered. "He's got a bullet in his shoulder and must be in some kind o' pain. Plus no food or water, unless he's melted snow. Still, he's no' goin' anywhere. Do ye want to take him now, or wait till morning?"

One by one, each man voiced his opinion. The consensus was to take him now, just so they could all sleep better for it.

"Fine by me," Greame said. "But what do we want to do wi' him? Take him alive or shoot him like the dog he is?"

Unanimously it was voted to just shoot him. He'd brought nothing but grief to their lives these past months, and nearly killed Gregor—twice.

Quietly, the small group carried two canoes out of the underbrush to the shore and paddled as silently as the frozen night itself. They flanked the *Revenge* and skillfully climbed aboard. Wearing moccasins proved invaluable to the stealth they needed to sneak up on the trespasser. Greame knew Blondie was in his cabin, probably making quick work of the whisky he kept there. It was probably the only thing that kept Blondie pain-free whilst he was healing.

One by one, the group climbed down below decks and followed their captain to his quarters. The door was closed when they arrived. Greame put his ear to the oak and heard grunts of pain on the other side. He wrapped his hand around the doorknob and flung it open, making it crash against the wall and startle Blondie in the process. Blondie jumped from the bunk searching for where he'd left his knife. Before he could reach for it, four pistols were trained on him.

The only sound heard on the ship was that of the waves lapping the hull. Not even a breath was heard.

Greame thought briefly about questioning the man, but he'd tried that before, to no avail. Besides, he didn't care anymore why or who or how. He only knew this was going to end tonight. Fear would no longer reign over the settlement.

Greame cocked his pistol, and his cousins followed suit. In what appeared to be a well-timed execution, Blondie lunged for his knife and was blasted to hell where he belonged. He landed on the floor with a deafening thud.

The four men went into the cabin, grabbed legs and arms, hauled the big man onto the deck, then tossed him into the freezing water without giving the carcass anymore thought than the rubbish it was. The currents were swift here and the body would be carried out to sea innocuously, or eaten by whatever lay in the depths. Either way, the terrorizing was over.

"It's really over?" Susan asked from the kitchen of Cat's house. Everyone was gathered there, except Gregor, who was probably furious beyond consolation by this time. Once again, Geoff, Kenny and Robbie told the tale.

Cat put on her cloak and grabbed her satchel.

"I'll come wi' ye. I dinna think I can stand to hear the next rendition—wi' embellishments," Greame snorted, as he draped his cloak over his shoulders.

Cat smiled, and they went to check on Gregor and relieve Thad from the Angry Giant for a while. Thad was indeed thankful.

"He's right sour tonight that he wasn't able to participate in the hunt," Thad whispered before he left the cabin.

Cat went right into Gregor's room and sat on the bed beside him.

He just stared at her with those menacing, deep-blue eyes. Cat never flinched.

Greame watched from the doorway, fascinated to see how she was going to lighten his mood this time.

Without a word, she pulled down the blanket and lifted his nightshirt. Greame saw a fleeting look of indignation, but the big man didn't try to stop her.

The stitches were looking well: no puss or weeping from the wound. She gingerly felt around the incision to see if there was any undo pain, watching his eyes the entire time.

"I think tomorrow ye can start eatin' soft foods."

He snorted and shook his head. "How long are ye gonna make me wait to hear o' what happened?" He bit out the words, hating to have to beg.

"That's why Greame came along."

Greame raised his eyebrows from the doorway as Gregor tore his searing gaze from Cat and trained it on him.

"Thank ye, Garnet," he clucked his tongue.

Cat pulled down Gregor's nightshirt and patted his shoulder, smirking the entire time it took her to leave the room.

"There's no' much to tell, man. We heard Blondie aboard the *Revenge*, just like ye said …"

Cat closed the door behind her and stepped out into the frigid night. It was so cold, her nostrils stuck together when she tried to breathe in. She covered her nose with her gloved hands, and looked up into the starry night. A star blazed its way to the ground, and a loon's eerie cry echoed from the water. She stood for a long time, just feeling. Feeling the cold, the quiet, the peace. The safety. Yes, for the first time in a long time, she felt safe.

She scanned the settlement, the snow squeaking under her boots as she walked the grounds looking at the cabins in the bright moonlight. The snow-covered land made it seem nearly as bright as a cloudy day. She could actually see shadows. Near the treeline, she noticed three deer browsing on the shrubs and what grass they could still find.

For a moment, she half expected Gent to come bounding out from the woods the way he used to, but she only heard the faint rustle of oak leaves in the breeze. Her feet were getting cold, so she turned for her cabin. Greame was waiting for her on the porch.

She smiled up at him. "Has Gregor been sufficiently appeased?"

He snorted. "Oh, aye, after three times o' the tellin' of it."

"And how far did ye hae to *embellish* yer tale?" Her grin was wide now, knowing what it must have taken to placate the big man.

"*Pffftt!* By the end o' the third time 'round, we all had cutlasses and had to hold off Blondie as he took pot shots at us from the cover of the ship." He held out his hand for her to step up on the porch.

Cat giggled at the vision in her head of swashbuckling pirates swinging from the ropes in a heroic attempt to reclaim their ship.

She walked into his arms and hugged his waist tightly. "I do so love ye, Greame Hay."

"Oh? Because I tell a good tale?"

"Ye can tell 'em wi' the best," she purred.

"Or is it because ye're seein' me as the pirate I am; darin' and dashin' and—"

She silenced him with a kiss that made him forget whatever else he thought he was.

27

Confession

WINTER'S ICY FINGERS HAD clawed into the Cape for the duration. The brutal winds howled relentlessly for days, peeling snow from hillocks and piling it in drifts four feet high wherever it suited nature's artistic whim. It was the end of February. The days were getting longer; the sun was warmer, but the cold never abated.

Kelvin, for the most part, remained in a semi-coma. Cat cared for him as best as she knew how, but held out little hope for his recovery.

Gregor, who was back to his old ornery self, entered Cat's house just after dawn, announcing that he had something he wanted to discuss.

"Chicory?" Cat asked, holding up a cup as Gregor sat beside Greame at the kitchen table.

"Aye."

"So, big man, what's goin' on in yer mind that couldna wait till a decent hour to discuss?"

Without any preamble he went directly to the subject. "I'll no' be goin' back to Scotland wi' ye in the spring."

He watched Cat's face for her reaction as he spoke. He'd given thought to it for more time than it was due because he didn't want to hurt her. But Scotland held naught for him. Here, in America, he could do what he wanted, go where he wanted, fight when he wanted. In a way, it would be easier not having Cat around. He cared for her deeply, perhaps as close to love as he would ever get, and that got in the way. Those feelings made him feel responsible for someone; made him think of someone other than himself. She was his weakness, and since he could never have her, he needed distance from her. It was the only way he could move on with his life. He'd lived forty-seven years on his own, after, at the tender age of ten, his father was killed by the Campbells.

Cat's eyebrows raised and her eyes held many questions, but as he'd predicted to himself, she'd ask none of the queries until she'd heard what he had to say first.

"I've grown right fond o' this place. No' just Maine, but New France and New York." Then he waved his big hand in dismissal and smirked, "Ye can keep Boston."

"Smiles at Everything and his people have been as much a family to me as I've e'er had," he continued. "No' to say ye and Greame here wilna always be my family." He met their eyes, but fixed them on Cat. "But I want to stay here."

Cat brought the cups of chicory to the table and sat without saying a word. She just stared out the window at the white wasteland, lost in her own thoughts.

Greame broke the awkward silence. "So, are ye plannin' on remainin' here in the settlement then?"

Gregor hadn't taken his eyes off Cat, but answered Greame. "For a time, or perhaps I'll follow the Indians."

He reached over and put his hand over Cat's. "Say something."

She tore her eyes from the snow and focused on Gregor's face, which seemed passive enough, but she felt his turmoil.

"I'll hae to be honest wi' ye, Gregor, I guess I just figured we'd all be stayin' together." She tried to smile, but she knew it was forced.

"But, ye're quite capable o' makin' yer own decisions and certainly dinna need my permission to stay here."

A look of disappointment flashed across his eyes. "Ye wilna even try to make me change me mind then?"

Cat raised her eyebrow. "Why? Would it do me any good?"

He hung his head. "Ye could at least hae put up a bit of a fuss, just to show me ye cared."

A smile blossomed on her face. She couldn't help it. Here was this giant, grown man who she'd known all her life, once the head guard for her clan chief, one who helped her locate her father during those hellish days after the Rising, and he wanted her to miss him and beg him to stay.

"What?" He nearly growled it out.

Still smiling, Cat stood and walked around the table to stand behind him. She wrapped her arms around his neck and kissed his cheek several times.

"Christ, Cat, ye dinna hae to get all mushy over me. I need to do this for meself. I need to stay," he told her, patting her arms and squeezing them.

Greame turned his head so Gregor wouldn't see him grinning.

"I ken ye do, big man. And all I've e'er wanted for ye is to be happy." She kissed him again, then asked, "Will ye take Sings Like Bird for yer wife?"

His body went rigid under her arms.

"Now, lass, why would I do that? I like me freedom. What would I need a woman for?"

"Companionship, love, someone to cook yer meals, mend yer wounds, tell ye how much ye mean to them—"

He unwrapped her arms from his neck and stood. "I had that here, for all the good it did me."

The smile froze on her face. She cocked her head looking up into those blue depths of his, finding he'd put up his shields.

"What are ye tellin' me, Gregor?"

"I'm no' tellin' ye anything." His tone was calm and devoid of emotion. He'd let his feelings slip out and now he had to rectify the situation. "I'm just sayin' ye've already done all those things for me, Cat, and I'm still feelin' that I need more in my life. What could any other woman do for me?"

She nodded slightly, still feeling his emotions and knowing he was covering them up tidily. "All right then. But, I'll—we'll all miss ye terribly. And ye ken ye can always come home when ye've a mind to."

"Aye. But I doubt wi' all me heart it'll happen." He downed his now cold chicory and left the house.

Cat stared at the door, then glanced over at Greame, who was smiling for some reason. She furrowed her brows and put her hands on her hips.

"What's got ye smilin' like a madman?"

He shook his head. "After all these years and this is the first he's e'er let it slip."

Confusion made her stomach twist. She was getting angrier by the second. "What are ye talkin' about?"

"Gregor's admission of love for ye." He sat braced for a smack and watched her carefully. Emotions flitted across her face and settled on doubt.

"Ye really didna ken?" He stood and stepped closer to her.

Cat looked into his eyes, those green eyes that saw too much sometimes, and shook her head.

"How long hae ye kent about it? And why didna ye tell me?"

Greame raised an eyebrow. "Oh, aye, and what would I hae said to ye? By the way, did ye ken our giant is in love wi' ye? And I've kent he's had eyes for ye from the first day he stepped ashore in the settlement."

Cat's mouth opened but nothing came out of it. Greame just laughed and patted her shoulder.

"I dinna ken what to do about this, Greame."

"There's naught *to* do. He kens ye dinna feel the same and it's time for him to move on."

She stared at him for a long moment before she spoke. "Were ye e'er … did ye think … what if …"

He put his fingers over her lips. "Garnet, if I e'er doubted that ye loved me, I would hae been the one to leave."

"But …"

He grabbed her shoulders and kissed her soundly. When he dragged his lips from hers, he whispered, "I ken ye love me, Catrìona."

Gregor all but disappeared for the next two weeks. In a way, Cat was glad he wasn't around like he usually was because after what Greame had told her, it was rather odd to know the man she'd grown up around was in love with her. She wondered just how long he'd felt that way. And how did *she* feel about it?

Sometimes she'd bubble with laughter at the thought of her and Gregor together. Somehow she could never quite picture it, but apparently he had. Just what had he pictured? she wondered.

"Christ O'Jesus, woman, stop it this instant!" she chastised herself while sitting in the freezing privy. She opened the door and nearly bowled into Gregor.

"Who were ye talkin' to in there?" Opening the door to see for himself.

"No one. Myself. Where have ye been?" she clipped.

"And good mornin' to ye, too."

"Sorry, just thinkin' out loud."

"I've been to see Smiles at Everything."

Her eyes widened. "Ye've been up to Pasadunkec?"

He nodded. "I told them I was stayin' in America and that I'd like to stay wi' them for a while."

"Ye mean after we leave, right?"

Gregor looked anywhere but in her eyes. "No. I thought it best I start my own way now."

Cat laid her cold-reddened hand on his arm. "Ye dinna hae to leave because o' me," she said quietly.

His eyes finally locked onto hers. "I ken ye think me daft for sayin' what I did, but God's truth, Cat, I just need a change." He refused to own up to what he'd let slip out. "And there's no time like the present to begin."

"I truly ne'er kent ye felt that way about me, Gregor." Her voice was soft and a bit shy.

He snorted. "I ken." He kicked at the snow, sending the sparkling white powder into the air to be whisked away by the breeze.

"How long?"

He scratched his beard and looked hard into her eyes. What could the confession hurt now. She'd just hound him until he answered her anyway. "Canna say as I can be puttin' a date on it," he said in a light tone. "But probably when we were tryin' to find yer Da."

"Oh."

That little sound spoke volumes to him. If there were any thoughts of her secretly feeling the same towards him and just not admitting it, they were just dashed. Just as well, he imagined. He had things he wanted to do and see, and she would never go along with him anyway.

"So." He stuffed his hands into the pockets of his cloak. "If ye dinna mind, I just came back to get some things o' mine and I'll be leavin' in the mornin.'"

"Gregor …"

"It's all for the best, lass." He laid a hand on her shoulder, turned and walked toward his cabin.

All she could do was stare after him.

❧

It was strange not having the big man around for meals, or anything else. He'd been an integral part of their lives for many years and was sorely missed. But as the first hints of spring began peeking through in the forms of running sap and budding trees and shrubs, Cat's mind turned to her trip home to Scotland.

A few days after Gregor's departure, Greame told her that Gregor had asked to have use of the settlement when he traveled with the Lobster clan of the Penobscot here to their fishing grounds in the summer. Greame said whatever Gregor wanted to do with the cabins was his business. They had never *owned* the property the settlement was built on. They were living off the land as the Penobscot had done for millennia.

❧

Kelvin showed no signs of returning to his old self, so they packed up around him, moving everything they owned onto the *Revenge*. Geoffrey was honored when Susan told him she would be proud to return to her husband's homeland with him, even though he would have remained in Boston if that's what she had chosen.

The date for departure was set for the first week in May, if the weather was favorable. They would head south to drop off Thad, who had no intentions of leaving America. When they left Boston in December, they informed the cousins who ran the teashop in Boston about their plans to return to their homeland. All of them were unsure whether they would remain or leave at the time. By now, they would've had ample time to decide and Greame would abide by whatever choice they made.

Only the barest of necessities to live on were left in the cabins. Everything from curtains to rugs and furniture was aboard the *Revenge* awaiting sail. The last of the household goods would be brought aboard when they left.

The week before they were to set sail, the strangest thing any of them were to ever witness happened. It was breakfast-time and Cat was getting ready to tend to Kelvin. When she opened the door to his room she found him sitting up on the bed.

Cat dropped the tray of broth and tea and inhaled sharply. The clatter of tray and china brought everyone in from the dining room to see what had happened. They all stared as if he was some newfangled contraption waiting to be revealed to the world.

Kelvin slowly turned to them and rubbed his scruffy beard. In a very hoarse voice, not quite his own, he asked, "How long hae I slept?"

Everyone stood with mouths agape, and it was a few moments before Greame had the wherewithal to answer his query.

"Four and a half months."

Kelvin shook his head and slowly reached around to rub his lower back. "Guess that's why me backend feels like I've spent too much time in bed, aye?"

No one knew what to say.

Cat finally regained her senses and went in and sat beside him on the bed. She lifted his hair from his forehead to check on the goose egg he'd been sporting since the accident. It was gone. She looked into his eyes. They were clear and lively.

"Can ye remember anything, Kelvin?" She poked and prodded his head and neck and back.

He looked her in the eyes and smiled. "We're leavin' next week. Thought I'd best get up if I was to be considered a fit helmsman."

Cat and Greame exchanged looks, reading each other's thoughts.

Without acknowledging anything was out of the ordinary, Greame asked, "Anything before that?"

"I heard voices all the time around me. I could hear ye all, but just couldna open me eyes. Oh, and I heard Blondie's dead, aye?" He caught Greame's nod. "Good. I think he was the one who tried to bash me head in."

As if permission had been given, everyone smiled and a few laughed, and finally, they all went in and patted Kelvin's shoulders and told him how pleased they were to have him back. Robbie told him he was glad that he'd woken from the land of the dead.

"Dinna think I was e'er dead, lad, but it 'twas a queer place, indeed."

He tried to stand but his legs were too weak to comply.

Cat steadied him back to a sitting position. "Kelvin, ye'll hae to work yer leg muscles some yet before ye can stand on yer own."

"What are we waitin' on then? We're to sail in a week, lass. There's no time to waste."

She chuckled, happy to see he still had a sense of humor. "I'm quite certain I can speak to the captain and push back the sail a week or two—but only if we absolutely hae to," she told him quickly when he began to argue his lack of readiness.

❧

It took Kelvin two full weeks of rigorous exercise to get his muscles back in working order. He still wasn't one hundred percent but pleaded to Greame that he could carry his weight.

"We've to sail to Boston first, anyway," Greame told him. "If George, John, Edward and Tommy wish to join us, they'll need time to pack. That should give ye more time to build yerself back up to yer former self, Uncle."

"I'll be ready."

28

Turning the Page

THE DAWN BROKE A CLEAR yellow. It was the thirteenth of May, Greame's birthday, when all nine of the settlement's inhabitants finished ferrying the rest of their belongings aboard the *Revenge*. By mid-morning, as the tide began its ebb, the sails were hoisted and the cool spring breeze filled the canvas to begin the voyage.

Gregor hid in the thick woods on the shore, cursing himself for behaving much like a child. Cat, and the rest, would have been happy to say goodbye to him, he knew, but he couldn't stand the thought of it. Possibly never to see her again. He had only himself to blame as the sails billowed, capturing the wind in a heartwrenching display of finality.

As he watched, he caught sight of her on the stern scanning the shore. Like a punch in the stomach, it brought back memories of the last time she'd sailed away from him. She didn't know he watched her then either. He knew she sensed him now—was looking for him. He wondered if he should he step out from his hiding place and bid her farewell. No. She might get the idea he wanted to join them, and he didn't. He stood by his decision to remain here, but damn it, he wasn't expecting it to be so hard. Just before her figure faded into the distance, he saw her raise her hand. He returned the gesture from the cover of the trees. It somehow made him feel better, even though she'd never know.

When the *Revenge* disappeared from the horizon, he walked down to the beach and sat on a large boulder. For hours he remained, as much a fixture on the shore as the rocks themselves. When the tide began its return, he stood, stretched his stiff muscles, and re-entered the forest.

Today was the beginning of another chapter of his life and he wasn't going to start it off on such a disheartening note. Smiles at Everything would surely find something to cheer him up with. Perhaps there were some English in the vicinity they could harry. Yes. A good fight and he'd be back to his old self again in no time.

❧

Cat felt Gregor's presence and wished he would show himself. She could feel him watching her, but the sails filled and they were on their way. Any change of heart Gregor might have had was too late to do anything about now. He'd have to find his own way to Scotland, if he chose to do so. In a show of faith she knew he'd see, she lifted her hand in farewell, but the gesture went unanswered.

She watched her Maine homeland grow smaller with an ache in her heart not that much different from when she had left Scotland nearly ten years earlier. The further she got from the fir-studded granite coast, the less she could distinguish exactly where the settlement was. It was disconcerting how abruptly this chapter in her life ended, but there could hardly be a segue for this sort of thing.

She was deep in thought when Susan came over to stand beside her after Sarah was put down for a nap.

"Are you sad to see it go?" Reading Cat's mind as she grabbed the railing for balance.

Cat nodded. "Aye, strangely enough. I've been torn for so long whether to stay or return home, and now I look back on my time here in America as a great adventure."

Susan smiled. "It seems my adventure is just beginning."

"Will this be the first time ye've sailed across the sea then?"

"Yes." She turned and faced Cat with those big, soft green eyes full of questions. "Tell me all about your voyage. What was it like?"

Cat snorted and shook her head, turning her hair to liquid fire in the breeze. "No, no, my friend. For if I do that, ye'll surely wish to remain in Boston."

Her eyes appeared a bit frightened now, so Cat hurried to explain, but in a milder form of the true horror she had dealt with.

"Ye see, the ship—if that's what ye'd call that floatin' tub o' death—was dirty and sickly and riddled wi' vermin of all sorts. We were ne'er allowed to come above decks for fresh air but once a week. There was no bathin,' no decent food, and too many souls aboard for its size. We were crammed in like rats in a nest." She laughed humorlessly. "No, make that we were crammed in *among* the rats in their nests."

Susan shuddered visibly. "How long does it take to cross?"

"Eight to twelve weeks, dependin' on the weather."

"What were the storms like?"

Cat glanced out at the relatively calm seas they were experiencing at the moment. It really could be beautiful to behold, but she knew all too well how deceptive the sea could be. One day, placid like today. The next, waves so high they swept over the decks, taking with them anything that wasn't battened down. And the wind, the wind that howled like the dead who'd been taken down into the deep by nature's whim. This time it was Cat who shuddered.

"Once again, I'll no' be tellin' ye about that." When she glanced at Susan and saw argument forming, she repeated sternly, "I'll no' be tellin' ye."

Susan saw in those amethyst eyes just how stone-like they could be when she'd made up her mind about something.

"Then I'll just go ask Geoff," she said, thrusting her chin out petulantly. "He'll not spare my feelings." And pushed away from the railing in a snit.

"Susan," she called, her face grim and set. "Ye dinna give him any credit if ye think so."

Cat sat on the crates and watched the land fade away to dusty blotches on the horizon.

A shadow fell over her and she waited for Greame to sit beside her.

"She wanted ye to tell her about the voyage."

Cat nodded, still trying to block out the stirred-up memories of that trip.

"Geoff said she's been askin' about it for a month."

Cat turned her head to look at him, feeling more hopeful. "Then he hasna told her?"

"No," he smiled. "He kens it'll be an easier voyage than ye had, but it's still no' an easy trip to make."

She caught sight of three porpoises leaping beside the ship and her mood brightened even more. "I dinna think if someone had told me what it would be like it would hae changed my mind. I *had* to find my Da. There was no choice in it. But to purposefully want the sordid details ground out is … well, depraved, dinna ye think?"

"Perhaps. But I think she's just worried for wee Sarah, as well as for herself."

"I ken that, too, but I've been talkin' to the sea and the wind and askin'—no beggin'—for clear sailin' and a fine, storm-free voyage."

Greame chuckled. "Well, lass, if ye hae those sorts o' powers, please do put them to good use. It would be a grand thing if we could make the crossin' wi' little or no incidents."

"Then I'll ask ye to join me in my plea to the fates."

"I'll leave that task to ye as I hae other matters to attend to." He glanced over at the helm.

"How is Kelvin handlin' the ship's movement?"

"I can tell he's strugglin,' but ye ken how he is, he'll put up wi' it until he breaks."

"Anything I can do to help ye? Find something for him to be doin' that wouldna involve standin'?" She watched Kelvin smoking his pipe and looking for all the world as if nothing was wrong whatsoever.

"*Tcha*. And what might ye hae him do, sit in his cabin and do the mendin'?"

She slapped his arm. "I dinna think ye hae enough faith in me abilities o' persuasion."

"Oh, I hae every faith in yer abilities, it's just that he feels his manhood is threatened if I so much as suggest that I take o'er and let him rest."

She clucked her tongue a couple times. "See, that's just what I'm tellin' ye. Ye dinna understand how men think."

He raised his eyebrow and folded him arms over his chest. "Oh, *I* dinna ken how a man thinks, eh? And why dinna ye explain it to me, my dear."

"Ye hae to plant a seed."

He furrowed his brows together. "Ye're gonna hae him plant a seed? Here aboard ship? We've no dirt."

Cat laughed out loud at the vision playing in her mind of Kelvin sowing seeds in rows of pots. When she regained control of herself, she said, "I can see I'll just hae to show ye what I mean. Stay here, watch and learn."

She walked over to the helm and stood beside Kelvin. He spared her a glance before his squinting eyes returned to the horizon.

"What might I be helpin' ye wi,' lass?"

"Oh, just gettin' the last breaths o' fresh air before I go below decks. Ye hae it easy up here, Kelvin. I've got to go through the ledgers for Greame, as he sometimes gets terrible headaches in the dim light. I'm no' nearly as good as he is wi' me sums, but he trusts me."

Kelvin glanced over at Greame who had heard Cat and was pinching the bridge of his nose, trying his best not to smile.

"Hhmmm. I was always better at sums than he." He bent closer conspiratorially and said in a low voice, "How about I pretend me legs are stiff and go through them meself for ye?" His eyes got wide for a moment in fear he might have hurt her feelings. "Oh, that's unless ye dinna want me to."

Cat looked at him cheerily. "That would be a great help to me … and Greame. But are ye certain, Kelvin? I dinna want to tear ye away from yer task at the helm …"

"Watch this. He'll ne'er ken I'm fakin' it."

He pulled the pipe from his teeth and hollered over at Greame. "Lad, come here for a moment."

Greame dropped his hand and walked over to his uncle, giving Cat a look that suggested she'd been far too clever for her own good.

"What is it, Uncle?"

"Seems me legs are done in, would ye take o'er for me?"

Cat was so proud. Greame played the scene perfectly. He laid a hand on Kelvin's shoulder. "Are ye all right?"

"Oh, aye. Just a bit stiff is all. I'm goin' below decks to rest up for a bit."

"All right then. I'll take o'er here. Ye come up when ye feel ye're ready, aye?"

Kelvin patted Greame's back, winked at Cat, and headed down.

"I'll be down to get ye some tea in a bit, Kelvin," she said to his retreating back.

He just waved, making a show of his stiff legs.

Greame grabbed her arm and pulled her close. "That was no seed, Garnet, ye planted a full-grown tree!"

"Does it matter so much how it was done? All that should matter is no feelin's were hurt and he's still performin' a useful task. Besides, I hate doin' the ledgers." Her eyes held a devious twinkle.

He barked out a laugh. "Ye've ne'er even done the ledgers!"

"Aye, but I ken I wouldna care for it."

❧

May was a tricky month, weatherwise. It could be deceptively warm one day, then all hell could break loose the next with cold rain or even snow. On the third day of their voyage to Boston, Cat wondered why the fates hadn't listened to her pleas for good sailing.

It began just before dawn. The wind picked up in earnest when Greame was at the helm. The waves drove the small schooner up and down in a sickening dance. Greame didn't need to sound the all-hands-on-deck bell; everyone already knew their places. In the hammocks below, the men could get no rest anyway, being tossed about like they were.

Kenny headed for the galley to secure the dishes and food, while the rest went topside to tend to the sails and riggings. Cat was on her way up when she ran, literally, into Susan trying to maneuver through the narrow passageway with Sarah, whose blue-green eyes were wide.

"It's easier on the stomach if we're topside in storms like this, but it's safer below. Best stay in yer quarters, Susan."

"Are you going up?"

"Just to see if Greame needs anything. Ye stay down here wi' Sarah. Sounds like a thunder storm."

Cat made certain Susan returned to her quarters, then headed up. There was no way she would remain below no matter what it did topside. She staggered over to the helm like a drunkard, while the men checked the ropes that tied down their cargo.

"At least it's no' snow," Geoff shouted to Greame as the rain came down in sheets around them.

"Aye, it's warmin' up." He shouted back, glancing at the lightning flashes in the distance. "Are ye sure ye want to be up here?" he asked Cat when she anchored herself to the helm. One look at her face gave him his answer. She was the color of parchment as the dawn smeared the eastern sky in an angry gray.

"Forget I asked," he said. "It shouldna last too long. Just moving some new air in."

Cat's only focus was on the horizon. She hated getting seasick; it ruined the entire day until she could sleep it off.

"I wish Kelvin wasna up here. He's no' strong enough for this."

As soon as he said it, Kelvin slipped and was sprawled out on the deck. Without thinking, Cat ran over to him and met with Robbie to help Kelvin to his feet.

"Are ye all right?" Robbie asked, grabbing his uncle's arm.

"Goddamn it to bloody hell," he swore. "O' course I'm all right." He wrenched his arm out of Robbie's grip and grunted, but righted himself on his own.

Cat returned to Greame's side, and he tossed her a questioning gaze.

Cat managed a grin. "He'll be fine."

"Glad to see ye wi' a smile on yer face."

"Aye, well, dinna get used to it too quickly. We're no done wi' this storm yet."

The dark gray waves were frosted with white and appeared large enough to swallow the *Revenge* whole. The wind whipped at the one sail that remained hoisted, and the sound it made through the ropes made Cat's skin crawl. She was seriously rethinking her desire to return to Scotland. And this wasn't even a big storm. What could she have been thinking? Nearly ten years on dry, unmoving ground apparently had made her forget what it was like.

She glanced over at Greame, who for all intents and purposes looked as if he were born at sea. The wind whipped at his hair, pulling wisps from his queue and flying them in all directions around his face. His eyes were steely and dark, concentrating on the wind direction and waves that threatened his ship. What she always enjoyed most about him in situations of intensity was his mouth. It was wide and kissable, but, as if enjoying the thrill of it all, a slight smile played with its corners.

She was just thinking what those lips were capable of when a bolt of lightning hit the water very close to the ship. The earsplitting thunder sounded at the same time, and the smell of brimstone whipped past her on the wind. As she scanned the ship, all the men had stopped short awaiting the next bolt. There was really nowhere to hide. Seamen took their chances out on the open ocean from all types of weather.

As she tore her gaze back to the horizon, she noticed a clearing line to the west. Greame was right, it wouldn't be a long-lived storm, but still fierce enough for its length. She lifted her fingers to the yellow band in the sky that would get larger as time went on, and Greame smiled.

"Told ye."

Well before the skies cleared, the winds died off and the seas quieted once again. Susan and Sarah emerged from below and breathed in the freshened air.

"That wasn't near as bad as I thought it would be," Susan said to Cat.

Cat raised an eyebrow. "Well, then, perhaps ye'll enjoy the voyage better now that ye ken what a storm feels like, aye?" She wouldn't let on that if this were as bad as it got, they'd all breathe sighs of relief.

Susan smiled. "If you had only told me, I wouldn't have been nearly as frightened as my imagination led me to believe."

Cat did her best to hide a scowl and walked over to where Kelvin was rechecking the cargo.

He spared her a glance. When he saw the look on her face his gaze immediately went to Susan. Then he chuckled.

Cat gave him the full fury of her scowl. "What?"

Kelvin chewed on his pipe stem for a few seconds before pulling it out and using it to point in Susan's direction. "The lass hae some opinion ye didna care for?"

His perception was a little too close to the mark. "Perhaps I should tell her that this wasn't a storm at all, but just a bit o' wind. I wonder if she'd act so proud o' herself then?"

He chuckled again. "Ye ken ye're just angry that she didna get sick."

She glared, growled and stormed off, hearing Kelvin actually laugh behind her.

Greame found her in the captain's quarters picking up and putting items down at random. He watched her in the doorway for a minute before she noticed he was there.

"Kelvin was right," she said quietly.

"Oh? 'Bout what?"

She sat on the bunk twirling her hair. "I *was* frightened. And she thought the storm was naught to be concerned wi.'"

"Garnet—"

She held up her hand. "I ken. She hasna been through what I've been through, but she didna hae to be so smug about it." She looked up at him trying to control her emotions. They ranged between punching something—or someone—and having a good cry. "I really wanted to slap her, then tell her what it was really like." She shook her head. "Not even sure why I feel this way. I'm just so angry."

He stepped into his quarters and closed the door. With a decisive click of the key, he locked it behind him. He was at the bunk in two steps and rested his knee on the mattress next to her leg, then ran his hands through her thick, fiery hair, pulling on it. When her head went back he plundered her lips. Oh, he knew exactly what to do with excess frustration.

29

The Road to Perdition

THEY DIDN'T SPEND TOO long in Boston, just a few days. Edward and Thomas Hay had decided to remain in Boston, both having found what they called their true loves. John and George had been packed for a month in anticipation of returning home. For Greame it was a bittersweet day because, while he was happy for his cousins in their new lives, he was sad to think he'd probably not see them again.

Susan said goodbye to her friends and, since her brother was actually home, she got to bid him farewell, too.

"Sister, I'm a man of the sea. There is always the chance that I may see you in Scotland." He'd tried to make it sound as though it were really a possibility, but she knew deep down he was only trying to make her feel better.

Emily and Claire were teary but happy for them to be able to return home.

"I can't believe Gregor didn't wont ta return with ya," Claire said in her thick London accent.

Cat felt her heart ache for the friend she'd come to love. She was certain Claire never really expected Gregor to fall in love with her, but Claire evidently held onto the hope of it.

"Well, dinna be too surprised if he shows up now and again in his travels," Cat told them. "I ken he'd at least stop in to say hello and see if there's any news of us, if he's in the area." She didn't say news of *her*. "I'll be sure to write often and I hope ye do the same."

Emily gave Cat one of her signature hugs that squeezed the life out of her, and that was the end of it.

Thad, who'd booked a room at the Rose Guest House until he decided what he was going to do and where he was going to go, gave her a hearty handshake and pressed a kiss on her cheek.

"I'll miss you all," he said. "But especially you, Catrìona. You are an inspiration of courage and determination."

"A blessing and a curse, I'm afraid," she said smiling. She touched his cheek, then left 35 Newberry Street and never looked back.

Cat walked the tree-lined streets she'd come to at least appreciate, down to the quay that brought her here all those years ago with nothing but the clothes on her back. When she saw Greame walking towards her, she smiled. She was going home.

He waited for her to reach him and extended his hand. She took it and they made their way through the throng of people down Long Wharfe to where the *Revenge* was docked. They were the last to arrive.

"Ye didna leave much room for John and me to store our belongin's," George said with a grin.

Greame patted his back and looked sideways at Cat, "It's *her* tub that takes up most of the cargo space in the hold."

She sent him a good-natured scowl. "Oh, aye, well, ye've no' complained about it on a cold day, my dear."

"Looks big enough for two," George said, sidestepping the slap he knew he'd get from Cat for the bawdy remark.

Greame barked out a laugh and didn't care that he got a reprimanding glare from his wife.

"Good to see ye've remained happy wi' her, Greame." George patted his back and strode across the deck to begin preparing the sails.

Greame walked Cat over to the helm and she excused herself. He watched her skirts sway across the deck knowing she was heading below to get out of the proper lady's attire she despised and into her breeks. He wished he could be there when she did, but the ship was ready to sail. John and Robbie had thrown off the lines from the dock and were climbing back aboard. Kenny, George, Geoff, and Kelvin hoisted the canvas, with Robbie and John joining in the tug of war with the ropes.

Greame slowly maneuvered the *Revenge* through the mass of ships that were coming and going in the crowded harbour. Once out in open water, the second sail was hoisted, and the westerly breeze—significantly warmer than the one in Maine—took them due east to catch the quick-flowing current that ships used on a regular basis.

Cat emerged sporting the breeks, and that sark Greame always found extremely arousing. Must be the way the wind plastered the blouse to her body. He shook his head. Hell, her dresses were more revealing, but that cream-colored linen always did it for him.

A smiled played along her full lips as she sauntered over to him. She knew exactly what he was thinking and was toying with him, knowing there was naught he could do while he was at the helm.

"I really dinna understand it, Greame." Looking down at herself, her voice teasing.

He tossed her a hard look. "Aye, ye do." He hadn't noticed she was carrying her cloak, but she slid it over her shoulders to chase the chill away. He wasn't sure if he was pleased she'd done it or not, but it helped put her body out of his mind. For the moment.

As the sun began its descent, sliding into the wide expanse of water that shivered with color, the men fell into the routine of the sea they'd never fully lost. It was a bit like getting reacquainted with an old friend, and by suppertime they all wore looks of contentment on their faces.

"God, I've missed this," John said, looking around the table with a lopsided grin on his face. "Hearin' the sound of the wind snappin' the sails, the sea rushin' under the hull, and havin' sup wi' me family again."

Greame and Kelvin caught each other's eyes and nodded.

"Ye've no' had the chance to be aboard ship like we've had in the past years, and I'm sorry for it, John. I ken ye've missed it." Greame lifted his glass of ale in a toast. "Here's to bein' back at sea."

Everyone around the table raised their glasses and drank deeply.

Cat stood, as she had in the past, to speak to her family. "I want to thank ye all for doin' what ye hae for me all these years. And now," raising her own glass, "I want to thank ye for takin' me home. To Scotland!"

The table erupted in a cheer, and the rest of the evening was spent telling tales and Kelvin playing his pipes.

❧

The days grew warmer, but the sea was still deathly cold. As long as the sun shone, it was comfortable on deck, but on those cloudy days, Cat chose to remain below decks in the warmth of her cabin.

Susan had taken to cooking all the meals, which relieved Kenny of the time-consuming task. He'd never complained about being the cook, but much preferred to be topside in the fresh air.

Susan had also taken to becoming a bit shrew-like for some reason. She was moody and seemed to want nothing to do with Geoff.

It was Geoff who'd knocked on the doorjamb when Cat was sitting at Greame's desk composing a letter. She turned to see who it was and smiled.

"What might I be doin' for ye, Geoffrey?"

He stepped into the cabin and sat in the chair next to the desk. If a man could wring his hands, he'd be doing it. She touched his arm and waited for him to say what was on his mind.

He looked up, finally, with storm-gray eyes full of apprehension.

"It's Susan," he began, then looked down at his hands again.

"What about her?"

"She wilna let me … we hae no' made … no' for o'er a month. I canna even kiss her!" Normally very easy going, he was now as frustrated as a man denied sex could be.

Cat nodded, confirming her thoughts on Susan's newly acquired moodiness. "She's carryin' yer child, Geoff."

She'd said it so simply, his mind took it as an excuse and was about to argue. Suddenly, his head snapped up and he met her eyes to make sure she wasn't toying with him. She smiled in verification. It all seemed to make sense now. Susan had been the same way during the first couple of months she was carrying Sarah.

He stood up, grabbed Cat by the shoulders and lifted her to her feet, then kissed her square on the mouth. The dash he made from the cabin was like he'd been scalded. All she could do was watch and smile.

She was still smiling a few minutes later when Greame walked in, relieved of helm duty for a few hours.

"What's got ye grinning like that? And Geoffrey, too. He flew up on deck whistlin' and workin' wi'out a care."

"Susan's pregnant."

"Ah. So that's why the change in moods."

Cat nodded. "Geoff told me she was the same wi' Sarah, but we didna ken her as well, then. Didna notice it."

It took him a moment to connect that Cat was the one who'd told Geoff. He tucked a stray strand of hair behind his ear. "Does Susan ken?"

Cat's eyebrows rose. "I'd hope so."

"Then why didna *she* tell Geoff?"

She shrugged. "I prefer to stay out o' their love life, Greame."

"But he came to ye. Why?"

"He couldna understand what was wrong wi' her. He wanted my opinion."

"He couldna hae asked her?"

A storm passed through her eyes. "What are ye sayin'?"

He dug the heels of his palms into his eyes and growled. "Forget I was here." Then he bolted out.

Cat stood there for a moment thinking for sure he'd be back, but he didn't come back.

"Christ, now what's a bee up his plaid."

After supper was cleaned up and all the cooking items put away, Cat found him at the helm. The sun had set and the sky was the color of ripe apricots.

"It's too long a trip to be takin' wi' ye when ye're cross," she told him, standing beside him at the wheel. "What's got ye angry? Susan bein' pregnant wi' us at sea? There's no cause for alarm, she's just but a few months along."

He shot her a look with dark eyes, then returned those eyes to the horizon.

"I'm no' leavin' wi'out an explanation, so ye might as well talk."

The sea and the slapping of the sails were all that was heard for quite a while. Cat had nearly forgotten why she was standing there when he finally spoke. The words were terse and nearly spit out.

"I want a child."

Cat opened her mouth, but could think of no retort.

He snorted derisively. "As usual, ye've naught to say."

Anger raged over her face. "And what would ye hae me say to ye, Greame? That I wish ye were a normal man who could get cock stand and make proper love to me? Who could father a child wi' me? Oh, aye, that'd make ye feel all better, now wouldna it?" She was so angry she shook all over. In retaliation for making her feel that way, she hauled off and slapped his face. It accomplished two things: One, it made her feel lots better, and two, it snapped him out of his self-pity.

"Goddamn it, that hurt!" he said, rubbing his cheek with a stunned look on his face.

"Good, it was supposed to, ye … ye bastard! How do ye think what ye just said made me feel? Hae I e'er complained about us no' bein' able to hae children? No. So what would ye hae me do, go off and get wi' child by some other man just so ye could feel better about yerself?" She was on a roll now with no indication of stopping. "Do ye think that's e'er been important to me, Greame? Ye ken if it was, ye'd no' be the man sharin' me bed! I'd hae found a *stud* to keep me wi' child all the time." She nearly spat out the words. Her fists were in tight balls, then she growled. "Christ!"

She stomped off without giving him a chance to counter. He stood, rooted to the deck, rubbing his jaw and thinking what he could do if he *could* get a cock stand. Just for one day. Hell, one hour! For some inexplicable reason, he wanted her. Badly. He also realized that having a child of his own would never be anywhere near as exciting as having her, in all her explosive moods and quiet times, beside him for the rest of his life.

He glanced around the deck and noted that nearly every one of his cousins was staring at him. At least none were wearing smirks or he'd have thrown them overboard. Though he was sure George was smirking, as he had his back towards him, shoulders shaking.

"What are ye starin' at?" he shouted. "Hae ye no' heard an argument before?"

John, who was standing nearby said dead seriously, "Dinna think it was the *conversation*, Cap'n, so much as it was the way Garnet threw a punch. I'd want her on my side in a fight."

So sincere it made everyone smile, then chuckle. It even made Greame grin a bit. He had to admit, she surely could handle herself. And him.

"Kelvin," he shouted. "Take o'er for me for a bit, aye? I've got some grovelin' to do."

❧

Three weeks into the trip, after the weather had been more than cooperative, the voyage to Scotland took the high road to damnation.

The sun rose a vermillion orb in the eastern sky. The calm air was thick with humidity for so early in the season. All the men were edgy, expectant of some catastrophe to come. Cat, too, read the signs in the sky. It might not happen today, but all hell was going to break loose within a day or two. It just wasn't normal. She scanned the horizon in desperate desire for land, someplace to hide from the storm's fury when it came. She was working herself up to a rare fine panic when Susan stood beside her on the deck.

"Odd day, don't you think?"

Cat bent her head. She had to tell Susan what was coming.

"Aye. We're in for a bad blow."

Susan placed her hand on Cat's shoulder and smiled. "It wasn't bad the last time. Why should it be any different this time?"

Cat looked her in the eyes. "I didna want to frighten ye before, so I let ye believe that was as bad as it got, but it's no.' That was naught but a bit o' wind. What we're likely to get from this is waves that crash o'er the decks, wind that can tear off sails and ruin masts, lightnin' so fierce ye'd think we'd all be stricken by bolts from the gods."

Susan looked angry. "I do not believe in your *gods*, Garnet. My God would never let anything that terrifying happen to us."

Cat's turn to get angry now. "And why no'? Because one among us believes it to be?"

"My God would never allow a woman with child to perish!"

Cat's mind snapped to her previous crossing. Those too sick to be tended to, or those who had gone mad, were tossed overboard by the captain and crew with little or no thought. She remembered an expectant mother holding her two other children who were speckled with what could have been the pox. The captain ruthlessly ordered his men to throw the two children to the sea, saying his entire ship could become infected. The mother screamed and begged, telling him she would do anything—anything at all—if he would let her children stay with her. That they weren't sick, it was bites from the fleas and lice. Her pleas fell upon deaf ears and the toddlers were heaved over with as much dignity as dead fish. Then, when she fought the seamen with her fists, she joined her children in the deep.

Cat didn't realize she had tears streaming down her face. Susan was beside herself trying to console her, but Cat had gone very far inside, to a place she seldom ventured. To a place too difficult to return from.

"I didn't mean it, Catrìona! I didn't mean it. I'm sorry, so sorry!"

When Greame heard Susan screaming and saw her shaking Cat, he ran over to see what had happened.

Susan explained it as best she could, and Greame knew exactly what had precipitated the event. Cat's first voyage was still touchy ground, and Susan couldn't have known never to tread there. He shouted for Kenny and Robbie, but most of the men were already at Cat's side when they saw her have the same spell that had her so incapacitated nearly eight years ago. All of them had hoped to never see that again.

Greame ran down to his cabin and retrieved the amethyst crystal and a jar of lavender his brother-in-law Lachlan told him to use when she went inside herself this way. When he returned topside, Cat's head was cradled in Kenny's lap and he was brushing the hair from her face with as much tenderness as Greame had ever seen in a man. The circle opened for him to fit into and he knelt down beside her to place the large crystal on her forehead. He opened the bag of lavender and held it under her nose so she could breathe in its soothing scent.

Slowly, Cat's eyes fluttered open and returned to their dusty-violet clarity.

"There, now, that's our lass," Kelvin said as he patted her hand he'd been holding.

"What … where?"

"Ye had a wee spell lass, is all," Kelvin told her, the color returning to his face.

She tried to get up, but too many hands were holding her down. She looked around and found Greame's worried eyes.

"Where'd ye go, Garnet?" he asked from above her face.

She had to think hard, then Susan spoke and reminded her. She raised her hand and placed it over her face so they all wouldn't see her tears. It didn't help.

"Let's give her some privacy, aye?" Greame said, and the crew reluctantly went back to their stations.

Geoffrey was holding Susan, who was crying herself now. They headed to their berth below decks.

Cat was sitting on the deck leaning her back against Greame's wide chest. He was kneeling and had his arms tightly around her, as if he could protect her from herself.

"I'm so ashamed, Greame."

"Shhh, now. There's naught to be ashamed of." He kissed her hair. Hair that smelled of chamomile and rosemary. "I take it ye were tryin' to explain to Susan what a real storm would be like, when ye had yer spell."

Cat nodded and hiccupped a sob. "It was so real, like I was relivin' it all o'er again. Dinna remember what happened after that."

"That would be when yer eyes got all glassy and it looked as though ye may hae left us, save for the steady stream o' tears rollin' down yer cheeks." He kissed one of those tear-stained cheeks.

She laughed humorlessly. "And what's goin' to happen when the storm really does get here, Greame? Will I spend it in our bunk driven mad by the thing?"

He couldn't honestly answer that question. He stared out at the darkening sky and made a silent plea to the weather gods—and any other ones who'd listen—for the storm that was gathering to not be as fierce as he feared it would be. But what chance did he have in gaining their protection if Cat's pleas had gone unheard?

30

Hungry Ocean

CAT REMAINED IN HER BUNK napping and crying for the remainder of the day. Before supper, Susan knocked on the door, walked in without waiting for permission, and sat beside Cat. She'd brought in a cup of warm broth and set it on a shelf next to the bed.

Cat smiled and held Susan's hand for a moment. "I'm sorry for givin' ye such a fright."

"Geoffrey told me what he knew about your first crossing." Her eyes were so full of compassion. "Garnet, why didn't you tell me it was that bad? I'm a grown woman who can rationalize that one voyage could be quite different from another." She brushed the hair off of Cat's forehead.

Cat closed her eyes and fought back the tears that threatened to surface again. When she'd composed herself, she opened her eyes and looked directly into Susan's.

"I think it was more because *I* didna want to remember it. Couldna bring myself to relive it." She looked away. "I'm sorry for no' givin' ye enough credit to make up yer own mind about it. Forgive me." The tears she fought so hard to hold in check coursed down her cheeks unabated.

Susan bent and embraced her tightly. "There's nothing whatsoever to forgive. I don't know how you did it—lived through it—and still remained so strong."

Cat let out a ragged breath. "I canna tell ye how frightened I am of this next storm, Susan."

"But you'll be in the capable hands of your husband, and all of us will be here with you, Garnet. You won't be locked in a dreadfully dark hold, and … I just cannot imagine what you've been through."

Cat didn't tell her that even *with* Greame at the helm, she hadn't been able to withstand the storms they'd sailed through without going into a full-blown panic.

❧

The hazy, uncharacteristically warm and humid day stretched into three. With each passing day, they inched closer to their destination. Closer to Scotland. Perhaps they'd outrun the front that was destined to change this heat into the more comfortable June temperatures.

But that was just wishful thinking. During the night, thunder was heard to the south. Cat woke in a sweat to find Greame beside her.

"Is Kelvin at the wheel?" she whispered, knowing she had woken him.

"Aye," he replied groggily. "Said he'd relieve me until dawn."

"I'm goin' up."

He got up on his elbow and pushed the hair out of his eyes. "Want me to come up wi' ye?"

"No," she said as she slid her sark over her head and stepped into her breeks. "Ye'll be needin' all yer wits about ye when the storm hits. Get some sleep."

She grabbed a lantern and made her way topside. It was breezy, but the sea was still quiet. The air was fragrant with the scent of rain. Lightning flashed on the horizon, taking many minutes before its accompanying thunder rolled over them. At the helm, Kelvin was illuminated by his own lantern. She walked over and stood beside him.

"It might stay south of us," he told her as he blew out a puff of aromatic smoke from his pipe. The wind stole its scent before she could enjoy it.

She snorted. "We could only be that lucky."

"We're in verra cold water this far north. There's a good chance the wrath of it will miss us."

Cat laid her hand over his arm. "Thank ye for givin' me a bit o' hope, Kelvin."

"I dinna care to e'er see ye in that state again, *a gràidh*."

She smiled at his craggy features reflected in the soft light, distant lightning throwing more light behind him. "I dinna care to be in that state again, either."

"It'll still blow fierce though, I'm afraid." He turned and sent her a wink. "Just make us get to Scotland quicker, aye?"

Despite herself, she giggled and nodded. "Anything I can help ye wi'? Get ye something from the mess?"

"No, lass. Just gonna catch as much wind in these auld sails as possible to keep us out o' harm's way. Why dinna ye get some sleep. We're fine up here."

"Dinna think I could sleep." She wrapped her arms around herself. "Just thinkin' o' what's out there will keep me from even closin' my eyes."

They fell into a long silence while the thunder rolled deeply on the water from distances too far to comprehend. The wind picked up now, filling the sails, making them look as though they were breathing.

Cat jumped when Kelvin spoke again.

"Are ye ready, lass? Here it comes."

The deck came alive with the Hay clan. Some were tying down items that might have a chance to move, while others manned the ropes in readiness to lower the sails if the wind got too feisty.

Cat turned when she sensed Greame emerge from below. He hadn't put his hair back in a queue yet and the wind whipped it around his head, making him look like Medusa. He walked over towards her as if the deck weren't heaving at all. He smiled at her in the lantern light and began capturing his hair. Cat would have loved the chance to tie it for him, but dared not let go of the railing at the helm.

"Looks like the brunt of it'll stay to the south," he told her. "We'll be in for a bit o' wind, though."

"Nearly exactly what Kelvin told me."

"Ye're stayin' here, then?" Referring to her death grip at the helm.

"Aye."

"All right. Here we go."

He no sooner said it when a gust of wind pitched the ship forward at an unnatural speed. Shouts and orders were barked and the sails were lowered halfway so they wouldn't catch so much wind. A broken mast so far from land would be their deaths.

As yet it wasn't raining, but with the lightning picking up in intensity, it probably wouldn't be long now.

It was beginning to get light. That would make it easier to see what was coming, good or bad. Cat's heart was beating rapidly against her chest, but so far the panic was kept in check. She kept thinking of Scotland, of *Slios Mìn* and what she was going to do when she got there. Well, besides kiss the ground she landed on and not leave it again for the rest of her life! Greame could sail where he chose, but she refused to take any more lengthy voyages.

It began with hail the size of pence. It pinged off the deck, off their heads, making stinging injuries. Thankfully it only lasted a few minutes. The deck was white with it when it turned to rain, soaking everyone to the skin immediately. The only thing any of them could do for the moment was hold on and ride it out.

As the wind blew stronger, the seas turned frothy and the rollers grew in size. Greame took over at the wheel because Kelvin just wasn't strong enough to fight the pull of the waves and wind. Without a word, Kelvin became Greame's eyes, watching for rogue waves that could swamp the ship from any angle. The sails were lowered completely and the *Revenge* was steered only by her rudder and the sheer determination of her captain.

Cat was terrified. She desperately wanted to close her eyes on the raging gale to visualize something else, but she dared not. She flinched as each giant wave relentlessly pounded the deck. At one point, George was swept off his feet and washed across the smooth boards to the starboard side, managing to grab hold of the rail before he slid off into the sea. He righted himself and hung on for dear life. There was nothing anyone could do if any of them were in trouble. It was every man for himself.

Cat heard Kelvin shout, *behind ye!* just in time to see a wave of frighteningly enormous proportions heading directly for them from the stern.

"Christ!" she whispered to herself and hung on with all her strength. It was mesmerizing to watch as it rose and fell, racing closer and closer, only to rise higher after each fall. It seemed to be searching for them, yearning to take them under.

Greame braved a glance behind at the behemoth to gauge his steering. Cat watched him make a slight adjustment to the wheel before he caught her eyes. He nodded, and she heard in her head, *I love ye.*

She managed a nod of her own just before the monster hit. The ship rose up on the wall of water, nearly black with depth. Higher and higher, before it crested over them, breaking over the bowsprit, taking it off as if it were a twig.

Cat hung on for dear life as the frigid current tore at her from all directions. She opened her eyes under the water to see Greame, still holding the wheel as his body rode the torrent, Kelvin right beside him. There was no up or down, no breath left in her lungs, no way to free herself from the depths. The icy fingers of death were grasping for her, but she wasn't ready to release herself to the greedy abyss just yet. Greame turned and saw her under the water and shook his head. Once again she could hear him in her head. *Don't leave me.*

Time stretched on and her lungs felt as though they would burst. Tiny white lights danced in front of her eyes. It would be so easy now to let death take her. Almost a relief.

Don't leave me! blared urgently in her head. No, she thought, she wouldn't leave. She wanted to return to Scotland, return home. This would be all for naught if she died now.

After what seemed like a lifetime, the water receded with a *whoosh.* Cat landed roughly on the deck next to Greame and gulped in the air she'd been craving. Greame released the wheel and grabbed for her, holding her tightly as she coughed and sputtered. He pushed the hair from her face and shouted over the fury of the storm.

"Ye're all right now. We're all right."

Cat could only nod as he pulled her to her feet and guided her hands once again to the rail. The storm was far from over.

Kelvin gripped the other side of the helm looking as frightened as she felt.

They scanned the deck to see if everyone was still aboard. The ship pitched and rolled, but one by one, the men righted themselves. Everyone was doing a head count of their own and came up one missing.

They all called for Robbie, searched between the crates that somehow managed to remain lashed together, but he was not on deck. Kenny and Geoff fought their way to the bow shouting to Greame that Robbie was missing.

The entire Hay clan, except Cat and Greame, was at the rails searching the water for their cousin. The waves were still smashing hard enough against the ship to push it forward, pitching it to dangerous angles. A man in the water didn't have a prayer.

An eternity passed before the men gave up looking. He was gone, taken to the merciless depths of the icy sea.

Robbie was the youngest, and therefore the one they all protected. Little good that did him today.

Cat was too terrified to cry. She knew she had to remain strong or she wouldn't get through this, and if everyone didn't stay to task, they'd all end up feeding the hungry ocean.

The storm raged on for the entire day. There were no more rogue waves, but that didn't diminish the destructive power of the beating they took. It wasn't until late afternoon that the storm slowly abated. As the sea spent herself, and the winds died down enough to hoist the sails once again, stock was taken by each person aboard ship.

Kenny and Geoff, who'd been closest to Robbie, wept openly. Kelvin, too, angrily wiped at his eyes.

When all hands didn't need to be topside anymore, a few of the men went below to get some rest. They'd take shifts sleeping for a few hours to regain their strength. Kenny went below to begin food preparations, as no one had eaten all day. Geoff went to see how Susan and Sarah fared.

When he opened the door to their cabin, he was hit with a sight that nearly buckled him to the floor. The room looked as though someone had taken a tantrum in it. Puddles of water covered the floor. Furniture and smaller items lay strewn about, all soaked. Susan was sitting on the edge of their bunk. Their bunk with his cousin Robbie lying in it, and Sarah curled up beside him fast asleep.

Geoff stood in the doorway with eyes bright with questions. He broke down as he stepped in and knelt beside the bunk.

"He's a bit banged up, Geoff, but nothing's broken that I can tell." Her voice was strangely calm after what she'd been through. "He comes in and out of sleep. Must have hit his head pretty hard judging from the size of the bump on it."

Geoff pulled her into his arms and cried for her, for Robbie, and for himself before regaining his composure enough to ask her what happened.

"I thought we were going under," she began. "Water poured in from everywhere and I held onto Sarah with all my strength. I tried not to scream, but I know I did. Things were bumping around everywhere down here, but one of the bumps moaned. I staggered to the door and opened it to find Robbie hanging by his arm from the ladder to the upper deck. I crawled out to see if he was all right, and managed to help him in here."

"No easy task, lass. Are ye all right?" Holding her hand, then pressing his hand over her belly. "And the bairn?"

She stared at him for a long moment as the tears flowed down her cheeks. Then she nodded and hugged him fiercely.

Kenny knocked on the doorjamb and nearly fell into their room at the sight of Robbie on the bed, alive.

"Christ!" He looked from Susan to Geoff. "How?"

Geoff released his wife and stood to pat Kenny on the shoulder. "I'd best go up and tell everyone we hae Robbie or Susan will be gettin' this same reaction from all o' ye."

He pressed a kiss on her forehead and left to share the good news with the rest of the crew.

31

No Option

IT TOOK THREE DAYS TO right the ship, but at least they managed it on sunny, dry days with light winds. Trunks and crates had been tossed about in the hold, breaking a few of them open. Water was mopped up and cabins aired out. The upper deck looked like a giant clothesline with blankets, linens and clothes being dried by the strong, late spring sun.

Robbie was up and about, bruised, but no worse for the wear. Cat watched as his cousins made an effort to pat his back when they walked past him, as if to reassure themselves he was real—and alive.

"How's the head?" she asked when he sat beside her on the crate. She reached up to feel his head.

"It's naught to be concerned wi,' Garnet." He looked out at the horizon. When he turned to face her again, he had a question in his eyes.

"What's on yer mind?"

He seemed to compose his thoughts before he spoke. "I dinna ken what I'm goin' to do when I get home."

Cat cocked her head, waiting for him to explain.

He stood and paced in front of her, fiddling with a thread that had come loose on the sleeve of his sark.

"I mean, when we were in Maine—or Boston, for that matter—there was always somethin' to do, somethin' excitin.'"

Cat smiled widely. "Ye're tellin' me, Robbie, that ye'll miss bein' a pirate, or bein' hunted by madmen, or rescuin' kidnapped women, or fightin' off demon Indians?"

He snorted and smiled, then all out laughed. "It was quite an adventure, wouldna ye say? See what I mean? How I am goin' to best that?"

"I'm verra sure that if ye stay around me, ye'll always hae some sort o' trouble to try and be gettin' out o,'" she replied in all seriousness. "I hae a knack for it."

He sat beside her again and brazenly took her hand. "I was hopin' ye'd say that. The stayin' around ye part, anyway. I dinna ken what I'd do wi'out ye and Greame and the rest. I dinna seem to be good at anythin,' but I feel useful when I'm wi' ye all."

Cat scoffed, "No' good at anything? Please. Ye're someone we can all rely on for anything, Robbie. Ye're a bit like Greame in that ye take to the sea like a cow takes to grass. Do ye think for one minute Greame's goin' to stay on dry land when we get home? He'll be needin' ye as part o' his crew, and he'll be lucky to hae ye."

Cat smiled when she saw him blush, still not all that comfortable with a woman scrutinizing his virtues. He released her hand he hadn't remembered holding, and turned away to let the wind blow the heat from his face. After a moment, he threw a quick look at her, thanked her, and walked away.

Cat's eyes followed him then rested on the man at the helm. Greame was smiling at her. He probably knew exactly what that conversation was about and enjoyed seeing Robbie struggle to face a woman, even one he'd known and lived with for nearly ten years. Cat returned the smile and turned to face the horizon.

The afternoon sun was warm, but the air was still chilly enough that she had to wear her cloak. Puffy white clouds drifted through the brilliant blue sky to the north. They must be halfway home by now, she thought. Three, maybe four more weeks and she'd be on land again.

Idly, she wondered what was happening in Scotland at the moment. She knew from what she'd heard in Boston that Highlanders were fighting for England against the French in New York, New France and Ohio. Many regiments were being shipped from Scotland to the colonies, just as she had seen in her visions, when she still had them. She also heard that England was trying to go to war with France. Again, just as she saw it, England would be at war with the world before it was over.

She shook her head to clear out those thoughts. She wanted a fresh start, one without wars involved. She hoped dearly to be able to find a place so secluded in the Highlands that the English wouldn't know she existed. Her thoughts again went to *Slios Mìn* and its six thousand acres. Would it still be standing? Would someone else have taken it over?

Like an omen a cloud covered the sun. Things wouldn't be the same as when she'd left. Trying to second-guess everything was an exercise in futility. Then she thought of the Sight. Would it come back to her when she returned home?

Did she want it to?

"I can hear yer thoughts too clearly, Garnet." Greame took a seat beside her and captured her hair in his hands. He loved the way it shimmered in the sunlight, all colors of reds and browns and black.

She turned to face him, the sun making her squint. "What do ye think?"

He grinned as his fingers ran through her fiery mane. "'Bout what?"

She clucked her tongue. "Thought ye said ye could hear my thoughts."

"I just said that because of the look ye get on yer face when ye're immersed in yer thinkin' about Scotland."

"Do ye think I'll get the Sight back when I return?"

"I've heard tell that it leaves when a seer leaves Scotland—though that was hardly true wi' ye—but I've no' heard that it e'er returns." He stopped his fingers from their task and scanned her amethyst eyes glistening in the sunlight. "Do ye want it back?"

Cat shrugged and turned away as if she could find the answer out to sea.

Greame got up and sat on the other side so he could see her face. This was important to her. And to him. She'd finally made peace with the fact that she'd lost her abilities. What would happen if they returned?

He grabbed her shoulders and made her look at him. "What do ye want?"

She brought his face into view and studied it for a minute. The deep lines around his eyes, those eyes that right now were the color of spring grass flecked with deeper greens of Maine spruce. His wide mouth, serious now, but when he chose to smile, could melt her heart. The way the wind always loosened strands of his long, chocolate-brown hair and sent it dancing around his cheeks.

His eyebrow quirked and a smile threatened around his lips. "Do ye remember the question?" he asked, smirking now.

Cat focused again and scowled. "Canna I even enjoy the sight of my man for a moment?"

"Oh aye, take all the time ye want, *after* ye answer my question."

She lowered her gaze and shook her head. When she looked up at him again, her expression was torn. "I dinna ken."

❧

She woke to the sound of rain. Gentle and soothing. When she stepped out of her bunk and looked out the window, all she saw was the ghostly gray of fog and the dead calm ocean. No wind meant no sailing. She dressed and went topside.

Susan was at the bow rail, alone. Cat walked over to stand beside her.

"It's so strange," Susan began in a soft voice; speaking louder would break the peace. "Like we're the only people in the world. Nothing else exists. Just us and this ship in a drop of water."

Cat nodded, understanding exactly what she meant. "I used to think tiny things lived in drops o' water, separate from anything else. But then I wondered what happened to those things when the drop dried up. I stopped thinkin' of it because it was too sad."

They were both silent, contemplating their thoughts while the soft rain glistened in their hair and on their lashes. In the distance, an odd noise cracked the quiet. It was a whooshing noise accompanied by the spray of water.

Apparently, they weren't the only ones who'd heard it, for it was Robbie who shouted, "Whale!"

Cat and Susan looked at each other grinning, then ran across the deck to the stern to where Robbie was standing, searching for the beast. The fog was so thick nothing could be seen, but the whooshing sounded again, followed by another right after it. There were two whales out there, and it seemed as though they were getting closer.

Most of the crew, who weren't busy due to the lack of wind, assembled at the stern to get a look.

"Gregor told me he saw one on his voyage to Boston," Cat said with a bit of awe in her voice.

Suddenly, from out of the mist slid the giant. Its dark-gray back cut through the water effortlessly, coming very close to the ship. Seeing it from above, Cat noticed it had white wings, making it appear as though it flew under the water. The second one emerged, and now Cat could see what the whooshing noise was from. The beast blew out water and air from a giant hole on its head, closing just before it dove under the ship, following the first one's path.

Greame saw her excitement and smiled. There she stood, her hair plastered to her head, drops of water coursing down her face, oblivious of the wet because of a whale. He watched as she followed it to the starboard then to the bow, her eyes never leaving the water for fear she'd miss it coming up for air again. When it surfaced right next to the bow, she was treated to the sight up close. She giggled, as did Susan, and reached out in an attempt to touch it. When the second whale came up beside the first, it stopped, and with its enormous, sad black eye, seemed to make a connection with her.

Cat knelt on the wooden deck and stretched her arm down through the rails, but was too high to reach it. Who would have thought to do that, but her? he wondered. He noticed Susan wasn't reaching for it. In fact, she had stepped *away* from the rail when it came up beside them.

Then he saw her speaking to it, but couldn't hear her words. His eyes widened in astonishment when the whale pushed itself up out of the water to touch her hand. The crew was silent, each of the men watching with amazement on their faces. When Cat and the whale made contact, she giggled again, rubbing the barnacle-like knobs on its head. Slowly, it sank back into the deep and *flew* away. Further in the murk, the other one surfaced, blowing out old air and water.

Cat stood and stared at her hand as if it weren't hers anymore. She wore a look of shear happiness. The crew assailed her with questions of how it felt, what did she say to it, and how she knew it wouldn't harm her.

"It was rough, like stones, yet slippery like an eel," she began, still staring at her hand. Then she looked up with a frown between her brows. "I spoke to it?"

"Yes, but in a language I didn't understand," Susan informed her.

"It was the *Gàidhlig*," Robbie said, searching her face. "But no words I've e'er heard."

"Oh. Do ye remember them, Robbie?"

He shook his head.

Greame walked over to hear her better. "Must be like when ye speak yer chants. Ye use the auld *Gàidhlig*."

Cat nodded, then smiled. "There was no reason for it to harm me. I could hear it …" She looked around at the crew, then looked at Greame, as if silently asking for permission to tell them more of her powers. He smiled and nodded.

"I could hear it talkin' to me in my heid."

No one said anything. No one laughed or gasped or made any sort of derogatory gestures, so she continued.

"It wanted to ken what *I* felt like, too. Was curious about me … us, the ship. It could see us all watchin' it from under the water."

They stared and remained silent.

Sheepishly, Robbie asked, "So what did *it* think when ye touched it?"

She smiled. "That I was verra soft, but a bit dry."

Slowly, the men smiled and walked away. A few of them looked at their own hands, wondering what it would have felt like had they dared to do what she had.

❧

Thankfully, the fog lasted just one day. By the next morning, only wisps of it were left as the day cleared off.

By mid-afternoon, white sails were spotted on the horizon.

"What colors do ye want us to fly, Cap'n?" John asked. "Probably no' the French, aye?"

Greame laughed, then put the spyglass up to his eye. "No, no' the French. Might as well fly the English one, since that's who it is. Man o' war. Must be provisionin' the colonies wi' more soldiers."

"Glad I'm out," John said flatly.

"And ye, such a fine man wi' a sword, John. Ye didna care to fight?" He set the scope on the helm.

John shook his head. "It's no' our war. No, I just want to settle down somewhere wi' me family and find me a fine Scottish wife to keep me warm at night."

The disclosure hit Greame hard. He'd never given thought of what his men wanted from life. It was all about him and Cat these past years. Why didn't it ever occur to him that they might have wanted something else? He studied his cousin's face. John was nearly the same age as himself, and he'd just celebrated his fortieth birthday when they left Boston.

"What would ye hae done if it werna for me keepin' ye in Boston for the past ten years?"

John frowned and played with his long moustache. "I think ye give yerself more credit than ye deserve, Cap'n. If I'd really wanted to go home, I'd be there by now." And with that he walked over to the ropes and gave them a tug.

Greame snorted. "Guess he told me."

"Takin' up talkin' to yerself?" Cat asked from behind him, noticing the sails on the horizon for the first time.

"Aye. Seems just when I start havin' a mind about my crew, thinkin' I did them a disservice by keepin' them wi' me for all those years, I get set straight."

Cat wasn't paying much attention to his answer as the ship inched closer. She was feeling the approaching ship, or rather the feelings of the men on the ship. The closer it got, the more intense the feelings became.

Greame had stopped talking when he noticed her face change. He could feel her anxiety build, but didn't know where it was coming from. She was staring at the man o' war. Could she be sensing something from it?

He touched her arm. Making her jump. "What is it?"

"I dinna think ye should stay in their path."

"Are they plannin' to board us?"

"No, they're plannin' to take yer ship." She looked at him with a bit of fear in her eyes. "Can ye outrun them?"

He stared at the ship. "No' out in open water like this. That's what the man 'o war does best. The *Revenge* is built for smaller places where that giant hulk canna go."

"Then ye'd better think o' something quick. I dinna care for what they're plannin.'"

Greame shouted for all his crew to assemble and told them what Cat had just said.

"We canna outrun them," Kelvin said, squinting at the English ship.

John smiled a devious smile. "Now this, this is what I've missed." He patted his cutlass.

"Ne'er mind that, ye auld pirate, we need a plan and we need it now."

"Sail directly at it." Cat's eyes were glassed over when he studied her face. She was in a trance.

"Are ye sure, lass?" he asked quietly. "It could be the end of us."

Her voice sounded far away. "At the very last moment, veer off. Its size'll prevent it from turnin' around quick enough to chase ye. It'll let us be. No' worth the effort."

Greame searched the faces of his men for any inkling of a better idea. With the exception of John, they seemed quite willing to do what she said.

"Let's man yer stations and do what she says then. I see no other option."

The deck came alive with shouts and activity. For good measure, John, Geoff and George went below to man the guns. Just in case. They'd not go down willingly to the *Sassenaich*.

Greame's scar tingled madly. He'd forgotten that happened when English soldiers got too close.

Cat stood like a statue in the wind, her eyes never leaving the English ship, seeing only what was to come.

It didn't appear that she was going to be given an option as to whether she wanted the Sight back or not, Greame thought. It *was* back.

He put the telescope up to his eye for a better look at the ship. Its deck was a mass of men scurrying around. Men were in the ropes, up in the sails, everywhere. Hundreds, he knew, it took to sail such a monstrosity. Cat was right though. They had no guns at the bow and it took a good long time to turn such a behemoth around. He only hoped she was right about the fact they'd let his schooner go. They had no chance otherwise.

Greame spotted the captain in his spyglass. He, too, was looking through a telescope getting a fix on the *Revenge*. Greame held his course, straight ahead. Any deviation the man o' war made, Greame adjusted to it to remain dead center of it.

"He's orderin' his ship to slow so they can get into position to board us," Cat said, talking as if she were dreaming.

"Perfect. Once he begins lowerin' his sails it'll take even longer to hoist them again to gain full speed."

"He's confused by yer course."

"Hell, I'm confused by my course! I'd no' hae tried this maneuver if ye hadn't suggested it."

The crew of the *Revenge* watched as the man o' war's sails dropped two and three at a time. They could hear its captain barking out orders and watched as the men did his bidding.

There were only a few hundred feet separating them now. Just a bit further, then Greame had to make his move.

The afternoon wind was freshening, making his sails billow like soldiers' chests puffing out with pride, scoffing at the enemy. All eyes of Clan Hay were upon their captain awaiting the signal.

Greame judged his distance, stepped away from the wheel and took a deep bow to the English captain. Then just as nonchalantly, stepped back to the helm and made his move.

The wheel was spun around and the small schooner's sails turned to catch the wind. The *Revenge's* hull tipped in the water from the severity of the turn, skirting the English ship and sailing away at a rapid speed, much to the amazed faces of the men on the man o' war. They stared open-mouthed at such a daring maneuver. Before the captain could react, it was too late. The *Revenge* had already sailed past. Past the guns that pointed out at her and past the opportunity to chase her down.

John came up from below, full of the devil, to stand beside Greame. "Want me to hoist our *true* colors, Cap'n?"

Greame sent him a smirk when he noticed the black flag under John's arm. "No, John, I do no.' I think if they saw us with the skull and crossbones hoisted, they'd make a whole-hearted attempt at catchin' us. And that back there was enough excitement for one day, thank ye."

Cat shook her head and came back to reality, rubbing her forehead. She looked back at the English ship, still trying to reset all its sails. It was getting smaller and smaller as the *Revenge* did the impossible.

Outrun a man o' war.

"I'm goin' to lie down. It's been too long since I've had one o' those and it's a bit hard on the heid."

She took a step, then collapsed onto the deck. Without a word, John took over at the helm as Greame lifted his wife and carried her below where she could sleep it off.

32

Homeland

IT TOOK THREE AND A HALF more weeks of sailing before the first gulls were seen. There wasn't a sweeter sound to Cat's ears when she heard their cries overhead. Land wasn't far away now.

Greame was below in his quarters when Cat burst in to tell him the news. He smiled at her beaming face as she wrapped her arms around his neck.

"We still hae about a week o' sailin' before we get to Port Erroll, ye ken."

She pushed back, releasing her death grip so she could see his face. "But we'll be in sight o' land soon, right?"

He smiled and kissed her cheek. "Aye, before the sun sets."

She squealed with delight and ran out to tell Susan.

As promised, well before the sun set, land was spotted in the distance. Cat was the first to see it, as she'd been hovering on the bow since early afternoon. The distant land was a dusty purple as the summer sun blazed over it. It would change colors many times the closer they sailed to it and she savored each changing hue. Granted, it was only England, but there was such a sense of relief it took all her strength to remain composed.

After a few minutes, she walked over to the helm to stand beside Kelvin.

"See it, do ye?" he asked through clenched teeth that bit his pipe stem.

She nodded. "I truly thought I'd ne'er return, Kelvin."

"It'll be good to be home."

She studied his face. "What will ye do when ye get back?"

Without even pondering for a second, he replied, "Sail wi' Greame when he's a mind to, fish when he doesna."

"Is that what ye did before ye turned pirate?" She grinned at his scowl.

"I ne'er *turned* pirate, Garnet, I've always *been* a pirate."

When she didn't say anything, he continued, in as good a mood as he'd ever been. "I'm sixty and six years old. Been 'round the world couple o' times, I reckon. Always been at sea, since I was eight, if I recall back that far." He grinned, but never took his eyes from the horizon. "My Da was a bit famous for his piratin.' That was way back when men truly feared the black flag. 'Course the King would pay men such as himself to capture the treasures of the French and Spanish. Oh, those countries had their own piratin' ways, but England had the lion's share of 'em."

Cat stared at him open-mouthed and shook her head. "I canna believe it took nearly ten years for ye to tell about yerself, Kelvin."

He snorted. A sound she rarely heard from him. "Ye ne'er asked, lass."

"So, did ye introduce Greame to piratin'?"

"No. We Hays all come from the same stock. We're a close band, and after his Da died, I took him wi' me as much as I could. But he ne'er liked bein' so far from his family. That's why he took on wi' Tullibardine so he could be reasonably close to them.

"Had a knack for the sea, our Greame. Seemed a waste when he decided to stay on land all those years."

Cat thought for a minute how fate had played such a big part in their meeting. If he'd been at sea, she'd have never met him at Blair Castle that day with Tullibardine. And yet, if he hadn't been at sea when Charles Carlyle had her kidnapped, he would not have saved her. Where would she have ended up? she wondered.

A hand touched her shoulder, startling her.

"Are ye all right, lass?" Kelvin asked with a worried look on his face. "Ye're no' havin' another spell, are ye?"

Cat smiled weakly and shook her head. "No, I was just thinkin' o' fate."

He turned to her now to study her face. "A dangerous thing, that."

"Thinkin' about it or the actual subject?" She brushed a loose strand of hair from her face.

"Fate, itself." He dragged deeply on his pipe and returned his gaze to the horizon.

"It's rather interestin' how ye can see how it played out when the event's past, but no' how it's goin' to manifest itself in front o' ye."

"Aye, what I said. Dangerous."

They fell into silence. Cat watched the sunlight turn the land a pinky-orange, just before the sun set. She went below when it began getting dark.

Greame was lying in the bunk with his arm over his forehead, his hair splayed out in a dark fan over the pillow. He opened his eyes when Cat walked in. She sat down beside him, resting her head on his chest.

"Anything wrong? Ye seem a bit quieter than when I saw ye last."

"Do ye e'er wonder where we'd be now if we'd ne'er met?"

He was quiet for a moment. Truth be told, he thought about it more times than he cared to remember, and didn't like any of the outcomes. "Aye."

She lifted her head to look at him. It was too dark to see his eyes, but she detected loneliness in his answer. She reached over him and turned the lantern's flame higher, brightening his face, then lay her full body onto his and peered into his eyes.

"Do ye think we were meant to find each other?"

That was a nice scenario. One where he was fated to meet her, no matter where or when, and always with the same result, that they'd be together like they were right now. "Aye."

"Terribly chatty, aren't we now."

He wrapped his arms around her and kissed her soundly. "My life wouldna be worth livin' if I didna hae ye, Garnet, therefore, I prefer to no' think o' such things."

Before she could continue on the subject, his mouth closed over hers again, and shortly after the subject was forgotten.

❧

Greame slid out of bed a short while later to relieve Kelvin at the helm. He could see lightning to the north when he got topside.

"How long's that been goin' on?"

"'Bout an hour or so. Seems to be headin' east. Shouldna bother us." Kelvin stretched his arms and yawned deeply.

"Garnet talk to ye about fate when she was up here?"

Kelvin nodded. "How a woman's mind works—especially that one's—I'll ne'er understand."

Greame barked out a laugh. "Tell me."

"We were havin' a rare fine conversation about piratin' when all of a sudden, out o' the blue like, she starts talkin' o' the fate." He blew out breath. "I couldna keep up, so I kept quiet."

"Wise man, Uncle." He patted Kelvin's back. "Wise man, indeed."

"See ye in the mornin.' Wake me if ye need me." He ambled off with his lantern.

Greame took the wheel with a smile. Fate or not, he was heading home. If this wind held, they'd reach Port Erroll in three days. He began planning his agenda for getting settled. First, was to see if his family home had survived the ravages of time and war. If so, they'd at least have a roof over their heads while he had a real home built for her. He had enough gold to build a castle, but that's not what she would want. No, instead she would want to have homes built for all the men she'd come to think of as her family, so that's what he was going to have done.

He also knew she'd want to see her childhood home again. There was a wealth of land there that belonged to her. He was pretty certain that if he paid the back taxes on it, she'd have it back, as long as it hadn't been taken over by someone else.

Six thousand acres would be a big temptation, and he knew it bordered Campbell territory. Too bad Gregor wanted to remain in America. He'd have been the man to run that land. He chuckled to himself when he thought of the big man having the Campbells to torment nearby, raiding the countryside, lifting cattle as his forefather did a few decades before.

The distant storm had cleared off, leaving only the starlit velvet black of night above him. Constellations he remembered as a lad were welcoming him home, stable and predictable as they were for his father and his father before. His eyes followed a shooting star that whisked through the heavens. He made a wish like a child. Only now he had the means to make his wish come true.

❧

Cat sat up straight in her bunk and scrubbed her face with her hands. The dream, though more likely a vision, was of a battle. Of course it was of a battle. It seemed that's all she was destined to see, and she fought to put it out of her mind.

"Gregor." She blew out a breath as if to dispel him from her thoughts. "Ye're gonna torment me from afar, aren't ye? Christ, I wish ye had just come home wi' us. There's naught I can do for ye from here, man. Ye're on yer own."

She looked out the window to see the first hints of dawn. The summer days were very long this far north. She got dressed and decided to go up and keep Greame company. She certainly didn't want to close her eyes and continue with the dream.

The wind was brisk when she got on deck. She hadn't bothered with her cloak, as it was stuffy in her cabin. She toyed with going back to retrieve it, but the sun would be up shortly to warm her, so she walked over to Greame and pressed a kiss on his raspy cheek.

"What are ye doin' up so early?" he asked, wrapping his arm around her waist.

"Dreamin' o' Gregor."

She'd said it as if it hurt, so he assumed it was a nightmare. "Oh? And what sort o' trouble is he in now?"

Cat snorted humorlessly. "That's just it. It doesna matter for I can do naught for him."

"Bad?"

"Some battle. I didna stay in the dream long enough to finish it."

"I was thinkin' of our friend, as well."

She turned to face him as the sky behind him turned the color of thistles. "Ye were? What about?"

"Thinkin' how he would hae been the perfect man to run *Slios Mìn.*"

She smiled and nodded. "Oh, aye. Campbells to the west, ripe for the takin.'"

He laughed at the picture in his head. "Was thinkin' the verra same thing."

The smiled faded from her face though. In a small voice, she asked, "Should I hae tried harder to make him return wi' us?"

Greame's lips thinned into a rigid line. "He's a grown man, Garnet. One who kens what he wants. Would ye take that from him?"

"No, but …" She began twirling her hair, something he hadn't see her do for a long time.

"He kens where we are," he told her softly. "If he wants to come back, he will. And he kens he's welcome to."

"Ye're right. Ye're right." The lock of hair was dropped.

The subject was changed quickly when she asked, "What's the first thing we're goin' to do when we reach Port Erroll?"

For the rest of the morning they made plans for their new life. It all sounded like a faerie tale, but Cat decided that she'd been run by her visions nearly all her life. Now it was time to make decisions based on what her heart wanted to do, instead of her head.

❧

Cruden Bay came into view three days later. It was what the village was truly called, but the locals, especially Clan Hay, called it Port Erroll for the Earl of Erroll, Scottish nobleman.

The sheer granite cliffs jutted out of the boiling sea like sentinels guarding what lay atop them. Lush green grass and ochre-colored lichen nearly covered the rocks, and wildflowers bloomed in riotous color in the nooks and crannies. Slains Castle rose as though carved from the stone it sat upon.

"Who owns the castle?" Cat asked Greame as she stared up at it.

"The fourth Earl of Kilmarnock, William Boyd. At least he did before I left."

"Doesna look like it's kept up verra well. If he was a Jacobite supporter, he may hae had it taken from him. Most werna able to keep their lands after the Risin.'"

He remained quiet, flooded in memories of his childhood. Just around the next jut of rock lay the small crescent beach that led to his home. Would the old stone croft still be there? he wondered.

He glanced up at the castle. Even when it was occupied, it always looked forlorn. The waves pounded the rocks with thunderous abandon. The white froth contrasted vividly with the light greens and aquamarines as it splashed and sent thin fingers of white bubbles through the water. He remembered those treacherous waves when storms ravaged the coast. That's how he'd obtained the *Revenge.* There were no souls left aboard when she floated onto his beach. They were lost to the tempest, yet their ship came away unscathed, as though destined for him.

The entire crew was on deck in preparation for lowering the sails and dropping anchor. Susan stood up at the bow with Sarah in her arms, anticipating what her new home would look like. Cat felt her fear. Susan was a city woman, used to shops, eateries, and social activities. There would be none of that here. Cat could feel the immense disappointment in her heart. She had to have known it would be this way. Geoff had to have told her what to expect, but Cat knew what it was like to do something for love. Susan would get used to her new surroundings in time.

She hoped.

They rounded the point and sailed up a narrow alley of sea ending in a pink sand crescent beach wonderfully protected from the brunt of storms. It was made for habitation. Cat smiled, feeling very comfortable with the location. It reminded her a bit of Maine. Oh, perhaps she could have it both ways! The rugged granite coast, the smell of the sea each morning, the gulls crying from above, yet she was home. Home, with the heather and gorse, the open land leading to mountains that reached for the clouds. Home where she could speak her native tongue, and …

The flash hit her with enough power to make her fall to her knees holding her head, for it felt as though it was going to fall off or explode. Or both.

It was as if she was receiving ten years' worth of images. Her powers returned with such ferocity, she felt sure she wouldn't live through it.

She saw the aftermath of Culloden, the years of starvation of her people, the systematic terrorizing by the Hanoverian troops, keeping the Scottish nation perpetually under their thumb, allowing them to live no better than dogs. Then, as crops failed, even more starved and died. An entire way of life, of joy, of tradition, of family, gone, destroyed, as though the Scots meant nothing and the world—at least the English—would be better off without them.

The vortex ravaged behind her eyes, blurred by their speed as they raced through, never stopping on any particular incident. Seasons flew past, sunrises, moonsets, lush greens, vivid purples, blinding whites.

Then, slowly, oh so slowly, it spent itself, leaving her sobbing in Greame's arms. He was shouting her name. For how long? she wondered. She looked into his face, so strong and worried, and through her tears she reached for him, saying it was all right, she was all right. He hugged her fiercely to his chest and rocked her back and forth, as if to comfort himself as well as her.

He released her from his death grip when she stopped crying. She looked up at him and smiled weakly, as he pushed the hair out of her face. Her eyes continued scanning her surroundings to see the frightened faces of her family.

"What happened? What did ye see? Are ye all right? Christ, I couldna make ye come out of it. And to try and locate the crystal in the hold would hae been impossible after the mess it was in after the storm."

"It all came back to me, as if I was gettin' caught up wi' all that's gone on since I've been away." She sat up, resting her head on her knees. "It was rather dizzyin' and painful, but aye, I'm all right. How long was I out?"

"Seemed like a lifetime, but I'm sure it was no more than half an hour," Greame told her, noticing her hands shaking. "Do ye want to go below and sleep for awhile?"

She lifted her head and saw that the sails were lowered. They were so close to land.

"No, I'd be verra happy to get on dry land and stay there for a verra long time."

❧

Cat and Greame stood in front of the Hays' family croft. It was a traditional stone, one-storey dwelling with a thatched roof. There was a hole in it on the east corner, but otherwise it had held up. All the thatching would need to be replaced, but that was to be expected after ten years in the elements.

Cat glanced at Greame, silently asking permission to go inside. His hand pushed gently on the small of her back and they walked in together.

There were windows in each room letting plenty of light in. Cat took in the kitchen with its counters and cupboards, all in need of updating. The ancient table where Greame and his family ate was still there, along with a few chairs. There wasn't a stove, but Cat knew that was easily remedied.

She walked into the keeping room that faced the sea. There was an enormous fireplace with small ovens on either side of it. That was the reason there wasn't a stove. There was a bedroom off of it only the size of the spare room she had in Maine. It certainly wouldn't fit her tub.

She walked back through the keeping room and kitchen to where there were two smaller bedrooms. She stood with her hands on her hips and shook her head. It was a good starting place, but would need a few additions to suit her needs.

Greame watched with a smirk on his face. He knew just what she was thinking, and he agreed. It would work for them in the meantime though, until he could build them a new one.

Cat turned and noticed his look. She smiled in return. "Aye, it'll do."

He walked over to her and wrapped her in his arms. "Mam would be pleased ye thought so. She loved this house dearly."

"What about yer cousins? Do they hae crofts nearby?"

He guided her outside and they walked up a small knoll behind the house. From the top she saw a small fishing village on a river that fed the sea.

"That's where my cousins live."

Cat could see them all walking towards their respective homes in a coming-home parade of sorts. Slowly, she saw people emerging from the crofts. More Hays, she suspected. When they began running towards Greame's family, and hugging and patting backs and shaking hands, her suspicions were confirmed.

"They've no' seen their families for nearly ten years. There'll be a lot o' catchin' up to do." She slid her arm around Greame's waist and looked up at him. "It's good to be home."

33

Settling In

TO REMOVE THE GOODS of so many people's lives from the hold of the *Revenge* took nearly a week. The very last thing to come off was Cat's copper tub. Greame told her he'd build her a separate building for it. She told him it was a fine idea, just as long at it had a fireplace to keep warm by.

Greame's family all found places to live, with the exception of Geoff and Susan. For the time being, they were staying with Cat and Greame, but it wouldn't do for long. Cat needed her private space.

Instead of the Hay clan falling back into the routine of fishing, they became builders. If there was one thing the settlement in Maine had taught them, it was how to build. Only here, abundant woods to cut for timber weren't available, so they had to rely on the time-tested methods of stone, which was in abundance.

With the gold recovered from long-gone pirates in their possession, Greame and his family were all in the market to buy land. After looking at several small pieces of property and noticing how, per acre, the small parcels were more expensive than the larger ones, it seemed the thriftiest method was to purchase one large tract to build several homes on.

A month to the day after their return home, the Hays of the Maine settlement bought a four-hundred-fifty acre parcel of rich farmland that bordered the sea just to the north of Slains Castle.

Cat stood staring out at the cliffs and the thundering sea far below, breathing in the sea-scented breeze. As the wind whipped at her, she closed her eyes, savoring the wildness of it all. When she sensed Greame approach she turned and smiled.

"Is it to yer likin' then?" he asked, the wind nearly taking his breath away.

"It's beautiful. So powerful." She captured her hair so she could talk without it whipping in her eyes. "But I've a question."

"Oh?"

"Where will ye moor the *Revenge*?"

"Are ye up for a walk?"

She nodded and followed him for about half an hour before they reached the top of a knoll. From its crest, she looked down onto a small inlet secluded enough to keep the ship out of the fury of the North Atlantic storms.

"It's deep water even at low tide."

She scanned the area, feeling the land speak to her. Again, she felt the similarities to the Maine coast. After a moment, she pointed to a slight dip in the land with a hillock behind it.

"There. That's where we should build our house."

"Let's hae a look then."

They walked over to the site and took it in. Cat could see it perfectly. A whitewashed stone house with lots of windows to capture the view and the sunlight. This house would have a wooden roof with heavy beams inside instead of the traditional thatching. She could picture a large kitchen for her herbs, and plenty of room to have the entire family over to dinner. A bedroom large enough to hold her tub, along with her bed, armoire and chest of drawers; and one spare bedroom, just in case Gregor decided to visit.

Her brows lifted, wondering where that thought came from. It was highly unlikely Gregor would ever see this place from what she kept seeing in her visions. Visions she refused to let run their course because she was terribly afraid she'd end up seeing his death in one of them. He'd made his decision and she was trying her damnedest to let him live his own life. It was easier to not see what he was up to. Sort of.

Greame's hand on her shoulder brought her out of her thoughts.

"Are ye all right?"

She rubbed her eyes. "Aye. Just thinkin' o' Gregor again."

"Ye need to let him go, Garnet."

She snorted. "I'm tryin,' but apparently it's no' as easy as I thought it would be."

"Did ye hae another vision of him?"

She shook her head. "No. Now I'm buildin' a spare bedroom for him."

He chuckled. "Well, we should hae a spare bedroom anyway, but I dinna think it will be just for him."

"I guess I just miss him."

"I miss him too, oddly enough." He rubbed the two-day growth of stubble on his chin. "The man could be a trial, yet he was also entertaining to hae around."

She remembered all they'd been through together, but it was time to let him go, and she was not going to think of him anymore if it killed her.

Without another word, she turned from Greame and began walking the borders of their new house. She took a deep breath and cleared her head, then began seeing how she'd like it to look. She knew she wanted a few apple trees for her precious pies, and perhaps a stand of spruce trees to remind her of Maine. The spruce would also serve as a windbreak to block the brunt of the gales that blew in off the water. Had she realized this part of Scotland was so tree-starved, she'd have brought some spruce back with her to plant.

Greame watched her and closed his eyes to see what she saw. It was easier that way, as her mind always had such detailed pictures. He liked her ideas and made mental notes of what he'd add to her vision. It would be a grand house indeed. They had time to begin the foundation, but that's probably as far as they'd get before the winter set in, halting the construction efforts.

Cat walked back to him smiling. "So, what do ye think?" knowing he'd seen what she saw.

"I like it. A lot." He slung his arm over her shoulder and they began the walk back to the croft discussing each detail, adding or altering the plans.

❧

Scotland was a very different place from what she'd left ten years earlier. The country was on the cusp of a new age. The Enlightenment had begun, and the Industrial Age was beginning with machines doing the work in the textile mills instead of women and children. Banking was big business, with the Bank of Scotland holding huge reserves.

New inventions were springing up for everything from new farming tools to automated machines that did the work of ten men. This had mixed results. While the farmers benefited from better tools allowing them to till the land better and drain off marshland to allow crops to grow, it eliminated the need for so many tenant farmers, therefore making many stewards of the land move to the cities for work. Cities grew rapidly, too quickly to prevent bad building practices. They, too, became overcrowded and soon there wasn't enough work there either. Many began to emigrate to the Americas to seek a better life.

Because the Hay clan had become wealthy, they were able to afford to live where they were happiest. Not one would have moved to the city, with the exception of Susan. Geoff would not submit to the idea, though, saying his children would learn to be self-sufficient as he had, and they would have their family nearby.

Cat listened to this argument nearly every day, wondering how she was going to make it through the winter with them under the same roof. Each day, she left with Greame at the crack of dawn to help with their new house so she wouldn't have to listen to them. At least Susan cooked supper for them when they returned each night, exhausted and sore from lifting the stones for the foundation.

Kelvin and Robbie were the only two from the Maine settlement not building their own crofts. Kelvin already had a house, and Robbie was content to remain with his parents, as he was the youngest and the only one still at home. He helped his family with the farming and fishing, benefiting them and himself.

Geoff was planning on remaining in Greame's parents' house. It suited his family for now, if Susan could be convinced that this is where she should stay to raise the children. An addition or two would make the house perfectly livable for their growing family.

❧

The autumn days grew shorter with each passing sunset. Cat was ready for a change of scenery and asked—no begged—Greame to take her to *Slios Mìn* to see how it faired.

It was the last week in September when they procured a pair of horses and began their four-day trip west. As in Cat's previous vision, the rolling, open moors were colored with fading heather and gorse. The late summer grasses were a rich gold blowing in the wind. It was truly breathtaking.

The weather was more like Maine, as it was actually mostly clear the first two days and nights. When they reached the hilly terrain, they were treated to more typical Scottish travel, with misty rain and low clouds that obscured the mountains. With each mile put behind them, Cat felt the land she remembered. It was a pleasant ache in her heart.

When they reached Blair Atholl, they stopped to look at Blair Castle from the knoll, shrouded in fog. Gregor had told her that the Hanoverians tried to destroy it, but the old stones proved too much for the cannon fire. Certainly, there was damage, but nothing that couldn't be repaired. The old tower, built by a squatter named Red John Comyns during the Crusades in the eleventh century, still stood, a testament to the craftsmanship of the era. Workers were busily rebuilding the walls as they rode past. She idly wondered if the Murrays still owned the castle. Not her concern, she decided. It's not as though she'd ever set foot in it again.

They were about to continue on when Cat caught Greame's eye. He was smiling.

"I was wonderin' if ye wanted to see the auld croft again," he told her, knowing that's what she was going to ask.

"Could we? It wilna take long."

At his nod, they turned their horses around and began the mile-long trek towards Anna Macpherson's cott where Cat lived after her mentor died. Cat wondered if it still stood. Instantly, she saw in her mind that indeed it did. She smiled at how easily the Sight came to her now, and so far it was easy on her. So far.

At the crossroads where the ancient pictish cross stood to mark the juncture, they took the path to the left that was now severely grown up with tall grasses and gorse. It didn't look like anyone had been down the road since she'd left. Out of habit, she searched the trees for a raven. Things had changed. There wasn't a black-eyed messenger anywhere in sight. She was a bit disappointed. But so much had happened here, it was to be expected.

They rode down the lane, rounding the bend to find, just as she'd left it, the old cott. The ancient apple tree still stood at the corner, laden with ripe fruit. Where the garden had been was now overgrown in weeds, with only a few of the perennial flowers left blooming. She dismounted and walked around the yard, remembering each thing that'd happened there.

She glanced at Greame who'd walked up beside her. "Do ye remember when ye dropped me off here?"

With a large grin on his face, the mist glistening on his hair, he said, "One o' the most confoundin' days o' me life."

She giggled, "Me, too. I'd ne'er had that emotion before, ne'er felt that way about anyone. And ye, takin' everything I said the wrong way." She threw her head back. "Christ, I was so angry at ye."

He laughed. "I remember slappin' the reins o' the coach and wantin' to get as far from ye as I could, yet all the while wishin' to go back and see ye again. No' that I would hae kent what to do when I got there."

"I wish ye had turned around …"

"It wasna our time yet, Garnet."

She stared into his eyes for a moment, remembering how captivated she'd been by them when they'd first met. How they still captivated her. She pressed a kiss on his mouth and hugged him tightly. "Fate," she whispered in his ear.

They released each other and walked into the cott. As suspected, no one had stepped in here since she'd left. Cobwebs overran each corner and she brushed them away. She sat on the edge of the bed, still covered in the once brightly colored quilt, faded now from time and the sun, and lifted the floorboards where she used to hide the *clach na brataich* and the ceremonial dirk left to her by Anna. It was empty.

"Yer own wee hidey hole?" Greame asked as he peered into the dark gap.

"I of't wondered if, in my haste to leave wi' Gregor, I'd left anything behind. Now I ken. Must've had more wits about me than I remembered."

She stood and walked over to the cupboards, opening and closing each one; bare as the day she'd left them. Then she walked over to the vision window and sat in the old rocker. The wavy glass made the outside world move and undulate in a strange dance. Out of habit, she gathered a lock of hair and began twirling it. Her eyes closed and it all came flooding back. Not good memories. Those last days before she went in search of her father were frightening. She wondered now how she did it. If not for Gregor, she wouldn't have been able to.

Oh, she missed him terribly.

She opened her eyes when Greame touched her cheek.

"Why are ye cryin,' lass?"

"We should go. Too many bad memories linger here."

"No, Garnet, they only linger in yer mind. When ye let them go, ye'll see how charmin' this place is."

He held out his hand and she took it, stood and looked around at the small croft.

"I was hopin' Anna might still be here, might visit wi' me one last time, but I guess she really has made the change from spirit to person again."

"Come on. Let's get some fresh air and clear yer heid." He guided her towards the door. She let him.

"How far is *Slios Mìn* from here?" he asked, taking in the surroundings and storing them for future reference.

Cat sent him a questioning look as she mounted her horse. She brushed the last of her tears away, smiling weakly. "I'd forgotten ye'd ne'er been there. It's a pretty ride … or it used to be. We'll be there tomorrow."

❧

The road that followed the River Tummel had been updated to such a degree that it no longer resembled a path. It was wide enough for two wagons to pass. It certainly made travel much smoother and cut the time it took to get to *Slios Mìn* by a few hours. No longer did they have to slog through wet moors with mud so thick as to remove one's shoes and nearly halt a horse's forward motion.

It was the only thing that had changed though. The land was still thickly forested in the foothills. The Grampian mountain range was to their right, but the misty air prevented them from seeing it. There was probably already snow on its peaks.

Cat's heart ached with anticipation as they rounded the knoll to where her family's home was. They rode in silence. When she saw the barn standing, then the stone two-storey house as wonderful as the day she left, she broke down and cried.

Greame understood her emotion, for he'd felt it to nearly the same degree when he saw his family home still standing. He gave her a few minutes to compose herself. The horses stopped at the barn, as though someone was there to tend to them. Cat and Greame dismounted and walked across the dooryard to the house. Cat stood at the door for a moment, then pushed it open to step into the past.

They stood side by side in the kitchen, one a generation more modern than Greame's Mam had. Here, the cupboards were fully stocked with dishes, pots, pans and bowls. As she looked around, she remembered everything she'd ever done in this kitchen, every chore that each item was used to complete.

She walked down the hall to the best room. The furniture was dusty, and cobwebs hung in every corner, but she saw past them, almost seeing her Mam in the rocking chair beside the fireplace knitting or mending the never-ending pile of clothes the men were so hard on.

She turned and went up the stairs, a bit afraid of what—or who—she might see up there. The last time, her oldest brother Seumas, who was just killed in the Rising, was sitting on his bed, in spirit form, wanting to apologize for his actions when he was still alive.

The doors to the three bedrooms were all open, letting light flood into the hallway. She sensed Greame behind her, though he remained silent. She stopped in front of her brothers' room and cautiously glanced in. Her breath was released when no one was seen sitting on any of the beds.

Continuing down the hall to her old bedroom, she was amazed she ever called it a room. A closet was more like it. It was just big enough for her bed and a small path to walk around it. She stepped in and walked over to the window to look out over the barn, her mind's eye so clearly seeing the sheep and cows that her family used to raise. The overgrown fields were empty now.

She turned, catching Greame's eye, and smiled, but they both remained quiet. She stepped back into the hallway then walked to the last room upstairs, her parents' room. This was where she saw her mother battling for her life with Willie Campbell, but could do nothing to save her from her fate. Again, everything was the same as when she left.

Greame was standing beside her. She slid her arm around his waist and leaned her head on his shoulder, as if it were too heavy to hold up any longer. He gave her a squeeze.

"Are ye all right?" His voice was so soft, she barely heard him.

"Aye. This was much harder than I thought it would be. There are so many memories here, good and bad."

"It certainly has held up well. I would say that no one has stepped foot in here since ye left."

"That's what I think, too." She looked up at him. "Do ye think I still own it then?"

"We'll find out soon enough when we locate the records. I'm fairly confident that if ye pay the back taxes, it'll be back in yer hands."

Cat nodded. "Then what? I mean what will I—we—do wi' it? As much as I love this place, I'd rather be on the coast."

He rubbed the back of his neck. "Seems a shame to just let it go." Then his head snapped up. "How do ye feel about havin' tenant farmers run it for ye?"

Cat lifted her brows and pursed her lips. "That would work."

"They'd hae to be Campbell savvy."

She barked out a laugh. "It was always a game to my Da. He'd hae a sense when to move his cattle to stay one step ahead o' the thievin' rustlers. Then he'd go on night raids and pick out a few o' their best. The next mornin' he hae a larger herd."

Greame smiled broadly. "I wish I kent yer Da a bit more."

"He was a good man." She looked around again, committing it all to memory, then turned to go downstairs. When she reached the bottom, she asked, "We're spendin' the night here, right? I mean there's no sense startin' out this late in the day and travelin' at night."

"I'll go see if I can snare a rabbit or two. Why dinna ye get the fireplace started."

Cat smiled brightly and, just as though it hadn't been ten years, went and got the broom to knock away the cobwebs, then went out to the shed to see if she could find some peat.

34

Homecoming

THERE ARE TIMES WHEN SO much has happened to a place that even the Earth itself feels it. Feels death, anger, pain, destruction.

While Cat and Greame were waiting for the rabbits to cook, they took a walk around the property with the intention of getting acquainted, or in Cat's case, reacquainted, with the land she'd lived on a lifetime ago.

They walked high into the sheilings where the cattle and sheep used to graze. There was barely a sound, not even birds, just the mist dripping off the trees. A great sadness emanated from the ground, though no battles were fought in this area that Cat knew about. She felt like sobbing, her heart hurt so.

At the top of a knoll that looked out over a long valley, the fingers of fog moving like specters across it, Cat touched Greame's hand.

It was cold, like her own. He turned to look at her, eyes bright with the same sorrow she felt in her heart.

"Even after all these years, what was done to the people here has remained," Cat said quietly.

"How can it be?"

"I think it's because there hasna been anyone here to change the anguish of what happened. If we stayed here for a little while, perhaps we could change the feel of the place, let the earth ken we humans hae made our peace."

He looked out at the lonely land. There was so much of it here. He pondered what she'd said. With Geoff and Susan bickering day and night, the thought of spending the long winter in that atmosphere wasn't all that appealing. He wouldn't be sailing or fishing anytime soon, there simply was no need. They also couldn't really work on their house until the weather broke in the spring. This would be a pleasurable retreat alone with her for a few months, with no relatives nearby to intrude. It would be peaceful, wonderful.

When he returned his gaze to her, he was smiling. "Let's stay."

A slow smile spread over her face at the prospect. "It would be nice, Greame. We'd be alone—truly alone—for the first time since we've been together." Then a different kind of smile blossomed on her face, one that mirrored Greame's previous thoughts. "And we wouldna hae to listen to Geoff and Susan peck at each other all winter."

He laughed, picked her up and twirled her around, planted a kiss on her forehead, grabbed her hand and ran down the hill like he was five, dragging her with him. The grass was wet and slippery, and before they reached the bottom, his feet slid out from under him. He landed in a heap with Cat falling rather ungracefully on top of him. They were laughing so hard, tears streamed down their faces.

Soaked through, they lay in the wet grass breathing heavily and grinning like fools. It was like a new beginning, and they couldn't have been happier about it.

They helped each other up and headed back to the house. Supper would be ready by now.

❧

The next morning, as the sun burst through what was left of the fog, they rode to Aulich proper, which had burgeoned in population since the last time Cat was there. It now even had a school.

To obtain the deed to *Slios Mìn aig Aulich* they had to apply for a Service of Heirs at the sheriff's court. When they walked into the office, Cat asked the rather skeletal-looking man how to go about the task.

The man at the desk looked them up and down and pulled out several pieces of parchment.

"We'll hae to get all yer information and send a retour to the Royal Chancery in Edinburgh," he told them in a rather nasally voice.

After Cat passed along all the pertinent papers and information, she asked how long it would take before they heard.

"All depends," he replied, adjusting his jabot with long, thin fingers. "If there's naught out o' the ordinary, perhaps a couple o' weeks to a few months. A Royal Messenger will bring the deed directly to ye." He squinted at them suddenly. "However, if there are contestin' parties, it could take years."

"I dinna think ye hae to worry about contesters, sir," Cat said. "There's no one left in my family to contest anything."

❧

They rode back to Port Erroll so they could let the Hay clan know they'd be spending the winter at *Slios Mìn*, and to bring their belongings—except for the tub—back with them. With any luck, by the time they returned, Cat would have the title to her property. But for now, they were content to make plans for their new life together.

The days grew shorter and shorter. When they reached Cruden Bay, Greame gathered his family and announced his and Cat's decision to winter inland. The news wasn't taken as well by everyone as they'd thought it would be.

Susan put her hand to her growing belly and asked, "Who's going to help with my baby?"

"He'll no' be comin' till April. Dinna fret. I'll be here for ye."

Geoff caught the "he" part of their conversation and gave Susan a start when he whooped with joy at the prospect of a son. He grabbed his wife in a gentle hug and told her they'd be fine for the winter, on their own.

Cat noticed the "on their own" was emphasized and it seemed to sound like a pleasurable prospect to Geoff. Perhaps he'd make Susan see how special this place was after all.

Three days later, Cat and Greame were driving west in a wagon loaded with essentials on the newly constructed roads that made travel nearly luxurious. They had timed the weather right, and though it was colder, at least it wasn't snowing or raining.

The trees were ablaze in golden hues now, the cold making them turn seemingly over night. The sky was as rich a blue as it could get, and not a cloud to mar its surface. When they reached the Grampian range this time, they were treated to its full glory. Snow covered the high peaks and the autumn colors rained off the sides like bright waterfalls.

Greame stopped the wagon and stared at the beauty before him. "No wonder ye missed this place, Garnet. As much as I will miss the sea this far inland, this has a certain appeal I could easily get used to."

Cat smiled and touched his arm. "I feel the same. This was all I kent until the Risin.' That was when I first saw the sea, in Inverness. It drew me in like naught had before, so I understand wholeheartedly why ye'll miss it. I will, too."

They made camp by the river before it got too dark to see. The moon rose brightly in the star-filled sky, a lazy, lopsided oval as if a drunkard drew it. By the moon's light, they watched a stag browse his way through the open meadow. His antlers, sharpened from the rut, glistened like lances on his head. Greame eyed him briefly, surely making plans for how many suppers he'd feed them for, but in the end, the beast went free. It just seemed a shame to spoil this moment with death.

The sun rose in a milky sky the next morning. They counted their blessings that they'd be home before the storm hit, and hopefully, get unpacked.

❧

The sky lowered the closer they got to *Slios Mìn*. When they rounded the corner by the barn Greame stopped to open the doors. It had started to spit snow, and the wind was picking up leaves, herding them into small whirlwinds in the dooryard.

Cat drove the wagon into the barn and jumped off; the dry dirt at her feet rolled up in a little cloud. Her mood was that of a teenager again. So many wonderful times here were floating through her mind. She made herself put the bad ones away.

Greame began unhitching the horses and whistling. She couldn't remember him ever whistling before and she smiled. He must have been feeling good, too.

She began picking through the trunks in the back of the wagon in search of food so she could begin supper preparations. The rest could wait until tomorrow to unpack.

There was peat in a small storage shed off the kitchen. She retrieved enough to start the stove in the kitchen and the fireplace in the best room. She shivered from the raw damp in the house, but knew as soon as she began working she'd warm up quickly.

Back to the barn once more for the rest of the staples Susan had packed for her. When she stepped back into the kitchen, the fires had caught and the rooms were beginning to warm up. She unpacked some lovely biscuits along with dried fish that would make a good stew. As she began cutting up some potatoes, a battle scene played out in her head.

❧

Greame was still in the barn brushing down the horses when he happened to glance out at the hills. A lone horseman was riding towards the house. He walked out in anticipation that it was the Royal Messenger delivering Cat's deed.

As the rider got closer, his hopes were raised even further.

❧

The skirmish was between the English and a band of Indians who looked like Mohawk. Cat couldn't seem to stop it from consuming her mind. She sat on the floor, huddled in the corner, holding her head while she watched, waiting for Gregor to appear in it. She assumed she was going to be watching his death, with no option to look away.

The scene must have been happening at this very moment. Most of the soldiers wore coats. The screams of dying men filled her head, and tears streamed down her face.

For an eternity the relentless fray persisted, so much like when she watched the battle at Culloden when her brothers were cut down nearly side-by-side. To continue watching would surely be her undoing, but the vision played on. Finally, she could take it no more and angrily willed her mind to stop, leaving her in sobbing ruin.

Perhaps he was already dead and she was spared having to see every gory detail.

"Damn ye, Gregor. Damn ye!" She sat rocking herself with a pain in her heart the likes of when her family had died. He may not have been blood, but he was still her kin and the only family she had left.

Guilt made its way in, chastising her for not *making* him come back with her. It was her fault, after all, for not asking him—begging him—to come along. Now, he was gone. She'd never forgive herself.

Couldn't.

In the waning light outside, she heard voices. Probably the Royal Messenger. His timing left a bitter taste in her mouth. She wasn't in the mood for visitors, especially one who'd want to be fed before returning home. She rose to her feet, splashed some water on her face and grabbed a linen.

Footfalls were on the porch now. She didn't have time to make it to her room feigning illness without being seen.

Greame opened the door and stepped into the warmth of the croft. The blazing lanterns illuminated the room, his eyes scanning the kitchen for her. He found her, noting her puffy, reddened eyes and wondered why she'd been crying.

Remaining in the doorway, he said, "I've news to take the sadness from yer heart."

He opened the door a little wider to let the visitor in.

A large man stepped into the room and closed the door behind him. As he turned towards her, the lantern light touched his face.

Cat stood there for a second trying to make sense of who stood in front of her. He was well dressed, clean-shaven and his hair was tied in a queue.

She lifted her hand to her heart when her mind registered him.

"Gregor," she whispered, running into his arms.

Greame grinned as her eyes lit up.

Fresh tears flowed down her cheeks as she hugged him fiercely. "Big man, I ne'er thought I'd see ye again."

"I couldna stay away, Cat," he said into her hair, holding her tightly. "All I did was try an' get into trouble to keep me mind from ye and the rest. Figured I'd be killed if I kept it up."

He ran a hand over her back, but then began chuckling.

She released him and looked up through blurry eyes, managing a watery smile. "What are ye findin' so amusin'?"

"Ye mean to be tellin' me, woman, ye ne'er saw me comin'?"

She choked out a laugh and shook her head. "It should please ye to ken that this time ye were a complete surprise."

Gàidhlig Glossary

A' Ghaoil Mo Chridhe = a GHOoil moe CREE-ee = love of my heart

A Gràidh = a GRY = dear

Bean-sìdhe = BAN she = faerie woman

Catrìona = kaTREEna = Catherine

Ceilidh = KAY-lee = party or visit

Ciamar a tha thu? = KIM-er ah HA ooh? = how are you?

Clach na Brataich = clack na BRA-teck = ensign stone

Duine Mor = DOON-ya mor = big man

Gàidhlig = GAAH-lik = the Scottish language

Greame = Graham

Lachlan = LAHK-lan

Mo Charaid = Mo-KAH reach = my friend

Pìob Mhor = Peep Vohr = large pipe (bagpipes)

Sassenaich = SAH-sen-ache = the English

Seumas = SHAY-mus = James

Slàinte mhath = SLAN-cha VAH = good health

Slìos Mìn aig Aulich = slees meen ek AW-lick = smooth slope at Aulich

Tapadh Leat = TAH-pah laht = thank you (familiar)

Here are a few words in broad Scots:

Ken = know

Kent = knew

Dinna = don't

Penobscot Glossary

Weliwoni = well-eh-WONI = thank you

ABOUT THE AUTHOR

Mary Duncan is an artist and graphic designer when not writing, and has designed each of her book covers. Her love of genealogy and history were the sparks that ignited writing about 18th century Scotland. Though not of Scottish descent (in this lifetime, anyway), she has a deep passion for anything Scottish (with the exception of haggis). Mary lives with her husband on the Downeast coast of Maine.

Visit her website at

www.eyesofgarnet.com

LaVergne, TN USA
17 February 2010
173389LV00003B/49/P

9 781596 637429